"I cannot be what you want," Alys said softly.

"And that is…?" Gowain questioned.

She shivered. "A—"

"Lover?" he whispered, pleased by the hike in her pulse.

She nodded and ducked her head.

Gowain grinned, stroking her forearm. She was still trembling, but not with uncertainty or fear. Nor was she trying to pull away. It was worth the strain on his self-control. "I want you to be comfortable with me, Alys."

"I am, but…" Her eyes locked on his, twin pools of startling blue, filled with trampled hopes. "This will not work."

"It can, if you want it badly enough." His gaze focused on her, his eyes as dark and mysterious as the forest at night. In their depths flickered a longing she understood only too well, for it mirrored her own. Loneliness, a yearning to belong to someplace and someone.

The ache in her chest grew, coiling so tight, she could scarcely breathe.…

Please address questions and book requests to:
Harlequin Reader Service
U.S.: 3010 Walden Ave., P.O. Box 1325, Buffalo, NY 14269
Canadian: P.O. Box 609, Fort Erie, Ont. L2A 5X3

Suzanne Barclay

Knight's Rebellion

Harlequin Books

TORONTO • NEW YORK • LONDON
AMSTERDAM • PARIS • SYDNEY • HAMBURG
STOCKHOLM • ATHENS • TOKYO • MILAN
MADRID • WARSAW • BUDAPEST • AUCKLAND

ISBN 0-373-28991-X

KNIGHT'S REBELLION

Copyright © 1997 by Carol Suzanne Backus

SUZANNE BARCLAY

has been an avid history buff all her life and an inveterate dreamer since she was very young. "There is no better way to combine the two than by writing historical romances," she claims. "What other career allows you to journey back to the time when knights were bold and damsels distressed—without leaving behind the comforts of central heating and indoor plumbing?" She and her husband of twenty-one years recently moved into a new house with a separate office where Suzanne can dream in blissful peace…when not indulging her passion for gourmet cooking or walking their two dogs, Max and Duffy.

Suzanne has prepared a comprehensive Sommerville family tree, detailing the marriages and progeny of all the Sommervilles and Harcourts…even those who did not star in their own stories. To receive a copy, send a large SASE to: Suzanne Barclay, P.O. Box 92054, Rochester, NY 14692.

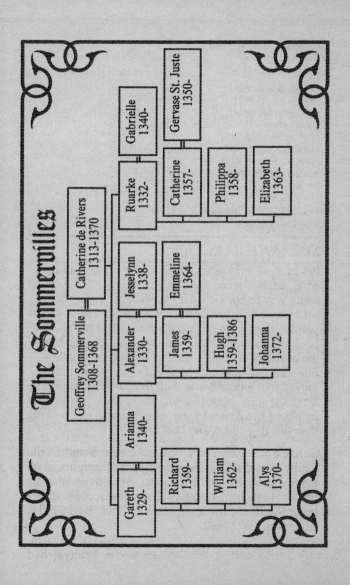

The Sommervilles

Geoffrey Sommerville 1308-1368 == Catherine de Rivers 1313-1370

- Gareth 1329-
  - Richard 1359-
  - William 1362-
  - Alys 1370-
- Arianna 1340-
- Alexander 1330-
  - James 1359-
  - Hugh 1359-1386
  - Johanna 1372-
- Jesselynn 1338-
  - Emmeline 1364-
- Ruarke 1332- == Gabrielle 1340-
  - Catherine 1357- == Gervase St. Juste 1350-
  - Philippa 1358-
  - Elizabeth 1363-

Prologue

England, April 1390

Night fell swiftly in this wild corner of the Peaks District, snuffing out the gray day and turning the hills black as the maws of hell. The wind rose, bearing with it a hint of rain, its chill fingers tugging at the shabby band of riders working their way down the rutted track between the mountains.

Gowain de Crecy hunched his shoulders beneath his threadbare tunic and rusted armor, his body's instinctive reaction to the cold his brain was too preoccupied to note.

Riding beside him, Darcy Beaufort, his second in command, sighed, weariness mixing with exasperation. Gowain was a born leader, wise beyond his six-and-twenty years, brave and possessed of tremendous willpower. He was the sort of man other men would follow into hell itself. If Gowain had a failing, it was that he sometimes forgot others were not as strong and invincible as he. "Dammit, man, do you never tire?" Darcy grumbled.

"What?" Worn leather creaked as Gowain turned and raised the visor of his helmet. Within its shadowed depths, his eyes glowed like green fire, but his chiseled features were as stark and forbidding as this rugged land of his birth.

Silently Darcy cursed the woman whose betrayal had

turned this idealistic man into a hard, driven one. "How much farther?"

"Eastham lies just around the next bend."

"Good. For I don't think the others could ride much longer."

Startled, Gowain looked back at the rest of his troop. Thirty soldiers, veterans of the wars in France and used to long, hard marches. Yet even they were drooping with fatigue from the desperate pace he'd been forced to set when they took the babe and fled from Blanche's home. Alarmed, Gowain sought the nursemaid riding in their midst.

Ruby's thin frame was swamped beneath Gowain's cloak, her shoulders bent as she shielded wee Enid from the elements. If the girl faltered, there'd be none to care for the two-year-old.

For an instant, remorse pierced Gowain's icy reserve. "I could call a brief halt so she might rest."

"Nay, we all need more than a few moments' respite, and we dare not tarry that long in the open."

Gowain nodded and looked forward. "We'll have rest and a safe haven, if we can just hold out for another league." Or so he hoped. A shiver of foreboding raced down his spine. He was even tempted to pray, though he knew God did not heed him.

"Are you certain your father will welcome us? It's been some years, and you said you didn't part on good terms."

"Warren de Crecy is not one to hold a grudge, especially against a wild lad too much like himself. He did not like it that I left Eastham, but he understood that I was young and hot-tempered, a second son determined to earn his fortune in France."

"And Ranulf?" Darcy asked. "Your wicked half brother?"

His head came around sharply. "I never called him that."

"Not in so many words, mayhap..." Darcy hesitated recalling whispered words exchanged in the black hell of a French prison, dark confidences shared by men who'd never expected to see light or freedom again. Yet they had, thanks to Gowain's sacrifice. "You told me your older brother resented you and your mother. If he made your early years unbearable, he'll doubtless not welcome us warmly. Mayhap we should bypass Eastham and press on."

"There is nowhere else to go," Gowain said flatly. The search for Enid had exhausted his funds. They had little food left, and no other hope of shelter. Damn, he hated returning home a failure, his dreams dashed, but needs must. "We will not stay long. I only want a place where we can rest for a few days, a week at most, and to ask my mother for the use of Malpas, her dower property. She offered it to me before…before I left Eastham…but I was too proud to take what was not mine."

"You will swallow your pride?"

"To save wee Enid, gladly." He'd sold his soul to save her, now he'd barter his pride, beg, if necessary, to provide his little daughter with food, shelter and, most important, a place where she could heal. Gowain lifted his face to the cold breeze, but the fresh air, smelling of earth and home, didn't scour away the past. "I wish I had written to them to find out how matters stood at Eastham. If they have not prospered, I'd not inflict an additional burden on them by appearing like beggars at the gate."

"Always you think of others instead of yourself."

"If I had thought at all, I'd not be in this mess," Gowain snapped. "God rue the day I took up with Blanche."

Darcy's broad face, weathered beyond his eight-and-twenty years, softened. "If you hadn't, there'd have been no Enid."

Gowain's chest constricted with pain and guilt. Enid, the child he'd got on Blanche a short time before he was captured by the French. The babe born while he was in prison and presumed dead. Poor Enid, born after Blanche wed another. They'd cast Enid out like soiled goods, Blanche and her noble husband. God, when he thought of the hovel where he'd found his daughter—

"Enid is only two," Darcy said slowly. "She'll forget."

"Forget!" Gowain snarled. "How can you say that, when she wakes screaming every night? You've heard her. Jesu, what can those beasts have done to make my babe so terrified? If only she would tell us what happened, mayhap I could help."

"Don't!" Darcy said. "Don't torture yourself, Gowain. None of this is your fault."

"I'd speak of it no more," Gowain said gruffly. He shoved the anguish to the back of his mind and shut the door on it. A skill he'd mastered as a child and perfected over the years. He didn't just hide his emotions, he ceased to feel them. 'Twas the only way he'd survived the French prison and Blanche's betrayal.

"Is that Eastham?" Darcy asked, pointing ahead.

"Aye." A sense of relief swept through Gowain as his weary eyes traced the familiar lines of his birthplace.

Set atop a rocky promontory, Eastham Castle's twin towers rose defiantly against the rapidly darkening sky. Strong and stalwart as an ancient warrior, it cast a long, protective shadow over the village huddled at its base. After all that had happened to him of late, Gowain had half feared he'd return to find Eastham shattered along with his other dreams and hopes.

"Do we bypass the village or ride through it?" Darcy asked.

"Through. The way is shorter." But as they approached the low wall of rocks surrounding the village, Gowain's unease returned. The wall looked unkempt, the cottages neglected.

"This place looks deserted," Darcy muttered.

"Hmm." Gowain leaned from the saddle to examine the road in the fading light. The track showed signs of recent traffic. "It could be nightfall or the approaching storm has driven everyone within." Yet no hint of light seeped out from around the tightly closed door and shuttered window of the cottage on his right.

Gowain knew who had lived there. Master Everhard, the tavernkeeper, and his daughter, Maye. Beautiful, lively

Maye had been pursued by half the village lads, himself included. He was half tempted to dismount and ask for news, of Maye and the castle.

"I like this not." Darcy loosed the loop of his battle-ax from the saddle. He was big as an ox, with arms like tree trunks. A good man to have on your side in a fight.

"Slip to the rear and alert the men," Gowain whispered. Slowly drawing the sword from its sheath, Gowain laid it across his thighs. Just in case. Around them, the wind whistled between the buildings, the only sound other than the ring of iron shoes on hard earth and the jingle of harness. By the time they cleared the village, Gowain had decided on a change of plans.

"I'll not let you go up there alone," Darcy protested when he heard what Gowain intended to do.

Gowain looked up the hill to the castle, set out against the billowing clouds, lights shining from the uppermost tower windows and flickering along the wall walks, where the guards no doubt made their rounds. Whatever awaited him there, he was used to facing his demons alone. "I need you to keep Enid safe. Dismount and hide the men in these rocks. After I'm assured of our welcome, I'll come myself to fetch you. Myself. If another should come and say I sent him, know that I'm taken, and flee."

"But—"

"I hate to leave you here in the wind and cold, but I will not be longer than is needful." Gowain turned away before Darcy could say more. For all his resolve, the ride up the steep hill to the castle was the longest in his life. Nerves stretched taut with dread, he drew rein before the drawbridge.

"Halt and state your business," a stern voice shouted down from atop Eastham's walls.

"Open the gates for Sir Gowain de Crecy," he called.

"The hell ye say," came the reply. "He's dead."

Gowain lifted the visor of his helm. "I'm very much alive, as you can see. I come alone, in peace, to see my father and—"

"Wait here while I see what His Lordship says."

Gowain stared at the closed drawbridge, unable to fathom that his father might not let him in. An interminable wait followed. Just when Gowain thought he might burst into a thousand pieces, the door of the sally port to the right of the drawbridge created open and a group of men rode out.

The tingle of apprehension in Gowain's belly became full-blown alarm. He backed his stallion up till he stood on the crest of the road. It was purposefully narrow, so that an invader might bring up only a few men at a time. At the first sign of trouble, he'd spur down the path.

As the troop drew near, he recognized their leader.

Ranulf!

It was like seeing their father as he might have been at thirty. Ranulf had their sire's fair hair and eyes the color of summer sky. How Gowain had envied Ranulf that link with the man he adored. How he'd hated the black hair and green eyes he got from his mother. Ranulf had known, of course, and taunted Gowain with it. Calling him "gypsy boy" and "black savage." The passing years had intensified Ranulf's resemblance to their father, Gowain saw as his brother halted before him.

"You are not well come here," Ranulf snarled. Though they were of a height, he glared at Gowain as imperiously as Zeus from Mount Olympus. "Get you gone from Eastham."

Gowain glared right back. Out of the corner of his eye, he saw Ranulf's men fan out, flanking him on the sides, but unable to get behind him on the narrow trail. So, they thought to take him. Reflexively his fist tightened on the hilt of his sword. "When I left for France, our father said I would always be well come in his castle," he said, calmly yet firmly.

"*My* father is dead, and I am lord here, now."

"Dead?" Gowain blinked, only years of absorbing physical blows keeping him upright. "When?" he whispered.

"A year ago...for all the notice you took."

"I...I was in prison."

"I am not surprised you ended up there."

Gowain barely heard the taunt as he struggled to absorb this latest blow without revealing the pain it caused. Ranulf had the ruthless instincts of a wolf. If he knew he'd drawn blood, he'd close in for the kill. It had always been thus between them. Gowain the outsider, though he'd been born at Eastham, and Ranulf, the heir, jealous of the young rival for their father's affection and for the wealthy estate.

"I truly did not know about Papa." Gowain tried to think what he should do next. "I will not presume further on your hospitality, then. I assume my mother has gone to Malpas Tower, and I will join her there."

"She has not gone to Malpas."

"Where is she, then?"

Ranulf shrugged. "Gone back to Wales, I should think."

"But why? Malpas was her dower property."

"Nay. Malpas is mine, not hers. Since there was no marriage twixt my father and her, she has no dower lands."

"What?" Gowain swayed. "That is impossible. They were wed."

"They were not." Ranulf sounded so certain, so smug.

"You lie. She was his wife. He...he called her wife."

"Then he did so to humor her, for there was no marriage between them." Ranulf smiled, his eyes cold, calculating. "No copy of their marriage lines could be found."

"You destroyed them, then, you bastard."

"I am not the bastard here." Ranulf's lip curled. "You are, entitled to naught, not even my father's name."

"Our father," Gowain said firmly. "My mother was—"

"Was a clever little Welsh whore who inveigled her way into my father's bed." He stroked his chin. "Mayhap you are not even his get. You've her looks, and none of Warren de Crecy's."

"What have you done with my mother? By God, if you've hurt her..." Gowain cried, lifting his sword.

"He raises arms against me! Seize him!" Ranulf shouted.

Gowain's bellow of denial was lost in the scramble as Ranulf's men surged forward. Instinct saved him, prompting him to bring his blade up to counter the first blow.

Ten to one, they had him, but he'd spent the past six years fighting the hard, unforgiving French; these men had doubtless spent theirs subduing unarmed peasants.

With his left hand, Gowain whipped the battle-ax from his saddle and flung it at the foremost rider, catching him in the chest. The man screamed; his horse reared, slamming back into those who followed. The noise and confusion were horrific as men struggled to control horses gone wild.

Gowain wheeled his horse and plunged down the dark path toward the village. Mentally he calculated his next move. Did he go left, toward the rocks where his men waited? Or right, drawing his pursuers into the forest where he'd played as a boy?

Right.

He'd not risk a confrontation when there was a chance he could lead Ranulf's soldiers away, lose them in the woods, then double back and get his people to safety. Where? Where could he take them that would be safe... even temporarily?

Behind him, he heard shouts. He risked looking back and saw he was pursued by six men. Ranulf was in the lead, weapon gleaming ominously in the gray light. Ahead, the forest beckoned. Dark. Mysterious. He plunged into it. The forest closed around him, swallowing him, wrapping him in quiet and shadow. The puny trail went right; Gowain headed left, into the thick brush. He couldn't hide the signs of his passage, but if he could go far enough, fast enough, he might be safe.

Briars snatched at his clothes; branches tried to scrape him from the horse's back. Ducking low over the saddle, he laid his face alongside the horse's neck and watched the woods flash by. He'd had no destination in mind, or so he thought, but when he saw the clearing and tumble of chalky rocks, he halted.

Here he used to play with Maye and her brother, Rob.

Slipping from the saddle, he led the stallion around behind the rocks, secured him, then crept back to watch. Faint light filtered in through the canopy of leaves. In the dimness, nothing moved. He could hear nothing, but as he pulled off his helmet and cocked his head, a twig broke behind him.

Gowain turned in one swift movement, crouching low as he brought his sword up.

"Gowain!" gasped a female voice. She stood a foot away, a peasant woman in coarse homespun. "'Tis me." She drew back the cowl of her cloak. "Maye," she added when he didn't speak.

Maye? Nay, the Maye of his youth had been slender and beautiful, a siren whose call he'd longed to answer. "Maye." His voice was as unsettled as his pulse. "What do you here?"

"Waiting for you...same as always." As she closed the distance between them, her features grew more distinct. Yet they were blurred in their own way, by six years' worth of lines and extra pounds. Still, it was Maye. "We heard you'd died."

"I'm too tough to kill." He looked around. "You cannot stay here. Ranulf comes...."

"He'll not venture far into the woods. Ranulf fears the dark. With good reason. 'Tis the outlaws' domain." Her eyes moved over his face, no doubt finding the years had marked him, too. "You've scarcely changed. I saw you ride into the village and wanted to run out and warn you, but Rob feared I'd be reported."

"To whom?"

"Ranulf." She spat the name, then smiled. "When Rob's back was turned, I came looking for you, and found your men instead."

"Darcy and the others? Where are they?"

"Safely away where Ranulf'll not find them, no thanks to that great, stupid bull of a man." She puffed up. "That...that Darcy feared I'd betray you."

"It's happened before," Gowain muttered.

"I'd never hurt you, Gowain." She laid a work-roughened hand on his arm. "Many's the time I wished I'd gone off to France with you instead of staying to wed John the Miller."

Gowain swallowed against the sudden tightness in this throat and looked away from her adoring gaze. In his youth, he'd lusted after Maye, but he'd never loved her. "'Tis in the past," he said gruffly. "Do you know what became of my mother?"

"Nay. She…she just disappeared. Rumor had it she was a witch who'd entrapped Lord Warren, and once he was dead, she turned herself into a raven and flew back to Wales." She snorted. "I say 'twas a bit of nonsense put about by Ranulf."

"Aye. Likely she's gone to Malpas Keep." At least that's where he hoped he'd find her. Gowain dragged a hand through his wet hair, more tired and dispirited even than he'd been in prison. "I've got to find a place where my men and I can rest till I decide where we'll go."

Maye smiled. "I know what you should do. You should join the others who've run afoul of Ranulf."

"What others?"

"The dispossessed ones. Families he threw off the land after he became lord, soldiers who refused when he ordered them to kill, poachers who took his game rather than see their children starve last winter. There's six score of them, at least, hiding in the caves. They'd fare better, did they have a strong leader to guide them." She glanced at him as she used to, as though he were the moon and the sun.

"I'm no rebel," he muttered. "And I'll not fight my brother, no matter that he just tried to kill me."

"You may not have much choice. Ranulf's hatred of you has grown over the years. He'll not rest till you are dead."

Chapter One

"I cannot go to Newstead Abbey?" Stunned, Alys Sommerville sank down on the bench in her mother's workroom. She barely noticed the sharp smell of hot metal in the air, a by-product of her mother's penchant for goldsmithing. From the time she was old enough to mind, she'd played in a corner while her mother fashioned beautiful artifacts from lumps of ore.

Lady Arianna, Countess of Winchester, sighed, her grimy fingers tightening on the gold candlestick she'd been fashioning when Alys intruded. "Not till your father's well enough to go with you."

"But his broken leg is barely healed. It could take weeks before he's up to so long a journey," Alys fought to keep her voice steady. A Sommerville did not rail and whine, even for good reason. "Surely William could escort me."

"He's gone to Scotland on your father's business. And Richard," she added before Alys could drag in her other brother, "sailed for France yesterday."

"He did? Why was I not told?"

"You were locked in your room finishing your book."

"Aye, but that is no excuse for ignoring my family."

Her mother chuckled. "I fear we are alike in that, my love. You lock yourself away with your herbs and potions, I with my metal and files." She traced the graceful line of the dolphin that formed the base of the candlestick. For all that she was a countess, her lovely face was streaked with dirt, and the linen coif covering her head was askew, leaking strands of blond and silver hair. She'd inherited her talent at metalworking from her goldsmith grandfather. How lucky she was to have wed a man who not only understood her need to pursue her God-given skill, but bit off the head of anyone who decried his wife's preference for goldsmithing over acting as chatelaine to their castle.

Would that I could be as fortunate, Alys thought. But then, any husband, understanding or otherwise, was denied her by the special gift that was both bane and blessing. "I know you are weary from nursing Papa though his broken leg, and I hate to add to your burdens, but I must go to Newstead. Surely we can find a way," she added, for her parents had never denied her anything.

"I know you enjoy your visits to the abbey and have gleaned much useful information from the sisters for your books, but..." Her mouth set in a stubborn line Alys saw seldom. Doting as she was, Arianna was fiercely protective. "'Tis too risky."

"This is no casual visit," Alys protested. "I have finally finished the books and would have the sisters copy them as a precaution." From the velvet bag in her lap, she withdrew ten slender leather-bound ledgers. Lovingly she traced the gilt letters on the topmost one.

The Healing Way by Lady Alys Sommerville. Volume 1.

"Oh, Alys. What an accomplishment." She wiped her hands on the skirt of her gown with typical disregard for the fine material and reached for Alys's treasure. "Nay, I am still too dirty," she remarked, glaring at her stained fingers. "Turn the pages for me, if you will."

Alys knelt beside her and opened the book. Though the floors of the great hall on the first story were strewn with fresh rushes and those in the bedchambers just below were covered with costly rugs from the East, this garret boasted neither, for fear a spark might catch them on fire. The cold seeped through her heavy velvet gown, but she scarcely felt the chill for her excitement.

The books contained every scrap of knowledge she'd been able to amass on the subject of cures. Penned in her own neat hand, they reflected her need to bring order and logic to a subject fraught with uncertainty and, all too often, failure. "The first three contain drawings of herbs." She turned the sheets of costly parchment, pointing with pride to the sketches she'd made of each plant, seed and blossom. "And in the second three are recipes for potions. The third group has lists of sage advice on healing, arranged by ailment." As she spoke, Alys shuffled the books and opened each for her mother.

"This is amazing." The blue eyes Arianna had bequeathed to her daughter sparkled with joy.

"If only Great-aunt Cici could have lived to see what use I made of the things she took such pains to drum into my head."

Her mother smiled. "She loved every moment you two spent together. Teaching you all she knew about healing and herb craft gave her a reason to live long past what any of us expected. What of the tenth? You've worked on it the longest."

"It was the hardest to write." Alys shifted the book to the top of the pile, but didn't open it. Her gloved hands clenched tight on the slender volume. "It's about magic. About the healing touch of freaks like me."

"You are not a freak!" Arianna cried, lifting a hand toward her daughter's cheek.

Instinctively Alys leaned back. "Is it normal to shy away, even from the caress of a loved one?" she asked angrily.

"Nay, but that doesn't make you... Oh, Alys." Arianna bit her lip, tears welling. "I did not know it pained you so." Her brimming gaze darted to the gloves covering Alys's hands.

Alys ached with the need to fling herself into the soft haven of her mother's arms, but that sweet sanctuary had been denied her from her thirteenth year, when the change had come upon her. Though her heavy clothes blocked most of the sensations, a stray touch on her bare face or neck would bring misery.

"I am sorry I said anything, Mama, for truly it does not bother me." Most of the time. "I am used to be-ing…separate. It helps me with my work." Yet it cut her off from so much of life. And caused her parents untold anguish. "I am grateful for my skills, especially when I can help someone."

"As you did your papa. If not for your gift, you never would have been able to set his leg properly."

Alys shuddered as she recalled that awful day when her father's squire had come racing back from what should have been a routine ride with one of the young warhorses her father had been training. "Lord Gareth's mount bolted and they both fell into a ravine," the lad had shouted. A rescue party had been quickly mobilized. They'd arrived to find the beloved lord of Ransford laying at the bottom of the gulch, sprawled like a broken toy.

"Your gift is heaven-sent, I know," her mother said. "But setting the bone was even more agonizing for you than it was for Gareth." Again her eyes strayed to Alys's hands.

"'Tis all right, Mama," Alys said gently. Inside the thin gloves, her hands ached with remembered torment. "It is hurtful to touch someone who is sore wounded, as Papa was, but if not for my skill, I'd not have been able to align the bones perfectly so he could walk again." She shook her head. "Better a few hours of pain then to see Papa a…" *Cripple.* She swallowed the word.

"You are so brave and uncomplaining, it humbles me."

"I am not brave. If I were, I'd be out using my gift to help others instead of hiding away writing books."

"But your books are a help, and the healing hurts you," said her loving mama.

"That is beside the point."

"Not to your papa and me."

The pealing of the tower bell intruded before Alys could protest that her gift should be shared, no matter the pain or risk to herself.

"It is time for supper." Arianna stood and shook the metal filings from her skirts, her expression troubled. "I know going to Newstead is important to you. Let me see if I can find a way."

Alys leapt up, forcibly reminding herself not to hug her mother. "Perhaps when Papa sees the books he'll understand. He prides himself on being a man of logic and learning."

"So I reminded him when his leg kept him confined to bed and he raged like a caged bear. Gareth has yet to forgive me for threatening to tie him to the bed. For his own good. He did that once to your uncle Alex, when he was being stupid." Their mood lightened as she recounted the incident. By the time they'd descended the two sets of stairs, they were smiling and laughing.

"You two are in a good mood," her father remarked, limping from the shadows into a circle of torchlight at the foot of the stairs. Despite his sixty years, he was an active, vigorous man, his ruggedly handsome face tanned from hours outdoors working with the warhorses he raised. Pain flickered in his midnight-brown eyes, and he still leaned heavily on a cane, but his steps were surer every day.

Needing to make some kind of a connection with him, Alys risked touching his arm. Through the rich velvet of his tunic, she felt iron-hard muscles and a surge of love so strong it nearly made her weep. Drawing back, she asked, "How are you?"

"Up and about, thanks be to your sacrifice."

"I was glad to do it, Papa."

"Still, it was not easy," he muttered. When they reached

the great hall, he added, ''I hope you do not mind a guest for dinner. The guard brought word that a Lord Ranulf de Crecy has come, begging entrance. He has a petition for me to hear.''

''Business?'' Arianna grimaced. ''Oh, Gareth, you are not yet healed and cannot ride off to settle some squabble.''

''The man wants a hearing. Which I am bound to give him.'' As a justice of the king's chancery court, the Earl of Winchester was often called upon to render judgment and mediate disputes between nobles.

Alys trailed unhappily after them as they slowly made their way across the rush-strewn floor to the high table. She'd not be able to propose her own plans to her father until he was done with this Lord Ranulf. Fuming inwardly, she took the seat beside her mother and propped her chin on her hands.

Sunlight slanted in through the high windows of the long, stately room, the shimmering rays bent into a dozen colors by the costly leaded glass. Bands of light fell on the brilliant tapestries depicting the triumphs of generations of Sommervilles. There had been many in the years since the first Lord Sommerville helped William of Normandy conquer England. Aye, her family had a proud heritage. The Sommerville men, and women, knew their minds and followed their hearts.

The bustle of activity in the hall caught her attention. A pair of brawny men in Sommerville livery were setting up extra trestle tables, while the maids scurried about placing manchet bread trenchers and cups at each place. Her father's pages dodged through the throng with pitchers of wine and new ale. Ordinary as these tasks were, an air of suppressed excitement hung on the air, along with smoke from the hearth and the scent of baking bread.

Oriel rushed up, her face flushed, her brown braids flying. She was the daughter of Ransford's former housekeeper, Grizel, and had recently taken over her mother's duties. "Do not fret, Lady Arianna, we've food aplenty for your noble guests."

"I am not the least worried," the countess replied. Which was probably the truth. Busy with her family and her smithing, Arianna paid little attention to domestic matters.

Alys looked over and caught her father smiling fondly at his wife. *Ah, if only I might find someone like Papa. Someone who accepted me for what I am,* she thought.

A commotion in the hall intruded. Ransford's portly steward advanced down the aisle between the tables. In Edgar's wake trailed a nobleman and a trio of rough-looking soldiers.

"Edgar's joints must be paining him again, for his steps are halting. I shall give him some of that bryony salve to apply to his knees," Alys whispered. "It may ease the stiffness."

Her mother nodded. "That tall man must be Lord Ranulf. Is he not a most handsome man?"

That he was, tall and blond, with the regal bearing of one of her Papa's warhorses. His close-fitting sapphire-blue cote-hardie emphasized the width of his shoulders and the fairness of his skin. If the quantity of jewels embroidering his tunic seemed a bit ostentatious, Alys was willing to overlook it, for he so resembled a statue come to life. The image of male perfection was marred somewhat by the stranger's dark scowl and haughty glare.

When they reached the foot of the dais, the man waited an instant, then turned his frown on Edgar. "Will you announce me to the earl, or must I do that myself?"

Pompous, as well as pretty, Alys thought, and the newcomer fell a mark in her estimation. Her cousin Jamie was even more handsome, yet he did not pose and swagger so.

Edgar drew himself up to his full height of five feet and five inches, pounded his staff on the floor in the manner of a court herald and bawled, "Lord Ranulf de Crecy, Baron of Eastham, lord of Malpas, Donnerford and numerous lesser holdings, does beg an audience with your grace.''

''I'll wager this Lord Ranulf never begged for a thing in his life,'' Alys muttered.

''I'll wager he never had to…leastwise not from a woman,'' her mother replied with a saucy grin.

''Mother!'' Alys exclaimed.

''Well, he is most wondrous to look on. With a sizable estate. Let him be your dining companion and see what comes—''

''Naught will come of it.''

''You will not know till you try.''

''How? If I cannot bear the touch of my own dear family, how could I stomach the touch of a strange man?'' Alys shook her head. ''It would be cruel to lead him on when I cannot wed him.''

''But if you left your gown and gloves on—''

''Even at night, in bed?'' Alys sighed. ''What man would want a wife he could not kiss or touch or couple with? No bed sport? No heirs?'' She looked over at the handsome Lord Ranulf and then at her equally handsome sire. ''Men, even those as wonderful as my papa, have not the patience or self-denial for that.'' Still it was hard not to hope, to wish for what could never be.

''Excuse me for not rising, Lord Ranulf,'' Gareth said. ''But I am just recovering from a broken leg.''

''My condolences. Does it mend well?''

''Very. My daughter is a skilled healer.'' Gareth beamed in Alys's direction, but Lord Ranulf continued to stare at him. ''What brings you to Ransford, sir?'' her father asked.

''Treason,'' Lord Ranulf growled.

''Treason!'' The word riffled through the room, stilling the hum of pleasant conversation.

''Against King Richard?'' her father asked slowly.

''Nay. This strikes far closer to home. My half brother has taken arms against me and is ravaging the land about Eastham.''

"Ah." Her father settled back. "How comes it that you bring the matter to me instead of your overlord? Whoever that—"

"James Hartley of Hardwicke."

"A good man," Gareth said slowly.

"I took the matter to him some months ago, when Gowain first turned rebel, but Lord James is too busy with his southern estates to heed my troubles," Ranulf replied, his tone flat.

"What has this Gowain done?"

"Killed the captain of my guard, attacked and burned two farms, pillaged the villages about my castle and raided every convoy bringing goods to me."

"These are strong charges."

"And true. Clive," Ranulf called over his shoulder. One of the soldiers who had been standing behind him, came forward. "Tell my lord earl what transpired the day Gowain returned."

Clive, a big, beefy man in scarlet livery, bowed to Gareth. "He killed Donald." The soldier went on to tell how Gowain FitzWarren had struck down the captain, who was attempting to protect Lord Ranulf from harm.

"What provoked this quarrel?" Gareth asked.

"My refusal to turn Malpas Keep over to Gowain." Ranulf held up a hand before the questions could fly. "Let me go back and explain that Gowain left home some six years ago, after a bitter argument over property with my father. Nearly a year went by before he wrote to his mother to say he'd taken a post with Sir Falsgraff and was part of the garrison defending Bordeaux."

"You speak of your father and Gowain's mother."

"Gowain is my father's bastard, gotten on the Welshwoman he brought home the year after my mother died," Ranulf said stiffly. "There was some talk he was not even my father's get, but old Warren was a soft man and raised Gowain as his own."

"Your sire is dead, then?"

"Alas, eighteen months ago."

"And his...er, Gowain's mother?"

"Disappeared, along with a chest of my mother's jewelry. I assumed she'd gone back to Wales. Lacking the funds to mount a war over a few baubles, I let the matter rest. Gowain returned in April. From the meanness of his clothes and armor," Ranulf added, flicking a speck from his fine tunic, "I judged he'd fallen on hard times and come to beg a handout. When I apprised him of our father's death, he did not grieve, but demanded Malpas Keep, which he claimed was his mother's dower property."

"Was it?"

"Though Elen sometimes portrayed herself as Warren's wife and chatelaine of Eastham, there was no marriage. Thus, no part of my property was hers...or her bastard's. Had it been otherwise, do you think she'd have run off to live in some hovel in Wales?"

"I suppose not." Gareth stroked his chin. "I am sorry for your misfortune at his hands, but why have you come to me?"

"I've come to you for a ruling in your capacity as magistrate of His Majesty's court. I want Gowain and those who ride with him declared outlaws."

"That is a serious step. And this seems a personal matter. Can you not capture him and bring him to trial yourself?"

Ranulf's jaw flexed. "'Tis not just a personal matter. He has aligned himself with a band of brigands who were hiding in the hills, runaway serfs and soldiers without a lord. They know every acre of land and every hiding hole in the district, and have managed to elude capture. Gowain has turned the experience he gained fighting the French all these years and now preys on his own countrymen. Is that not so, Clive?"

"Aye." Clive's hamlike fists clenched at his sides. "He's a black one, is Sir Gowain, wild and bloodthirsty as any Scots riever, but canny, ye understand. He favors swooping down on unsuspecting merchants, kills the leader right quick, then forces the rest to surrender. We laid a trap for him, with my men posing as merchants. Gowain sent the leader back to us in pieces.''

A shocked silence fell over the hall.

"These are grievous charges," Gareth said slowly.

"Aye. If you declare him an outlaw and put a writ about, those who have been helping him will cease, lest they be outlawed, too," Ranulf said quickly.

"He can also be hanged without a trial," Gareth muttered.

"'Tis no more than he deserves for killing innocent men, women and even children.''

"Children," Alys whispered, appalled by the story.

"What proof do you have of his deeds?" Gareth asked.

"Proof?" Ranulf scowled. "My storage sheds lay empty, for he's stolen my supplies. My captain is dead and others with him. Several farms have been burned to the ground.''

"Was Gowain seen perpetrating these crimes?"

"I know he is guilty," Ranulf growled.

"Hmm." Gareth stroked his chin. "Still, I'd not act hastily in this matter. Will you sup with us ere I think it over?"

"Of course," Ranulf said smoothly, but his clenched fists and narrowed eyes betrayed his anger over the delay.

Nor could Alys blame him. "Papa, surely you will grant his request," she blurted out. "This Gowain must be stopped.''

Ranulf turned and stared at her so intently her cheeks flamed. "Who is this charming lady who pleads my cause?''

"My daughter, Lady Alys," Gareth said with pride. "May I also present to you my wife, Lady Arianna?''

Ranulf bowed deep, first to her mother, then to Alys. "You seem in need of a dining companion," he said to Alys. Mounting the dais, he took the seat to her left.

* * *

Within minutes, Ranulf's plans changed. Oh, he still wanted Gowain outlawed and eliminated. But he also intended to wed the wealthy, well-connected Lady Alys.

Ranulf's gaze narrowed as it wandered over the great hall's costly furnishings, carved chairs, lavish wall hangings, pristine white tableclothes set with silver plates. The candlesticks gracing the head table were wrought of pure gold, the intricate designs matching the goblets from which they drank. He was calculating their worth when the Lady Alys spoke.

"What your brother has done is monstrous. How horrible to be turned upon by your own kin."

"It is." Ranulf gave her his most charming smile. She was a pretty enough thing, if your taste ran to tiny blondes got up in yards of blue velvet. Her gown was so voluminous it hid her shape completely, but her features were lovely. Not that looks mattered, when a girl was heiress to a fortune.

Ranulf had made it a point to learn all he could about the Sommervilles before coming here. He'd known about Gareth's broken leg and that the two sons of the house were away on their father's business. These facts had made it unlikely the earl would offer to help fight Gowain. That was the last thing Ranulf wanted. Even with a larger force, it could take months to find Gowain's hiding place and eliminate him. Time Ranulf didn't have.

Every day, Gowain grew stronger and more daring. Soon he might become bold enough to attack Eastham or Malpas. Precious as his castle was to him, Ranulf was more worried about Malpas. Thus far, he'd managed to keep the area cut off and the outside world ignorant of what he was doing there. If word got out...

Jesu, he didn't even want to think about that.

"Do not groan, Lord Ranulf," Lady Alys said gently. "I promise to aid you in convincing me father."

"I thank you for your good wishes, Lady Alys." He'd learned she was a healer of some repute and unwed because, if you could believe it, her parents had left the choos-

ing of a husband to her. Now he meant to be that man.
"Will you have some of the roasted fowl?" Ranulf set
himself to charm. No easy task, for she was a skittish thing.
The meal was an extravagant one, fit for a feast day, but
she ate little and drank even less. She also had an annoying
habit of avoiding contact with him. Even in such lavish
surroundings, with plenty of room for the diners, it was
inevitable that hands brush or thighs touch.

Despite Ranulf's efforts to capitalize on this, Lady Alys
managed to keep her distance. Even more curious, she wore
gloves. They were of the finest-quality leather, thin and pale
as her own lovely skin. But gloves nonetheless. Mayhap
she'd been burned or she suffered a skin rash. Not that he
cared. He'd have taken her if she had two heads and no
legs.

"Gareth, you need to stretch out and elevate your leg,"
Lady Arianna said as the servants began clearing the tables.

"I must speak with Ranulf," the earl replied.

"Why do the four of us not repair to my solar? You
could be comfortable there and converse with Lord Ranulf
in private."

Ranulf could scarcely credit his luck. Dining with an earl
and now invited into the Sommervilles' inner sanctum as
though he were already part of the family. The Fates had
surely smiled on him...a blood connection with a noble
family, a large dowry and a toothsome bed partner to ini-
tiate in all the ways he liked to be pleasured. He was less
pleased when they reached the richly appointed solar and
he heard what Lord Gareth had decided.

"I regret that I cannot issue a writ against Sir Gowain
without sworn warrants of his deeds," the earl said. "It
may be that someone else has done these things and im-
plicated Gowain."

Ranulf ground his teeth together. "Your honesty and
sense of duty to the law do you justice." *And I curse them
both.*

Lady Alys exclaimed, "Surely Lord Ranulf's word is enough."

"'Tis not a matter of his word, Alys." Gareth frowned. "Have you forgotten what nearly happened to us?" He turned to Ranulf. "Years ago, my family was wrongly accused of treason, solely on the strength of rumor and the false witness of villainous men. We managed to outwit them and unmask the true criminals, but 'twas a near thing. Though I am certain your proof is solid, I'd not outlaw a man without making certain he is guilty."

"But, Papa..." Lady Alys began.

"'Tis all right," Ranulf said. He'd rouse the earl's suspicions did he complain. "I will provide whatever you need."

As Lord Gareth enumerated the proofs he would require against Gowain, Ranulf took a sip of the wine, rich, smooth Bordeaux wine, not the sour stuff they kept at Eastham. When he and Alys were wed, he'd eat and drink only the finest. He'd refurbish Eastham from cellar to turret. Of course, it would never be as grand as Ransford.

Hmm. Ranulf cocked his head, considering yet another course of action. If something should happen to her brothers, Ransford and the wealth of the Sommervilles would be hers. And his.

"I am sorry to disappoint you," said the earl.

"Disappoint me? Never. Your caution and concern are proof the king chose wisely when he named you his justice. On the morrow, I will return home and begin gathering information."

"If you and Lord Ranulf are done, may I ask a boon, Papa?"

"Of course." The earl gave Alys a dazzling smile.

Lady Alys lifted a velvet bag from a nearby table and withdrew from it a stack of books. Kneeling at her father's side, she handed him the top one. "I have finished my herbal."

"Alys!" the earl cried. "What a tremendous accomplishment!"

"Thank you, Papa, but I am anxious to have them copied ere something happens to the originals. Please say you'll let me go to Newstead Abbey." Her pleading smile would have melted iron.

"You know I'd let you go if I could, but I'm weeks away from being able to ride, and I'd not send my precious love unescorted."

"I could take Sir Miles and a goodly troop."

"Nay." Tears sprang into the earl's eyes, and he looked to his wife for support."

"Mayhap we could send to London for some lay brothers to do the copying," her mother offered.

Lady Alys shook her head. "The nuns' work is the finest in the land. They alone can do justice to my books."

Ranulf thought the lot of them stupid and sentimental. But he also saw a way to achieve his goal. "If I might offer my services, my lord. I have with me a fighting force of five knights and thirty mounted men. No one would dare strike at the lovely Lady Alys while she was in my care."

"Thank you, Lord Ranulf. Oh, Papa. Please, please."

"Well…" Lord Gareth murmured.

Ranulf sensed him weakening. "If we started early and set a brisk pace, I could have her there by vespers," Ranulf said.

"Very well." The earl's grudging permission was drowned out by Lady Alys's shrieks of delight.

Ranulf's pleasure was quieter, but just as sharp. Silently he planned a small detour on the way to Newstead.

Chapter Two

"Are you certain we are not lost?" Alys asked.

Lord Ranulf started. "Nay, I know exactly where we are. You can trust me to see you safely to our destination, dear Lady Alys." His smile was patronizing yet smug, as though he knew something she did not.

Above all things, Alys hated lies and secrets. She shifted in the saddle, uneasy, suddenly, with a man she'd dismissed as a harmless fop. "I've twice traveled to Newstead, but nothing about this wild country seems familiar." Not the rugged mountains glaring down at her from on high, nor the black forest crowding close to the narrow road.

"Surely you do not mistrust me."

"Nay." There was no reason for Ranulf to deceive her, yet the notion that he hid something persisted. She did not have her great-aunt Cici's ability to read minds, but with her special healing gift had come an awareness of people's nature. Her first instinct about Ranulf had been wariness. In her eagerness to leave for Newstead, she'd ignored that vague unease.

Well, her family often warned that someday her impetuous nature and penchant for wanting her own way would get her into trouble. Mayhap it had. Feeling lonely and afraid for the first time in her life, she studied Ranulf.

The raised visor of Ranulf's helmet shadowed his

smooth, pleasant features. Too smooth, mayhap. Ranulf had shown her many faces in the short time since they'd met. The bland one he had on now, the furious mask he'd worn when he'd demanded her father outlaw his rebellious brother, the beguiling face of the flatterer he'd put on for her parents. Who was he, really?

Her stomach clenched, and her palms grew damp inside her gloves. Why had he gone out of his way to escort her?

"I'd not take even the slightest risk of something happening to you," he said silkily, maneuvering his horse closer to hers.

He sounded as annoyingly protective as her family. That must be what had ruffled her. Not some nefarious intent, but his stifling attitude. "I am not some fragile violet, sir knight. My father is a horse breeder, and I an excellent horsewoman, able to ride long distances even over rough terrain."

"I am sure you are." He patted her hand.

Alys flinched and drew away, but an impression filtered in through her protective glove. Something dark and murky. Her own fears or something in him?

"Forgive my forwardness," Ranulf said stiffly, frowning at her gloved hands.

Alys sighed. "'Tis I who should beg pardon, my lord, and thank you for not peppering me with rude questions about my gloves. The truth is, my skin is very sensitive."

"Ah. You are wise to protect your delicate self from the elements. And to wear such a modest costume for traveling." He cast an approving eye over her gray gown and matching cloak.

Made from wool of the cheaper sort, the garment was devoid of fancy trim and cut full to resemble the serviceable robes worn by the nuns. She would be living among them for several months and wanted to dress as they did. Also, she hoped to further some of her experiments with herbal cures. Though her mother had insisted she bring along a few velvets and silks...just in case...Alys had packed her simplest things for this trip.

"I want to thank you again for escorting me," Alys said. "Especially since I know you must be anxious to return home and begin gathering evidence against your dreadful brother."

"Not at all. Not at all." He smiled that eager-puppy smile that had won over her parents when he'd proposed escorting her to the abbey. "I would climb the highest mountain, ford a raging river, to see you safe."

Alys sighed. Merciful heavens, but his devotion and courtliness were annoying. For several reasons, she'd be glad to reach Newstead and bid her courtier farewell.

"Are you tired, my lady? Should I call a halt?"

"Nay." Alys straightened in the saddle. She'd not delay the journey even for an instant. "I am fine."

Lord Ranulf smiled like an indulgent auntie. "You have only to say if you are weary, and we will rest. Or I could take you up before me so you might—"

"Perish the thought!" Alys exclaimed.

Ranulf blinked, his smile faltering for the first time all day. "I assure you I meant no impropriety. I had hoped you looked upon me as a friend anxious to help you."

What could she say? How could she explain that she'd sell her soul for but one embrace, one hug that wasn't fraught with tension and apprehension? Alas, it was not to be. "You are a friend," she said gently. "Had you not offered your help, I'd not be making the journey to Newstead till my father's leg was healed or one of my brothers free of responsibility."

"They value you greatly." Ranulf smiled and again edged his palfrey so close his mailed leg brushed her skirts. "I would gladly be more to you than a temporary guardian."

Alys fought the urge to retreat. "What do you mean?"

"I should speak with your lord father first, I know, but we left so quickly there wasn't time. I'd have you to wife."

"You what?" she cried.

"I'd wed with you."

"Oh." Drat. "I—I am conscious of the honor you do me," Alys stammered. "But it is not possible."

He stiffened. "I grant an earl's daughter could look higher, but I've two castles and am engaged in a venture that will yield me wealth beyond your wildest dreams."

"It isn't a matter of property or money."

"Your father said you had the choosing." He sounded faintly appalled. "Yet you've not found a man to your liking." He grinned. "Till now. We deal well together, I think."

"I am sorry, Lord Ranulf, but it is impossible."

His smile developed a hard edge, and his eyes turned cold. "You would change your mind…in time."

Not in a hundred years. Alys bit her tongue to keep the words back. "We will not have time. We part in a few—"

"I realized that. Which is why I decided we'd detour to visit my castle at Eastham."

"What?" Alys's heart raced. "You are kidnapping me?"

"Never!" he exclaimed. "Only giving you a chance to see what kind of life I can offer you."

"But—" Alys was torn between fear and outrage.

"Milord." Clive and another man pounded toward them from their places at the head of the column. "Egbert reports there are abandoned wagons up ahead."

"Why trouble me to report some farmers have deserted their goods?" Ranulf snapped. "Can you not see I am busy?"

"But I think they are your wagons," said Egbert, a chunky man with a wicked scar across his forehead. "The ones sent to London to fetch the winter supplies."

"What? Was there evidence of foul play?" Ranulf's eyes narrowed as he scanned the forest up ahead. "This is far from his usual range, but it may be Gowain."

Egbert shuddered. "There was no one about. Not the guards sent from Eastham or the wagon drivers."

"That makes no sense," Clive muttered. "If Gowain, or some other bandits, had waylaid them, why leave the goods behind?"

"Because they heard us coming and took flight," Ranulf replied. "Or…" His eyes widened suddenly. "Or they are still—"

A bloodcurdling cry cut off his words. Men sprang from behind the trees and rushed onto the road. They were roughly dressed in tattered tunics and hide boots, some mounted on shaggy horses, the rest afoot. Their weapons glinted in the dimness of the tiny glade. At their head rode a mail-clad warrior, his long black hair flowing from beneath his helmet, his sword aloft.

"Bastard!" Ranulf roared. Drawing his sword, he spurred forward, crying, "Take them. A hundred silver marks to the man who kills the bastard!"

Ranulf's men surged after him, a great screaming tide of mail and muscle. The two groups met with enough force to shake the ground, then dissolved into knots of men striking at each other with blade and ax and mace. The clash of steel on steel, the shouts of the warriors and the shrieks of the wounded rang off the trees till they filled the air.

Left behind, Alys sat transfixed, her fists clenched so tight her bones ached. She'd seen the men of her family practice on the tiltyard and attended several court tourneys, but never had she imagined real war would be so horrible. She held her breath, watching as Ranulf and his opponent exchanged blows in the center of the chaos.

The focus of the fighting shifted like a restless tide, surging back and forth across the road and into the verge of the forest. Men began to drop from view now, outlaw and soldier alike slipping from sight beneath the dreadful thrust of shimmering steel to the flailing mass of hooves below.

The healer in Alys cried out to aid them. Instinct urged her to flee while she could. If Ranulf won, he'd press his claim for her hand. If the outlaws won, she might be in worse trouble. Either way, she was in grave danger.

Just then, a man crawled out of the fighting. Blood covered the side of his tunic. He held one arm against his body. When he was halfway to her, his strength gave out, and he collapsed in a heap.

Heedless of her own safety, Alys slipped from her mount and moved toward him. Kneeling beside him, she touched his shoulder with her gloved hand. "Let me see where—"

He rolled over, a stained knife clutched in one gory hand.

Alys gasped and jerked back as the blade sliced the air just shy of her ribs. "Hold! I'd tend your wound."

His pain-filled eyes widened, then softened. "Sister?"

Alys debated for only an instant. If it helped him to trust her, she'd lie and claim to be the nun she obviously resembled. "Aye. I'm Sister Alys. Let me see…"

He flopped onto his back, eyes shut. "I'm done fer, I fear, Sister. If ye could give me the last rites."

"Let me see." She parted the bloody rent in his tunic and winced at the long, jagged gash. "It'll want stitching." She looked at the mass of fighting men. They surged over the roadway and into the forest, careless of anything in their path in their quest to kill. "We have to get away from here."

Though he was small, the man was heavier than he looked. She half dragged, half carried, her patient off the road and into the brush, then collapsed panting beside him.

"Sister," he whispered.

Alys sat up and leaned over him. "I'm here."

"Promise ye won't leave me to die alone."

"I won't leave you…but neither will I let you die. If I can get the bleeding stopped and the flesh stitched—" She raised her skirts and tore a strip from her chemise. In deference to the cool, damp weather, it was wool, but it was soft and finely woven. She folded it into a pad and pressed it against the wound.

Her patient moaned softly. "Feels like I'm dying."

Poor man, Alys thought. Then she took a good look at his face. Beneath the dirt and blood, his skin was freckled and hairless as a baby's. "How old are you?"

"Th-three-and-ten."

"A child. Who would send a child out to fight?"

"My lord needs every man who can heft a weapon," he said weakly. "Least with me gone, there'll one less to feed."

"Indeed." Alys was torn between pity and fury. What dire circumstances landed people in such straits? She pressed harder on the pad, then lifted it, pleased to see the wound wasn't as long as she'd feared. But it was deep. She had needle and thread in the pouch at her waist, but her medicine chest was with her baggage. God alone knew where the carts and horse had gotten to. Wait, there was a small pack of herbs in her saddle pouch. If she could just reach it…

"Stork, I'm called…'count of my long legs," the boy murmured. "But my real name's Dickie…Dick of Newton. Just wanted ye to know…fer the prayers. Ye will pray fer me?"

Tears filled Alys's eyes. "You're not going to die, Dickie. I'm going to fix you up good as new." She stood and looked toward the road, suddenly aware that the sounds of battle had faded. Either the trees were masking the noise or the fighting had moved farther away. If she hurried, she might be able to find her horse while it was still relatively safe. "I have to get my medicines." She placed his hand on the makeshift bandage. "Press here. I'll be right back."

Alys dashed away. Anxious as she was to return to him, she hesitated at the edge of the woods. A stand of young oaks and gooseberry bushes blocked her view of the road. But she could hear nothing over the thrum of her pulse against her temple. What had happened? Had they wiped each other out?

Parting the brush, Alys looked out onto a scene straight

from hell. The bodies of men and horses littered the ground. It seemed no one lived.

"Oh, Sweet Mary have mercy." Alys crossed herself, then hesitated, reluctant to walk among them. But Dickie would be added to their number if she didn't act. She lifted her skirts and walked slowly down the edge of the road, trying not to see the details of the horror spread before her while she searched for her horse. There, a few feet into the carnage, she recognized the red-and-black trappings her father's squire had put on her mount. Was it only this morn? Merciful heaven, but it seemed a lifetime ago.

Alys picked her way to the horse, then knelt and untied the pouch from behind the saddle. As she stood, someone grabbed her from behind, lifting her off the ground and pressing her back against a rock-hard body.

"Who the hell are you?" growled a hard voice.

The question broke through her shock. Alys erupted into action, lashing out with her feet, twisting her body. Her scream was cut off by a wide, callused hand. Instantly she was bombarded by her captor's emotions. White-hot rage. Dark, seething frustration. Terrified, she whimpered and went limp.

"Bloody hell." His grip gentled. Remorse now warred with his earlier fury. "I will not hurt you. Swear you'll not scream again, and I'll release your mouth."

Alys managed to nod. When his hand lifted off her lips, she dragged in a lungful of air and tried to steady herself. His skin was no longer touching her skin, linking her with his deeper feelings, but the sizzle of his violent emotions remained. "Please," she whimpered.

He spun her around to face him, and she got another shock. It was the black-haired man who'd led the attack.

Oh, no! Alys's knees went weak. She'd have fallen over if he wasn't holding her upright. He towered over her, his massive chest and wide shoulders straining the links of his mail shirt, his face concealed by a dented helmet.

"You!" he thundered. "You were riding with Ranulf."

Anger sparked then, and Alys flinched. "I—"

"Sister Alys!" Dickie staggered out of the brush.

The giant released Alys and wheeled around, bringing his sword up. "Stork. What the hell are you doing here?"

Alys forgot her own fear. Drawing the knife from her belt, she darted between him and the boy. "Get back. Leave him alone."

"'Tis all right, Sister," Dickie said. "We are saved. This is Lord Gowain."

"G-Gowain." The air left Alys's lungs in a rush; the knife wavered in her hand and her courage with it.

"Sister Alys?" Gowain raised the visor of his helmet and eyed her skeptically. What she could see of his face, shadowed by his visor, was even less reassuring…glittering dark eyes, roughly chiseled features as stark as the surrounding mountains. "You wield a blade right surely for a nun."

"I—I was not always one. I—I had brothers who taught me to defend myself," she stammered, more grateful by the moment for her disguise. If the brigand dared attack Ranulf, what would he do to a mere woman? Doubtless the gown that so resembled a nun's robe and her healing skills were all that stood between herself and ruin. "Desperate times call for desperate measures."

"A sentiment I support."

"Is that meant to justify your unprovoked attack on us?"

"Us?" His mouth thinned. "What are you to Ranulf?"

Alys rued her hasty tongue. "He was my escort."

"How went the battle, milord?" Dickie asked.

"Well enough. Ranulf fled when the battle turned against him. My horse was cut from under me, but the other lads gave chase," Gowain replied, his eyes remaining locked on Alys. "Where was he taking you?"

"Newstead Abbey," Alys replied.

His gaze hardened. "I know that place, but it is many leagues east of here."

"Aye, well…" She could hardly tell him of Ranulf's

insane notion to wed her. Not and maintain her unanticipated but fortunate guise as a nun. "We became lost."

"In these woods? Ranulf knows this land right well."

Drat. "I...I do not know."

He grunted. "Ranulf only cares for that which profits him. What did he hope to gain by escorting you to Newstead?"

Oh, dear.

"Sister Alys," Dickie called, weaving unsteadily.

"Dickie." Alys dropped her knife and reached for the boy. As she wrapped an arm around his back, she fancied she could feel the life draining out of him. Dickie slumped against her, nearly dragging Alys down with him.

Gowain rescued them both by sweeping the boy into his arms before he hit the ground.

"Lay him down right here in the grass and remove his tunic," Alys ordered. She hurried over to retrieve her knife and pack. When she returned, she found the knight kneeling beside the boy.

"Whatever possessed you to follow us?" Gowain asked. His voice was low, gentle, as he stroked back the boy's sweaty hair.

"I heard them say how important it was to get the food," Dickie whispered. "You needed every man."

"That I did, Stork, but I also needed men to stay behind and watch over the camp. Men I could trust to follow orders."

"I'm sorry, my lord." Dickie shivered.

Gowain drew off his mended cloak and laid it over the boy, the gesture surprising and touching. "Just lie still." He glanced around and glared at Alys. "Damn, I thought you'd run off."

"I would never leave someone who needs me." Alys fell to her knees on Dick's other side.

"You'd be the first, then," Gowain muttered.

"Sister, am I going to die?"

"Not if I can help it."

"It hurts."

"I know." Alys longed to remove her gloves and touch him, to let the warmth of her flesh soothe him. But if she did, his pain would engulf her and she'd be useless. She stroked his cheek with the backs of her gloved fingers and let all her concern, all her confidence and, aye, all the love she felt for this skinny boy, show in her smile. "Trust in me, Dickie of Newton."

He smiled. "I do." His lashes fluttered, then closed.

"He's fainted, thank God," Alys said.

Gowain tugged off his worn helmet and tossed it to the ground. Leafy light gleamed dully on sweaty, well-chiseled features, a wide forehead, high cheekbones and a square, cleft chin. His hair, black as a raven feather, curled wetly against his bronzed skin. But it was his eyes that caught and held her. They'd looked black in the shadowed depths of his helmet. Now she saw they were green. A rich, velvety shade of green that reminded her of the forest at night. He might have been counted a handsome man, if not for the coldness in those dark, merciless eyes. Aye, he was all hard angles, a harsh face and remote eyes. Unforgiving. Uncompromising. "Can you save his life, Sister?"

"Aye. I need hot water, clean cloths for washing and—"

"You'll have to make do without."

"Do you want him to die?"

A twig snapped behind them. Gowain leapt up, sword in hand, and stood over them, as protective as a wolf defending its mate and cub. The bushes parted, and a mountain of a man stepped out.

"Ah, here you are," he fairly sang out. "Lang Gib said he'd seen you taking to the forest with a wench, but I could scarcely credit that." He looked down at Alys and her patient. "*Dieu*, it's Stork!" His hand hovered over the boy's head. "Is he dead?"

"Nay," Alys replied, touched by his concern. "But he needs immediate care. If you could get me water and—"

"I've told you we haven't time." Gowain sheathed his

sword with an angry motion. "Darcy, rig one of the wagons we captured to carry the wounded. Sister Alys will ride in it and tend them. Be ready to travel in a quarter hour."

"Sister." Darcy's wide face was all smiles. "'Twas a lucky thing we chanced on you."

"She was with Ranulf," Gowain growled, making Darcy's smile dim. "What happened after my horse faltered? Did you manage to capture the scum?"

"He got clean away, though he left many a dead man behind. Wounded, too." Darcy sighed. "Damn, I thought you had him."

"So did I, but he maneuvered me into a corner. I could not take him without killing him."

"Ranulf deserves to die," Darcy exclaimed.

"But not by my hand." Gowain's jaw tensed. "I'll not kill my own brother."

"Aye, well. I expect there'll come another day when we can take him and stop this."

"I pray so." Gowain cursed and ran a hand through his hair. "Damn. It would have saved us so much if we could have captured him and forced him to yield to our demands." His hand fell to his side, clenched into a tight fist. "Losses?"

"Not bad." Darcy rattled off the name of one who had died. "We've a handful with minor injuries and three others sore hurt.... Mayhap you'd see to them when you finish with Stork, Sister?"

"Certainly. I need hot wa—"

"We've no time to tarry," Gowain said. "Ranulf could return at any time. Bind their hurts as best you can. We'll see you have what you need when we get to camp."

"I can't go with you. I'm needed at Newstead."

His gaze turned icy. "So you said, but Newstead Abbey is miles from here...in the opposite direction from the one in which you were traveling, I might add."

What could she do but try to bluff? "That's impossible. Ranulf told me—"

"Then he lied. My dear brother has a way of twisting things to suit himself."

"He did not lie about you," Alys snapped.

"What did he say about me?" he asked softly.

"That you robbed, burned and murdered. That you attacked innocent travelers...just as you did us a few moments—"

"Ranulf is no innocent."

"So you say, but I think—"

"I've no time to trade insults with you, Sister."

"Fine. Give me a horse, then, and I'll be on my way."

"And leave the wounded behind to die?" he asked in that silky voice she was coming to hate. "Is that not against the oaths you swore to aid mankind?"

"I did not vow to aid criminals."

Gowain tsked. "I did not know the church made such distinctions. Are not all men worthy in God's eyes?"

Alys stiffened. He might be a brigand, but he was a clever-witted one to trap her so. "I could have ridden away when the fighting started," she said with a calm she didn't feel. "I stayed to help Dickie, and I will gladly see to the others. All I ask in return is an escort to Newstead when they are well. Is that too much to ask?"

"Nay, it is not," Darcy said quickly.

Gowain's glittering green gaze remained locked on her wary one, holding it so that she couldn't look away. "Providing you are not Ranulf's spy. 'Twould be folly to let her go if she means to betray us...especially now."

The last must have held meaning for Darcy, because he nodded, expression dour. "I will set someone to watch her on our ride to camp."

"If you move Dickie, you consign him to death," Alys said. "For jolting about in a wagon with his wound unstitched would kill him. I will not, I cannot in good conscience, leave till he's properly—"

"I cannot spare more time," Gowain snapped. "If you

are so concerned for them, I suggest you use it to bandage them rather than issue edicts." He turned and stalked away.

"Clod, cold, unfeeling clod," she muttered.

"Nay, he is not that," Darcy said. "You do not know him, so you cannot see what it cost him to give that order. But there are many lives depending on him. We must reach our camp, and swiftly, lest Ranulf return."

I hope he does, Alys thought. I hope he comes and kills you all. Fortunately, she was wise enough not to voice such an unruly hope aloud. Nor did she really want all these people killed, but it would give her great satisfaction to see Gowain meet an outlaw's just rewards...the hangman's noose. As she bent to tend Stork, her hands shook so badly she could scarcely bind the wound. Partly it was sharing a measure of the pain the young boy felt; partly it was fear for herself.

What would happen if they discovered she wasn't a nun?

Chapter Three

"You were rude to Sister Alys," Darcy said when they were well away from the scene of the battle.

"I have greater worries than hurting the feelings of a spoiled, prideful nun," Gowain growled, his mind on the perilous journey to safety. They rode at the head of the swiftly moving column, with a rear guard as well as men afoot to sweep away traces of their passage. It had taken time and work, but his rebel band ran as smoothly as the king's army in France.

"She is uncommonly beautiful for a nun."

"I did not notice." But he had. He could still recall the feel of her small, slender body against his. His nerves still tingled from the spark that had passed between them. One instant he'd been furious with her, the next, swept by desire. Jesu, he was truly a lost cause if he lusted after a nun. And one who might well be in league with Ranulf.

And yet. She had the softest eyes he'd ever seen. Large, expressive blue eyes so dark they'd appeared black in the dim forest glade where she'd tended Stork, Sim and Martin.

"We are fortunate she was there, else we'd have lost three good men," Darcy said.

Gowain grunted. She had spared him the terrible weight of Stork's death, yet he didn't want to be in her debt. In the brief few moments they'd been together, she'd made him feel things he didn't want to feel. Especially for a nun.

"Curious she is not wed." When Gowain refused to be drawn in, Darcy went on. "Though she is one of the most comely women I've seen, she is not a tender young maid, I think. No girl would have such fire. How old would you judge her to be?"

"Why, thinking of bedding her?" Gowain asked nastily.

"Of course not. I did but speculate."

"Cease prattling about her and speculate instead on whether what we took today is enough for our purpose." Word that a trio of supply wagons moved along the road toward Eastham had prompted Gowain to risk a daylight raid. The guards and drivers had abandoned their cargo and fled into the woods without a fight.

"We hadn't the time to examine everything," Darcy said. "But I saw sacks of beans and flour, which we sorely need, two kegs of ale and several of salted beef." He patted his belly. "'Twill be good indeed to eat something besides root soup."

"Welcome as the food is, I'd rather we had taken Ranulf." Gowain's hand tightened on the reins. "Then we could stop living like hunted animals."

"Soon," Darcy said gently. "This haul brings us that much closer to making our move against him."

"Aye." But the knowledge that it would soon be over, one way or the other, brought little solace. Thus far, he and his men had fought defensively, to stay alive, to free those oppressed by Ranulf and to get food with which to feed them. The next step was a huge one. The taking of Malpas Keep itself. The battle required careful strategy and superb timing. "But even if all goes according to plan, we still may suffer heavy casualties."

"The men know that. They are prepared to sacrifice—"

"Well, I am not," Gowain exclaimed, thinking of Stork and the others, possibly bleeding to death in the wagon because a delay might cost more lives. "Jesu, do you think I want to buy back my estate with their blood?"

"It is not just your lands we fight for," Darcy reminded him. "It is our very lives. We could not last the winter without food and better shelter. Nor can we provide for the increasing numbers who flee from Ranulf's tyranny. The people who've joined us are nearly more desperate than we are." He paused a moment, considering Gowain's unyielding posture. "If only the king would grant your request for a hearing."

"King Richard has no time for dispossessed men such as we," Gowain said bitterly. "He's too busy granting grand titles to his favorites to even respond to my letter." It had been sent by a priest a week after Gowain took to the woods. Father Bassett had assured him the letter was handed to the court functionary, yet no word had come from London.

"Then we must look to ourselves and take back that which Ranulf has stolen from all of us," Darcy said firmly.

"Aye, we must." And God save us all. "I will ride back along the line and see how the men fare," Gowain said, as much because it was his way to check on things himself as because he was restless with the dozens of worries that beset him.

The pair who rode directly behind him were seasoned veterans who'd followed him from France. Despite long hours in the saddle, Robert Lakely and Jean de Braise sat tall and alert, ready to spring into action at any sign of trouble. Seeing Gowain change direction, they moved to accompany him.

"Keep your places," Gowain said. "I'll be right back."

"I'd go with you, just in case there is trouble," said Jean, older than Lakely and prone to pessimism.

"I'd have you here, for that reason," Gowain replied and headed down the column. He nodded to the men he passed, noting keenly the condition of each. His soldiers had borne the brunt of both the attack on the wagons and the skirmish with Ranulf's men, yet the farmers and tradesmen turned warrior looked the most haggard. A few sported red splotches on their rough tunics.

Arthur Jenkins was by far the worst, bent over and wavering slightly in his saddle. "Not far, now, Arthur," he called. "Can you make it, or would you ride in the wagon?"

"Nay. I think my arm's broke, and the wagon'd jostle it worse than my horse does," he said through lips gone white.

Gowain's jaw tightened with suppressed fury...against Ranulf, King Richard and even God. These good people did not deserve the suffering that life had thrust upon them. Damn, but he wished he could find a way to take Malpas without their help.

When he came abreast of the middle wagon driven by Henry Denys, Gowain turned to ride with it. "How goes it?"

Henry shrugged and jerked his head toward the back of the wagon. "Better ask my brother. I've been that busy trying to avoid the worst of the ruts."

Ralph Denys sat in the back of the wagon, arms folded over his chest, dour gaze fixed on the nun ministering to her patients. "Nobody's died...yet," he muttered.

A sigh of relief hissed through Gowain's teeth, and he moved a bit closer. "Sister, you have saved—"

"No thanks to you." Her eyes were not soft or gentle, now, but blazed like hot coals in her ashen face.

Gowain drew back, the praise he'd been about to offer catching in his throat. "I do not answer to you."

"And you can be grateful for that. If you were my father's man, he'd whip you raw for such callous disregard of human life."

"Would he, now?" Gowain's eyes narrowed, studying the regal tilt of her head. "And who might your illustrious sire be?"

She blinked, then lowered her lashes, effectively shielding her eyes. "No one you would know."

"Ah. But I might have heard of him."

"Not all men's names are whispered about like an ill wind."

"I long ago ceased to care what others said of me." He gathered the reins to leave.

"Wait." She stretched out a hand to him, and he noted she yet wore her gloves, stained from her night's labors. Odd she should keep her hands covered, for the air was not that chilled. "How much farther to your camp?"

"A mile, no more," he said curtly.

She nodded and fell back on her haunches beside Stork. "Good. Send ahead and bid them heat water. I will also need bandages...clean bandages," she added, eyeing his filthy tunic.

"You are adept at issuing orders, Sister."

"And you slow to follow them," she snapped. Her raised chin and contemptuous expression clearly showed her willfulness. "If you do not value their lives, think how hard it may be to replace them with other boys willing to follow you into battle."

"On the contrary, Sister," Gowain said icily, straining to contain a temper he usually had no trouble controlling. "It is easy to find boys who will fight for me. The water will be waiting." He spurred his horse forward so swiftly a cry went up.

"Are we attacked?" Henry called as he passed the wagon.

"Nay." But he was beset by a sharp-tongued shrew of a nun. He'd thought Blanche haughty, but this one left her in the shade. He wanted her gone, wished he could send her on to Newstead. If she was in league with Ranulf, however, she'd quickly tell his half brother about the size of Gowain's force and location of his camp. Gowain could not afford to take that chance.

Nor could he be without a healer till the wounded recovered. None of the other women in camp had her skill. Much as he hated to need anyone, he needed the nun.

"We're here, Sister." Henry halted the wagon.

Alys shifted on her numb knees. The forest through which they'd traveled most of the night still surrounded them on three sides. Ahead lay a ridge of jagged mountain peaks. Set out against the gray sky of early dawn, they seemed to growl at the heavens like the teeth of some great, defiant monster. What a bleak, fitting place for an outlaw band, yet she saw no tents or lean-tos. "Surely you do not live in the open."

He chuckled, revealing broken teeth set in a face as craggy as the mountains. "Nay. Camp is up there wi' the crows."

Alys tipped her head back and looked where he pointed. "All I see are stone and sky."

"Aye. 'Tis what's made it nigh impossible for Ranulf the Cruel to find us. There's caves up there, the entrance hidden well back among the rocks. The trail's narrow, tricky as hell…er, if ye'll pardon my speech, Sister…and well guarded. Even if Ranulf did find it, he'd not drag us out in a hundred years."

Alys groaned faintly. She'd hoped Gowain's camp would be in the forest, so that she might slip away into the trees and escape. Once trapped in the mountain, how would she ever get out?

Her throat constricted as the enormity of her situation truly sank in. She was the prisoner of a vicious outlaw, protected only by her habit and his necessity. Had Stork not assumed she was a nun, had they not needed her to keep the men alive, she'd be dead, or worse….

What would happen if they discovered she wasn't a nun?

Alys clasped her arms around her shivering body and struggled to stay calm. There had to be a way out. She'd keep her wits calm and her eyes open for a chance to steal a horse and ride off. Better to be lost in the woods than to be the prisoner of such as these. Mayhap she could find her way to Eastham and Ranulf.

Ranulf, of course.

Alys nearly laughed aloud in relief. Ranulf had wanted to wed her. Surely he would not leave her to the outlaws' mercy. He'd either send trackers to follow them to this hideout, or ride to Ransford for her family. Once it was known she'd been taken prisoner, they'd come to rescue her. If her father couldn't sit a horse, he'd send for her uncles, Ruarke and Alexander, and her cousin Jamie, hero of the wars against the French.

"I thought you were anxious to see the wounded cared for," growled the object of her thoughts. Gowain had dismounted and stood beside the wagon, eyes glaring a challenge from deep within the dark sockets of his helmet. Behind him, his crew of thieves busily transferred the stolen goods from the wagons to packhorses. They worked briskly and efficiently, doubtless with the skill of long practice.

"Come, I will take you up with me," Gowain said, holding out his mailed hand.

"I prefer the wagon, thank you," she said coldly.

"The wagons are going to a farm nearby, where…"

"From which you doubtless stole them."

"What I steal, I generally keep. The wagons are mine. The farmer stores them and the horses for me betweentimes."

"Between raids. What of the wounded? Do they walk?"

"Nay. We'll carry them up on litters. 'Tis a long hike, and I but thought you'd be weary after your long night." He shrugged, as though the matter were unimportant. "Suit yourself, but don't fall behind."

Pride kept Alys from calling him back. She rued it during the long walk up the mountain. Her low riding boots were soft-soled, and the stones bit through the leather. Blisters sprang up on her heels and toes; her muscles, cramped and bruised from jolting about all night, screamed with every step. It took all her will and concentration to keep moving.

Soon even the men carrying the wounded had outdistanced her.

"Hoping to fall back and escape?" demanded a familiar voice.

Alys spun, and would have fallen if Gowain's hard hand hadn't reached out and grabbed her arm. Though three layers of wool clothes separated her from his touch, the contact sent a sizzle across her skin, raising gooseflesh in its wake. It was not his anger or annoyance. What was this strange sensation?

He felt it, too. His nostrils flared, and his eyes widened, then narrowed. "What the hell?" he whispered. His gaze moved over her. Some emotion she couldn't name flared his eyes so that the green burned bright. "*Dieu*, surely I am cursed," he spat, dropping her arm and severing the connection.

Alys exhaled sharply. What had happened? She hadn't felt his emotions, not exactly. This was like nothing she'd experienced before. "What... Where is your horse?" she asked lamely.

"Why do you wish to know?"

"I...I do not care where he is." She tossed her head, fractious and confused. "You had offered me a ride, yet—"

"I felt the urge to stretch my legs." He executed a bow that would have done a courtier proud, if not for the cynical twist of his mouth. "After you... Sister."

Alys picked up her skirts, took a step and winced.

"Have you hurt yourself?"

"My boots are soft and not made for walking."

"Like their owner, no doubt." Before she guessed what he was about, he knelt and tugged at the hem of her skirt.

"Nay." Alys tried to jerk free, but he held her fast.

"Show me your foot."

"Nay." She wore woolen hose, but it might not protect her from his touch.

"Your modesty is ill placed. Stick out your foot."

"I do not want you to touch me."

His expression hardened. "I have yet to stoop to ravishing nuns," he snapped. "I am trying to help."

"A first, I am sure."

Gowain stood in a swift, lithe movement. "I've no time to bandy words with a spoiled nun. We must be inside the caves, and quickly, lest we're spotted." He swept her off her feet.

"Oh!" Alys waited to be rushed by his emotions, but felt only the sinewy strength of his arms around her back and under her knees, the thunder of his heart against her ribs. Yet, beyond those ordinary things, she sensed power held in check, feelings blanketed by rigid control. The realization that he was able to hide from her was more frightening. "Put me down! How dare you!"

He tightened his grip on her. "Stop wriggling, or we'll both fall down the side of the mountain."

Alys glanced over his shoulder at the treetops, far, far below them and stopped struggling, but the feeling of being surrounded by some terrible force persisted. She'd seen a tree once, struck by lighting. It had simply exploded from the inside out and burst into flames. Now she understood why.

"Relax. I won't drop you." His breath fanned her forehead, warm and soft.

"I...I am not used to being handled so." Was that her voice? She sounded breathless and faint.

"You are the first nun I've carried, also. 'Tis a bit... disconcerting. Aye, that must be it," he added, so low she barely heard the words.

"It, what?" Talking eased her, gave her something else to concentrate on besides him and the feelings he concealed.

"Nothing." He climbed steadily despite her weight. "How old were you when you felt the calling to be a nun?"

"Thirteen," she said without thinking, for that was when her life had changed...and not for the better.

"Ah. I am told females do irrational things at that time."

"Irrational! What is irrational about taking the veil?"

"Nothing, if you are suited to it. Which you are not."

"You are an expert in such matters?"

"I know women," he said with a contempt that grated.

"I am sure you do...and all of the low sort."

"Tsk, tsk. Did not Christ have compassion for them? Why did you wish to become a nun?"

"Because...because I wished to serve God." Oh, how the lie stuck in her throat. *Forgive me, but I have no other choice.*

"Ah. There are far too many who enter the church to avoid marriage rather than because they have a true calling."

That stung. "I'm pleased you approve."

"I do not." He shifted her, ducking as he stepped forward. Instantly the dark swallowed them up. He set her on her feet, but surprised her by keeping an arm protectively around her back to steady her.

Alys instinctively braced a hand on his chest. Beneath the iron links of his mail, she felt the pounding of his heart. It raced a bit, matching her own pulse. Why this sense of connection with him, of all people? "Where are the others?"

"They are forbidden to come to the entrance lest any be spotted from below." His low voice echoed faintly off unseen stone walls. "I but wait for my eyes to adjust to the darkness."

Alys stood perfectly still, senses straining to pick up clues to what lay ahead. From farther inside the caves, she heard distant scurrying sounds and muted voices as the outlaws settled their stolen goods. Yet she was more keenly aware of the man towering over her in the gloom. The rasp of his breathing reminded her of the steep climb he'd made, burdened by her weight. And that on top of a fierce battle and a long ride.

If she was exhausted, he must be doubly so. She looked

up, measuring him in the faint light. She'd not realized before how large he was, taller even than her father and brothers, his mended mail seemingly stretched to accommodate his powerful frame and bulging muscles. She'd been a fool to chafe at him. A shiver worked its way down her spine.

"Come. You grow chilled." He raised a hand to take her arm, then dropped it when she shied away.

Her eyes must be used to the dimness, for she saw the bitter twist of his lips. It is not your fault, but mine, she wanted to tell him. Though why she should care, she didn't know.

"Hang on to my cloak or my belt, then," he said gruffly. "The way is rough and twisting. I'd not want you to trip and break your neck till I'm certain my men are like to live."

"Thank you for reminding me of my worth." She stumbled along behind with her hand clutched on his cloak.

"I'm a plain-speaking man." He forged ahead, down a set of stone steps, ducking through low archways and around impossibly tight turns with her close behind.

A square of light bloomed ahead as they rounded a particularly sharp bend in the tunnel. The air was warmer and smelled faintly of past meals and stale, sweaty bodies. Alys wrinkled her nose. "Whew! It stinks worse than—"

"Gowain!" A woman dashed up the set of steps they were descending and wrapped her arms around his waist. "There were wounded, and I feared—" She stopped, frowning as she looked around him at Alys. "Who is this...this woman you've brought?"

"She's not a woman, Maye. She's a nun." Gowain loosened Maye's arms, then turned her and guided her down the steps ahead of him with the care a man bestows on his loved ones.

Alys followed, shocked by the keen sense of disappointment she felt. Fool. Of course a handsome, virile man like him would have a woman, be she wife or mistress.

At the base of the stairs, Maye stopped again, and glared at Alys. She was plump and older than Alys had first guessed. A hint of silver showed in the long brown braids draped across her ample bosom. Doubtless she'd been a beauty in her youth, might be still, if her features were not contorted with anger. "From whence did she come, this nun? Why did you bring her here?"

"Gently," Gowain said wearily. "We met Sister Alys on the road. Her healing skills saved Stork, Martin and Sim."

"And I am staying only till they're well," Alys said firmly. "Then I'll be continuing on to Newstead Abbey."

"As soon as I decide if it is wise," Gowain interjected. He raised a hand to cut off her objections. "Your patients await you in one of the caves." He looked over Maye's head toward the fire in the center of the cavern. "Bette. Would you show Sister Alys the way and make sure she has whatever she needs?"

A woman detached herself from the crowd around the hearth and crossed to them. "Of course. Come with me, Sister."

Bette was older than Maye, and far friendlier, chattering on about the camp facilities as she led Alys from the central cavern to a smaller one. But as she looked back over her shoulder, Alys saw Maye and Gowain walk off, heads bent close in companionable conversation. The sight caused an odd lurching in her midsection. Though he was a rough brute of an outlaw, he and his woman had something Alys envied. Closeness.

Fool, Alys chastised herself. She should not waste time yearning for what she could not have, but spend what energy she had on finding a way out of this terrible predicament.

Chapter Four

It was an hour before sunrise when Ranulf spurred his tired horse across the drawbridge and through the gates of Eastham, what remained of his men straggling along after him. The castle keep was dark when he reined in before it and slid from the saddle. "Where the hell is everyone?" he screamed.

The steward rushed down the stairs, hair disheveled, still struggling into his tunic. "M-my lord. Welcome home. We didn't know when to expect you, but I can have a meal in—"

"Silence!" Ranulf backhanded the man, sending him sprawling in the dirt. "How can I think what to do with you posturing and babbling?" He stepped over the cowering servant and stomped up the steps, pulling off his gloves as he went. They were stiff with blood. "Pity it is not that bastard Gowain's."

"Aye, milord, that it is." Clive hurried after him. "What will you do now?"

"Do! Do! I'll wipe him out, that's what I'll do." Ranulf tossed aside the gloves in disgust. "A hot bath...in my chambers. At once," he bawled over his shoulder as he threw open the doors to the great hall and stalked in.

The wooden doors struck the wall with a resounding crack. The sleep-rumpled servants jumped, then froze in the act of setting up the tables. Several clung together, whimpering. An old woman crossed herself and tried to slink away.

"You, there, bring wine." Ranulf threw himself into the massive chair before the hearth, where a new fire struggled to get started. "Curse the luck," he growled, for the hundredth time in the long hours since the disastrous rout. "If he hadn't had so many men...if I hadn't had to protect Lady Alys..." Ranulf moaned and buried his hands in his face. "Damn. I came so close to having her to wife... daughter of an earl...heiress to a fortune."

"Poor Lady Alys." Clive gingerly leaned his tired shoulder against the mantelpiece. "Do we go after her?"

"What use?" Ranulf raised his head. "Where the hell's that wine?" he bellowed.

The steward materialized at his elbow. A livid bruise marred his cheek. His hands trembled as he offered a silver cup engraved with the de Crecy arms. "W-will you break your fast?" he asked.

"Can you not see I am too overset to eat? My dear betrothed torn from my arms by that bastard who dares call himself my kin." Ranulf gnashed his teeth, then drank deep of the wine.

Clive licked his parched lips, but dared not upset the delicate balance of things by asking for a drink. Then he spied Janie, a skinny wench who'd warmed his bed of late, bravely holding out a wooden cup. Clive thanked her with a nod and gratefully downed the sour ale Ranulf purchased for the servants. Then he waited for his lordship to make his will known.

"Wine!" Ranulf commanded, holding out the cup. "Must a man who's risked death to save his love, then rode half the length of England with a broken heart, die of thirst in his own castle?"

The only things Ranulf had loved about Lady Alys were her name and her money, Clive thought. "I could take out a fresh troop, milord, mayhap find their trail and follow it to their hiding place,'' he added. The time for that was hours past. Coward that he was, when the tide of battle had turned against them, Ranulf had fled with nary a thought for poor Lady Alys.

''What makes you think you'd have any more luck finding their camp than you have before?'' Ranulf sneered. ''The whole country hereabouts is behind him. The peasants wipe out his tracks when he passes and send us looking in the opposite direction from the one he has taken. You know that for a fact.''

''Aye.'' Clive had stood by as Ranulf's executioner tortured a young farmer into confessing just that.

''What I need to do is turn them against him. I need to make them see he is the villain, not me.'' Ranulf drained the cup the steward had refilled, then stared into the fire. The leaping flames cast wild images across his face, igniting an odd light in his dark eyes. ''If only Lord Gareth had been willing to declare him an outlaw, but no, he wanted more proof. But now...'' Ranulf sprang from his seat, the silver cup rolling across the floor and into the ashes. ''That's it!''

''What is?'' Clive retreated a step, for Ranulf was known to kick out at those about him when something went amiss.

''Her father will be only too quick to sign a writ when he learns how his daughter was killed by that heinous criminal.''

''Killed? But we do not know that, milord. It is possible she was taken prisoner.''

''She's as good as dead to me,'' Ranulf snarled. ''Think you I'd wed with her after Gowain has used her? Nay, but...'' He stroked his grimy chin and began to pace. ''You are right about one thing, though. We must convince her father she's dead.''

''Wouldn't it work just as well if he thought her kidnapped?''

''Rumor has it these Sommervilles are soft where family is concerned...even their womenfolk. I saw for myself that he's the type to talk his way around a problem. He'd send messages to Gowain offering to ransom the girl.'' Ranulf shook his head. "Besides, there isn't time. The next shipment of Blue John is due to leave Malpas in a month's time, providing the roads are safe and we get more workers for Bellamy. Have you seen to it?"

"And where am I to get them?"

"Raid the farms. Clear the streets of Eastham village."

Clive frowned. "If we take people so close to home, questions will be raised." The mining of a rich vein of costly fluorspar had remained secret thus far because they'd sealed off all communication with the keep and village. The gemstones were worth a fortune to Ranulf, and he'd promised Clive a fat bonus. "If we took folk from hereabouts and one alarmed relative followed our men, they'd know what we were doing."

"All right." Ranulf raked a hand through his fair hair, grimacing at its sweatiness. "Send a patrol to the west of here. They're to attract as little attention as possible. Raid what farms they can and bring back every able-bodied youth for immediate transport to the mines."

"What if they run into Gowain's men? They may look like an undisciplined mob, but they fight like seasoned warriors," Clive said with grudging respect.

"Damn. He is a continual thorn in my side. He not only starves us by stealing our supplies, he threatens my plans. Well, I won't have it," Ranulf snarled. "I've worked too bloody hard at this scheme to let that bastard ruin it."

"Shall I hire more men to guard the roads?"

"Nay. There's no time. Find me a body."

"A body?"

"Aye. Young, slender and blond. It will have to be suitably marred, of course, so no one will realize it isn't Lady Alys."

"What isn't?"

"The body in the casket, you idiot." Ranulf whirled and studied the cowering servants again. "You there, all who are between the ages of thirteen and twenty and fair, step forward.''

No one moved.

''Clive!'' Ranulf growled, fixing him with that wild, piercing stare of his. ''See to it.''

Clive looked from his lord's implacable expression to the servants' terrified ones. He couldn't do this. But he'd not live if he didn't. Well he recalled the long, lingering death of the man who'd been reeve of the mine before Bellamy. Black Toby had foolishly thought to skim off a bit of Ranulf's mine profits and been skinned alive as punishment. Clive's own back crawled, then he recalled Janie weeping over the death of a childhood friend. ''I have heard that a young woman died in childbed a few days ago,'' he murmured. ''Let me go into the village to ask the priest what she looked like and if she has yet been buried.'' Lowering his voice further, he added, ''Why deprive yourself of a servant if a body is to be had?''

Ranulf nodded. ''Aye, I've few enough to serve me as it is, what with those faithless jades who've run off to join him.'' His fist clenched. ''Gowain must be eliminated before he grows stronger. Go at once to the village. When I've washed away this filth and rested, we'll make plans for the sad journey to Ransford to inform Lady Alys's family of her unfortunate demise.''

Alys tucked the rough blanket under Dickie's chin and sighed. He looked so still and fragile.

''You've done all you can for him, Sister,'' Bette said.

''Pray God it was enough.'' Alys stood, arching her back against the ache put there by hours of bending over her patients.

''Ach, you're that done in, up most of the night. Let me show you to your bed,'' Bette said. ''Bab, that's my oldest girl—'' she nodded in the direction of a capable young woman sitting beside Martin's pallet ''—she and Dame Dotty will watch the lads. If only there was some way we

could show our gratitude," she went on. "But our caves
are short on comfort, I fear. Still, you'll have a chamber to
yourself with a brazier to warm it."

"Thank you." Alys smiled at the woman who'd stayed
by her through it all. Primitive the caves certainly were,
but the womenfolk who'd helped her tend the wounded had
been unbelievably kind and compassionate. Not at all the
rough criminal lot she'd expected. Their clothes were worn,
their supplies limited, but their capacity for giving had surprised her.

"Come, I'll show you the way. These tunnels are so vast
and winding even I sometimes get lost." Bette shoved aside
the blanket that served to cover this chamber's doorway.

Numb with fatigue, Alys ducked under it and into a
gloomy corridor, lit only by a single torch. The rough stone
seemed to ooze damp chill. Shivering, she chafed at her
arms. "What I'd really like is a hot bath."

Bette brightened. "That we can supply."

"Really?" Alys glanced down the dank hall. It stank of
smoke and past meals and too many people living close
together.

"Hot springs within the mountain. Gowain discovered it
shortly after he joined us. 'Twas he decided 'twould make
a good place for us to wash clothes and such. He and Darcy
like to soak in them," she added as she lit a torch from the
one on the wall and started down the hall. "Me, I'm not
much for such things." Light flickered as she shivered.

"The others must share your opinion," Alys said dryly.

Bette chuckled. "It does smell a bit ripe when you come
in from the outside, but after a bit, the nose gets used to
it." She tromped on in silence through the complicated
maze of tunnels.

"Do you know what time it is?" Alys asked.

"Near midnight, I should guess. Without the sun, it's
hard to gauge. We've a sand clock in the great hall. Bertram, that's my husband, he's in charge of turning it. He

was headman in Eastham village before Ranulf took over
and put in his own man.''

"Is that why you came here? Because he lost his post?''

Bette paused, her round face creased with pain. '''Twas
more than that. Osbert—that was the new bailiff—he took
all we had. Our cottage, our garden plot, even our animals
and household things.'' She shook her head, eyes watering.
"When I think of that man eating his swill out of me
mam's best bowls…''

"Couldn't you protest to the manor court?''

"Lord Ranulf is judge and jury there, Sister, and 'twas
by his leave that Osbert ran us off.''

"That is monstrous!'' Alys exclaimed.

"Aye.'' Bette gave her a watery smile. "But worse than
that was done to other folk, so I can't complain overly.
Come, you'll catch a chill standing here listening to me
blat on.''

Alys followed, her mind in turmoil. True, it was no crime
for a lord to deal with his people as Ranulf had Bette and
Bertram, but a Sommerville would never condone such callous, heartless behavior. Her parents had taught her an overlord owed his people protection, justice and honesty.

"Mind how you go,'' Bette said as they mounted a set
of stone steps. "This here's a natural bridge.'' She started
across, holding the torch higher. Its pale wash revealed a
steep drop on either side of the span, into a seemingly end-
less pit so dark it swallowed the light.

"Oh, my.'' Alys hung back.

"Don't worry. It's strong and sturdy. Gowain made sure
of that before he allowed any of the rest of us to use it.''

Alys gingerly crossed the bridge, certain to stay in the
center. "How can decent people like yourself stay with a
murderous rebel like Gowain?''

At the other side, Bette turned and waited for her. "Gowain's no brigand. Leastwise, not like you mean. Oh, he's
done his share of fighting, but in a just cause. If not for
him, the rest of us would surely have starved to death, or

been caught by Ranulf's men and butchered like the others.''

''What others?''

''The ones who stayed in Eastham village...the farmers who resisted when Ranulf ordered them from their land or tried to take their children away.''

''What would he want with farmers' children?''

''To serve at the castle, he said, but the maidens were made to entertain his guests, and the lads were never seen again.''

''Dear God.'' Alys shivered, and not from the cold.

''Just so. Bertram and I fled in the night with our young ones, taking only the clothes we wore. Others did the same, Letice Cardon, the brewmistress, Percy Baker—who's wed to my Bab—Henry and Ralph Denys, Velma, Maye and her wee Johnny.'' Bette shook her head. ''Each one has a sad tale to tell, but—'' she straightened her shoulders ''—we've survived. Thanks to Gowain.''

''Hmm,'' Alys said noncommittally, not ready to elevate a ruthless brigand to sainthood. Mayhap he needed an army to fight his battles and saw a way to gain one by helping these people.

''Here we are.'' Bette ducked through an archway, then stood, torch aloft. Light glinted off the vaulted stone ceiling, danced on the dark surface of the bubbling water below it. The warm air smelled damply of sulfur and other minerals. ''The water's deep at the far end, but shallow over here.'' She led the way down a narrow, boulder-littered path along the water. ''We beat our clothes upon these flat stones, and rinse them in this pool. I'm told it's the best for bathing, too, for there are rocks below the surface where one may sit without drowning.''

''I can swim,'' Alys said, though at the moment she doubted she had the strength to paddle far. ''Are there soap and towels?''

''Aye.'' A ledge had been turned into a storeroom, with bowls of soap and lengths of linen toweling. ''Help yourself to what you need. I'll give you a bit of privacy while I go and make certain the brazier in your chamber is filled with coals, then I'll return to show you the way back. Can I bring you anything from your saddle pack?''

If only she had her chests of clothes. All she had in that saddle was a fresh chemise, gloves and her precious herb books. ''Thank you, no. I'll put this robe back on when I've washed and sort through my things when I get back to my room.''

The moment Bette left, Alys ducked behind a large rock and shed her clothes. The boots came first. She wriggled her aching toes, and set the woolen hose aside for washing. It was a relief to remove the soiled robe and confining headdress. On the morrow, she'd find a way to clean both. Beneath the linen coif, her coronet of braids felt matted and untidy. She longed to unplait her hair and wash it, but the hip-length mane took hours to dry, so she merely reseated the wooden pins.

Clad in her chemise—for the thought of bathing nude in foreign surroundings made her uneasy—she sat on a smooth rock and dipped her toes in the water. ''Ahh.'' The seductive warmth chased the chill from her feet and moved up her legs. Sighing again, Alys slid onto a lower rock and submerged up to her chin. It was a bit hotter than her usual bath, but she welcomed the burning sting to banish her aches, soon grew used to it, in fact.

''How delightful.'' Slithering around, she rested her back against a warm rock and soaked up the heat. Eyes closed, she let her arms drift in the buoyant water. Her mind drifted, too, mulling over all that had happened since her departure from Ransford. It seemed weeks, not a day and night, had passed.

Getting home again was her first priority, but she was loath to leave until she knew Dickie and the others were out of danger. Once they were well, would Gowain honor his promise and escort her to Newstead? Impossible to tell.

What a curious man he was, she thought, shifting uneasily as his face swam in her mind. Though she sensed volatile passions simmering beneath his cold, hard exterior, he masked them with a control she greatly envied. How did he do it?

Bah! Likely fear and weariness had made her mistake the matter. Either that, or he was the one person in the world whose emotions she could not read.

Alys sighed and forced herself to relax, to think of something besides her enigmatic captor. The hot water bubbled around her, tickling over her skin like a hundred tiny touches. Or a hundred hugs. The comparison made her wistful. It had been so long since she'd felt anything like this. The sensation was soothing, yet oddly sensual. A lover's caress.

Why had she thought of that, when she'd never been closer to a swain than the lines of a romantic ballad? Nay, but she'd dreamed of them. Dreamed of being held and kissed and cuddled. The bubbles prickled and tickled and enticed. She began to imagine what it would be like to—

Alys sat up abruptly, ending the sweet yearning for what could not be. "Stop tormenting yourself," she whispered.

She stood, scattering water, and waded the two steps to the bank of the pool. Quickly stripping off her chemise, she dried her trembling body, her movements stiff, brisk and practical. Her gown felt grubby and unappealing. She was just belting it when she heard the sound of a voice in the tunnel outside.

Bette?

Nay, the voice was deep, male.

"Trust me, sweetheart, you'll enjoy a hot soak," it said.

Gowain!

Alys gasped, her heart racing beneath her clammy clothes.

"Here we are. See. Is the pool not lovely?" His voice was soft and crooning. A lover's voice.

Alys didn't wait to hear the woman's reply, certain it was Maye. Just as certain she'd die of embarrassment if forced to face the trysting pair. Instinctively she backed away from the bathing pool, scrambling to hide in the rocks behind it.

"We'll sit over here." Footsteps scraped on the stones, coming closer, pausing at the spot she'd recently vacated.

Alys held her breath, dying inside. If only she could sneak out without being seen, but Bette had said there was only one entrance. Gowain and Maye were between her and that doorway.

"Shh. Easy, now, dearling," he crooned. "First let us get your clothes off."

"Oh, no," Alys mouthed.

Muffled rustling followed, accompanied by Gowain's gentle murmurs. "How does that feel?" he asked.

"Mmm," said a small, sweet voice.

Alys groaned and tried to cover her ears.

"Sit here, put your feet into the pool," he urged.

"Oh!" someone gasped.

"It feels hot at first, but you'll grow used to it. See?" A splash marked the entry of a big body into the water.

Alys shivered, trying not to imagine what those wide shoulders and broad chest would look like without chain mail. She'd seen her father and brothers shirtless, but some inner sense told her this wouldn't be the same. The soft voice of Gowain's companion reminded her he wasn't alone. Wasn't for her.

"Ready, sweetheart? Let me lower you into the water," Gowain coaxed. "That's it."

A breathless feminine squeal followed, chased immediately by a rumble of male laughter. Water splashed, chuckles ensued, and Alys's imagination flitted down amorous paths. She'd seen lovers dallying in Ransford's gardens. Seen and envied them the lingering touches, the closeness forever denied her.

"Your skin is so soft," Gowain said. "Especially on your belly. Mmm. Does it feel good when I rub it?"

Alys bit her lip to keep from groaning aloud in shame and misery. She had to get away before things went farther.

"Sister Alys," Bette sang out.

Alys did groan then and scrunched down.

"Oh, Gowain. I didn't know you were here," Bette said. "Sorry to intrude, but I am looking for Sister Alys."

"Here?" Gowain growled.

"Aye. She spent the whole night tending the wounded. I thought a soak might ease her aching muscles."

"I did not see her when we arrived." He sounded wary.

"Oh, dear. I hope she didn't come to some harm. She said she could swim." Footsteps came closer. "Sister Alys?"

There was no help for it. Better to stand and face trouble than to be found cowering like this. Generations of proud Sommerville breeding stiffening her nerve, Alys got to her feet. "Here I am, Bette." She kept her gaze on the woman for fear she'd see more of Gowain and his mistress than she wanted.

"Sister, whatever were you doing back there?" Bette asked.

"Er, lacing up my boots."

"They must reach to your knees," Gowain dryly observed, "for we've been here a goodly time."

Alys's eyes flicked toward him, then away. It was enough to see he stood in waist-deep water, torchlight emphasizing the planes and hollows of his heavily muscled chest. Something fluttered in her midsection. She prayed it was nausea. "I am ready to go back, now, Bette." She sounded strained.

"Of course." Bette smiled at her, but bent toward the pool.

"Are you enjoying your bath, lovey?"

"Hot," said a small voice.

Alys glanced down and saw a tiny sprite of two or so sitting bare-naked on the hollow rock where she herself had rested.

"My daughter, Enid," Gowain said.

"Oh." Heat crept up from the neck of Alys's gown, burning her cheeks. "I thought—"

"Did you, now?" he asked archly. "Shame on you, Sister."

"Aye, well..." Thoroughly mortified, Alys nonetheless raised her chin and left with as much dignity as she could muster.

"Good night, Gowain," Bette said. "Wait, Sister, or you'll get lost in the tunnels."

"I hope so," Alys muttered under her breath.

Gowain's chuckled. "Don't be shy, Sister Alys, you're welcome in my bath anytime."

Alys fumed all the way back to the sleeping chambers. When she saw the one assigned to her, her smoldering temper erupted. "I cannot stay here." Her horrified gaze moved over the damp, mossy walls and the thin pallet spread on the stone floor. A brazier glowed in one corner, but it didn't take the chill or the smell of mildew from the place.

"'Tis the best we have," Bette said, wringing her hands. "Gowain's own, in fact."

"His?" The heat drained from Alys's face. "Surely he does not expect me to share his bed."

"Nay!" Bette exclaimed. "He moved his clothes and the trunk with his papers into his counting room so you might have the largest chamber...and the brazier to warm you."

The lump in Alys's throat thickened, a tangle of fatigue, misery and, aye, fear. If only she hadn't dismounted to aid Dickie. Nay, she'd had no choice in that. Nor did she have a choice now, it seemed. Swallowing hard, she managed to nod. "I—I am sorry to seem ungrateful, but at home..." She swallowed those words, too. Kind as Bette had been, 'twould not do to let these brigands know her father would pay all he had to ransom her. She'd gotten herself into this.

She'd get herself out. Tomorrow. When she was dry and rested. "I am just tired, is all."

"'Course you are." Bette laid a hand on her shoulder and squeezed gently. The purity of her compassion seeped through the fine wool to soothe Alys's troubled heart. "You've had a rough day and night, but you've naught to fret about. You're safe here with us. Gowain will not let any harm befall you."

Alys managed a noncommittal murmur. When Bette left, she stretched out on the lumpy pallet, still dressed in her robe. Her eyes were gritty; her head pounded with weariness, yet sleep refused to come.

Chapter Five

"Do we have what we need?" Darcy asked.

Gowain looked up from the tally sticks Bertram had prepared, the notches cut into the sticks providing a count of their supplies. "Barely, if we ration the food, especially the flour."

"Flour." Darcy sighed, his eyes drifting shut. "Ah, to have real bread again. I'm sick to death of dry oatcakes."

"Percy the Baker does the best he can with—"

"With what little we have. I know, I know. The miracles he performs are second only to the parable of the loaves and fishes, but man was not meant to live on beans and root soup."

"Especially one your size."

Darcy sniffed. "When will we march?"

Gowain leaned back in the low stool and braced his back against the wall of the small cave that served as his counting room. Though it was not yet suppertime, he was bone-weary. He'd grabbed a few hours sleep after his swim, then risen to oversee the countless details of camp life. His eyes were gritty, and his mind was crowded with plans and worries. Not the least of which was leading these people into battle. "Soon, for the weather will not hold much longer."

"Agreed." Darcy took the other stool in the cramped

room and extended his hands toward the brazier of coals struggling to keep the chill at bay. "These caves have served us well these past few months, but we all grow tired of living like moles. People need sunlight and fresh air. Nerves are frayed, tempers uneven."

His own included. That must be why he'd reacted so oddly to the nun. "Aye. Even Maye, who normally insists we take in every stray sheep we find, shouted at me for bringing the nun here."

"She's jealous of Sister Alys."

"Of a nun?"

"A beautiful nun."

Gowain shrugged. "Why should Maye care? What was between us ended years ago, by her will. I begged her to go with me when I left Eastham, but she didn't trust me to provide for us and wed John the Miller instead."

"Does it pain you still?"

"Nay," he said curtly. It had taken him a long time to get over Maye's betrayal. She'd been his first love, but she'd lied about loving him or she never would have stayed behind. It was Blanche's betrayal, however, that had convinced him to commit to no one and nothing. "I am grateful to Maye for warning me about Ranulf and for leading us to the caves. Nothing more."

"Maye loves you still," Darcy said slowly.

"You are mistaken. We are but friends."

"If only she were convinced of that." Darcy poured two cups of ale from the flagon on the chest and drained one in a single long swallow. "Then I might stand a chance of winning her."

"You and Maye?"

"Why not? I am not totally repulsive to women."

"I did not mean that," Gowain said quickly. "'Tis just you have never seemed to favor any one woman."

"When have I had time for courting? We were two years in that French prison, then months searching for wee Enid.

Now we are outlaws scrambling to stay alive. Besides, I had not met the right woman till now.''

"There is no such thing. Maye will only break your heart. It is not in a woman to be true or honorable.''

Darcy blinked. "I know Blanche gave you a distaste of ladies, but surely there are good, loyal women. My mother was one, God rest her soul, and your lady mother—"

"Aye, my mother.'' Gowain lifted the other cup and drank, but the mellow ale bound for Ranulf's own larder and stolen in yesterday's raid, did not wash away the bitterness or the ambivalence. "She was a good person, a loving mother. Still, it is possible she lied about Warren being her husband. Mayhap my whole life was a lie.''

"But that doesn't change your concern for her.''

"Of course not. She is my mother. No matter if she lied to me, it tears at me not to know where she is or even if she lives.'' He closed his eyes briefly. "Did she flee into Wales as Ranulf suggested, or does he hold her prisoner in Malpas Keep?''

"Would he do such a thing to a woman?''

"I pray not. And yet…'' Gowain shivered, remembering the cruelties Ranulf had perpetrated as a youth, maimings and torturings too horrible to relate, even to Darcy. Or was he afraid that his friend would not believe him any more than Warren had? "It would explain why Ranulf has closed Malpas and blocked the roads into the area…to prevent me from rescuing my mother. Even so, I must believe she is alive and whole, or I will go mad.''

Darcy crossed himself. "God will it be so. If only it had not taken us so long to gather the men and arms we need to take the keep.''

"It couldn't be helped.'' Gowain sighed. "What worries me most is that we've been able to learn nothing about what goes on inside the keep or the village.'' Ranulf's patrols blocked the only road through the mountains and into the area. The only traffic allowed on the road was Ranulf's men and supplies.

"I do not understand why he would isolate the region."

"Nor do I, but it bodes ill, my friend. It gnaws at me that we've been unable to move till now, and yet..."

"You have second thoughts about this."

Gowain nodded. "I do not like having to risk these people's lives to regain my property and, hopefully, rescue my mother."

"Your plan is sound, and the men have trained hard to hone their fighting skills."

"Aye, but under their stolen mail, they are still farmers, shopkeepers and runaway servants. The flotsam and jetsam cast out of Eastham when Ranulf inherited."

"They were that when we arrived at the caves. A disorganized mob bickering amongst themselves. They would have starved or been killed off by Ranulf's patrols had you not taken them in hand."

Gowain's chest tightened. "I am no hero. I lead them because I needed men to fight against Ranulf."

"Tell that to the people whose lives you saved."

"What shall I tell those who died in our raids or the ones who will fall in the assault against Malpas? What of Stork and the other boys who will surely follow us into battle the next time?" Gowain asked savagely.

"'Tis not your fault the lad disguised himself and sneaked out to ride with us."

"It isn't...and it is." Gowain stood and paced the few steps across the chamber, jamming one hand through his hair. "Jesu, but I've wrestled with this demon for weeks. Before I came along, they were Ranulf's victims, entitled to the world's pity and compassion. In my thirst for revenge against Ranulf, I turned them into rebels. If we fail to take Malpas and are caught, they will hang, and the fault will be all mine."

Darcy rose and went to him. Laying a hand on his friend's shoulder, he squeezed gently. "You gave them hope where they had none. If we turned outlaw and stole, it was only to survive. And we took only from Ranulf or those loyal to him.''

'''Twill be small consolation to those who die.''

"Remember what Bertram said when you proposed we take that first supply wagon? 'Better to die fighting for freedom than to live a hundred years under the heel of Ranulf the Cruel.'''

"I suppose.''

Darcy clapped him on the shoulder. "Ranulf has given us no choice. We must leave the caves before winter sets in. There will be no supply wagons moving on the roads then, no herds to raid, no crops to take. If we don't freeze to death, we'll starve.''

"With you, it is always food,'' Gowain said, forcing a smile. Bad enough he must endanger these folk. He'd not doom them with a weak, distracted leader. "I've decided to send the wounded and the children to a safe place till the fighting's done.''

"Where?''

"To Newstead Abbey.''

"Newstead? But that is miles in the opposite direction from Malpas.... Oh, I see, you've decided to escort our nun there.''

Our nun. Sister Alys had looked most unlike a holy sister last night, her damp robe clinging to a surprisingly lush body, her eyes blazing with a temper no nun should possess. Aye, that was part of it, she was too vivid, too passionate and vital to be immured in some musty abbey. And as for the rest...he found it damned difficult to ignore the current of awareness that flowed between them. "She doesn't belong here. She's a distraction. To Maye,'' he added, lest Darcy think he meant himself. "I am counting on Maye to organize our supplies for the march.''

"You don't worry Sister Alys will betray our hiding place if you let her leave here?''

"She's seen little of our camp.'' Except the hot springs, but Gowain was not about to discuss that meeting with

Darcy, for fear his friend would see too much. "She knows nothing of our plans. She won't have the chance to get word to Ranulf, if, in fact, she's in league with him. She'll be blindfolded during the journey, and I'll leave Ralph Denys at the abbey to make certain she does not try to get word to Ranulf."

"Not the most caring of keepers," Darcy grumbled. "He'll surely resent being kept out of the fighting."

"'Twill make him a zealous guard, then."

"We may have need of her healing touch before this is done."

"She's too soft and pampered to be of help to us." Gowain snorted. "Bette says she pitched a fit when escorted to my chamber. The sister demanded a decent room and a bed…a real bed, not a musty pallet on the ground."

Darcy grinned. "I seem to recall you lamenting the lack of all three on more than one occasion."

"So do we all, but we've grown used to doing without. She never would." His jaw tightened. "Not that it matters. A nun has no place with a group of outlaws."

Someone was watching her!

The feeling dragged Alys from a restless sleep. She lay very still on the thin straw pallet, senses alert, straining for some clue to what had roused her. The darkness pressed in on her, smothering and disconcerting. Even in the deepest winter night, some faint light came in through the shuttered windows of her chamber at Ransford. Here, there was nothing. No light. No sound. It was like being blind and deaf.

Panic clogged her throat. She had to get out. Which way lay the blanket that covered the entrance to this miserable hovel?

"I think she's awake," someone whispered, the voice light and childish.

"Mama?" asked an even younger voice.

"Nay. Sister Alys. She's an angel. My mama said so."

Alys relaxed. "Who is there?" she called softly.

Wool rustled somewhere to her left as the blanket was thrust aside. Two children, one no more than a toddler, stood silhouetted against the pale light from the corridor.

"Are we disturbing you?" one asked. "Mama said we mustn't."

"I'm very glad to see you. Glad I can see at all." Alys sat up, wincing as her tired muscles reminded her of yesterday's violent activities. Or was it yesterday? "What hour is it?"

"Dunno." Hand in hand, the children crept in, a thin-faced girl of seven or so, and a tot of barely two who hid her face in her companion's rough brown robe.

"I'm Birdie," said the older one, eyes solemn, dark hair sleep ruffled. In her left hand she clutched a bit of blue cloth. "Bette's youngest." She stuck her thumb into her mouth.

"Oh, of course." Dimly Alys recalled Bette rattling on about her brood as they tended to the wounded. There were five children in all, their names beginning with the letter B. Bab, the oldest girl, was wed to Percy Baker. "And who is this with you?"

"Enid," Birdie said around her thumb. "She's afeard of folks." The little girl patted the babe's glossy black hair. "'Tis all right, Enid, nuns ain't like ordinary folk. They have to be good and kind...my mama said so."

Enid turned her head, staring at Alys with the startling green eyes she'd inherited from her father.

"We met last night at the springs, though I do not understand why Gowain had a child up at that hour."

"She doesn't sleep so good. Nightmares," Birdie whispered.

"Oh. I'm so sorry," Alys murmured. She'd lain awake more than one night fighting her own demons.

"She's a bastard, but Mama says that ain't her fault, so we love her anyway."

Alys's opinion of Gowain dropped lower. "Is Maye her mama?"

"Nay. Ruby, that's Enid's nursemaid, says the Lady Blanche is Enid's ma, but Gowain stole her away."

"He stole a child from its mother?" Alys was appalled.

"Maye wants Lady Blanche to roast in hell, and my mama says 'tis no more than her due."

Alys frowned, trying to make sense of this. Bah! His lack of morals mattered not to her. The important thing was to check on her patients and find out when she could leave for Newstead. "Can you tell me if it's morn or night, Birdie?"

The girl shrugged. "Morn, I think, for folks are just beginning to stir. Without the sun, 'tis hard to tell."

"Mmm." How sad. Alys untied the thong at the end of her braid and began to unplait the strands. She longed to ease these little ones, but had scant experience with children, beyond the dispensing of hugs and telling of stories to her young nephews.

"Oh...your hair's like the sun." Birdie crossed to her, Enid clinging to her side like a burr. "Can I touch it?"

Alys stiffened. Nay, she wanted to say, but the words stuck on the lump of pity in her throat. "Of course." Her hair fell nearly to her hips, and she held out a hank of the end. If Birdie didn't actually touch her scalp, it would be all right.

Birdie abandoned her thumb and reached out with both hands. Her mouth rounded as her fingertips sifted through the hair. "It's even warm...like the sun. Feel, Enid."

The babe raised her head, and Alys's heart clenched. Enid's leaf-green eyes were shadowed, haunted by fears no one should experience, especially not a tot. What happened? Who hurt you so? she longed to ask.

Instead, Alys held out a bit of her hair. "It is all right, Enid," she said in her softest voice, the one her father had taught her to use on a frightened horse, the one that worked equally well on wounded humans. That Enid's injuries were not physical made Alys all the more eager to heal her.

Keeping her terrified gaze locked on Alys's coaxing one,

Enid slowly reached out a single finger. She touched the hair, then drew back as though she'd been singed.

Alys's heart cracked. Poor lamb. She ached to take the child in her arms and rock her as her mama used to do. Impossible. Tears welled up in Alys's eyes, tears of pity, frustration and anger over the things she could not change. "Touch it again."

Enid looked up at her and blinked. "Angel?" she whispered, and reached not for Alys's hair, but for her face. Slender fingers grazed Alys's cheek.

Fear. An icy, relentless fear of darkness and a man who'd stalked her in the night.

Alys felt Enid's terror and helplessness in the instant before she pulled back, severing the connection. Sweet Mary! Who was the man? What had he done to Enid?

Enid whimpered.

"I'm sorry, poppet," Alys murmured, struggling to regain her calm. "You just startled me."

"He stole it, you know," Birdie said, rubbing her fingers over the bit of hair she still held.

"Who stole what?"

"Ranulf the Cruel. He stole the sun. We have to live here, in the darkness, till Gowain takes us to the promised land."

"Oh." Alys struggled to separate fact from childish invention. "Where is this land Gowain has promised you?"

"Mal-something. We'll be safe there 'cause he won't be able to get us. My mama said so."

"Ah." Alys reclaimed her hair, rebraided it, wound the braids atop her head, then stuffed on her wimple and headdress. She felt rumpled and grimy, in need of food and a change of clothes. But another need was even more pressing. Standing, she shook out her wrinkled robe. "Could you show me the privy?"

Birdie nodded, but her thumb went back into her mouth as she gazed up at Alys. "You've hidden the sun."

"Nuns keep their hair covered."

"And their hands, too?" She looked at Alys's gloves.

"Mmm," Alys replied. "The privy?"

The garderobes proved to be an improvement over the hole in the ground Alys had been expecting. Birdie led her to a small cave with a blanket draped door for privacy. Three holes cut into a narrow ledge formed the seats. Water rushing beneath them carried away the filth. "This is ingenious," Alys exclaimed.

"Gowain's men made it. We have a pot in our room, in case I have to go during sleep time."

"Pity they aren't as eager to use the baths."

Birdie wrinkled her nose. "I hate baths."

"Hot and nice," Enid said.

"Aye, that it was, sweetheart. I left my chemise there last night. Could you lead me to the pool, Birdie?"

"Aye, but I'm not allowed to go there alone."

"Very wise of your mama, but I'll be with you."

With Birdie as her guide and Enid trailing behind, Alys went on a tour of the rebel encampment. Birdie's thumb was in her mouth, except when she spoke. Alys wondered if the child was not old for such behavior. Richard's sons had both sucked their thumbs for a time after they were weaned. Looking for reassurance, their mother had said, and predicted they'd soon outgrow it. Which they had.

How could people bear to live like this, buried under mounds of rock? What little she'd seen of the place last night, when they'd arrived had made her shiver with disgust.

The lump in Alys's throat grew. What if she never saw any of them again...her parents, her brothers or Oriel. What if she never got home? Nay, she'd not think like that. Gowain had promised her an escort to Newstead in exchange for saving Stork and the others. Alys tried to memorize the route they took, but the corridors had more twists than a garden snake. "This mountain must be combed with caves," she remarked.

"At first we played hide-and-seek in them," Birdie said.

"But it's not so much fun." She stopped in front of a huge iron-banded door and shoved it open. "We're not supposed to come here, but it's ever so exciting."

Alys's jaw dropped as she looked around at the heaps of stuff. Armor, mail, pikes, piles of longbows and barrels bristling with arrows. "There's enough here to equip an army."

"What are ye doing in here?" The large pock-faced man who'd driven the wagonload of injured last night glared at them.

"I'm showing Sister Alys about," Birdie said.

The man grunted. "Well, this is no place for brats or females. Be off with ye, now."

Alys was only too happy to comply. As they rounded a corner in the tunnel, she dimly heard sounds ahead. Muted grunts and the clash of steel on steel. The sound had grown to a roar by the time they reached a large cavern.

Torches rimmed the vast room, casting an eerie glow on a battle scene enacted by nearly a hundred men. They fought each other with sword and lance, with pike and knife. Some shot arrows at straw-stuffed figures, while others feinted and parried in a mock battle with long quarter-staffs.

"Oh, my," Alys breathed.

"What are you doing here?"

Alys gasped and turned to find Gowain staring down at her. "What is going on?" she asked faintly.

"I should think that obvious.... I'm training my army."

"Mercy, you really do intend to ravage all of England."

"Is that what Ranulf said?"

Alys started, conscious of the suppressed tension radiating from him despite his bland expression. How easily he seemed to control his emotions. "What do you plan to do, start a war?"

"Nay, finish one."

"I see."

"I wish you had not, for now I cannot afford to let you go."

"What? But...but you promised."

"That was before I caught you sneaking around my camp...spying for Ranulf."

Chapter Six

"**Y**ou cannot go back on your word!" Sister Alys cried, hurrying down the corridor after him.

"I just have," Gowain replied without breaking stride. Behind them, he heard the clatter of booted feet as his men trailed along behind, eager witnesses to the upcoming drama.

"But you promised."

"And you said you'd not wander about." Mentally he braced for her shrieks of outrage. Or was she a weeper, like Blanche? Damn, there was nothing that unmanned him like tears.

"I...I was looking for the pool."

The vulnerability in her voice tugged at him. Hard to ignore, but he was used to difficult tasks. "The why matters not, Sister. I've said you must stay, and stay you shall."

"You are the most dishonorable—"

Gowain stopped and turned; she halted, bumping into the wall to avoid a collision. It irked him that she'd prefer a bruise to contact with him. Fool. She's a nun. Naturally, she doesn't want to be pawed by a man. "You've called me outlaw several times," he growled. "Why are you surprised that so loathsome a creature as myself should break his word?"

"I...I trusted you."

"Don't."

"I did save Stork's life."

He winced. "What makes you think a man who would lead a child into battle cares if he lives or dies?"

"Because…because of the way you looked at him," Alys said.

"Ah, you can read men's intents as well as heal them?"

She cocked her head and smiled ruefully. "In a way, I suppose, but we stray from the discussion."

"There is no discussion. I say you stay, and that's final. 'Tis the way of tyrants, is it not, lads?" He looked over her shoulder at their rapt audience.

His men snickered. "Oh, aye, he orders us about something fierce," one called out.

"Forces us to steal food to feed our starving families."

"Damned impertinent for a nun if ye ask me," grumbled Ralph Denys. He stood directly behind her, menacing as a graveyard specter. Ralph was slight and wiry, a bully, who'd been the self-appointed leader here before Gowain's arrival. His ugly temper made Gowain sorry he had not done something about Ralph.

Sister Alys must have sensed something amiss, for she glanced over her shoulder, then took a step toward Gowain.

That simple gesture pierced him like a cry for help. Gowain closed the gap between them, taking care not to touch her.

"Sister Alys disobeyed my orders, but she is still a guest here and under my protection. Is that clear?" he asked, fixing first Ralph, then Henry and the others with what Darcy called his menacing stare.

"Ye're the leader," Ralph snarled.

"By the people's will, not mine," Gowain said, a not-so-subtle reminder that the rebels had chosen him over Ralph.

"Let us go in to supper," Darcy called from the rear of the pack. "I cannot quarrel on an empty stomach."

"You cannot do anything on an empty stomach," Gowain shouted back, and the tension dissolved into hoots of laughter. With the sound vibrating around them, Gowain looked down at the nun. "I suggest that in the future if you've a bone to pick with me, you do it in private. I may be lower than offal in your eyes, but these men and I have been through much together, and they tend to see me differently. I'd hate to see that sharp tongue of yours land you in more trouble than you already have."

She nodded and swallowed, her eyes so huge they filled her face. "I...I will try."

Satisfied fear would keep her in line, he swiveled his head toward the men. "The good sister's presence causes me to think that turning rebel has made our manners go begging. If you'll allow me to escort you in to sup." He held out his arm to her and bowed as precisely as an elegant courtier.

She trembled, then seemed to gather herself. Hesitantly, as though expecting to have it chopped off, she extended her gloved hand. It hovered over his forearm, then settled. "Oh, it...it is all right," she whispered.

All right? Gowain sucked in a quick breath. Light as her touch was, it sent ripples of awareness through him. He'd sworn off women, but he'd have had to be dead not to recognize the emotion. Thrice cursed he was, to desire a nun. Obviously he'd been celibate too long. He'd have to do something about that, but how and with whom, he wasn't certain.

"I do not understand how you do it," the nun said.

Gowain struggled to shake off his sensuous thoughts and make sense of her comment. "What are you talking about?"

"Nothing. Nothing at all." Her smile seemed forced. "Let us go into supper. I vow I'm hungry enough to eat a horse."

Frowning, Gowain led her down the corridor. Damn, after making such a fuss over keeping her here, he wanted her gone, out of sight, certainly out of touch. The feel of her small hand riding on the crest of his arm ate at Gowain's control. Why had he insisted she take his arm? By the time they reached the double-wide arch of the great hall, his head ached from trying to keep his baser feelings locked away.

"Oh!" Sister Alys stopped on the threshold.

"Impressive, is it not?" Gowain asked. The cavernous room was twice the size of any normal hall, the ceiling so far above the stone floor that the light of the torches set in the walls was swallowed up before reaching it. The walls themselves sparkled as the light caught on shiny grains in the stone.

"What...what is that horrible smell?" she whispered hoarsely, nostrils pinched, eyes watering.

"Smell?" Gowain sniffed, then wrinkled his nose. "The chimney must have backed up again. 'Tis just a hole in the rock through which the smoke can drift out. Sometimes an animal builds a nest over the—"

"Do they never wash?" she asked.

Gowain took a deeper breath and winced. "These folk are not used to bathing."

"Well, you should speak to them, insist on at least a weekly wash and a change of clothes."

"I fear such niceties are hard to come by," he muttered. "Some people have only what they're wearing."

She blinked. "Really? But—"

"'Tis Sister Alys," a woman called.

As one, folk turned toward the door. A great cheer rose to reverberate off the stony dome. People leapt up from their benches and started toward her, hands outstretched.

"Oh, my." Sister Alys backed into him.

Gowain steadied her, then himself. "They want to thank you."

"Please...please do not let them touch me."

He stiffened. "Of course. I'd forgotten your fear that our filth will rub off on you. Hold," he called out. "Would you frighten off the good sister by mobbing her?"

The crowd stopped, and Bertram stepped forward. "I am Bertram, former headman of Eastham. On behalf of the folk here, we want to thank you for saving Stork, Sim and Martin," he said gravely. "Please forgive our zeal—we want only to thank you. Because of Gowain's successful raid yesterday, we can offer you a meal worthy of your deeds." He gestured toward the trestle tables, set with bowls and cups.

"Do not even think about refusing," Gowain growled in her ear. "They've worked since dawn to do this for you."

"I wouldn't dream of letting them down." Straightening away from him, she entered the hall. "My thanks, one and all," she said graciously. "I did what I could for your wounded comrades and did not expect to be so honored."

Another cheer roared through the cavern and people hastily returned to their places.

Bertram bowed. "This way, Sister." He escorted her toward a high table of sorts, set perpendicular to the rows of makeshift tables where the rebels of Eastham sat with Gowain's men.

Trailing behind, Gowain gave the sister high marks for poise. Not by word or gesture did she react to the stench of so many unwashed bodies. A stink that had either grown worse while he was out raiding or gone unnoticed because he was preoccupied with other things. Whatever, he'd speak to Bertram after they supped, he decided, watching the nun negotiate the narrow aisles between the tables.

She walked as proudly as a queen, head high, shoulders square. There was a fluid grace to her movements that bespoke familiarity. He'd seen that posture, that regal bearing in dozens of ladies at the court in Bordeaux. Blanche among them. Sister Alys had perfected it, adding the slow glide, the sensuous sway of hips that caught a man's eye. He knew, then, that he'd been right about her origins. Sister Alys was no merchant's daughter, but that which he hated most...a wellborn lady.

The chill of that realization should have doused the fires

of desire she had kindled in his blood. Instead, he found himself likening her gentle dignity to his mother's.

Bertram stopped by the table, bowed, then hustled off to alert the cooks, leaving Gowain to seat their honored guest. It was going to be a long meal. Still, he'd faced worse trials.

"That was well said, Lady Alys," he muttered as he helped her step over the bench they would share.

"Thank you, I..." Her voice trailed off as she realized what she'd admitted. Sinking down onto the rough-hewn bench. "I told you I was not always a nun."

"But you did not say you were a great lady."

"You needn't make it sound a curse."

"In my eyes, and those of many here, it is."

"Because of Ranulf?"

"Among others." Like Blanche and her foul husband.

"Not all noblemen are like Ranulf."

"Nor are all rebels fiends."

She inclined her head to acknowledge his wit. "Yet I have not found they keep their promises."

He sighed in exasperation. "I would have let you go had you not seen so much of our camp."

"I will tell no one," she vowed, expression earnest.

"I cannot afford to trust you," he said stonily.

"Why? I have not lied to you."

"Have you not?" He regarded her narrowly. "I would say there is a great deal you have not told me." He glanced down at her gloves. "Why, for instance, do you keep your hands covered?"

She shoved her hands into the folds of her robe. "That, sir, is my own business."

"Have you hidden something inside one of your gloves? Mayhap a map showing the location of this mountain?"

"I would never do such a thing." She raised her chin. "Even had I wished to, I spent most of that horrible journey trying to keep Stork from bleeding to death while we jounced over these miserable trails at the breakneck speed you insisted—"

"I would have stopped if I could."

She opened her mouth, then sighed, color fading. "I know you are not an unfeeling man. I saw it in your eyes when you looked at the wounded. I shouldn't have struck out at you."

A woman who apologized? A rational, logical woman?

"'Tis just that I feel so helpless, and I'm not used to it. I fear frustration goads my temper." She slanted him an unhappy glance. "Nor am I used to being distrusted for no reason."

Touched, Gowain unbent enough to share a bit of himself. "Neither was I before this started. It hurts, does it not?"

"Aye." She looked out over the boisterous crowd, cocked her head and smiled faintly. The smile was tinged with sadness when she turned to him. "They remind me of home and our people. Mama often likens them to a brood of pups, full of energy and high spirits, sometimes difficult to control, but dear nonetheless."

"Who is this family whom you love so much?"

She started. "No one you would know."

"You are afraid I'd hold you for ransom?"

"Mayhap, though they've little wealth to give up."

She was a liar, but surely one of the worst he'd ever seen. Those expressive eyes gave her away, along with the blush that was the curse of many fair-skinned folk.

"Your...your rebels are not what I'd expected."

Gowain let the subject of her family drop, for now, but he'd not rest till he knew who her people were and why she concealed their identity. "Not all rebels are ruthless brigands. Some are good, God-fearing people who inadvertently broke a few laws."

"But if the laws are overthrown, there will be anarchy."

"What if those in power have bent the laws to profit themselves and harm those they are sworn to protect?" he asked.

"Then...then you should protest to your overlord. To the king, if need be," she said evenly.

"The king is too busy for the likes of us."

Her eyes rounded. "You've tried?"

"Aye. We did not choose this path, it was forced upon us."

"By Ranulf?"

"And other nobles, as well. I sent messages to my father's friends, explaining what was happening at Eastham, asking for news about Malpas." Begging for news of his mother, for the truth about her marital status. "They did not believe me." He looked her full in the eye, watching those dark blue pools drink in his every word. Intelligence sparkled in them, yet they were still the kindest eyes he'd ever seen. Eyes a needy man might drown in, if he wasn't careful. Good thing she was beyond his reach.

"I—"

"Stew, Sister Alys?" The cook stood before them, his fleshy face shining with pride.

"Of...of course."

He ladled a thin soup into her bowl and stepped back, smiling expectantly. "I'm Percy, former baker at Eastham village, but since being driven from my shop, I've done my best to feed those fortunate enough to find sanctuary here."

"I fear we've not given you much to work with," Gowain said.

"Nay, 'tis truly a challenge to serve a filling meal when there are few fresh vegetables and even less meat. But after yesterday's raid—" he grinned, deepening the grooves around his eyes "—we've salted meat, beans and flour."

"All of which must be carefully rationed," Gowain warned.

"To be sure. Despite our wish to honor you, Sister, I've used only what was necessary to make a tasty stew. I hope you'll find it to your liking."

"It smells delicious, Master Percy." Sister Alys picked up the wooden spoon, dipped it into the stew and lifted it to her lips. Barely waiting for the steaming liquid to cool, she gulped it down. "Delicious." She set about emptying the bowl with a speed that rivaled Darcy's.

The beaming Percy served Gowain, then moved on. Silence descended on the hall, broken only by the rhythmic slurping of a hundred hungry souls.

Gowain ate with one eye on the rest. 'Twas the first hot meal he'd had in days, and the warm glow in his belly nearly made up for the heavy price they'd paid for the pleasure. Nearly.

Head down, Sister Alys cleaned her bowl with unladylike haste. When the last drop was gone, she looked up. "Oh, dear, I fear Mama would be appalled to see me attack my food so, but it seems years since I last ate." She looked expectantly toward the doorway of the makeshift pantry. "What is the next course?"

"There isn't one."

"Oh." Her stomach growled its disapproval, bringing a flush to her cheeks. "Bread, then?"

Gowain shook his head. He rather enjoyed watching her cope with things. She didn't rant or rave, didn't break into tears. She merely…adjusted. "Oatcakes."

"I've never had them. Are they good?"

"A bit dry," Gowain said.

"But…but what of the wagonloads of salted beef and other things you took? Surely there is more than this."

"We must ration what we have, or we'll starve tomorrow."

"I see." Her flush deepened. "On my father's estates, no one, not even the lowest serf, goes hungry. I had not thought much about what it would be like. Especially for the children." He followed her gaze to the nearest table, where Birdie ate with the rest of Bertram's brood. All had finished their stew and were looking around for more.

"It breaks my heart," Sister Alys murmured.

Oddly, he believed her.

The arrival of the girls with the baskets of oatcakes was

greeted with a cheer. The cheer became a roar when Percy announced there was butter to spread on them.

Sister Alys was the first one served. She accepted the large slice of the flat cake with a smile. "How wonderful, it's still warm." She spread butter on it, then sat staring at it.

"The butter eases the dryness, and they're filling," Gowain said around a bite of his.

"I'm certain it is delicious, but I fear it would stick in my throat." Before he could guess what she was about, she rose and went to Bertram's table. Breaking the cake into four pieces, she gave one each to Birdie, simpleminded Benje and the twins, Bertie and Bradley.

Sister Alys's smile lit up the room as she crossed back to the head table and sat.

Gowain stared at her, the food in his own mouth turning to dust. "I was wrong about one thing," he said slowly. "No matter your noble birth, you are well suited to your holy calling."

She gave him an odd look, soft and vulnerable, and then a glint crept into her eyes. "Does that mean you'll let me go?"

"I should." For the sake of my sanity. "But I cannot."

Tom the Reeve approached the table. "I've posted the guard like you asked, Gowain. Want I should take the nun to her cell?"

"Cell?" Sister Alys asked, turning wounded eyes on Gowain.

He winced, but could not back down. "I regret that I cannot give you free run of the camp."

"Well, then I shall just have to try harder to convince you I am trustworthy." She left the hall as she had entered, head high, dispensing smiles to those who called out to her.

Sister Alys didn't belong here.
She was going to ruin everything.

The nun wanted to leave. 'Twas Gowain who demanded she stay.

Which meant getting her away from here wouldn't be easy.

Long, skinny fingers drummed erratically on the ledge of a stony outcropping around the bend from the nun's room. Hostile eyes peered through the concealing gloom at the soldier posted outside the blanketed doorway. Not easy at all.

Still, it was necessary. Which meant another way must be found to eliminate her.

Eliminate?

'Twas a sin to harm a holy sister.

Still…the fact remained, Sister Alys had to go.

"Ouch. Drat, drat." Alys yanked the comb out of her hair and contemplated the blond hair caught in the teeth. She'd been at this for so long her fingers were numb and her head aching. Still, her hair felt like a disorderly bird's nest, so filled with knots and snarls she'd never be able to rebraid it.

Sitting cross-legged on her pallet, Alys sighed and thought wistfully of the effortless skill with which Mabel had always tended her hair. "I regret taking you for granted, dear friend. When I get home, I promise to make up for it. If I get home."

Depressed, she leaned her throbbing head against the wall of the cave. At least she didn't have to grieve in the dark. Bette had stopped by earlier with a supply of candles, an extra blanket and fulsome apologies.

"'Tis shameful of Gowain to treat you so," Bette had said. "I told him so, too, the ingrate. After all you've done for us…"

"He is grateful, but he cannot bring himself to trust me."

"Not surprising, given all that's happened to the poor man. I'm not one to blaspheme, Sister," she'd added in a whisper. "But that damned Lady Blanche near ruined his life with her betrayal. She gave him good reason to distrust highborn ladies.''

''How did she betray him?''

''He doesn't speak of it, but from his men I've learned that Lady Blanche bore the wee mite, then abandoned her like an unwanted puppy. Had Gowain not gone looking for Enid, the babe might have died. She still suffers from terrible nightmares and never smiles. It tears at Gowain's heart something fierce.''

Remembered fear raced down Alys's spine. Enid's fear. Who was the man who stalked her? Surely not her father, for his gentleness with his daughter last night had been eloquent.

A scream tore through Alys's dark reverie.

The high, thin wail of a child in pain.

Alys leapt up and flung aside the blanket. ''Where did that cry come from?'' she demanded of her guard.

''Little Enid's chamber.'' He pointed to the left. ''But 'tis nothing unusual. Happens near every night. Just ignore it, and—''

''I will not.''

''Wait. I'm supposed to see you stay in your room.''

''Come with me, then.'' Alys brushed by him and started down the corridor. The cry came again, higher, wilder. Alys ran to the door, flung aside the blanket and stopped. The room was dark except for the light filtering in from the hallway. That faint pool illuminated a scene familiar to many parents.

Gowain knelt on the floor beside a pallet, his hand extended toward Enid, who cowered against the wall.

''Shh, sweetling, 'twas only a nightmare,'' he murmured.

''Dark,'' Enid whimpered, eyes wide and dazed, still trembling in fear from the things that had chased her.

Alys seized the nearest torch, wrenching it from the iron ring in the wall, and carried it into the chamber.

''What the devil?'' Gowain's eyes narrowed against the light.

"Hold this." She thrust the shaft of the torch into his hand, then went to Enid. "'Tis all right, Enid. 'Tis only your papa. See, he's brought a light to chase away the bad things."

Enid blinked. "P-Papa?" she asked uncertainly.

"Aye." Alys reached out to offer comfort and realized she'd left off her gloves. Panic raced down her spine; her belly roiled. Draw back, common sense warned, but Enid's need outweighed her own. "Shh." Steeling herself, Alys stroked the little girl's cheek. The fear leapt between them like a living thing. It clogged Alys's throat, made her pulse race.

Someone whimpered. Dimly Alys realized it was her.

"Sister? What is it?" Gowain touched her shoulder. His hand was warm, solid. It radiated concern. It offered a haven.

Blindly Alys turned toward him. "Help me," she whispered, shattered by the fears that tore at Enid. "Hold me."

Strong arms wrapped around her, dragging her against the muscular wall of his chest. Beneath her ear, Alys heard his heartbeat, strong and steady, a measured counterpoint to her own wildly galloping one. She focused on the sound as if it were a lifeline, used it to settle her own ragged pulse. The fear receded, and her mind began to function again.

"Shh, shh. 'Tis all right." His breath ruffled the hair at her temple and warmed her icy skin. He held her securely, one hand splayed across her back, the long fingers gently kneading the tension from her spine.

She should have felt trapped; she felt safe. Why was she not linked to his emotions? Lifting her head, she stared into his leaf-green eyes and knew these were his emotions. She felt safe because of his overwhelming urge to protect. Never had she been this close to another yet felt so keenly aware of herself. He dwarfed her, made her conscious of her own smallness and softness in contrast to his size and strength. Power held deftly in check, she thought. Tenderness where she'd least expected it. Deep inside her, something stirred, like a flower unfurling its petals to the sun.

"Alys." His fingers contracted, pressing her closer so the heat of his body enveloped her. An odd light kindled in his eyes. The tiny flames beckoned and beguiled. His features sharpened; his breath came faster, racing with his heart.

The melting sensation in her belly spread, grew to an uncomfortable tingling ache. "Gowain?"

"Aye, I feel it, too." He lowered his head and brought his mouth down hard on hers.

Fire! Hungry and urgent, it swept through her.

Alys screamed, the sound muted by his kiss. Panicked, she pushed against his chest and bit him.

He jerked back with a startled cry, a drop of blood on his lower lip. "Damn!" He sounded as shocked as she was.

For once in her life, Alys didn't care about anyone else. She had to get away from him. Twisting from his arms, she got to her feet and stumbled from the room.

"Papa, where is the angel going?" Enid asked.

"She's not an angel," came the snarled reply, "but another temptress sent to try my soul. Damn her."

We are both damned, Alys thought as she fled.

Chapter Seven

"Bless me, Father, for I have sinned," Gowain murmured. "I am sure that does not surprise you." He stared at the candle burning on the table in his counting room. The flame sent shadows writhing along the bleak stone wall, but cast no light into his troubled soul. Who could blame God for giving up on him?

Sighing, Gowain raked a weary hand through his hair. He'd left Ruby strict instructions to stay with Enid and came here seeking peace and some much-needed sleep. His conscience allowed him neither.

He'd kissed a nun. Mayhap not the bloodiest crime besmirching his soul, but a weighty one.

His gut twisted. Worse, he'd terrified and repulsed a woman he'd come to respect for her gentleness and compassion. Those qualities had proved a more dangerous lure to a lonely man like him than her natural beauty. Not that that excused his behavior. Tomorrow, he'd apologize. He'd tell her…what? That he'd been celibate too long? That her kindness to his daughter and the others had overridden his good judgment and morals? Doubtless she didn't think he had any.

Gowain shut his eyes, but the image of her wild blond hair and flushed cheeks haunted him still. She hadn't looked like a nun as she gazed up at him with those soft, alluring blue eyes. She hadn't felt like a nun, clinging to him, trembling with some nameless fear he'd sought to calm. But she was.

"Sister Alys," he murmured. "Sister Alys, the healer." He repeated the phrase several times. It didn't still the yearning. That single, disastrous embrace had changed everything. He no longer saw her as a nun, but a desirable, passionate woman.

She was so young, so vibrant. Why had she chosen to lock herself away in an abbey? Could he somehow change her mind?

God, he was truly cursed to even wish for such a thing. He buried his face in his hands.

She had never felt so miserable in her life.

Head down, Alys pretended to nibble on the hunk of hard cheese Bette has saved especially for her, barely conscious of the others breaking their fast in the hall. Her crime weighed so heavily on her that she couldn't swallow a morsel. Nor had she slept at all after returning to her room last night. Despite her guise as a nun, she had begged Gowain to hold her, had practically invited his kiss, then had made him feel like a rapist.

"Sister?" A skinny woman stood before her, toying nervously with dark braids even more lumpy and ill braided than the ones Alys had stuffed beneath her own headdress this morn.

"I am Velma of Newton...Dickie's sister." Tears seeped down her careworn face.

"Is he worse?" Alys asked, ready to leap up.

"Nay." She wiped her face on the frayed sleeve of her loose-fitting robe. "He is awake, complaining of boredom."

Alys relaxed. "Well, that is good news indeed. I'll check on his bandages as soon as I've broken my fast."

"I...I wish I had more to offer you than my thanks, but

we were forced to leave everything behind when we fled Ranulf.''

"I am so sorry," Alys said. The same heartfelt but useless words she'd given to all those who'd suffered under Ranulf's ruthless heel. Who could have guessed from meeting him that so handsome an exterior hid a rotten core? "But the pleasure of seeing Dickie well and strong is all the thanks I need.''

"You are indeed a godsend, Sister.''

Alys cringed inwardly. I'm a freak, a cheat and a liar. She longed to stand and shout the truth to the assembly, but she was afraid. Afraid they'd hate her. How ironic that fear of what these rebels might do to her had spawned this damnable lie. Now she was stuck with it till she could escape or her family came to rescue her. After last night's disaster, she was doubly anxious to leave the caves. "I do what I can.''

Velma smiled shyly. "I want to be a nun, too.''

"You do?" Alys looked at the unmistakable bulge in the young woman's robe. "But what of the babe you carry?''

The light in Velma's eyes winked out like a snuffed candle. "Babe? I'm not carrying a babe.'' She turned away, the soft folds of her robe molding to the mound of her belly.

Alys stared after her, confused. "But...''

"She is with child, Sister," Bette said gently. She set a cup of ale down before Alys. "Velma's not been quite right since the day Lord Ranulf and his men swept through the village looking for a bit of sport.''

"What happened?''

"Lord Ranulf ravished her, the fiend, and killed her betrothed." Bette sighed, her concerned gaze following Velma's progress out of the hall. "She refuses to accept the fact that his seed caught in her.''

"You...you mean 'tis Ranulf's child she carries.''

"I'm afraid so, since she's been with no other man before or since. When we first learned she was expecting, I feared Velma would take her own life. But the mind's a strange thing, Sister. Velma's is pretending none of it happened.''

"What will she do when it comes?" Alys asked, appalled.

"I do not know. That's why we were doubly glad you saved young Stork. He's the only family she's got left, and she depends on him as though he were the elder, not her. Ah, here's Gowain come down to eat at last.''

Alys spied him working his way through the crowded room, and her will quailed. For all that he carried himself with the unconscious arrogance of a warrior, he halted to speak with each person who hailed him. He was sober-faced himself, yet whatever he said left smiling people in his wake. It struck her, then, how kind and considerate he could be…when it suited him.

She did not suit him, nor he her. There was a tension between them that could only have been made worse by what happened last night. Suddenly she couldn't face him. "Well, I'd better look in on Dickie," she said briskly.

"You've not finished your food," Bette protested.

"I…I'm not hungry." She'd fast as a penance for her lies. When she turned, Gowain's big frame blocked her retreat.

"A moment of your time, Sister Alys." Seen at closer range, he looked as wretched as she felt, his face pale, his eyes fastened on something over her head.

"I…I am needed in the sickroom," Alys said, lamely.

"'Twill only take a moment.''

"You two sit," Bette said. "I'll fetch your cheese and ale, Gowain," she added before scurrying off and leaving them alone.

Alys sank down on the bench, her knees suddenly weak. He knew she wasn't a nun. No holy sister would have run about with her hair unbound or clung to a man like a harlot and let him kiss her. Her cheeks burned with shame.

"Thank you for not running off," Gowain said gruffly. He stepped over the bench and sat as far from her as was possible without falling off the end. The space between them seemed charged, like the air before a storm. "Though I'd not blame you if you did." He traced the wood grain with one finger, then cleared his throat. "I apologize for my behavior last night."

"Oh, well, it…it was late. Enid's nightmare had us all a bit upset and…and confused."

"That does not excuse my…my unseemly behavior," he said stiffly. "The only excuse I can offer is that I have been living like a monk since we broke out of de Grise's dungeon—"

"Dungeon?" Her eyes widened. "You were locked up?"

"By the French, not the English. It happened while I was part of the garrison at Bordeaux. Our crime, my men's and mine, was being ambushed by a superior force of the enemy."·

"Oh. I didn't mean to imply…"

"I'd not have you think worse of me than you already do." His gaze met hers, then skittered away, but not before she recognized an anguish that went beyond her petty shame. "I've done many things of which I am not proud, but frightening you, after all you've done for us, is surely the worst."

"Please do not fash yourself," Alys pleaded. "'Tis I who deserve most of the blame, bursting into your daughter's sleeping quarters with my hair down, throwing myself at you…"

"It was Enid's nightmare, wasn't it?" he said suddenly. "It affected you very strongly, though I'd not realized that till now. That was why you were upset enough to turn to me."

Alys nodded mutely, dreading the next question.

"How did you know what she feared?"

Because I felt her fear. "All children are afraid of the dark at one time or another."

He frowned, his gaze piercing. "You knew it was a man

she feared. Not me, you said. A bad man. What did you mean by that?''

"I—"

"Here we are." Bette plunked down a plate of hard cheese and a pitcher of ale. "I brought you a bit of sausage, too, Gowain. You're looking a mite peaked today."

Alys leapt up. "Speaking of which, I've patients to check on and bandages to change." She made good her escape before Gowain could object, but she knew he'd not let the matter drop.

Not till he'd laid bare all her secrets. She had to find a way to leave before that happened.

"You'll not believe what we've found." Jean de Braise, the French scout, gestured for Darcy and Gowain to precede him into the storeroom where the weapons were kept. "I had the men put the coffers in here till you could see them for yourself." Jean closed the door behind them and barred it.

Gowain scowled at the mound of wooden chests. There were a dozen, all alike, finely crafted of dark oak with fanciful designs of birds and flowers carved into the tops and sides. He could have fed his rebel band for a year on what it had cost to make these trunks. "Where did you find them?"

"A league from where we ambushed Ranulf," Jean replied, tugging at the black mustache that drooped over his lips. A Gascon by birth, he had survived the French prison and come to England to help Gowain search for Enid. Gowain had bidden Jean scout the battleground to see if any weapons or horses had been left behind. "We followed the tracks of two wagons through the woods and came upon them, abandoned at the crest of a steep gulch. The wagon drivers apparently panicked at seeing their way blocked, took the horses and fled."

The chests could belong to Ranulf, but there was something intrinsically feminine about the designs. Gowain's gut tightened. "Open them."

Jean bent and pried the lock from the nearest one with the point of his dagger. He threw back the lid to reveal neatly folded stacks of clothing. Lifting out a bit of silk, he smiled appreciatively. "The garments of a fine lady."

"Aye." Gowain fingered a length of emerald velvet. It was soft as butter, more costly even than anything Blanche had worn. "The owner of these must be wealthy indeed."

"Were the wagons traveling with Ranulf?" Darcy asked.

"Me, I would say so. And yet…" Jean shrugged one shoulder. "The nun with the face of an angel was the sole woman we saw with that pig."

"Exactly." Gowain crushed the velvet in his hand, the only outward sign of the anger he contained. She was not a nun. She'd lied to him, coerced him into believing her story against his better judgment. The betrayal burned like acid in his gut. How she must have laughed over his halting confession this morn. "She's not a nun," he growled.

"Now, Gowain, we do not know that. 'Tis not just to accuse her till we have the facts," Darcy said.

He thought of her long blond hair, the fine chemise. "Do not talk to me of justice," Gowain snapped.

"Wait, there is more," Jean said. "This chest here…the one set off by itself…is so heavy it must contain coin or plate."

Gowain hefted a corner of the trunk and grunted. "Open all of them. I want to see what we've got before I confront the little liar." Damn her for making him trust her, for making him think she was one of the few good women on this earth.

The heaviest chest was filled with books. Some were leather-bound volumes on plants and medicine, others were ledgers filled with a flowing script. "Written by Sister Alys's hand, no doubt," Gowain muttered. Sister Alys. Damn, but it made his blood boil. "These three trunks are filled with pots," Jean reported. Each had been wrapped with a length of wool to prevent breakage on the journey. He pried the wax seal from a small one and sniffed. "This one's some kind of sweet-smelling cream."

Gowain snorted. "Doubtless the secret of Sister Alys's soft white skin."

"There's more clothes in the rest. Some are plain woolen robes, but finely woven," Jean added.

"This one, too." Darcy slammed the lid down and sat on it.

Gowain turned. "Let me see."

"A fine thing when you do not believe your own second in command," Darcy grumbled.

"You've not the face for lying."

Darcy sighed, rose and threw open the trunk. It was filled with gloves. Small leather gloves made of the softest leather and individually wrapped in linen.

Gowain raised one brow. Cocking his head at Darcy, he asked, "You still think these things aren't hers?"

"Nay, I grant they may be, but—"

"What other woman do you know who never removes her gloves...even when she's nursing the wounded?"

"Mayhap she's a glove merchant."

Gowain snorted. "Aye, and I'm the king of England."

"Why would she wear these?" Jean asked.

"Her hands could be burned or scarred," Darcy said.

"Nay," Gowain said. "I saw her hands. They are not scarred."

"Then she does remove her gloves."

"When she sleeps, apparently. Enid had a nightmare, and her screams roused Sister Alys."

Darcy frowned. "Why would she pretend to be a nun?"

"Because she is Ranulf's spy," Gowain snapped.

"I do not believe she'd be in league with him," Darcy said. "She saved the lives of Stork and Martin."

"To lull our suspicions, to make us bring her to the caves so she could gather information."

"As I recall, she did not want to come here," Darcy said.

"So she claimed." Gowain began to pace, his anger too hot and wild for him to sit. "She's clever, but she'll not get the chance to betray us. Not this time."

Darcy grabbed hold of his arm. "What do you intend to do?"

"Watch her. We'll detail a guard to follow her. When she tries to leave, we'll follow. Mayhap we'll be lucky enough to catch Ranulf, too," Gowain added, relishing the moment when he'd expose the beguiling little nun for spying on him...and making him trust her. He damned her for that most of all.

Maye drew back into the shadow and watched Gowain pass by. As his footsteps died away down the corridor, she slumped against the wall outside the weapons room.

Sister Alys was not a nun.

The knowledge struck terror in her heart. The heart she'd hoped Gowain would claim. Not so long as Alys was around.

Maye had watched them all through the meal yesterday and in the hall this morn. Even when they were arguing, there was an air of suppressed tension between them that wasn't entirely anger. She'd seen enough men battling desire to recognize the signs in Gowain. Especially in Gowain, for he'd looked at her just that way years ago. Features stark, nostrils flared, body as tense as a stallion scenting a mare. And wanting her.

"Damn." Air hissed between her teeth as Maye began to pace in the corridor. "Why could he not look at me like that?" He'd gently yet firmly rebuffed her subtle attempts to pick up where they'd left off years ago. Her feelings had been hurt till she'd realized he was doubtless not over Blanche. From Darcy and the de Braise cousins, she'd learned more of the woman's betrayal. Thinking he needed time, Maye had resigned herself to wait till he was over his pain. Seeing the way he looked at Sister Alys had been a shock.

"Maye?" Darcy lumbered down the passageway toward her.

Drat. Was there no end to her suffering this day?

"I was hoping to find you." His dark eyes moved over her face, burning with the light she wanted to see in Gowain's. "I am going down to the farm, and I wondered if you and young Johnny would like to come along?"

Maye hesitated, weighing the risk of making him think she returned his interest against the lure of a few moments in the fresh air and sunshine.

"It's a beautiful day," he added. "And I thought the boy might perk up if he felt the sun on his face."

"You do not play fair, Sir Darcy."

He grinned. "'Tis my only fault, I swear."

"Hmm." Maye rolled her eyes, noting without meaning to what a big man he was, tall and as square of shoulder as he was decent. If Darcy Beaufort took a wife, he'd not be diddling with the maidservants the way her John had. "I suppose..."

"Excellent." He took her arm in his big paw and escorted her back toward the hall as though she were a grand lady instead of a miller's widow. "I only wish I could take them all...the children," he added, "not their mothers. It's damned hard seeing them so pale and wan, cooped up here day after day."

"Not long, now, and we'll be leaving. Gowain said what with the supplies he took from Ranulf and the men's training being complete, we'd be ready to move in a week or two."

"Aye." Darcy frowned.

"What is it? Surely not some hitch in the plans."

"Not exactly." He looked around, then down at her. "We suspect Sister Alys is not a nun, but a wealthy lady."

Maye groaned softly. The confirmation of what she'd overheard Gowain say rang in her head, sounding a death

knell to her hopes. No wonder he'd been drawn to Alys.
She felt violated, cheated. Gowain would not have had the
camp or the rebel army if not for her. Now that they were
on the verge of success, he'd toss her aside and wed a lady.

"So he won't let her go?"

"He fears she may betray us to Ranulf. After all, she
was traveling with him, and obviously not so she could join
the other nuns at Newstead Abbey. She may be a friend of
Ranulf's."

"So," Maye breathed. If Alys was anything at all to
Ranulf, Gowain wouldn't want her. "She must be Ranulf's
mistress. Why else would she go about with him unescorted?"

"Hmm. She does not seem like a man's mistress,"
Darcy said, frowning. "She is too shy and virginal."

"Not to mention a gifted mummer," Maye snapped.

"I will mention it to Gowain...later. Just now he is not
sane when it comes to the subject of her."

Hardly comforting news. "What does he intend to do?"

"Watch her, wait to see if she incriminates herself by
sneaking off to meet Ranulf."

"What if she doesn't? What if there is some other reason
for her pretending to be a nun?"

"My thoughts exactly. Your quick mind is but one of
the things I love about you, my sweet." He caught hold of
her chin and kissed her before she could pull away.

Maye scowled. "I am not your sweet."

"Not yet...but when you realize I am twice the man
Gowain is, you will love me as I—"

"Let go of me, you overgrown bear." She plowed her
fist into his belly, but she was the one who grunted in pain.
Darcy might look soft, but he was hard as iron.

Darcy released her chin and rubbed his stomach. "Damn,
but you pack a wallop, Mistress Maye."

"'Tis Madam Maye."

"Nay, John was no husband to you. I, on the other
hand—"

"You are full of grand notions that are no more than a puff of smoke." Maye turned and stalked down the corridor, her mind racing with grand notions of its own. Somehow, she had to get rid of Lady Alys.

"Will you still come away with me?" Darcy asked, keeping pace easily with his long strides. "Down to the farm?"

Come away. That was it, of course. If Lady Alys left the mountain, Gowain would assume she'd gone to meet with Ranulf and betray him. Mayhap she could pay Farmer Donald to take Alys to Newstead Abbey. "I'll come," she said. "But only so Johnny's not cheated of an outing, do you understand?"

"I understand you very well, Maye mine," Darcy said, eyes glittering. "Better than you think."

"Why are you doing this?" Alys demanded. Maye had accosted her as she left the sickroom that evening and, without preamble, proposed aiding her escape from the rebel camp.

Maye sighed in exasperation. "You should thank me instead of asking a lot of stupid questions."

"I am grateful," Alys said, well aware why Maye wanted her gone. Jealousy. There was no reason to be. Since tendering his apology this morn, Gowain had avoided her, even to staying away from the evening meal. It was just as well, for there could never be anything between them. Leaving was her only option. "I am desirous of reaching Newstead Abbey. Are you certain this farmer will take me there? Gowain says it is many leagues away. I have no coin to pay him now, but once I reach Newstead—"

"Aye, aye, it is all agreed." She hustled Alys into a side tunnel, unlit save for the torch Maye carried.

"Are you certain you know where you are going?"

"Aye. In the five months we've been here, we've explored every bit of these old tunnels...me and Gowain."

"Bette says it was you who brought Gowain to them."

"Aye. And a good thing I saw him riding up to the castle that day, or Ranulf and his men would have killed him for sure."

"Why?"

"There was always bad blood between them. Ranulf resented his father bringing Elen into the house so soon after his mother died, and he hated the child she bore a few years later."

As she hurried after her guide, Alys tried to understand. Richard had never begrudged Will anything—had, in fact, sold him a tract of prime land for a pound. "Did their father ignore Ranulf in favor of Gowain?"

"Nay. Old Warren loved them both equally, if blindly in Ranulf's case. He was a kindly man, who took his duties to his family and his retainers seriously. Gowain is much like him in that. He could have gone back to France and sold his sword as a mercenary if not for Enid. He wanted to make a home for her. And then, when he came here and saw how poorly these people did with no one to lead him…" She shrugged, making the torchlight writhe along the walls. "He took it upon himself to care for them, to set up rules and establish order."

"And got himself not only a cadre of loyal followers, but an army with which to prey upon the countryside," Alys muttered.

Maye rounded on her, eyes bright as the torch. "Gowain is no brigand out for plunder. His cause is just…noble."

"Murder is never just or noble."

"Ha! How little you know him." She tossed her dark hair. "Gowain has ever hated senseless violence. He kills only when he must…to survive. 'Tis why I refused when he begged me to go with him to France six years ago. I feared he'd fail as a mercenary and we'd both starve. So I stayed behind to wed safe, prosperous John Miller instead. Bah! The rutting wretch." Her glittering eyes narrowed. "I'll not let Gowain down again. I'll do whatever is necessary to see he regains all that was taken from him."

Alys nodded, touched by Maye's devotion. All the rebels viewed Gowain as a cross between king and god. He was a hard man, but not the cruel, wanton murderer Ranulf said he was. Almost, she wished she could stay behind and help. Clearly Gowain expected a battle...sometime soon. There would be wounded.

"Come, it grows late." She grabbed hold of Alys's sleeve and tugged her along.

The tunnels grew narrower and more twisted, plunging through the heart of the mountain. At last Alys felt fresh air on her face. Moments later, they emerged into the dark, velvety night. Stars dotted the sky like a spray of diamonds, and a brisk breeze ruffled through the trees at the base of the mountain. Relieved to be free of the tunnels, she threw her head back and breathed deep. "How do you stand being cooped up inside?"

"Better that than Ranulf's dungeons," Maye snapped.

Alys shivered and wrapped her arms around her waist, chilled as much by apprehension as the fall air. "Where is this farmer?"

"Donald's son will meet you at the bottom of the trail." She pointed to a path winding through the rocks and into the brush.

"You aren't coming with me?"

"Nay. I have to get back before I'm missed. Gowain will not be best pleased to find you gone."

Alys nodded, feeling oddly bereft at the notion of not seeing him again. Nay, 'twas better this way, for them to sever whatever connection there was between them. It would come to nothing, anyway. "Well—" She turned resolutely toward the trail that would take her away from the mountain and the rebels...and Gowain. "I hope you all get whatever it is you are seeking."

Maye didn't respond.

Alys looked over her shoulder and found herself alone. Shivering, she began to gingerly pick her way down the moonlit path. It was steep and narrow, little more than a wild-animal trail. Small wonder anyone scouting this area wouldn't bother to investigate it. When she came abreast of the trees, she hesitated. The woods were thick, black and intimidating.

"Farmer Donald," she called softly.

No one answered.

Feeling exposed and vulnerable, Alys slipped into the woods and flattened her back against the rough-barked trunk of a towering oak. "You are fine," she whispered, the words nearly drowned out by the rapid thud of her heart.

When she was young, she and Will used to play hide-and-seek in the old apple orchard in Ransford's lower bailey. Though this was very different and far more frightening, she clung to the memory, remembering how good she'd been at waiting and listening for Will to make some noise that would betray his presence.

Somewhere nearby, a twig snapped.

Alys turned toward the sound, her heart pounding so wildly she could barely hear over it. Straining, she waited.

There…there it was again. Closer.

Should she call out? Nay, some instinct for survival bade her keep silent till she knew who was there. The limbs of the oak were low, sheltering. If worse came to worst, she'd see if she remembered how to climb a tree.

A few feet away, the brush quivered, then parted. She'd been expecting a face, but it was a long, furry muzzle that thrust cautiously through the bushes. Slanted yellow eyes gazed straight at her…then narrowed.

Sweet Mary! A wolf!

Chapter Eight

A chill wind whistled down the mountain, moaning through the pines at the edge of the forest, bringing with it the scent of rain. Overhead, steely gray clouds raced across the moon and stars. The turbulent night suited Gowain's mood exactly.

"Where the hell is she?" he snapped, scanning the barren stretch of rocks between the mountain and woods. A quarter hour ago, Darcy had caught Maye returning from her self-appointed mission to rid them of Lady Alys.

"She cannot have gotten far, alone and afoot," Darcy said in a mournful voice.

"Stop trying to make me feel sorry for her. If she's already met up with Ranulf, she's neither."

"How could Ranulf have known that Maye would pick tonight to help Alys escape?"

"He could have had someone watching. Ever since the battle, his patrols have ranged further afield." Gowain had increased his own scouting parties and alerted the farmer to keep watch.

"If Ranulf knew our camp was in these mountains, he'd have brought an army and besieged us. You are letting your anger dull your wits, my friend. Ranulf is tucked up safe in Eastham, and Alys is out here somewhere, lost and frightened, waiting for an escort who will never come."

Gowain looked around at the inhospitable terrain, and his rage momentarily faded. "Whatever could Maye have been thinking of, asking Donald's son to take her to Newstead?"

"Obviously Maye isn't rational, either. 'Tis as I told you earlier. She's jealous and wanted Alys gone." He shook his head. "I lectured Maye on the perils of sending poor Alys out alone."

"Oh, I'm sure that will aid your suit of her."

Darcy rolled his eyes. "She told me to do something that is physically impossible." He tsked. "When we're wed, I'll have to do something about her improving her speech."

"That I'd like to see."

"Hmm. Still, I blame myself for this. If only I had kept my mouth shut about the trunks, none of this would have happened."

"Aye, well, it proved my theory. Lady Alys…if that is her real name…is a liar and worse. See how quick she was to flee."

"Who can blame her? Maye told her that her ruse had been discovered, and we knew she was not a nun."

"And Lady Alys ran." Gowain stood in his stirrups and scanned the area. "With the foliage twisted this way and that by the wind, it is hard to see if anyone's about. We'll split the men into pairs. Post a lookout on the road at the other side of the woods, in case she makes her way through it. Send men also to the farm. 'Tis unlikely she got so far, but I'd leave nothing to chance. The rest of us will fan out and search the forest."

Darcy nodded and passed the word down the line of mounted men. The soldiers paired up and rode out, leaving Gowain alone with his dark thoughts.

Darcy was right, and he a fool to think his half brother was nearby. Still, that did not mute his fury with Lady Alys. When he caught up with her, he'd make certain she paid, both for lying to him and for making him feel like the lowest of sinners.

Jaw set, Gowain walked his stallion toward the woods. The wind knifed through his hastily donned mail, making him shiver. Or was it dread that iced his skin? Furious as he was with her, a tingle of worry intruded. If some harm should befall her, part of the blame would be his for holding her prisoner.

Inside the tree line, he stopped and lifted the visor of his helmet. The cool air and the familiar scents of loam and leaf washed over him, easing his mood. As a boy, he'd spent many hours exploring the forest of Eastham, both for pleasure and to avoid confrontations with Ranulf. His eyes trailed slowly over the trunks of stalwart oak and slender birch. He studied the shadow-draped bushes huddled at their base for some sign of disturbance.

Nothing. All was silent, save for the swish of wind-driven leaves stirring overhead. Yet he could not shake the feeling of impending doom. Loosening his sword and laying it across his thighs, Gowain kneed Traveler into motion. Well trained, the big horse began to pick his way between the trees, instinctively using a path where wild game had trod. Long moments passed as they worked their way deeper into the forest.

Suddenly Traveler stopped, head cocked to the left, ears perked forward. His nostrils flared, and a shiver of excitement raced beneath his glossy black hide. But he was too well lessoned to make a sound.

"What is it, lad? What do you smell?" Gowain tugged off his helmet, the better to hear, and headed toward the left at a wary pace, his senses on alert. He heard the gush of a stream off to the right, and then, below it, a sound that chilled his blood.

A low, feral growl.

Traveler shied and blew softly.

"Wolves!" Gowain hissed. He controlled the horse with the pressure of his knees and raised his sword. Though nearly wiped out closer to civilization, packs of the savage beasts still hunted in the wild Peaks.

What of Alys?

Gowain swore, his rage drowned by an icy wave of fear. Heart in this throat, he leaned forward, straining to pick up some clue to what was happening. Where was Alys? Where was the damned wolf? The growl came again, close by. To his right.

Gowain tugged on the reins. Traveler hesitated, then plunged into the brush. A dozen quick but careful paces brought them to the edge of a small clearing.

Here the trees were thinner, allowing pale gray light to filter in through the dancing leaves. It illuminated a scene straight from his worst nightmare.

Alys stood with her back to an aged pine. Before her, a wolf crouched low in the waving grass, ready to spring.

Gowain set his heels and gave Traveler his head. As they raced across the field, he cried, "Alys! Don't move! I'm coming!" The wolf leapt like a scalded cat and disappeared into the brush an instant before Gowain reached it. Sliding from the saddle, he threw himself between Alys and possible danger.

"Protect, Traveler," he commanded. "Protect."

The stallion pawed the earth and faced the spot where the wolf had vanished, ready to do battle with his steel hooves and snapping jaws if the predator returned.

"Alys." Gowain half turned, grabbed her around the waist and dragged her into his arms. "Jesu, are you all right?" She felt so small, so vulnerable trembling in his embrace. He was shaking, too, with fear and something that went deeper than mere relief. It welled up inside him, a tangle of raw emotions. Fighting for control, he pressed his cheek against hers.

Fear! It raced from Gowain into Alys, stunning her. He was terrified for her. Never had she felt its like. "Gowain?"

"Shh." He stroked her back, the jagged edge of terror softened by compassion. "Are you unharmed?"

"Aye," she whispered, her pulse as unsteady as her thoughts. "You worried about me."

He lifted his cheek away from hers, yet held her body even tighter. "Of course. What if you told Ranulf where we are?"

"You don't really believe I'd do that."

"Nay, I suppose I do not."

He glanced away from her, toward the woods. "But this must wait till I've dealt with the wolf."

"Dog," Alys said.

"'Twas a wolf, hopefully hunting alone. If there is a pack of them…" Gowain stopped, not wanting to frighten her. A lone wolf he could manage. A pack was another matter.

"Drat. It took me ages to coax her to come even that close to me. I nearly had her."

"What?" Gowain glanced down into her wide, dark eyes. They glittered with something suspiciously like annoyance. "You wanted to capture a wolf?"

"She's a dog. Someone's pet, I think, for she has a bit of rope tied round her neck."

Gowain glanced at the brush, then back at the woman in his arms. "Terror has overset you."

"I am not terrified." Alys's hands splayed over his chest, her eyes wide and pleading. "Oh, I was frightened when I first saw her step from the brush, and thought as you did that 'twas a wolf. But when I realized she was a dog, I tried to get close…"

"You are mad. You tried to capture a wild dog?"

"Not wild, just alone, scared and hungry. Please, you have to help me find her and her pups."

"Pups? You truly are mad if you claim to have seen—"

"I didn't see the pups, but I could tell she's nursing. She was afraid of me…more afraid than I was of her. The only reason she came close to me is because I fed her."

"You fed her." Gowain was beginning to feel like a fool, echoing everything she said to him. "What did you feed her?"

"The cheese Maye had given me for the journey to Newstead."

"Of course." Gowain's anger returned. "How could I have forgotten about that?" He released her, and his arms felt oddly empty without her. "Come, I'll take you back to the caves."

She crossed her arms and regarded him stonily. "Not without my dog and her pups."

"You are in no position to issue orders, *Lady* Alys—if that really is your name."

"Of course it is." She sounded insulted.

"Why not lie about that, too? You've lied about everything else," Gowain snarled.

"Aye, well…" She looked down, gloved hands fiddling with the ends of her belt. "I…I did not set out to deceive you. It just happened. Dickie thought I was a nun, and when you came upon us, looking so ruthless, your sword red with blood, I…I was afraid."

"So your first thought was to lie."

"My first thought was that if you knew I was a lady traveling with the man you had, for all I knew, just killed, I might be the next victim of your thirst for revenge."

Gowain grunted, in no mood for logic. "And later, when we had welcomed you into our camp, honored you for saving our comrades, did you not feel safe telling us the truth?"

"I…" She foundered, looking uncertain for the first time. "There didn't seem to be a good time to say so."

"Last night might have been an excellent time," he snapped. "Or this morn when I poured out my apology for defiling one of Christ's chosen. Would that not have been a good time to ease your conscience and mine?"

"Aye," she whispered. A flush stained her cheeks, but her gaze did not waver. "I am sorry. I hated seeing you suffer."

"But what? With you, there is always a *but*."

Her gaze shifted away. "I was ashamed of what happened."

Gowain stiffened, recalling all too vividly her frantic fight to get free of his embrace. "You made your feeling clear. I but mistook the reason for your revulsion."

"I was not revolted," she said quickly. "I was... surprised." She gave him a half smile. "I've never been kissed before."

Gowain stared at her mouth, the pure lines of her face, the slender column of her neck, the rapid rise and fall of her breasts beneath the ugly robe she wore. Then he looked again at her mouth. The taste of her lingered in his mind. He wished to hell it didn't. "The lady who owns the gowns and costly bits in those trunks must be overwhelmed with suitors."

"My family has protected me from that."

"Why? Are you promised to some great lord?"

She shook her head. An indefinable sadness flickered in the depths of her eyes. "No suitors, no betrothed."

"Why?"

The sadness grew; the faint sheen of tears glinted in the shifting light. "'Tis a long, boring story, and one you would not believe, anyway." She sighed. "Suffice to say, I wished to remain unwed, and my family has allowed me to do so."

Unwed. Promised to no one. His fickle heart skipped a beat. His errant body quickened. He was suddenly aware of how close together they stood—so close the scent of woman and rosemary filled his nostrils. Her compelling eyes were full upon him, soft and mysterious. Despite his misgivings about her, something inside him shifted. He wanted to reach out and touch her. Nay, he wanted to clasp her tight against his body and never let go.

Far away, thunder rolled across the heavens, and the wind sliced through the glade. It tugged at her headdress, freeing a lock of pale hair. He remembered how it had looked last night, tumbling down her back like molten gold.

In the hours since, he'd thought about her hair more than once and cursed himself for wishing he could run his hands through it, see it spread on his pillow. A strand whipped across her face and caught on her mouth. Without thinking, he captured it. "Soft as silk," he murmured, sifting the hair with his forefingers.

"It's tangled. I've not been able to comb it properly," she whispered back, her voice low and husky.

The sound ruffled through his mind like a hot wind, charging the space between them with more tension than the approaching storm. "I could do it for you," he heard himself whisper.

"I—I think I would like that."

"No more than I." Gowain studied her in the half-light, torn by conflicting urges. She was wrong for him, a proud, pampered lady. Yet she'd proved herself made of finer stuff than any other lady he'd ever met. And he wanted her, more with each passing moment. He thought she wanted him, too, though she was wary as a woodland doe. "Are you afraid of me?"

"Nay, of...of this." Her helpless gesture took in the two of them and all the unspoken tension. "When you kissed me, 'twas like being plunged into a firestorm. It frightened me."

Gowain nodded. That night, the backlash of Enid's nightmare had stripped him of his customary control. He'd taken with little regard, less care. His mood was not much calmer now, latent fear still edging his pulse. Still, the need to hold her was a growing hunger deep inside. He'd fought it from the moment they met.

"Alys." Her name—minus the "Sister"—tasted so right. He gave in and put one hand on her shoulder. Through the wool gown, her flesh felt warm, resilient. So good. When she didn't back away, his fingers curled reflexively, kneading lightly. "I am sorry I startled you. There's little gentleness left in me."

"But there is." Her eyes full on him, she covered his

hand with hers. "You have a great capacity for kindness and compassion, but you hide it as skillfully as your other feelings. I do not know how you do it."

"Practice," he muttered. "'Twas the only way I survived two years in a French prison."

"Oh, Gowain."

He shook his head, not wanting her pity. "'Tis in the past. As is what happened last night. Now…" He stared into her eyes, thinking a man could drown in them. "Now all I want is to wipe away that memory. If you'll let me." He lowered his head and brushed his lips over hers.

Alys jumped as heat bloomed. The press of flesh on flesh was brief, yet the tingling lingered. "Oh," she breathed.

"Aye." She looked as dazed as he felt, mouth parted, eyes smoky. He wanted more…much more…but she wasn't ready. He measured her shock in the pulse leaping in the hollow of her throat. She was stunned, not frightened. It would have to do for now. "Come, it's time we were getting back to the caves."

She trembled. "What of Maye?"

"Leave her to me."

"I do not want to cause trouble."

"You won't," he lied, knowing she was a distraction he could ill afford.

"But…"

Traveler snorted and pawed the ground.

Gowain turned in time to see a dark canine head part the bushes and look out. Slanted yellow eyes regarded them narrowly.

"Oh. She came back." Alys pushed past him and knelt, fumbling in the pocket of her robe. She held out her hand. "Come out, love, I've got some more of the cheese."

"Alys, get back," Gowain snapped.

"Wait. Look, she's coming."

The dog, a brindled mastiff to be exact, crept out of the brush. Hesitantly, one eye on Gowain, the other on Alys's outstretched hand, the hound inched forward.

"Alys…"

"She won't hurt me," Alys cooed softly.

The dog stopped a few inches shy of Alys, stretched its neck out. Sharp white teeth nipped the cheese from her palm, and then the dog took off running.

"Quick…follow her." Alys hiked up her skirts and dashed after the fleeing hound.

"Dammit, Alys, come back." She didn't. Swearing, Gowain charged into the bushes. Briars tore at his mail, branches swatted him in the face. "Alys, wait." She didn't do that, either. A long, frantic minute later he finally caught up with her. She was down on her knees in the moss, watching three eight-week-old pups greet their mother. The dam dropped the hunk of cheese, and the trio fell upon it, gnawing and growling.

"Oh, they're near starved," Alys whispered. So they were, ribs visible through their matted fur. "We'll have to take them back with us. They need food, a bath."

"They are wild things, likely half wolf."

"What does it matter? Their mother is domesticated. They'll learn from her. And from us. Please. We cannot just abandon them here. We have to give them a chance."

Gowain's objections stuck in his throat. Had he not thought the same thing when he'd finally found Enid, thin and neglected, in that squalid hut? He'd bartered his soul to give her a chance. "Very well," he said gruffly.

"Oh, thank you." She hopped up and gave him a hug. There was nothing seductive in the gesture, but it made his blood hum all the same. "Think how delighted the children will be." She looked like a child herself, bright-eyed and eager.

Gowain stilled, his inner armor cracking as his spirits lifted. "Think how much work they will be."

"I do not mind." She bent to fondle one of the pups. The thing was filthy, yet she let it lick the crumbs from her fingers, then gently stroked its head.

Charmed, Gowain hunkered down beside her. He tried

to imagine another fine lady cuddling a mangy, half-wild animal, but couldn't. "You are very good with them."

"I've been around animals all my life. My father raises and trains horses."

"Apparently he does quite well at it," he said dryly, thinking of the velvet gowns and costly books.

"Aye, he does." Her gloved hands skimmed the pup's head. "If I sent word to him, he could look into the matter of your claim on Malpas, then no blood would be shed in taking it."

"How did you know about that?" Gowain asked.

"From Ranulf."

His brother's name fell between them like an angry bolt of lightning, shattering the easy mood. "What exactly did he tell you?" Gowain asked through his teeth.

She blinked, and he could see the cogs in her fine mind turning. "That you wanted your mother's dower property, and when you learned that she had not been wed to your father, you rebelled, began pillaging the countryside."

"I see. Did he also say I planned to attack Malpas?"

"Nay." She frowned. "'Twas Birdie who first mentioned it, I think, though everyone in the caves speaks of it."

Gowain relaxed a fraction. "Come. We'd best get back."

"You are angry with me again."

"Nay, with this damnable situation we find ourselves in."

Chapter Nine

Damn Ranulf for coming between them, Alys thought as she watched Gowain fashion a sling from his own cloak to carry the pups. Despite his anger at her, he showed no rancor toward the pups, who leapt about, tugging at the wool as he tried to tie it.

The easy camaraderie between them had been killed by the mention of his brother's name. She never should have spoken of Malpas, wouldn't have if she wasn't concerned for Gowain's safety and certain her father could help. If Gareth Sommerville knew what sort of cruel fiend Ranulf was, he'd see that Ranulf faced his accusers in the high court...one Ranulf could not hope to sway as he obviously had the one at Eastham.

Gowain, on the other hand, was undeserving of the label *outlaw*. He was intelligent and well-bred. A complex man. Strong enough to keep a band of rebels in line, ruthless enough to raid to feed them. By his own admission, what softness he possessed, he kept as carefully hidden as Alys did her sensitive hands. She'd glimpsed it on many occasions, like now, as he carefully lifted a wriggling pup.

The pup squealed; its mother rushed in and tried to wedge her nose between Gowain and her baby.

"Easy. I mean your little one no harm," he crooned. He fondled the mother's head, and she quieted instantly. "You are right,'' he said, glancing briefly at Alys. ''The bitch has not been so long in the wild that she's forgotten men.'' He examined the pup, turning it this way and that. ''Still, I cannot tell if she mated with a wolf or not.''

Alys stood mute, deeply affected by the sight of the tiny thing engulfed by his big hands. He could break it with ease, yet the dogs sensed they were safe with him. ''Animals are better judges of human nature than people are,'' her father had often said. ''They see past the masks people put on to fool others.'' Obviously the dog and her offspring liked what they'd seen and trusted Gowain instinctively.

''Ready?'' Gowain asked. He'd bundled all three pups into the pouch and tied it on behind Traveler's saddle. He swung up into the saddle and held out his hand. The dam stood at attention beside his stirrup, trembling, but otherwise taking the situation in stride. Which was more than Alys could say for herself.

''You expect me to ride with you?''

'''Tis either that or walk. Traveler will scarcely feel the added weight. Come, we've dallied overlong as it is. Darcy and the others will think I've run into trouble.''

Alys hesitated, wary, yet a bit excited at the thought of sitting before him. What would it be like to have his arms around her, her back pressed against his chest? She wanted to know, wanted it so badly her skin tingled and her heart raced. She lifted her hand, then hesitated. ''You are still angry with me because you think I side with Ranulf.''

The light in his eyes died. He shook his head. ''I do not know why you were riding with Ranulf, but I don't think you came here to spy for him.''

''He was taking me to Newstead…or so I thought. I may not be a nun, but I visit there each year. To study healing.''

Questions flickered in the gaze that held hers so steadily. Instead of voicing them, he nodded and extended his hand again. ''We'll talk of it when I've got you safe inside the caves.''

His protectiveness drew her. She held out her hand,

struck by the ease with which he lifted her up before him. Settled against his chest, one arm around her waist, she felt secure and nothing more. If he was still angry, either their clothing masked it or his control did. She was relieved and grateful.

He clicked the stallion into a walk and glanced over his shoulder. "The bitch is following us."

"Did you think she wouldn't?"

"Nay. We've got her babies. 'Tis a powerful lure."

"Speaking of babes, Enid would sleep better if there was a light in her room. 'Tis the dark she fears."

"When we get to Malpas, she can have torches aplenty, but her sleeping cave is too small. I fear she'd overset a candle and be burned."

"How long till we leave for the keep?" When he hesitated, she sighed. "I'm sorry I asked."

"'Tis not that I do not trust you."

"But the fewer who know something like that, the better. I understand." Trying not to feel hurt, she changed the subject. "I am very glad you came for me. These woods are dark and lonely."

"Maye will be punished for—"

"Nay." Alys turned toward him. "Please don't. She tried to help me reach the abbey."

"Darcy says the farmer wasn't coming," he muttered. His arm tightened fractionally on her.

Alys shivered. If Gowain hadn't come looking for her, heaven knew what might have befallen her. "She does not like me."

"'Tis no excuse."

"Punishing her will only make matters worse. It might be best if you could find a way to get me to Newstead."

"Is that what you want?"

"It would be best," Alys repeated, heart heavy.

His arm tightened fractionally on her waist. "I would like it if you stayed."

"Really?" she said quickly.

"We have need of a healer."

"Is that the only reason?" she asked in a small voice.

His own was low and husky. "You know it is not."

Alys shivered. "I would like to stay. But...but..." She could not utter the words.

"You are still afraid of me." His chest expanded and contracted, as though he sought to steady his nerves.

Her own were raw with pain and sorrow. "Not in the way you think, Gowain."

He ducked to avoid a low-hanging branch, his breath fanning her cheek as he murmured, "If you truly fear me, say so, and I will leave you alone."

He could do it, too, she thought, recalling the control he exerted over his emotions. "I do not fear you," Alys whispered. "But there are reasons why we cannot be together."

"You are not wed or betrothed. What other reason is there?"

"None you would understand, I fear."

"Then you will explain it to me...once we are back in the caves," he said with arrogant certainty.

Alys was just as certain she could not trust him with her secrets, and so the silence spun out, taut and uncomfortable, each of them lost in thought, though he held her close.

A fine mist had begun to fall by the time they left the forest. Darcy and the others appeared out of it like fairy sprites. Armed sprites, their faces as dangerous as their unsheathed swords in the seconds before they recognized Gowain.

"You've found her," Darcy said, grinning. "Safe and unhurt?"

"For the most part," Gowain growled. "We've picked up a few more strays. A mastiff bitch and her three pups." He gestured at the dog, who hung back at the edge of the woods.

Alys bristled. "They are starved and afraid."

"Are not we all?" Darcy quipped.

"Don't encourage her, Darcy," Gowain warned. "We'd

best set our patrols and get back up the mountain.'' He dismounted and lifted her down from the saddle.

Cold without his heat, dreading the confrontation to come, she wrapped her arms around her body and shivered.

Gowain ordered one of his men to give Alys his horse and ride double with another. The pups were tied on behind Alys's saddle. ''Tom Reeve, go along with Alys and make certain she gets back to camp safely,'' he added before turning away to set up patrols for the night. In addition to the riders on the lookout for Ranulf's soldiers, several men were detailed to wipe out all traces of their passage.

Clearly Gowain was a man who left nothing to chance.

''Come along. I ain't got all night,'' growled Tom, a skinny, surly-faced man. He kneed his horse into motion.

Alys mounted and rode after him. Though being with Gowain made her skittish for some reason, she felt equally uneasy about leaving him. Especially with so much unsettled between them. She looked back, finding him quickly despite the gloom, a tall, armored spire in the center of his dark cloaked men. The mist made Gowain's mailed body glow with a strange silver fire.

Power, she thought. Power and confidence.

He had both in abundance. Pity she could not persuade him to give up this mad rebellion and allow her father to put the case before the king. Richard was a foolish, vain man at times, but he did have a strong sense of fair play.

Alys turned the problem this way and that as they rode up the mountain, but could see no solution that didn't involve risk to her family. She abandoned that dilemma for a more personal matter. What would she say when Gowain pressed her for answers? Could she bear to tell him she was a freak and watch his desire turn to revulsion?

''We're here,'' grumbled Tom, halting just inside the entrance to the caves.

Alys slipped from the saddle before he could help her. Her mind shifted from trusting Gowain to the more pleasant prospect of showing the pups to the children. ''Please bring the pups inside." Their dam hesitated, eyes wary, but she'd followed them this far and would likely stick close to her babies. "We'll take them to the kitchens, I think, for there'll be a fire there to heat water. I'll need some toweling or old blankets."

"I'm not your maid, Your Ladyship," Tom snapped.

"Of course not," Alys said hastily. She'd issued the orders without thinking, used to having a dozen people leap to do her bidding. 'Twas a sad commentary on her life that she expected others to perform tasks she could well do herself. "I can manage." Standing on tiptoe, she untied the makeshift sack. The pups were so quiet she feared they'd smothered. But when she lifted them down, they exploded into action, whining and pawing at the confining sack. It heaved and writhed like some frantic monster, while Alys struggled to keep hold of it. Sharp claws pierced the wool and laid a scratch down her arm.

"Ouch." Alys shifted her heaving burden and looked expectantly at Tom for help.

He stared at her, unmoved and unmoving.

Of all the rude, uncaring... Alys struggled for a better grip, overbalanced and fell heavily on her rump. The sack landed on her chest. Air whooshed out of her lungs, and spots twinkled before her eyes.

Tom's raucous laughter was drowned out by hurried footsteps as they were joined by Bradley, Bette's eldest son.

"Are you hurt, Sister, er, Lady Alys?" Bradley asked. He was a genial lad of ten-and-six, but like all the cave folk, he was pale from lack of sunshine and far too thin.

"Mostly bruised pride." She glared at Tom, who glared right back at her. Such brutish behavior would not have been tolerated by her father for one instant.

Bradley squatted beside the quivering sack. "What game have you bagged?"

"Not game...puppies."

"Puppies!" Delight wiped ten years from his face.

Alys's trampled spirits soared. Gowain's worrisome desire and Tom's rancor no longer mattered for she'd found a way to please the children. She untied the cloak and grinned as the pups came tumbling out. "Gowain and I came upon them in the woods. They're in sorry need of a bath, food and love. But dear, nonetheless."

"Aye, they are that." Bradley laughed softly as the pups gnawed on his knuckles. "Wait till Birdie sees them."

"We'd best get them cleaned up, first. Your mother will not appreciate having Birdie covered with dirt."

"Can I help?"

"I'll be going back down and telling Gowain you've found yourself a lackey," Tom snapped and rode off.

"I didn't mean to order you about," Alys called.

"Pay him no mind. Tom's a bit daft about such things. He was reeve at Eastham village in Lord Warren's time, but when Ranulf inherited, he replaced Tom with one of his own men. He doesn't take kindly to being no one, does Tom."

Alys understood the feeling all too well. She'd fallen from beloved daughter to despised prisoner. "I'll remember never to ask him for help."

"Especially not with so menial a task."

The pups, having realized Bradley's hands weren't going to yield any food, began to whine again.

"Hush," said Alys. "We cannot have the children finding you before we've gotten you clean enough for them to handle."

"Will you let me help?"

"I would appreciate it." Alys vowed she'd never again take another's assistance for granted as she had in the past. "But only if you're sure you want to."

Not only was Bradley eager, his help was invaluable. He bundled the pups back into the cloak and carried them to the kitchens while Alys led their mother. Once inside, he filled the big cook pot with water and set it to heat while Alys explained to the dubious Percy what they planned.

"I've never been one to let animals into my kitchen,"

the cook said, scowling, "'less they were bound for the pot."

The pups were penned up in a crate, but the intriguing smells of past meals had overcome the dam's wariness, and she was busily poking her nose into everything. Alys winced when the dog unearthed a scrap of meat from a crevice in the rock wall.

"Drop it," Alys commanded.

The dog ran past her outstretched hand, but instead of making for the door with her prize, the dam ran over and dropped it into the crate with her pups. They fell on the meat, sucking and slurping.

"Poor things, they are so hungry," Alys whispered.

Percy sniffed. "'Tis foolish to take them in when we have scarcely enough to feed ourselves, but..."

"They can have my share," Bradley said.

"Nay. You need to eat." Alys's hand fisted in her skirts. "What of the supplies Gowain brought in?"

"You know they are rationed by his order." Percy hustled over and unlocked a stout door. Inside was a pantry of sorts, the walls lined with shelves, the floor stacked high with kegs and sacks. "Still, I might be able to find something..."

"There's enough here to feed the lot of us for weeks," Alys said angrily. "Why does he ration the food?"

"'Tis part of his plan. He said the sacks and kegs must remain full and intact."

"Why? It makes no sense."

"I am sure he knows what he is doing," Percy said stoutly. "Gowain's a clever man, and he's not led us wrong yet." He reached over the pile of stolen goods and snagged a small kettle from the shelf. "There's a bit of soup left from yesterday. I'd thought to add it to tomorrow's stew, but we'll not miss it." He offered the pan to the dog, who began to lap greedily.

"What of the pups?" Bradley asked.

"If their mother's well fed, she can nurse them," Percy said. "Milk'll be better for them at any rate."

"Can I give them their bath?" Bradley asked.

"If you like," Alys said absently, pleased the dogs had a protector, but troubled by the rationing. "I'm going to speak with Gowain. It is not right to keep food from hungry people."

"Are you certain you should?" Percy asked. "Gowain always knows what's best for us, but he does not take kindly to having his orders questioned or disobeyed."

Tyrant, Alys thought. "He'll listen to me." She stalked off, filled with righteous indignation. She'd heard him say he'd return to the caves after setting those stupid patrols of his. Likely she'd find him in the main hall.

Alys lost her way and had to ask directions of a surly guard. She didn't recall his name, but the bandage on his hand covered a sword slice that she'd stitched herself. Such discourtesy was unheard-of at Ransford.

Pausing on the threshold, she searched the cavernous great chamber for her quarry. Gowain was not there, but some kind of entertainment was apparently in progress. Though why they should hold it so late at night, she couldn't understand.

Women in brightly colored clothes paraded back and forth before the hearth. They took no care of their garments, letting the hems drag on the dirt floor. Firelight caught on the gems that banded the necks and sleeves.

Where would they get such costly things? Alys wondered. She recognized Maye at the head of the group, her ample body stuffed into a lovely emerald green gown.

"Bow down, you serfs," Maye sang out. She postured and preened like royalty.

The half-dozen men at a nearby table hooted and pounded their wooden ale cups on the tables. The floor about them was littered with broken crockery, and a pile of what looked like books was heaped dangerously close to the fire.

Frowning, Alys stepped into the room. Books? Costly clothes? Where had they gotten such things? Were they part of the plunder taken with Ranulf's supply wagons? As she drew nearer, Alys recognized the leather binding on the books and choked.

They were her journals! Her precious herbals!

"What are you doing with my things?" she cried.

As one, the revelers turned toward her.

"Betrayer!" someone shouted.

"Liar! Scum!" they screamed. And worse.

Alys halted. She glanced about the smoky room, conscious of the angry faces and accusing eyes of those who had so recently sung her praises. The wall of hatred made her stomach clench, but she was a Sommerville, and they did not quail before adversity. "By what right have you taken my things?" she asked.

"You lied to us." Maye stepped forward, her pretty features twisted with contempt. "You claimed to be a nun, when all the while you were one of *them.*"

"Them?" Alys asked, baffled.

"You're a noblewoman."

"Oh, well, that is not a bad thing."

"To us, it is." Ralph Denys rose from a bench. "You and your kind have starved us, taxed us off our land and hunted us."

"But I am not responsible for that. I—"

"These are yours, are they not? The fancy clothes, the books and fine leather gloves," Maye snapped. "Bought and paid for by the money wrung from downtrodden folk like us."

"My family's retainers are not downtrodden."

"See, she admits it." Ralph's eyes glittered with savage triumph. He took a step forward.

Alys's heart skittered, but she stood her ground. "You are mistaken. We are not like that. But I must insist you return my things to me."

"You insist?" Ralph's laugh was harsh and nasty.

"You're in no position to make demands, Your Ladyship. These things are ours, now. Spoils of war."

Alys looked around at the resentful eyes and set jaws. For once, pure will would not prevail. "You may keep the clothes," she said evenly. Her eyes flicked to the books, her life's work, so close to the hungry flames. "But I want the books."

"Henry," Ralph called.

"Aye." He shuffled forward, a hulking brute with the mind of a child. There was no anger in his expression, only blind loyalty to his older brother. "What ye want, Ralphie?"

"I want you to burn those books."

"Nay!" Alys screamed and darted forward. Ralph caught her around the waist. The force of his rage sizzled through her, numbing her. So great was the pain, she couldn't speak.

"Hold her, then, while I do it." Ralph threw her at Henry.

The big man's arms came around her. "I ain't never held a lady before."

She felt his confusion, his gentleness and took heart. "Please...please don't let him burn my books."

"Gotta do what Ralphie says. He knows best."

"Let me go." Alys pushed against this arm. It was as unmovable as solid rock.

"What are you doing to Lady Alys?" Velma pushed her way into the circle of militant bystanders.

Ralph frowned. "This is no place for you, Velma."

"What is going on? Why is Henry holding Lady Alys? Why is everyone dressed in... Oh, those are her books." Velma glared at Maye. "You've no right to take what doesn't belong to you."

Maye scowled right back, hands on her hips. "She's Ranulf's friend, mayhap his mistress. He could have bought her these things with what he stole from us. That gives us the right." Behind her, the other women nodded and muttered in agreement.

"Go back to your room, Velma," Ralph ordered.

"Not without Lady Alys and her things."

"They can have them...all except the books," Alys said.

Ralph snatched up one of the journals and flipped through the pages, his grimy fingers leaving smudges on the parchment. "What's in these? An account of what Ranulf took from us?" Clearly he couldn't read, for he had the book upside down.

"They are recipes for herbal cures."

"Ha!" Ralph started to heave the book toward the fire.

"Please don't. They are important."

"Not to me. Revenge, that's what's important." Ralph's eyes narrowed. "See this...? He fingered the scar that bisected his forehead. "Little souvenir of the day Ranulf came calling on Velma. She was to wed my brother Hob. Lost them both that day, we did. Hob's dead. Velma as good as."

"I am so sorry, but why do you blame me?"

"You were riding with Ranulf," Maye said.

Ralph's lip curled. "I say we drive her out."

"Drive her out." A hunk of oatcake sailed over the crowd and hit the wall just above Alys's head. It was followed by a half-eaten apple and a wooden bowl. The air filled with food and coarse insults.

"Stop!" The command cut through the chaos. Gowain strode into the hall, Darcy at his side. "What the hell is going on?" Gowain demanded, his piercing gaze full on Alys.

"Stay out of it," Ralph snarled. "'Tis between us and her."

Gowain's head whipped toward him, his hand flashing to the hilt of his sword. His expression was fierce enough to melt stone. "What trouble are you brewing now?"

"She's the one causing trouble." Ralph backed up a step.

"Somehow, I think not." Gowain looked at Henry, his gaze gentling. "Release her, Henry," he said softly.

Henry frowned. "But Ralphie said I was to hold her while he burned those evil books."

"Books?" Gowain scanned the room, his lips thinning when he saw the gowns, crocks and books. "What have you people done?" Even Maye seemed to cringe before his accusatory stare.

"It isn't right she should have so much," Maye said. "Likely Ranulf bought these for her with coin he stole from us."

"They were bought by her sire, a prosperous horse trader," Gowain snapped.

"Horse trader?" Ralph looked from Alys to the profusion of costly garments. "Never. 'Tis another lie."

"I say it's the truth." Gowain stared them all down, till even Ralph avoided his gaze. "Damn," he exclaimed. "What is wrong with you? You act like a mob of Ranulf's thugs, not decent men and women who have ample reason to know what it feels like to be the victim of such ruthlessness. This," he added, arm sweeping to encompass the ruined gowns, crushed pots and defaced books, "this is likely why Alys pretended she was a nun. Because she feared she'd fallen in with a band of outlaws and would be robbed or murdered."

"I thought she'd be gone," Maye said.

Darcy put an arm around her. "'Tis a bad thing you've done."

Maye pulled away. "Gowain, please do not be angry with me."

"I'll speak to you later." He fastened his chilling gaze on Ralph. "Now, I want Alys released and her property returned."

Ralph's scar stood out white against his scarlet face. "Aye, Your Lordship." He turned to the crowd. "Didn't I tell you you'd be better off trusting me than one of them?"

No one moved.

Ralph wheeled around. "Here's your book, then." He
threw it at Alys. Henry still held her; she had no way to
duck aside.

Velma darted in front of her. The book caught her in the
temple, and she fell to the ground.

"Velma!" Ralph rushed to her.

Henry let go of Alys. "Ralphie, why did ye do that?"

"Sweet Mary!" Alys knelt beside the fallen woman.
"You've knocked her out." She looked at the blood welling from the gash, then up at the circle of appalled rebels.
"Don't stand there. Fetch my medicine chest, hot water
and blankets."

A dozen people scrambled to obey.

"Will...will she die?" Ralph whispered.

Alys glared at him. Then she saw his stricken expression,
and her own gentled. "I will do my best to see she does
not."

Chapter Ten

It must be near dawn, Gowain thought, judging by the grittiness of his eyes. He'd dozed a bit, his back propped against the wall of Velma's chamber. Mostly he'd kept watch over Alys and her patient.

Alys hadn't wanted him here, but he'd insisted. He felt guilty enough over what had happened without leaving her to single-handedly deal with the consequences.

The fire in the brazier had nearly burned out; the candle in the floor stand was a mere nub. He cursed this living in perpetual dark. It reminded him too much of de Grise's dungeon. When Malpas was his, he'd knock out the walls in the hall and put in huge windows. Glass would be beyond his means, but he'd have shutters made for the cold weather, and leave them open in good. Never again would he live in the dark. Sighing, he stretched his long legs out before him to ease the cramped muscles.

"Why do you not seek your bed?" Alys asked.

He started and looked at the figure on the stool. If he was tired, she must be doubly so. "I thought you were asleep."

"Somehow I cannot when I'm sitting vigil with a patient."

She had a strong sense of duty. He thought of Blanche—vain, selfish and coldhearted enough to abandon her own babe. Alys was as different from her as sunshine from shade. Sitting here through the night, watching her tend the unconscious woman, had heightened his appreciation of Alys's fine qualities. He'd not thought to wed again, but if he did, he'd pick a wife for her kindness, not her beauty. Alys had both.

"I admire your dedication," Gowain told her.

She ducked her head shyly. "Thank you."

"I apologize for what happened."

"'Tis not your fault."

"I should have done something about Ralph long ago."

"Bette says he was the leader here before you came, and resents it because people preferred you to him."

"Aye, though *tyrant* might be a better word. He's cruel, disruptive and vindictive, but I could not bring myself to kill him, and feared he'd betray us if I turned him out."

"I admire your sense of honor."

He shrugged. "It has grown lax over the years, as you've been reminding me from the moment you arrived."

"I cannot fault you for wanting to punish Ranulf." She shivered. "Everywhere I turn, every tale I hear only confirms that he is not the knight he seems, but a ruthless wretch. Still, I wish you could find some other way. If the king knew—"

"He'd side with Ranulf. Power always clings to power."

"You cannot know that till you try. You...you could go to London and beg an audience with His Majesty."

"I cannot take the chance he'd believe Ranulf, not me. Do you know what would happen? They'd hang us.... Not just me and Darcy and the lads who came with me from France. They'd hang the boys, as well, and the women..." He shook his head. "I do not want to think what would happen to them."

"But surely..."

"It would not work." He turned his gaze on Velma. She lay on a pallet before the brazier. The purple bruise at her temple contrasted sharply with her white skin. It had been hours since the incident, and as far as he could tell, the woman had not moved at all. "I know little of such things, but should she not have regained her senses by now?"

"It...it is not a good sign that she is still unconscious." She nibbled on her lower lip. "If only I hadn't insisted on having the books back."

"They are your property."

"More than that, they are books on herbal cures, which I compiled myself. It took years to complete them." She looked at Velma. "But what is that compared with a life?"

"You've done all you can for her."

"Have I?" She looked down at her gloved hand, flexing them so her knuckles showed through the thin leather. "There is one thing I have not tried."

"What?"

"It may be that I can determine what is wrong, but..." Her troubled gaze flickered over Velma's still form. "If only I were not such a coward."

"You are no such thing. When I walked in and saw you, held fast in Henry's grip, yet defying Ralph..." Gowain's chest tightened. "I feared I'd not reach you in time."

A faint smile tugged at her lips. "I have never been quite so glad to see anyone as I was when you came."

"If only I'd been sooner."

"Or Ralph's temper less volatile." Again she flexed her hands. "I owe it to Velma to try." She began to peel off her gloves. Beneath the leather, her skin was unnaturally pale.

"I wondered why you did not remove your gloves to tend your patients. Surely it would be easier."

"It's a great deal more difficult." She glanced at him, her features drawn, her eyes haunted.

Alarmed, Gowain went to kneel beside her. "What is it? What are you going to do?"

"Touch her, nothing more."

Yet it terrified her, Gowain realized. Before he could

frame another question, she leaned forward. Eyes closed, she hesitantly put her fingers on Velma's forehead.

"Oh!" Alys shivered convulsively.

"Alys?"

"It's all right." Her eyes were still tightly shut, her breathing was short and choppy. "Mostly all right. She is deeply unconscious. That…that helps some."

"Helps what?"

"Shh. I have to concentrate." Alys bent closer and moved her hands across Velma's sweaty brow. Gingerly she brushed her fingertips over the wound itself. "Oh, there it is." Another shudder worked its way through Alys.

Gowain reached for her, then stopped, afraid to intrude on whatever she was doing. What the hell was she doing?

"Pressure and pain," Alys murmured. "Have to ease the pressure." She was gasping for breath, trembling.

"Alys. Stop." Gowain took her shoulders and gently pulled her back, forcing her to break contact with Velma. "I know you do not like me to touch you, but…"

"Just give me a moment to steady myself." Her hands fisted in the front of his tunic; she burrowed into him like a child seeking comfort.

The unconscious gesture roused his protective instincts. He stopped thinking of her as a woman he desired, and held her with a tenderness he had thought had died with Blanche's betrayal. His hands moved down her supple spine, kneading away the tension, soothing the tremors. Gradually he felt her relax, and a rare feeling of awe washed over him. The prickly Alys trusted him.

Alys basked in the enveloping warmth of his body. Using her gift made her weak, dazed and disoriented. Somehow she seemed to draw strength from Gowain's powerful body. The slow rise and fall of his chest beneath her cheek steadied her breathing. The feel of his arms grounded her. But there was more…so much more. It was wonderful to be held by someone after what seemed like a lifetime of yearning for such closeness. Too wonderful for words. She could have stayed here forever, Alys thought in amazement, but there was much she must see to.

Reluctantly, she raised her head. "I know what to do."

"You are not going to do anything," Gowain growled. "You are exhausted. I'm taking you to your room and putting you to bed."

"I can help Velma."

"You've done enough." His jaw set, he touched her cheek. The hazy heat of comfort was replaced by a flare of temper.

Singed, Alys jerked away. "Don't…"

"Damn, but you blow hot and cold."

Alys glared up at him. "Do you think I *want* to be this way?"

"What way?"

"I…I am a healer, but not all my skills are of the normal sort." The skepticism in his face hurt, though she'd seen it in dozens of others. "'Tis a gift, of sorts, that runs in my mother's family. My great-aunt was an herbwoman, whose ability to heal was aided by the fact that her patients did not have to describe their ailments, she could read their minds."

He stared at her as though she'd grown two heads. "Go on."

"My mother never developed her talents, though she knows exactly what my father is thinking. And I…"

"You can read my mind?" Now he looked appalled.

"Nay. When I touch someone, I—I can feel the things they feel. Anger, happiness, pain—"

"That's why you wear the gloves."

"And the loose robes. Though my hands are the most sensitive, it can be painful to touch someone who is in the grip of strong emotions."

"Why did you not tell me before?"

"'Tis hardly the sort of thing I boast about, sir. You've no idea how many folk think such skills qualify me as a witch."

There was so much she wanted to tell him, to try to explain, but if she was right about Velma, steps must be taken soon. "When I touched Velma, I learned why she has not awakened. The bruise on her forehead has swollen inward. I—I could feel the bad blood pressing on her brain. She will die if the pressure is not reduced."

"You want to bleed her?"

"Cupping would not help, for it would take the blood from her arm, not her head. 'Tis too dangerous to plunge a knife into her head, but if we found some leeches and applied them to the bruise, they would hopefully draw out the bad blood."

"Leeches." He nodded and climbed slowly to his feet. Expression shuttered, he stared down at her for a moment. "I will go down to the river and gather your leeches."

Alys sagged back against the wall, drained by the healing and the confrontation with Gowain. She thought longingly of the few moments when he'd held her as though she was the most important thing in his world. The wonder of it awed her still. To be held and cherished by someone who cared for you...surely there was no more moving experience.

The knowledge that it would never happen again made her throat tighten and tears well. Nay, Gowain would never touch her again. Doubtless he either despised her or feared her.

A single tear slid down Alys's cheek.

She'd been better off not knowing that the power of his embrace could send her heart soaring with joy and hope, could warm her blood and make her pulse pound. The fall from the dizzying heights of what might have been left her cold and shaken.

Maye stood the moment Gowain entered the great hall. His clothes were wrinkled and his face was haggard. Still, she rushed over to him. "Gowain. Please say you aren't angry with me."

"You are lucky I found Alys unharmed."

"Of course. I did not mean for her to be hurt."

"Did you not?" He looked down at her with open contempt. "Oh, and how was she supposed to survive alone in the woods?"

"I asked Donald's son Donald to escort her to that abbey. I did," Maye insisted. "I gave him my mother's ring as payment."

Gowain rubbed a hand over his stubbled chin. "When Jean searched their farm, Donaldson was drunk in bed."

"That sot. He must have used my ring to buy ale."

"Hmm. I suppose that is not your fault. Still, you should not have suggested the plan in the first place. Particularly since I had ordered Alys kept here under close watch." He cocked his head. "You probably hoped I'd think she'd gone to Ranulf."

Maye twisted her hands in her skirt to keep from reaching for him. "Gowain..."

He sighed and placed his hands on her shoulders. "Maye, I thought you were my friend."

"I am," she said quickly, but she cringed inside, already guessing where this conversation would lead.

"Good." He squeezed gently. "Then you will understand when I say that I value your friendship, your support, your loyalty."

Maye nodded, the lump in her throat thickening. "I have tried my best to help you."

"Aye, that you have." He smiled wistfully. "I will always need you for my friend, Maye."

But nothing more than that. Maye heard the words as clearly as though he'd spoken them. It spared her pride that he had not.

"Years ago, I rashly asked you to come with me when I ran away to France. You were wise enough to know that it would not work out between us."

"I regretted it."

"Had you been with me, you would not have. 'Twas a

rough-and-tumble life I led. I'm glad you were spared the worst of it. Till now, that is.''

''We are going to win,'' Maye said quickly, glad to have something else to latch on to. ''We will take Malpas.''

''If so, 'tis in large part because of you.''

She smiled. ''Thank you for that.''

''You deserve the praise, but I hope you will not take it into your head to devise any more schemes to get rid of Alys.''

''Is she staying, then?''

''For the moment. We have need of a healer.'' The sudden flare in his eyes spoke of other needs and wants.

Maye sighed and nodded, heartsore but resigned. Since returning from France, Gowain had not shown her anything more than friendship. 'Twas her own fault if she'd dreamed of more. ''What of Velma? Is she any better?''

''We will know presently.'' He gave her shoulders a final, friendly squeeze. ''I'd best go back and see if Alys's bold new cure is working.''

Maye watched him walk from the room, so tall, strong and proud. What a fine man he was. How she wished he were hers.

''Ale?'' asked a familiar voice. Darcy stood at her elbow, a cup in one hand, a sympathetic smile on his face.

''I do not want your pity,'' she snapped.

''Pity is the very last thing I feel for you, Maye mine.'' Taking her arm, he deftly steered her to a dark corner, then sat her down on a bench. ''Are you going to be all right?''

''Aye.'' Sniffing, she took a sip of the ale. The strong liquid steadied her. ''I'll not cry over losing something I never really had.''

''That's my lass.'' He took the cup and drank from the spot her lips had touched. ''Is he still angry with you?''

''Disappointed. Which hurts worse.'' Maye touched his hand. ''I really did arrange for Donaldson to take her to Newstead. I—I did it when you took Johnny and me down to the farm.''

"Ah. And was that the only reason you went with me?"

Maye looked away from his earnest gaze. "Aye, but I had a good time in spite of myself."

"Did you now?" His fingers curled around hers. "Well, that's something. Will you take the noon meal with me, Maye? Even if it's just to show folks you aren't alone and pining."

She gazed at her hand, sheltered in the palm of his. 'Twas a good feeling, she decided, being cared for. "Aye, I'll sup with you, Darcy Beaufort, but not to bolster my pride."

"Thanks to Alys's healing skills, Velma is awake and possessed of her senses," Gowain announced at suppertime.

The cheer that swept the hall was deafening. Even Ralph managed to put aside his surly frown long enough to accept the heartfelt good wishes of the assembly.

"I must admit, when Velma did not immediately regain consciousness, I did not think she would live," Maye said over the din. "How did Alys do it?"

"Leeches." Gowain was surprised at the steadiness of his voice. Even now, hours later, he could scarcely believe what Alys had told him about her strange skills.

"Where is she, that we might thank her?" Maye asked, with surprisingly little rancor.

"I sent her to bed. She was exhausted." *Dieu,* he could still recall the trip to Alys's chamber a few short hours ago. She'd been beyond weary, so drained she could hardly walk. Yet she'd refused his aid.

"I would be able to feel your disgust of me, and that would only make matters worse," she'd said before setting off down the corridor, a hand braced on the wall for support.

The sight of her, weak and exhausted, yet beyond his help had angered him. "You do not disgust me," he'd snapped.

She'd studied him a moment in the smoky torchlight. "You are in the grip of some strong emotion. I see it in your eyes. 'Tis another skill I've developed, to avoid unpleasant surprises. Whatever it is would only do me harm." She'd moved on.

Gowain had gone with her, awash in helpless rage and frustration. It was not his nature to ignore another's suffering. He'd wanted to carry her to her chamber, comfort her till she slept, yet he couldn't help without hurting. He took pride in his hard-won self-control, but he'd known at the moment it was stretched thin. He'd learned to appear unaffected, to stifle his anger, pain and disappointment at the nasty blows life dealt him. While inside he seethed and bled. These things he couldn't hide from Alys. If he'd touched her, she'd have been stung by his rage.

Dieu, 'twas almost better when he thought she despised him. Now that he knew why she shied from his touch, he wanted to find a way to—

"You love her, don't you?" Maye asked.

Shaken from his thoughts, Gowain stared down into her glum expression. "'Tis as I told you, I've lost the ability to love."

"Nay, you only think you have, but time heals. The heart forgets. I know. When I first learned John dallied with other women, a part of me died. Oh, I didn't love him as I did you—still, he was a good husband, kind out of bed and considerate in. Practice, I suppose, of which he had a great deal. 'Twas the death of a dream that hurt. I'd convinced myself we were happy together. 'Tis awful to know you've been betrayed by someone you trusted with your innermost self."

"Aye, it does. Worse, it makes you afraid to trust again."

"Darcy says it comes of putting too much stock in appearances and not enough in actions."

"I suppose that's true." A dozen images crowded into his mind: Alys soothing Enid's nightmare, facing him down to tend Stork's wounds, defying logic to rescue a hound and her pups. All the marks of a good, kind woman. Gowain discovered there was something that hurt worse than betrayal. It was knowing that there was no way he could be with Alys.

"It must be true," Maye said, chuckling. "For Darcy is much smarter and wiser than he looks."

Gowain shrugged off his own pain. "He is the best friend a man could have…or a woman, either, for that matter."

"Aye, he is." Maye turned toward the spot where Darcy stood talking with Bertram. Her son leaned down from his perch on Darcy's big shoulders and said something that made both men laugh. Grabbing hold of the boy's arms, Darcy lifted him, then swung him about in a slow arc.

"Mama! See, I'm a bird!" Johnny shouted.

Maye grinned and waved back at him. "Darcy's patient with my Johnny, something his own father never was, for all the pride he took in having a son."

"He's been patient with you, too, Maye."

Her smile faded. "I didn't ask him to court me."

"But you've not turned him down, either. I'd hate to think you were toying with him. He's far too good a man for that."

"I…I know." She stared full into his eyes. "I am not sure of my own mind, yet, but I do like Darcy." She covered his hand with her own and squeezed.

The press of flesh on flesh, doubtless meant to convey caring and closeness, hurt immeasurably. It reminded Gowain that even so simple a gesture was impossible between Alys and him. He sighed and looked out over the crowded hall. "I am glad, Maye."

"It's Alys!" someone shouted.

Gowain spun and saw her standing in the doorway, her gaze fixed on himself and Maye. He knew how it must look, the two of them standing close together, hand in hand. He saw the hurt in Alys's pinched features and felt it bite deep in his gut.

Chapter Eleven

"It does not matter. It does not matter," Alys muttered as she hurried away from the hall. She should have been glad Gowain had someone to ease his loneliness.

Instead, she'd wanted to scratch Maye's eyes out. The surge of hatred had surprised and unnerved Alys. It made her wonder if she was not as good and kind as she'd always thought.

The truth was, she wanted Gowain for herself, even knowing she could not hold his hand as Maye had, much less be a true mate to him. If only she could turn this gift of hers off and on like a water spigot. If only she'd never inherited it to begin with.

Peals of laughter rang down the corridor.

Laughter? Alys stopped. In the days she'd been here, she'd not heard anyone laugh. Head cocked like a hunting hound's, she listened. There it was again. Curious, she traced the joyful sounds to the large room where the children spent most of their time under the watchful care of Ruby and several of the young mothers. The few times she'd chanced by, the boys had been listlessly playing with a set of wooden horses, while the girls learned the rudiments of sewing.

Alys paused on the threshold, unable to believe her eyes. A dozen youngsters, including Birdie, Johnny and Enid, dashed about the room, playing tag with the hound pups. The children's faces were flushed, their eyes bright as new pennies. Dickie of Newton sat on the sidelines, his chest bound with thick bandages. The mother hound dozed beside him, her head on his thigh.

"They are having a wonderful time," Bab said, coming up to Alys. "Thank you so much." Her thin face radiated joy.

"'Tis a miracle, Sister," Ruby added as she joined them.

"I am not a nun," Alys said gently.

"To me, you're a saint." Ruby grabbed Alys's hand and kissed it, her gratitude warming through the glove. "I'd never thought to see wee Enid smile, much less laugh. Only wait till I tell Gowain. He will be so pleased."

Even the mention of his name brought a pang of longing. "It is the pups' doing, not mine," Alys said.

"You insisted Gowain bring them here. My mama said so," Bab added. "She says you are the most selfless person she's met."

Alys shook her head. If she was, she'd be happy for Gowain and Maye, not resentful. "I am not—"

"Sister Alys!" The children raced over and clustered around her, all shouting at once.

"Can we name the pups?"

"Can one sleep in my bed?"

They clutched at her knees and grabbed hold of her hands. Nearly overwhelmed by their happiness, Alys swayed.

"Easy, you lot," Bab chided. "You'll knock Alys over."

"'Tis all right." Alys knelt among them, soaking up their pleasure as they pressed against her back and sides. For once, she found joy in her gift. "I am so pleased you like the pups."

"Can we name them?" Johnny asked, brown eyes sparkling.

Alys smiled. "Of course."

"But no arguing about it, mind," Ruby said sternly.

"We could draw lots," Dickie called.

"An excellent idea." She looked around at the eager faces. "What names do you have in mind?"

"Wolfspawn for the largest male," said one boy.

"Devil Fang for the other," Johnny said.

Alys frowned. "Hmm. Why not something more peaceful?"

"Let's call the female Lily," piped up a little girl whose mother bore that same name.

"Well, I am not certain your mother would like that." Alys looked to the other women for help.

Ruby cleared her throat and Bab grinned.

As though sensing they were being discussed, the pups trotted over and flopped down on their bellies, tongues lolling so that they appeared to grin at her predicament.

"Angel." Enid grabbed the small female pup around the middle and wormed her way through the circle lugging her burden. "Call her Angel, for you."

Alys slid her hand under the pup's hindquarters and helped to support it. "We'll have to see what the other children think."

"Angel," Enid said, more firmly. She laid her head on Alys's shoulder. Instead of fear, she exuded happiness.

"Alys, what is going on?" asked a deep, familiar voice. A dark shadow fell over them.

Alys started and looked up into Gowain's concerned face.

Enid looked up, too. Her contentment vanished in a spurt of pure terror. She tried to burrow into Alys.

Fighting to distance herself from Enid's fear, Alys said, "'Tis only your papa, sweetheart." She stroked the quivering body, needing desperately to ease things between them. Let that be her gift to him. "See, he's come to play with the pups."

Enid peered upward and shivered. "He's too big to play."

"Not really. He probably does not realize that he seems big, towering over us like this." Alys was vaguely aware of Bab tactfully taking the other two pups and the children to the far end of the room. Bless her.

"I am sure he does not." Gowain hunkered down beside them, his thigh brushing hers.

His warmth, his solid support, felt good. "See, Enid, he's just our size now. Mayhap he'd like to play with the pup."

Enid frowned. "Girls play. Boys play. Men do not play."

"Papas play," Alys insisted, recalling the countless hours her own father had spent on his hands and knees serving as her first horse. Loneliness surged through her. Would she ever see her beloved father and mother again?

"They do?"

Alys shook off the ache of longing. "Aye. Did you know that your papa found these pups and brought them back here?"

"He did?" Enid's eyes rounded.

"He helped." Gowain plucked the pup from her precarious grasp. "She's a sight cleaner than when I last saw her."

"We bathed her." Enid left the security of Alys's arms and ventured a step closer to Gowain.

"And fed her, too, I'll wager." Gowain rolled it onto its back and tickled the full belly, making the pup wriggle.

"Me do it." Enid attacked the pup with such zeal it whimpered and edged away, but Gowain saved the situation.

"Gently, Enid." He took her hand and backed it off. "Stroke her with just your fingertips, because she is small and delicate."

"'Mall and del'cate." Enid's tongue crept out between her lips as she concentrated on the task. She giggled when the pup raised its head and licked her hand. "She likes me."

"'Course she does. We all like you." Gowain glanced

up at Alys, his eyes misted, like rain-washed leaves. "If only you could relax and let us show you how much."

Alys's heart cracked. "If you sit on your papa's lap, you could hold the pup much better."

"He hasn't got a lap."

"He can make one." Gowain shifted, sitting and crossing his legs. A expression of pure wonder flickered across his face as his daughter plopped down on his lap.

"Gimme Angel," Enid demanded.

"Please?" Alys prompted.

"Please." Enid grinned when Gowain settled the pup across her thighs and watched as he petted little Angel. "Papa stroke her nice. Me too." She brushed the pup from chest to belly as she'd seen Gowain do. "We no hit or pinch like the mean man."

Alys went cold inside as the implication sank in. Enid's nightmare. She looked up and caught Gowain's hard stare.

"No one here will hit or pinch anyone," Gowain said gruffly.

Enid's hand stopped moving. "But it's dark here."

"The dark isn't bad."

"I don't like the dark. Bad things come in the dark."

Gowain sighed. "Soon we'll go to a place where it isn't dark, where you—"

"Go?" Tears filled her eyes. "Not leave me."

"Nay. Of course not." Gowain brushed his hand over her cheek. "We will all go."

"Angel, too?" Enid glanced at Alys.

"Well…" Much as she hated lying to a child, Alys also knew how damaging a lie could be. "We shall have to see."

"Angel go, too." Enid's small jaw stuck out in a gesture reminiscent of her father.

"She got more than her green eyes from you," Alys remarked.

"Are you saying I'm stubborn?"

"Mmm. As a stone."

"Please?" Enid asked, obviously having recalled the magic word that had gotten her her way.

"Stubborn and clever." Alys shook her head. "A dangerous combination." And she didn't only mean Enid. "Very well, you little minx, I'll come along if your papa wants me to."

Enid glanced sidelong at Gowain. "He does."

"You're a crafty lass, Enid," Gowain said, cuddling her. When she didn't pull away, he grinned. The smile transformed his face, easing the care lines. "We want Alys to stay with us because she wants to, not because she feels trapped."

The color drained from Enid's dusky skin. "Trapped?"

Gowain breathed a word in a tongue Alys was just as glad none of them spoke. "Enid…"

"Your papa misspoke, Enid," Alys said quickly. "He meant he didn't want me to have too many tasks. You know about tasks, don't you? Like when Bab washes the pots for Percy."

Enid nodded warily. "Angel no wash pots, Papa."

"Agreed." He ruffled his daughter's hair, but his jaw was rigid, and his eyes were hot with anger.

"The puppy is teething on the hem of your tunic, Enid," Alys said. She snagged a headless wooden horse. "Why don't you give her this to chew on instead?"

Enid happily accepted the suggestion, giggling as the pup champed down on the toy. Soon she was absorbed in fondling her pet's ears and watching it worry the battered horse.

Alys let out a cautious sigh of relief.

"My thanks," Gowain murmured. "You are very good with her."

"I've had a bit of practice with my brother's two young sons, but she's even more quick-witted than they."

"And fragile. So damned fragile, it breaks my heart." His voice was harsh, pained.

Alys glanced at him, realized too late that it was a mis-

take. His gaze was focused on her with searing intensity.
The air between them seemed charged, as though a storm
were about to erupt. She knew she should look away, but
was powerless to move.

"I am glad you decided to stay, Alys."

"Maye won't be."

"She understands now that she is my friend, naught
more. We were discussing it when you came into the hall."

"You were holding her hand."

The undercurrent of pain goaded him. He took her
gloved hand and, before she could react, slid one finger
under the sleeve of her gown, seeking and finding satiny
skin.

Alys gasped and tried to move away.

"Easy. Tell me what you feel."

"W-warmth...calluses."

He smiled, fighting to keep his emotions even. "And?"

"Happiness...I think."

"Because you are staying." Beneath his finger, her pulse
began to settle. "We can do this," he murmured.

"I am un-unnatural."

"You are as God made you, beautiful, kind, generous..."

"I cannot be what you want."

"And what is that?"

She shivered. "A...a..."

"Lover?" he whispered, pleased by the hike in her pulse.
She nodded and ducked her head.

He grinned and stroked her forearm. She was still trembling, but not with uncertainty or fear. Nor was she trying
to pull away. It was worth the strain on his self-control. "I
want you to be comfortable with me, Alys."

"I do, too, but..." Her eyes locked on his, twin pools
of startling blue, filled with trampled hopes. "This will not
work."

"It can, if you want it badly enough." His gaze focused
on her, his eyes as dark and mysterious as the forest at

night. In their depths flickered a longing she understood only too well, for it mirrored her own. Loneliness, a yearning to belong to someplace and someone.

The ache in her chest grew, coiling so tight she could scarcely breathe. She wanted...dear God, how she wanted...to take up the gauntlet he'd thrown down.

"Mayhap you do not want to take up with a murdering rebel."

"Do not say that about yourself! Your cause is just!" she exclaimed. Tears filled her eyes, blurring his features as surely as her previous view of right and wrong had been changed by meeting him and those he fought to save. "It's not you, it's me," she whispered. "I'm the one who is flawed."

"You are wrong. After what Blanche did to me and to Enid, I swore never to trust another woman. Yet in the few short days we've known each other, your gentleness, your pureness of spirit, have made me think otherwise."

"Gratitude," Alys said, wondering why it hurt so to know that he, like countless others, admired her healing skill.

"Hardly." A slow, roguish smile spread across his face, softening his features. So he must have looked before fate and a fickle woman tempered him, carefree and unbearably handsome. "I assure you that gratitude is the last thing on my mind." The huskiness in his voice slide down her spine like hot honey.

Alys shivered. "Please stop looking at me like that."

His smile thinned. "You would deny what is between us?"

"I have to," she replied with brutal honesty. "You do not understand what it is like to touch another and suddenly be thrust inside their skin, prey to their pain, their physical and emotional anguish. With Velma it was not so bad, because she was not conscious. But there have been times when a healing has left me so weak I could not move for days."

"Is it as horrible as that when I touch you?"

"Nay." She cocked her head, considering. "There have been times when I've known you were angry, yet you concealed it even from me. Now, for instance. I know you are disappointed by my answers, but I cannot feel it."

"You see...there is hope."

Alys was not so certain. "I do not see how it can work."

"Nay?" Mindful of Enid drowsing in his lap, he leaned forward till his lips were an inch from Alys's. She could have leaned back. It pleased him that she didn't. "Kiss me."

Her cheeks went red, then paled. "Kiss you?"

"Aye. Press your lips to mine, and when you do, think only of what you feel." He waited, coaxing with his eyes and nothing more, his smoldering desire held carefully in check.

The brush of her mouth was as light as the beat of a butterfly's wing and just as quick. It trapped the air in his lungs and made his blood hum.

"Again," he whispered and braced himself. This time her lips lingered, soft and sweet as honeyed wine.

The rush of sensations caught Alys off guard, the heady wash of warmth that sent her heart racing and her stomach fluttering. She wasn't certain whose emotions she was feeling. His, hers, they seemed to mesh in one dizzying, mind-numbing flood. Inbred caution warned her to break contact, some greedy impulse had her slanting her mouth and searching for more. He gave, his lips answering the pressure of hers, moving lightly and slowly. It wasn't enough. She groaned in frustration.

Instantly his mouth was gone. "Alys?"

She kept her eyes closed, savoring the moment.

"Are you all right? Did I frighten you?"

"Frighten?" She lifted her lashes and smiled into his scowling face. "Nay. It was..."

"Was what?" he demanded.

She searched for the right word and settled for "Exciting." Like riding a fast horse...too close to a tall cliff."

"It was that." He sat back and reclaimed his hand from the folds of her sleeve, looking supremely smug.

Alys licked her lips. They tasted of him. It was pleasant, yet disconcerting, because she already wanted another sample. But first she needed to know more, needed to know it was safe. Not only for herself, but for him. "Why is it different from the other night?"

He shrugged and looked down at his sleeping daughter and at the pup snoring in her arms. "I was caught off guard, not in control of the situation or myself."

"Today you were?" Even without his nod, she knew it was true. Hadn't she envied him that control? "Is that why I feel nothing when I touch you?"

He smiled wryly. "I had rather hoped you felt something."

The heat crept back into Alys's cheeks. "You know I do. The strange thing is, when I kissed you just now, it was difficult to tell what was me and what was you."

"Aye, it was." His gaze was steady, a burning green flame.

"Is it always like that?"

"It never has been for me...till now."

"How can you tell? It was only one kiss."

"I can tell." His lids lowered; his eyes smoldered. "If we weren't in the middle of the playroom, I might steal another one...just to make certain."

Alys waited for the skitter of alarm. It didn't come. "I would like that." Still, she was woefully ignorant about exactly what went on between men and women. She'd heard things about pain and animal lust, and she recalled enough from his first, fierce kiss to worry. "But what if you lose control again?"

"I won't." He brushed his knuckles over her cheek. The tenderness was unexpected, given the set of his jaw. "You are too precious to me."

"Could you teach me to block out what I feel when others touch me?"

He considered that a moment. "Nay. You are too open, too giving and generous. You could never cut yourself off that way."

"I could try," Alys said. "Think of it. I would be able to lead a normal life. No more robes, no more gloves, no more shying away from even the most basic of human contact."

"'Tis no way to live, Alys."

"Neither is the way I have been. Please say you will try."

"It would never work, and even if it did, I do not want to change you in any way."

"It would not change me, it would make things better. It may be my only chance to lead a normal life."

Filled with misgivings, Gowain looked away from her glowing eyes and determined chin. He spotted Lang Gib standing in the doorway and motioned the man in.

Lang Gib's expression was somber. "You're needed below. Chaffin's come with a message. Says it's urgent."

Gowain nodded. "I'll be right there." He looked down at his daughter. "Could you put her to bed, Alys?"

"Of course," she said at once. "Will you be long?"

"I pray not." He touched her cheek, pleased that she obviously felt none of his trepidation. If Chaffin had come so late, the news must be grim. "But don't wait up for me. You are still tired from nursing Velma."

She gave him an sunny smile and turned to kiss his knuckles. "If I do not, how will I convince you to help me?"

Gowain groaned. The brush of her lips, freely given, was more persuasive than a hundred impassioned pleas could have been. Much as he wanted to help her, he feared the plot was doomed. He'd never be able to teach Alys to cut herself off from the world. From him.

Chapter Twelve

Gowain hurried down the mountain, hoping Maye's older brother brought good news. The dour expression that greeted him, said otherwise. "What brings you hither so late at night?"

"A bit of news that wouldn't wait." Christened Robert, he was called Rob Chaffin for his bald head. Though his heart was with the rebels, Chaffin had remained in Eastham village, dispensing drink at his inn and gathering information for Gowain. "A squad of Ranulf's men stopped by my tavern last night. They wanted ale—not a flagon, mind, but every keg I had." He grinned. "Seems the shipment of supplies to replenish the stores at Eastham Castle and Malpas went astray."

Darcy chuckled. "And right fine ale it was. Tasted all the sweeter for knowing we'd deprived Ranulf's men of it."

"I was glad you were able to intercept the wagons."

"Thanks to your information." Gowain shifted and looked over his shoulder at the mountain, set out black against the night sky. Was Alys even now putting Enid to bed? He wished he could be with them, sharing the moment. Like a family, he thought, not at all surprised to discover the notion was pleasing. It was too soon, the voice of reason warned. There were obstacles to overcome. Not the least of which was her gift. But he had faith. Faith in his ability to win what he wanted. Alys. Then Malpas.

"Ranulf's loss is definitely our gain," Darcy was saying, patting his belly. "I'll wager he was furious."

Rob Chaffin nodded, his bald head gleaming in the torchlight. "His men said he near killed the horses getting back to Eastham, then set about preparing to march out again."

Gowain came away from the rock. "Does he know where we are?"

"Nay," Chaffin said. "They left Eastham at dawn today, Ranulf, Clive and a hundred men, riding east."

"Where were they going?"

"The soldiers who came into the tavern did not know. They had been patrolling the northern boundary of Eastham looking for you. 'Tis very odd," Chaffin added. "According to them, Ranulf has called in all his patrols to guard the castle."

"You mean, he is no longer hunting us?" Gowain asked.

"So it seems. Even stranger, Hick the Carpenter was pressured into making a burial casket of the finest oak...overnight, mind. Ranulf took it with him, in a wagon, which will slow him down."

Gowain frowned. "Who was in the casket?"

"They didn't know that, either. Clive made the arrangements."

"Mayhap one of Ranulf's knights was killed in the skirmish with us," Gowain said. "A knight with important connections."

Darcy cursed. "If so, Ranulf may think to rouse this knight's family against us, gain their aid in wiping us out."

"Possible." Gowain frowned, considering. "Did Ranulf's men happen to mention a lady who was traveling with him?"

"A lady? Nay, they did not, but they had little on their minds except ale and a dry bed."

Gowain nodded. "Likely Ranulf was too furious with me to worry over the daughter of a horse trainer." He clapped a hand on Chaffin's shoulder. "We are again in your debt, my friend."

"'Tis a pleasure to serve you." Chaffin grinned. "I only hope it hastens Ranulf's downfall. If ever a man deserved to die, it is surely that foul bastard."

"That may be, but not by my hand," Gowain replied.

Chaffin grunted. "Well, then, I hope the day soon comes when you sit as lord of Eastham Castle."

"I've told you," Gowain said gently, "that much as I deplore what he has done, I'd not oust my brother from his rightful place. I want only what is mine, Malpas, and a chance to live there in peace and raise my daughter." And win Alys.

"If you ever change your mind, you have but to say the word and the countryside between here and the sea will rise up to support you against him," Chaffin said solemnly.

Gowain shook his head. "Bad enough I've led astray those who already ride with me. I could not live with myself if I endangered any more in my fight."

"Our fight." Chaffin sighed and mounted his horse. "You always were too damned noble for your own good." He raised a hand in silent salute. "See if you can pound some sense into his thick skull, Darcy. Oh, and good fortune winning my sister for yourself," he added before he wheeled and rode off.

"How did he know?" Darcy asked.

"Chaffin is a rare man," Gowain said. "I wish he were going with us to Malpas, for I've no doubt the keep is in ruins and we'll need help to make it run smoothly again before winter."

"Do you still plan to leave for the keep in two weeks' time?" Darcy asked as they began the climb up to the caves.

"Nay. We'll go day after tomorrow if possible."

"So soon? Do you think the men are ready?"

"They'll have to be. With Ranulf and most of his men away, 'tis the perfect time for us to strike. And if Ranulf has gone to secure more troops, we must be safe inside Malpas before they come hunting us.''

Darcy grunted. ''We've much to do, then.''

''Aye.'' They reached the mouth of the caves, and Gowain turned toward the storeroom. ''I want to take another count of the weapons we have. We'll send Jean out to make certain Ranulf really has withdrawn his men. Set up training sessions for early tomorrow and ask Maye to set the women packing our things.''

And pray God we are ready for this, he thought.

What Gowain wasn't ready for was returning to his counting room and finding Alys asleep on the thin pallet he'd been using as a bed. She lay on her side, her left hand tucked under her chin, her hair tumbled over the pillow like tangled silk. His comb was held loosely in her right hand.

Beautiful, Gowain thought, but it wasn't her beauty that punched the air from his lungs and weakened his knees so that he sank down on the floor beside her. She looked so fragile, small and delicate as spun glass, her silky skin juxtaposed against the rough gray linen sheets. She didn't belong here, was his first thought. She deserved better, was his next.

When Malpas was his, he'd work tirelessly to make a proper home for her. That she was doubtless used to better than he could ever provide worried him.

Even as the thought formed, she stirred. Her lashes lifted, blinked over unfocused eyes. Then widened.

''Hmm. Gowain.'' She stretched and rolled onto her back. Her robe molded to high breasts and a narrow waist.

He started to reach for her, then remembered that he couldn't...not with desire running hot. It took a moment for him to master the urge. ''What are you doing here?'' he asked.

''Waiting for you.''

He had a fleeting image of coming into the keep each night to find her waiting, smiling, welcoming him. ''I like that.''

"So do I." She smiled back. "I sensed you were upset when you left, and I wanted to make certain you were all right."

His weariness, the press of the dozens of things that needed doing before they left for Malpas, vanished in a twinkle. How long had it been since anyone except Darcy had worried about him. "I am fine. Did Enid give you much trouble?"

"She went right to sleep." Alys sat up, shaking the hair back from her face. "Ruby is with her."

He nodded. Awkward, he reached for a trailing lock of hair. With a life of its own, it curled around his finger, releasing the scent of rosemary. "You washed your hair."

"Aye. I was attempting to comb out the tangles when I fell asleep myself." She sighed. "Impossible task, I'm afraid."

Gowain picked up the wide-toothed wooden comb he'd whittled for himself. "I've never done this before." He dragged it through the lively curl, wincing when it caught on a knot.

"It'll take more force than that. Don't be afraid you'll hurt me."

"But I am." Aware he wasn't only talking about a few pulled hairs, Gowain turned to the task. He toiled in silence for a few moments, drawing gently, anchoring the hair between his fingers to minimize the pain. Working his way from bottom to top, he reached her scalp. He felt her tense just before his hand touched her head. A reminder of the challenge they faced. Carefully blanking out his fears, he laid a hand on her crown and gently pulled the comb through her hair from root to curling end.

She relaxed beneath his touch. "Mmm. That feels good. You've a knack for this."

Gowain grinned, surprised at how the task had relaxed him, too. "'Tis not difficult. Like currying—"

"Careful," Alys teased.

"Traveler's mane…only much softer and sweeter-smelling."

She giggled and brought her knees up, encircling them with her arms. "I love having my hair combed. For years it's been my only form of human contact."

The pain behind her simple words hurt him. To prove something for both of them, he slid his fingers through her hair and stroked her neck. A quick shiver moved under her skin, followed by a soft moan. "Alys?"

"I'm fine…better than fine. It's wonderful."

Gowain smiled and pleasured them both by touching her again, trailing his fingers up her throat and cupping her chin. It occurred to him that he had done a lot of smiling since she came into his life. He tilted her chin up. "Aye, it is wonderful," he said and kissed her gently.

Alys's eyes were still closed when he lifted his head. "I've dreamed of this," she said, senses humming. "Of being with someone whose feelings do not swamp me."

"What makes you think you aren't feeling what I feel?"

She blinked. "But—"

"We want the same thing, Alys. Each other."

She colored prettily. "I'm not used to this."

"Neither am I." Because he didn't completely trust himself in the quiet room alone with her, he went back to her hair. Her sigh of disappointment had him grinning behind her back. Slow and easy was what she needed…whether she knew it or not.

"Did Chaffin bring bad news?" she asked after a moment.

Gowain tensed, worries flooding back. "Not precisely."

"What is it?"

"Ranulf has taken most of his men and left Eastham."

"Is he coming here?" she cried.

"Nay. He rode east."

"Why?"

"We think he has gone to get more men from a powerful lord."

From her father? Nay, he'd made his position clear. Besides, Ranulf would not dare face her father and tell him he had lost the daughter entrusted to him. "He could have gone to his overlord, Lord James. Oh, Gowain, could you not send a message to this man and ask him to intercede? If he knew—"

Gowain snorted. "He's a nobleman. He'll likely give Ranulf the troops he wants, but I mean to make damned certain they are too late to stop me from taking Malpas."

"You mean to move soon?"

"As soon as we can be ready...a few days at most."

"Gowain...mayhap Lord James would listen if you told him what Ranulf has done."

"It doesn't matter." Restless suddenly, he put the comb down and rose to pace the narrow room. "Don't worry, we'll be inside Malpas before Ranulf can muster his reinforcements."

"But won't he try to retake the keep?"

"It's virtually unassailable."

"Then how can you hope to conquer it?"

"By stealth and guile. Once inside, we'll be safe from attack. Winter will render the mountain trails impassable."

"But when spring comes, surely Ranulf will try to lay siege to the keep."

"He can try, but I doubt he will. Malpas is less than nothing compared to Eastham. My half brother is not really interested in the place, except to prevent me from having it. He'll not waste his men and money for such a small prize." He extended a hand to her. "Come, I'll see you to your chamber."

"I am not ready to leave you yet. Could we not sit and talk a bit longer?"

Gowain started, surprised but pleased. "I'm loath to part with you, too, but we both need our rest. The next two days will be busy ones."

Nodding, Alys let him pull her to her feet. She looked at their joined hands, hers gloved. "I want to touch you."

His senses spun, sizzled. "Sweetheart..."

She was already pulling off the thin leather. Before he could brace himself, her fingers slid up to frame his face. Her gasp of pain was like a lance to the heart.

"Alys." He took hold of her waist to steady her, scrambling to shore up his own defenses. "I'm sorry. So sorry." He fought for control, seized the tattered reins and held on.

"It's all right." Her hands slid away from his face, coming to rest on his shoulders. "I—I was just surprised. The heat..."

At least she was not completely repulsed by what had happened. "I'm sorry, love. You took me by surprise, too."

A tear slipped down her cheek, more terrible than a flood would have been. "I thought... I hoped..."

"I know." Steadier, sure his barriers were in place, he gently touched her cheek. "Better?"

She nodded and managed a misty smile. "If only I could do what you do. If only I could shield myself."

Gowain sighed and rested his forehead against hers.

"You are annoyed with me for saying so."

"Never." But he did not think her plan would work. "We will find a way to be together. That I promise you." They had to.

"Lord Ranulf. What brings you here?" Gareth Sommerville asked, staring down from the high table.

"I fear I bring grave news, my lord," Ranulf said solemnly. The crowd in Ransford's great hall fell silent.

"About Alys?" Lady Arianna clutched the edge of the high table, her face as white as the cloth that covered it.

Ranulf had arrived to find them in the middle of the evening meal. The steward had thought to detain him because the earl and countess were entertaining John, duke of Lancaster and the king's own uncle. But Ranulf had brushed past the old man and swept into the hall, anxious to impart his news. Now he studied the waiting Sommervilles, gauging how best to draw out the drama and gain the desired end. Gowain's downfall.

To think, he could have been the Sommervilles' son-by-marriage, dining off silver plates and rubbing elbows with royalty. Damn that Gowain for ruining everything.

"She's dead, I fear."

"Dead!" Gareth's shout rang off the rafters far above, was echoed back by the scores of retainers.

"Nay!" Lady Arianna shrieked.

"'Tis true. She was murdered," Ranulf said, pitching his voice over the swelling din. "By my fiend of a half brother." He was hungry and wet, but he knew it would be ages before his needs were seen to. Straightening his shoulders, he began the story he'd composed on the long ride here. "I've brought her home to you for burial," he said at last, the hall quiet except for the hiss and crackle of the fire in the huge hearth.

"Let me see her." Lady Arianna surged out of her chair. "I'll not believe it till I do."

Ranulf stepped closer, looked the earl in the eye and shook his head. "'Twould not be...best."

"Oh, merciful God." The lady collapsed into her husband's arms, sobbing so piteously even Ranulf was moved.

The shrieking and crying rose to such a pitch that Ranulf felt dizzy, but he stood firm. He answered the low-voiced questions of a grizzled warrior named William, accepted a cup of wine from a serving maid and let the grief wash over him. By the time the tide subsided, tears were streaming down his own face.

"M-my lord," Ranulf stammered. "I would stay only long enough to see my love properly buried, then I shall set out to track him down."

"Your love?" growled a raspy voice.

Ranulf glanced up into the hard face of Duke John. "I... That is, we had formed an attachment of sorts on the journey, and—"

"What sort of attachment?" the old man demanded. The

passing years were heavily etched into his features, but Lancaster's dark eyes were sharp and relentless.

"Nothing untoward," Ranulf said hastily. "I...I fell in love with her when we first met, and she did do me the honor of saying she returned my affections. But I swear, I did not touch her."

"Humph. 'Course not. No one did." His thick brows slammed together over his beak of a nose. "Go on."

"What is it, Your Grace?" Gareth leaned over the high table. "Ari's women have taken her to bed, and I must go to her, but first I'd hear what you've learned."

"This young pup says he was in love with Alys."

Gareth winced, and his eyes, already red and swollen, filled again with tears. "I cannot believe she's gone."

"'Tis true." The quaver in Ranulf's voice was real. If he did not get through these next few minutes, he'd be lost. "We were nearly to Newstead when we were set upon."

"Why did you not protect her?" Gareth demanded.

"When I saw we were outnumbered, I sent her back the way we'd come, with a goodly escort," Ranulf said. "They had orders to ride for Millwood Priory and take refuge there."

Gareth nodded and sagged back in his chair. "Come up to me, I beg you. I cannot stand with this cursed leg, and I'd hear the rest, even though the hearing near kills me."

The broken leg, of course. Ranulf nearly smiled. Here he'd been wondering how he'd get men from Sommerville without having to bring the too-honorable earl along.

Ranulf mounted the dais and took the chair Lady Arianna had vacated. It was large and handsomely carved, the down-filled velvet seat so soft 'twas like sitting on a cloud. First chance he got, he'd have one commissioned for himself.

"Go on," Gareth said hoarsely.

"The battle was fierce," Ranulf began. "I took a sword cut to the arm." He pulled back his right sleeve to display the bandage. A nice touch, he thought. "Still I fought on, knowing I had to put a stop to Gowain's ruthlessness. Eventually, we routed the brigands, but..." Ranulf hesitated. "As they fled from us, they overtook my men...and Lady Alys."

Gareth drew in a shuddery breath. "My daughter, was she...?"

"She must have put up a gallant struggle," Ranulf said.

"Oh." Gareth slumped over the table, his head in his arms.

"No more," said Duke John. Tears streaming down his seamed face, he laid a comforting hand on the earl's heaving shoulders. "Spare yourself the details, man."

"I...I could not bear to repeat them," Ranulf said, nearly choking on a bubble of elation.

Gareth raised his head, handsome features twisted now with pain. "Are you certain 'twas Gowain's doing?"

Ranulf ground his teeth together. Damn, even now the man could not just strike without being certain. "'Twas he who rose off her sprawled body," Ranulf said, painting as brutal a picture as he could. "If another of his men had her, too, I—"

"Shut up," the duke snapped.

"I...I am sorry." Ranulf looked down, fingering the fine linen table cloth. Flemish, mayhap, or even Italian. "I loved her, too, yet my grief has made my tongue outpace my sense."

"You loved her?" Gareth croaked.

"Who could meet Alys and not fall in love with her? Such a beautiful, gentle soul." Ranulf wiped his eyes. "We talked on the journey and found much in common. We agreed that we would exchange messages while she was at Newstead. I...I had intended to write you and ask for her hand."

"Alys agreed to that?"

Ranulf nodded. "I nearly died myself when I realized what Gowain had done. Please, my lord..." He threw himself on his knees before the grieving earl. "Please give me leave to hunt him down and kill him. For Alys's sake."

Gareth nodded slowly. "I'm not a man given to violence, but clearly this man…this animal…is a menace and must be wiped out. Tell me what you need, men, arms, anything."

"Just issue the warrant giving me leave to hunt him down and dispose of him. That is all I ask."

Chapter Thirteen

Malpas. The word was on everyone's lips when Alys entered the hall the next morn.

"Is it not wonderful?" Bette exclaimed as she handed Alys a cup of ale. "We leave on the morrow."

"Wonderful," Alys echoed, yet the thought of the fighting to come chilled her.

"No more living in the dark," Bertram said, plopping down on the bench beside Alys and reaching for a cup.

"No more oatcakes," Bab added as she set a platter of the despised items down on the table. "We'll have meat, cheese, and real bread...with butter."

The chorus was picked up by a group at the next table, and soon the hall resounded with cries for those things people had missed most. The refrain most often heard was "Freedom."

"Freedom." Bertram sighed, his fleshy face flushed with joy. "When we lived in Eastham, I never gave much thought to the simple things of life, like coming and going as I pleased. Breathing a bit of air that hadn't just been exhaled by my neighbor." He sighed again and reached for his wife's hand. "Watching the sun rise over the hills with someone you love."

"What a beautiful sentiment, Bertie." Bette beamed at

her spouse. "But anxious as I am to leave these caves, we mustn't forget that if not for this haven, we'd all be dead."

"Or worse," Bertram muttered. "Ranulf would have hunted us down like vermin. Makes you wonder what we'll find at Malpas," he said darkly. "Mark my words, there's something bad been going on there, or else he'd not have cut off all communication."

Bette and Bab exchanged troubled glances. Around them, people shivered and crossed themselves.

Alys ached for them. How shallow and frivolous her life seemed compared to the hardships these people had endured. She'd thought herself noble and, aye, even put-upon, because her healing gift brought her a degree of suffering. She'd taken pride in the herbal books she'd labored over. Nay, 'twas more than pride, she thought, self-disgust growing. She'd felt a certain arrogance and superiority, as though her learning and her gift set her above others.

Oh, she'd never said so. She'd never even thought so till this moment. Still, her cherished accomplishments now lay like ashes in her mouth, a sour taste that wasn't washed away by a quick swallow of Ranulf's fine ale.

Gowain had been right to call her spoiled and pampered.

"Alys, you are not eating," Bette chided.

"I am not very hungry."

"I know the food is unappealing, but you'll need your strength, for there is much to do before tomorrow morn."

"Speaking of which," Bertram said, "I must be about my chores. The foodstuffs and weapons must be recounted and parceled out for the journey." He kissed his wife's forehead and hurried off, drawing with him young Bradley, who was learning to cipher.

Alys absently ate the dry cakes, her mind on how she could make amends for her shortcomings. "What can I do to help?"

"Well, Maye is supervising the packing, Percy the preparation of food for the journey. Have you any experience in the kitchen?"

"None." Actually, there wasn't much she could do, beyond healing, drawing and writing. Here, too, her family had indulged her. Instead of learning to manage a household, as did other daughters of noble houses, she'd pursued her studies of herbs and healing. "I can organize the medicines. My crocks of herbs will come in handy, both in case anyone is wounded and to plant at Malpas."

Bette frowned. "I do not think there will be room to bring them. There is barely enough wagon space for the women, children and the supplies."

"What?" Alys exclaimed. "I spent weeks gathering those plants, and cannot just leave—" She bit off the rest, but too late, for Gowain materialized beside them.

"What is wrong?" he asked as he slid onto the bench at the other side of the table. Lines of fatigue bracketed his mouth, a dozen concerns shadowed his beautiful eyes.

"Nothing," Alys said quickly.

"Alys is worried there won't be room to bring her herbs and books," Bette said.

"It is not important."

Gowain reached across the table and took her gloved hand. "Alys, I know how greatly you value your books, but—"

"'Tis all right," she said hastily, squeezing his hand. "I understand that all the room is needed for the people. I—I ask only to bring the herbals I wrote and enough of such medicines as may be useful in case there are wounded."

"We will make room for all your books and plants," he said, but she guessed it would not be easy.

Alys shook her head. "I don't want special treatment."

"You are special." His voice was low and husky.

"I'll leave you two to argue this out," Bette said. There was a knowing twinkle in her eye as she bustled away.

Alys huffed in exasperation and reclaimed her hand. "I am no more special than anyone else here."

"What has brought this on?" he asked, frowning.

"I—I have realized you were right. I am spoiled and

selfish. From my earliest days, my family gave me everything I ever wanted. I've never been hungry, cold or frightened. Well, mayhap I was a little afraid when my gift first came upon me, but even then they cosseted me. Our retainers and servants were told to take care not to touch me, even accidentally. Gloves and thick robes were made to protect me in case someone slipped. My father gave up his counting room so I might have a large chamber in which to pursue my study of herbal cures. My brothers left off their knightly training to escort me when I gathered plants.''

"Are you done?" Gowain asked.

Drained, Alys nodded and looked down at her hands.

"Why does all this make you angry?"

"Because…because I am not worthy of so much.''

"I think you are." He reached out and traced the line of her chin, his touch betraying his sympathy. "Your abilities make you unique and vulnerable, Alys. They were right to encourage your mind and protect you from harm.''

"'Tis not them I blame, but myself. Over the years, I have grown arrogant and judgmental. I do not like learning that about myself, but 'tis true. I am not good and kind. I expect to have everything done my way. I order others about as though it was my right, and…and I was jealous when I saw you with Maye.''

He chuckled. "Ah, Alys, you have merely discovered you are human. Some people never learn that about themselves. If you have a fault, 'tis that you worry too much about others.''

"That is not true.''

"It is. For proof, I have only to remember the things you've done to help these people. Velma, Enid, myself…even Maye. Never once did you demand she be punished for putting you in harm's way. Nay, but you urged leniency.''

Alys sighed. All he said was true, yet it didn't ease her feeling of unworthiness. "I am useless outside the herb room or the sickroom," she protested. "I want to help prepare for the trek to Malpas, but there is naught I can do."

Gowain's expression sobered. "There will be wounded, I fear, Alys. Bring what you think is needful to treat them."

Alys nodded and began to make plans. She didn't relish the task, for it meant suffering, but it was better to be prepared.

"You do not look as though you slept any better than I last night," Gowain said, his voice dropping to a whisper.

"Nay." Alys watched desire flare in his eyes and felt an answering flame kindle deep inside her. "I want to be with you, but it seems impossible."

"Never say that. We will find a way. Once we are settled at Malpas, there will be time for us to spend together."

"If only you would teach me to shut off my feelings..."

"Nay." Shaking his head emphatically, Gowain stood. "You could not do it. Nor would I want you to cut yourself off from everything and everyone. Especially me."

I already am, Alys thought, but now, in the middle of the crowded hall with a dozen worries hanging over their heads, was not the time to argue this out. Rising to her feet, Alys said, "We will speak of it later. I'd best get busy with the medicines."

Nodding, Gowain stepped around the table. He bent to plant a kiss on her mouth. A careful, controlled kiss that made her yearn for the burning ones they'd shared last night.

This would never do...for either of them. Somehow, she had to find a way around her problem, she decided as she watched Gowain stride from the hall. But first things first.

Alys went to the table where Velma sat with Dame Dotty. The old woman had been asked to subtly keep an eye on Velma, lest the poor girl try to harm herself or the babe.

"I wonder if you two might help me?" Alys asked.

"Anything," Velma said quickly.

"I need help preparing some of my herbs and medicines

to take with us." Commandeering a table under one of the torches, where the light was best, Alys set the women to sorting through the pots originally intended for the abbey. The bathing soap would be useful at Malpas, the cream for softening the skin would not...no matter how much Alys regretted leaving it behind.

"Do you think there will be many wounded?" Velma asked as she sat rolling strips of linen to protect the pots and also serve as bandaging material.

"Gowain will do his best to see there aren't," Alys said neutrally. "But we had best be prepared." Two other women had joined Velma and Dame Dotty in helping Alys. They had had a hand in destroying her things, and had offered red-faced apologies before starting in to work.

Young Bradley staggered in, carrying another of Alys's chests. "This is the last one that has herbs in it. Do you want me to bring the one with the books in it, too?"

"Nay, the chest may be useful to pack other items, but we'll be leaving the books behind." Except for the ten precious herbals, which were stowed in her saddle pouch.

Maye walked in just then, glanced about the room and frowned when she saw Alys and her circle of helpers. As she started toward them, Alys braced for a confrontation.

"What are you packing in these chests?" Maye demanded.

"Herbs and medicines," Alys said levelly.

"Why was I not told? There's little enough room in the wagons for the food and the people who must ride."

"I'm taking only what is essential. There is no telling what, if any, medicinal stores we will find at Malpas."

"That is so." The sternness left Maye's round face, making the signs of sorrow more obvious. "I—I have something I would show you, Mistress Alys, if you would walk with me."

Wary but curious, Alys gave a few instructions to her helpers, then followed Maye out into the corridor. The dimness, the sense of isolation, fed Alys's unease, but she kept pace to the branching of the next tunnel. "Where are we going?"

"Just here." Maye stopped beneath a torch, the circle of harsh light emphasizing her stark expression. "I wanted to apologize for leaving you in the woods."

"There is no need—"

"Aye, there is." Maye nibbled on her lip, then thrust it out. "I'll not deny that I wanted you gone from here." Her tone said she still did. "But I did not mean you to come to harm. I paid Farmer Donald's son, Donald, to take you away. 'Tis not my fault he got drunk before he was to meet you."

As an apology, it was not much, but Alys accepted it with a gracious smile. For Gowain's sake. "Thank you for telling me. You are Gowain's friend, and I'd not have ill will between us."

"Aye, I am his friend. And for that reason, I give you fair warning. If you hurt him, I'll find some way to make you pay."

"I'd never harm him."

Maye snorted. "You don't belong with us. You're too soft, too used to fine things. Even when we reach Malpas, times will be tough and lean. There'll be no place there for a fine lady in her rich velvet gowns." To emphasize her point, Maye grabbed hold of Alys's arm and gave her a little shake. "Do you understand?"

The bolt of anger made Alys gasp, but she couldn't, wouldn't, reveal her weakness to this woman. She tried to ignore the sensations that bombarded her like the stings of hostile bees. *Don't feel. Look inward. Think of something else.*

In answer, Gowain's image rose in her mind. She clung to it as if it were a lifeline. She thought about last night, about how she had felt held securely in his embrace. She remembered the healing balm of his compassion. She thought so hard she forgot about Maye.

"Bah, what's the use? You wouldn't understand because

you've never been poor or needy." Maye let go of her, freeing her.

Alys swayed for the briefest of moments, then focused her mind back onto what Maye was saying.

"What is it?" Maye's eyes narrowed suspiciously. "Are you ailing or something?"

"I am fine," Alys said, surprised to find it was true. Maye's anger had affected her very little. "Just startled you would think me so shallow. I am not a nun, but for several years I've gone to Newstead to study healing with the sisters. The life there is stark and austere, yet I found it suited me right well."

Maye grunted in obvious disbelief.

"But I am certain words will not convince you. When we get to Malpas, you will see your fears about me were groundless." Alys straightened the cuff Maye had crushed and smiled at her adversary. "If you will excuse me, I'd best be getting back."

"I have work to do, as well. I but wanted you to know I had not lied about the escort to Newstead."

Nor, Alys thought, had she lied and said she was glad Alys was going with them to Malpas. Still, she was Gowain's friend. "Thank you. I'm pleased to know you do not bear me any ill will."

"Nay. I do not." Maye managed a half smile before she walked off in the direction of the washing pool.

Alys waited till Maye had rounded a bend in the tunnel, then grinned. Sweet Mary, she'd done it! She'd actually resisted another's feelings. Joy bubbled up inside her. She wanted to laugh and dance and cry. She wanted to tell Gowain.

Whirling, Alys set off in search of him. Two steps down the corridor, she stopped. It was too soon to take him her news. Her years of experimenting with herbal cures had taught her an important lesson. A thing that worked once sometimes did not work again. Or did not work in the same way. She needed more study.

'Twas disappointing, but not crushingly so, for one used to waiting and trying and testing. A determined bounce in her step, Alys returned to the hall. The tunnel no longer seemed so dim, nor the future so bleak. If she could do it once, she could do it again...mayhap for longer. The possibilities were dazzling. She entered the hall to find the others waiting with anxious faces.

"You were gone a long time," Velma said.

"What did Maye want?" asked Dame Dotty, a weathered old crone with wispy gray hair and a sharp tongue.

"To discuss...the size of the packs," Alys said, hedging. Gowain had decided that each person could bring only those personal possessions that would fit in a small sack.

Dame Dotty's beetled brows slammed together. "She's a jealous one. Thought mayhap she was up to more mischief."

"All is well between us," Alys said. Another lie, but a necessary one. Dissension could only harm everyone.

"I was worried, too," Velma added. She'd become devoted to Alys, even allowing her belly to be examined. The babe would be born in a few weeks, but Velma still refused to acknowledge it. "You should let her have Gowain," the girl added. "I don't like the way he watches you all the time."

"Velma..." Dame Dotty scolded.

"'Tis all right," Alys said, then turned to her staunch supporter. "He's grateful to me, Velma, for healing people."

"He doesn't look grateful. His eyes go all hot-like when he watches you." Velma clutched at Alys's sleeve. "Take care he doesn't get you off alone the way...the way *he* did me."

Alys gingerly patted Velma's arm. 'Twas the first she'd reached out to anyone...except Gowain. She was as anxious to test her theory as to comfort Velma. "Not all men are like Ranulf."

Velma whimpered and turned her face into Alys's shoulder.

Alys felt the fear and shame welling up in the young woman. For an instant, they dizzied her. *Stop. Don't be pulled in.* Once again, Alys thought of Gowain, drew strength from him. Brick by brick, she built a shelter for her own feelings, then looked out to help Velma.

"I know this is painful for you," Alys said. Her voice was strained, but she was in no discomfort. "What he did was horrible, terrifying, but it is over and done." With every word, Alys gained confidence. She could do this. She could. "Ranulf can never harm you again. You must put the past behind you."

"How can I when it grows in me? I wish it would die." Velma shivered. "There, I've said it, and now you hate me."

"Nay. I understand," Alys said from the heart. Despite her shields, she felt the empty, aching cold inside Velma. She felt it, but it didn't freeze her. "You are not alone in this, Velma. And no one, least of all me, hates you. It was not your fault."

Velma sniffed. "I tried to fight him, but Ralph doesn't believe that."

"Ralph is an insensitive clod," Alys exclaimed. "He has no idea what it is like to be small and fragile."

"Do you think he meant to hurt me when he threw that book? Did he hope I'd die, and it with me?"

"Nay. He was aiming at me. You saved my life, Velma. Had you not rushed in, he'd have struck me between the eyes and felled me for certain."

"And you saved me." Velma touched the bruise.

"Because you are worth saving, you and your baby."

"It...it will be here soon."

Alys nodded, aware the moment was delicate. "A month, mayhap less. I'm no midwife, but I'll be there for you."

"I do not know if I can bear to look at it. What if it resembles him?"

"What if it is the exact image of you?"

Velma blinked. "I'd not considered that."

"The babe is half yours—more than half, really—for you've carried it, nourished it, all these months."

Velma's hand stole down to her belly and hesitantly touched it. As if in reply, the unborn child kicked. "Oh!" Her eyes rounded, with wonder, not revulsion. "It does that in the night." She rubbed the mound thoughtfully. "Do you think it's a girl?"

"There is a good chance, but if not, if it is male, you will raise him to respect women."

"I will." Velma's chin came up, her eyes less dazed.

Smiling, Alys stepped back. Inside, she felt a little shaky, but otherwise none the worse for what could have been an ordeal. A successful experiment with a good outcome... both for herself and for Velma.

"I'm hungry," Velma said.

"Let's see if Percy can spare a bit of cheese for a mother with a growing babe," Alys said. At the door to her room, she stopped. "I'll put these herbs away and join you in a moment." She smiled to herself as she watched Velma waddle down the dimly lit corridor.

The scrape of stone warned Alys she was not alone. As she turned, a hand fell on her shoulder. Heat enveloped her. Heat and a rush of strong, dark power. She gasped, and the sense of being swept away immediately gentled.

"Sorry," Gowain murmured in her ear.

"Gowain." Alys smiled and turned to wrap her arms around his lean waist. His surprise and pleasure rippled through her.

"Alys. Sweetheart..." He hugged her in return. The warmth of his body enveloped her. "Are you all right?"

"Aye." She muted his concern by concentrating on the wonder of their embrace. "It feels so good to be held, simply held."

"I told you we could do this," he whispered.

She considered telling him what she'd learned to do, but

'twas too early to boast of her newly acquired skill. And, too, his control made her task much easier.

"Ah, Alys." He nuzzled the top of her head through the headdress. "Someday I want to see your hair loose. I want to see it spread out across my pillow."

Alys trembled, the suggestive words firing her imagination. Or had the temperature of his body risen? "You are very warm."

"Are you certain it is not you?"

"Nay, I am not."

"Good." Sighing, he loosened his arms and turned her to face him. "But if we stand here much longer, I may give you more of a lesson than you are yet ready for."

"Lesson?"

"In trusting me." His hands rested lightly on her shoulders. Beneath their warmth beat a frantic pulse. Rather like the distant pounding of fists against a barred door. Desire, carefully controlled. One day soon, she hoped she'd be strong enough in her own right that his control wouldn't be necessary. "I much admire the way you soothed Velma. Do you think she will be all right?"

"I hope so. At least now she will speak of the babe. That is a step in the right direction...for both of them."

He nodded, then dropped his hands to his sides, leaving her oddly bereft. "I came to see how you were doing."

Alys smiled. "You must have a hundred more important things to do than that."

"I think I've whittled my list down to an even dozen, but nothing is more vital to me than your well-being."

"I know." Alys gently touched the corner of his mouth, giggling when he nipped at her finger.

"See, you are easier with me every moment."

"That I am." She gazed deep into his eyes, intrigued by the green flames dancing in them. A fire she no longer feared.

"I am glad." His hands were on her shoulders again,

drawing her up on her tiptoes. "Very glad." His lashes drifted shut, and his mouth closed over hers.

Alys stiffened, expecting to be attacked, ravished. Her fears melted under the warmth of his lips. Soft as butterfly wings, they brushed across hers, once, twice. Her mouth began to tingle, and the heat spread, spiraling through her. Then they were gone. Whimpering, Alys opened her eyes and saw dazed wonder in the face so close to her own. "Gowain," she whispered.

"Aye." His nostrils flared, his breathing raspy in the darkened corridor. "What did you feel?" he muttered.

"All hot and shivery inside."

"Me, too. But..." He looked around at their bleak surroundings. "This is neither the time nor the place to kiss you as I'd like. But when we get to Malpas..." His eyes blazed with sensual promise.

Alys shivered as a delicious answering warmth kindled low in her belly.

"We'd best get you to the kitchens and I back to my duties before I forget my good intentions."

"You would never do that," Alys said. But if he did, she was determined to be strong enough to survive. To win.

"At times like this, I'm not so certain." Taking her arm, he escorted her down the corridors. From his air of preoccupation, Alys sensed his mind was filled with plans for the march to Malpas and the scheme to take it.

When they reached the kitchens, he rapped on the door.

"Whoever it is, go away," cried a harried Percy.

"'Tis Gowain. I've Alys with me."

The bar grated in its holder, then the door opened. "Come in. Come in." Percy's face was red, and his hair stood on end. Behind him, the kitchen seethed and broiled like a hive under attack. "We could use another pair of hands, Alys. Gowain, I've done as you suggested and divided the hard cheese into small portions. Each person will be given cheese and an oatcake."

Alys frowned. "Will you cook meals en route?"

"Nay," Percy replied, but before he could add more, a pot boiled over and he ran to head off disaster.

"A fire would be too dangerous," Gowain said. "We will make up for it with a feast once we take Malpas."

What if the victory wasn't swift? Alys thought of the worried, frightened people in the hall. "They'll need food to keep up their strength and spirits." She walked over to the mountain of grain sacks, glanced at the wall of kegs waiting to be loaded on the wagons. "Can we not eat some of this?"

"Nay. I plan to put my men in Ranulf's livery and have them approach the gates to deliver this delayed shipment."

"Using it as a diversion."

He grinned. "Exactly. We will arrive at night, just as Darcy's band is scaling the back walls. According to reports, the captain of the guard carefully inspects any persons or wagons seeking to enter Malpas. So the goods must be intact. Still, I hope the ruse will save a few of our lads. You've likely never been in a keep when a much-needed shipment of food arrives. Men, even good ones, are drawn from their posts by the excitement, the prospect of a full meal after days of rationing."

"Oh, I understand that." Alys scowled up at him, hands on her hips. "You have likely been too busy to notice, but the people in our own hall are in similar straits."

Gowain liked that "our." It boded well for their future together. "They are sick of oatcakes, that's true, but—"

"They are afraid, the women and children especially."

"I am sorry for that, but there is nothing I can do—"

"Food might help."

"How?"

"My father says men and beasts are both stronger on a full belly," Alys replied.

"Is there a problem?" Percy asked, mopping his face with his apron. In the other hand, he held a tray of small rolls. They scented the air with the mouthwatering smell of yeast.

"You've been making bread," Alys exclaimed.

"Gowain let me have one sack to make a few small loaves to take with us."

"Magnanimous indeed. Could they not have the bread tonight, instead?" Alys pleaded.

"They'll need the food more when we're on the march."

"Agreed. Could Percy not make more before we leave?"

Gowain scowled. "Then the shipment would not match the tally sticks, and the guard might become suspicious."

A knock sounded at the kitchen door. Bette opened it, and Birdie catapulted into the room. Close on her heels came Enid, black curls bouncing.

"I smell bread. Oh!" Birdie launched herself at the tray. Percy lifted it out of her reach. "Careful, 'tis hot."

"It smells like real bread." The girl licked her lips.

Enid danced in a circle. "I want some." She looked at Alys and added the magic word. "P'ease."

"You will have to ask your papa," Alys replied.

Gowain glared at her, then knelt. "Enid, we have to go on a long walk tomorrow, and you'll be hungry—"

"Hungry now. P'ease." She batted her feathery lashes.

Gowain knew he was lost. "All right, poppet." He took a roll from the tray and broke it in half. Steam rose in a fragrant cloud. "Let it cool a moment."

The girls nodded, so excited they jogged from one foot to the other as they waited.

Alys looked down at their pale, animated faces, and her heart twisted. Such joy for such a little thing. At Ransford, they ate off white-bread trenchers and gave them to the poor or the pigs when the meal was done. How wasteful that now seemed.

"Now, Papa?" Enid asked after a moment.

"Aye."

Enid and Birdie squealed with delight, then bit into the bread like starving wolves. Enid ate half of hers, then stopped chewing and looked up at Alys. "Angel have some?"

The lump in Alys's throat grew. "I'll have some later."

"It's berry good."

Alys nodded. "I'm sure it is." She waited till the girls had finished eating and wandered over to stare at the fresh batch of rolls Percy was pulling from the bake oven. "Could you not fill the flour sacks with something else and put them on the bottom of the pile? Surely this captain will not open every sack...particularly in the middle of the night."

"Hmm. Truth to tell, I'd not thought of that."

"He may be as excited as his men, or anxious to return to his bed." Alys smiled. "They may even bring the wagons in and wait to examine the contents in the morning."

"Possible," Gowain said slowly. "But what could we fill them with? Damn!" The corners of his mouth hiked up, and he struck himself on the forehead. "Why did I not think of it sooner?"

"What?"

"The Trojan horse." Gowain started for the door, turned and planted a kiss on her open mouth. "Percy, bake as much bread as you like, only save me a half-dozen sacks' full. Oh, speaking of which, keep all the sacks intact." In a blink, he was gone.

Alys stared after him, wondering what that was all about. Then the door popped open again, and Bette peered in.

"I thought I smelled..." She walked over to the tray sitting on the worktable. "Bread." Her hand hovered over it, as though it might disappear if touched. "I thought wishful thinking had gotten the better of me. Is it for the journey?"

"So I thought, but Alys has persuaded Gowain that we should bake more and eat this for supper," Percy said.

"Ohhh..." Bette drew the word out.

"Did you hear?" Birdie jumped up and down.

Alys smiled in pure, unadulterated joy. Never again would she take bread for granted, she vowed.

Percy set two crews of women to kneading dough.

Velma began to hum a working song, and the others took it up. Soon the kitchen was redolent with yeast and camaraderie.

Alys took off her gloves, rolled up the sleeves of her robe and pitched in to help with the dough. It was inevitable that her hands should brush Bette's and Velma's in the sticky mass. The first time it happened, she started, but recovered. After a few more such episodes, she scarcely noticed the contact. 'Twas rather, she decided, like drinking strong wine. The first sip shocked and burned the senses, but the surprise lessened with repetition.

Alys's heart did a slow roll. Was the answer to her problem as simple as these two things...becoming more used to touching people and concentrating on her own reactions instead of theirs? The more she thought on it, the more convinced she became that she could be with Gowain after all. She worked the dough with renewed vigor, anxious for the moment when she could speak with him, tell him what she'd learned about herself.

"Whatever has happened to Velma?" Bette whispered when the girl went for more flour. "She seems almost like her old self."

Alys collected her scattered thoughts. "I think she has come to terms with having the babe."

"And not a day too soon, if I'm any judge."

"Aye. We should still take care she's not left alone. And if you see Ralph talking to her, find a way to interrupt."

"Ralph? Has he been mean to her?"

Alys told Bette what Velma had said, confident the tale would go no further. "He may not have meant to hurt her."

"You are being overly generous with him. He's a bad one, mark my words. I'll tell Bertram to watch him."

Alys nodded absently and went back to kneading, her mind too full of Gowain for her to worry about Ralph.

Two hours later, Percy began pulling more trays of bread from the deep bake oven. Bette piled them into wicker baskets. "I used to serve bread on a wooden tray engraved with sheaves of wheat,'' she said wistfully. "I had to leave it behind when we fled. Never regretted it till now. Such a treat deserves a fine display."

"Folk'll be too overcome to notice the tray," Velma said.

Percy locked the door behind them, then they all set off for the dining hall. He, Alys and Bette carried the large baskets. Velma balanced a crock of butter on her stomach. Enid walked beside Alys, carrying a small loaf, while Birdie raced ahead, shouting the news like a town crier.

"Bread. We've got bread!"

Heads popped out of blanket doorways, alarmed faces giving way to frank amazement as they beheld the procession.

"Come, pause to sup with us," Percy urged.

The rebels needed no second urging. They dropped what they were doing and joined the crowd, which had swollen to fill the tunnel by the time they reached the large chamber where Gowain and the men practiced with swords.

"What is going on?" Gowain demanded. His scowl deepened as he listened to Percy's explanation. "There is much to do to prepare for tomorrow's journey."

Behind her, Alys felt people shift, their good mood fading. Please, please, they need this bit of happiness. Before she could voice her plea, Gowain nodded.

"But we must eat," Gowain said, with a lightness she sensed he didn't feel. "Go on, all of you. Enjoy."

"Papa coming?" Enid asked, bread clenched in her hand.

He bent down and kissed the tip of her nose. "Papa is too stinky for polite company. I'll be along as soon as I've washed."

Alys smiled inwardly, a plan forming in her mind. "Go along with Ruby, Enid," she said gently. "I will wait for your papa."

"What is this about?" Gowain asked as the crowd left. He looked filthy and disheveled. His hair clung wetly to his head and neck; sweat dripped from his face to the links of his mail shirt. To Alys, he'd never looked more desirable. Or maybe it was the realization that there was hope for them.

"You will see," she said cryptically.

Chapter Fourteen

"I do not think this is such a good idea, Alys," Gowain grumbled as they crossed the stone bridge to the hot springs.

"I do not see why not." She fairly skipped along beside him. "You wish to wash before you eat. I have something important to discuss with you in private. We save time by combining the two."

Time wasn't his concern. Alys's virtue was. Gowain glanced down at her sunny smile, illuminated by the torch he carried, and hadn't the heart to turn her away. He could be alone with her without acting on the passion that smoldered inside him. Still, the cavern had never seemed so dark and intimate as it did today, he thought as they ducked under the archway.

"I'll light a few more torches," Gowain said briskly.

"Candles would be softer. I put some in here yesterday." Alys walked to the wall niche and pulled out two thick candles. "Beeswax. I was bringing them to the abbess. There's also toweling and soft soap. Much nicer than the lye stuff."

Gowain couldn't argue with that. Still, he shifted from foot to foot, nervous as a virgin bride all the while Alys bustled about setting out the things for his bath. She bade him put the torch in the iron ring in the wall, lit the candles from it, then set them at either side of the bathing area. The bowl of soft soap was placed close to the water's edge, the toweling safely out of the way. When she was finally done, she stood and smiled.

"Ready?" she asked brightly.

Every muscle below Gowain's belt tightened. "Aye," he said hoarsely. Hoping the water would subdue what he could not, he strode toward the low, sloping rocks where the water was shallow.

Alys sat down on a nearby ledge, her arms around her bent legs, chin resting on her knees. "What I wanted to tell you—"

"Are you going to watch me undress?"

"What? Oh." She colored. "I was not thinking." She scooted around so that her back was toward him. "Tell me when you are in."

Gowain knew he was well and truly doomed if every remark she made heightened his arousal. Shucking out of his clothes in record time, he eased into the water. He needed to wash and get out of here while he still had some control over himself. Standing in the waist-deep water, he dipped his fingers into the soap and lathered his chest.

"Can I turn around now?"

"Aye." Gowain set his teeth and scrubbed faster.

She moved to face him. Her eyes widened, and fire bloomed in them as they traveled over his naked chest in a caress that was nearly palpable. His nerves scrambled; his mouth went dry.

"What did you want to say?" he managed to ask.

"Oh, Gowain. You are so beautiful…like some pagan god."

Gowain groaned, the desire in her expressive face inflaming his senses. "You should not say such things."

"Why? They are true." She cocked her head. "You do not want me to find you attractive?"

"Of course I do, 'tis just that…that…"

Her smile crumpled. "You have changed your mind?"

she whispered. "You do not want to be involved with someone like me."

"Nay. 'Tis nothing like that." He forgot about himself, forgot about caution and restraint as he lifted a hand to her.

She scrambled off the ledge and knelt at the water's edge. Her fingertips grazed his, igniting a spark. She felt it, too, for she gasped.

"I'm sorry." He drew back, then realized her hand was bare. "Alys. Your gloves."

"I took them off while we were kneading the bread dough. That is what I wanted to tell you. I...I have been experimenting today. When someone touched me, instead of reaching out for their feelings, I drew back inside myself. I know you did not think I could do it, and I am not certain I could long ignore someone who was in pain, but it did work."

"That is wonderful," Gowain said cautiously.

"Aye. It is. While we were working in the kitchen, my hands brushed Bette's and Velma's. It shocked me at first, but I grew used to it. I think it possible that being so isolated from others contributed to my sensitivity. When someone touched me, I expected the worst, which magnified their emotions. Do you know what the best part is?" She fairly glowed with excitement.

"What?"

"We can be together."

"Alys." Gowain put a knee on a half-submerged rock and reached up to cup her shoulders. He waited for her to start or retreat. She did neither, just gazed into his eyes with a wonder that mirrored his own. "Alys, I..."

He didn't know whether she read his needs or acted on her own when she leaned down to kiss him. Their mouths met and clung. Her soft sigh of acceptance sent passion leaping. Emboldened, he tried an experiment of his own, slipping his tongue past her parted lips. If she couldn't accept this mating, the deeper joining would be impossible.

Alys gasped as his tongue flicked over hers, so intensely

intimate, so shockingly unexpected. And yet so exciting. A shiver ran through her, and the tingle went with it. Her body warmed from the inside out, a melting kind of warmth. An odd pressure coiled tight in her lower belly. All too soon, he moved back, severing the connection.

"Alys?" he whispered.

She managed to open one eye. His were dark and hooded, glittering with sensual mystery. She was determined he'd unlock every one. "More," she murmured.

His laugher was low and rich. "Your wish is my command."

This time, when his mouth met hers she was ready. Lips parted, tongues tangled in an alluring dance. Alys followed where he led, then tried her own wings and sent them both soaring. She was dazed and winded when he tore his mouth free.

"Alys." His raspy breath matched the ragged beat of her heart. "You...you should leave."

"Nay." Alys reached for him, her arms sliding around his slippery neck. Her hands splayed over his wet, naked back. It was like grabbing hold of lightning. The heat sizzled through her. Heat and hunger, raw, aching hunger. "I want you," she whispered. "Oh, Gowain, I want to touch you, to hold you close." She leaned forward, overbalanced and slid into the water, robe and all.

"Damn," he exclaimed, but he caught her around the waist and supported her. "You're soaked."

"I do not care." She pressed against him, frustrated by the yards and yards of wet wool that came between them.

"Alys, I do not think—"

She stopped him the best way she could. With her mouth. He jerked, then groaned and gave them both what they wanted, deepening the kiss and drawing her up against him. His big hands skimmed down her back, stroking her. It was not enough, not nearly enough. Her whole body seemed to swell and pulse with the need to be closer. She loosened her hold on his neck and began to tug at the ties lacing the front of her robe.

"What are you doing, sweetheart?"

"Taking this off."

"What? Nay, you cannot... We cannot. This...this is not a suitable place. Someone might come in...."

"Everyone is in the hall." She swore as the ties knotted. "Help me," she pleaded, looking up at him.

Gowain took one look at her passion-hazed eyes and knew he was lost. Still, gallantry dictated one more attempt. "I want you, too, my love. But we should wait...till we're at Malpas."

She shook her head, the fears that plagued him ghosting her gaze. What if something happened? "I do not want to wait. Please." With trembling hands, she framed his face. "I know you need me. I need you even more. Please," she said again.

Gowain sighed, the urge to give in warring with the instinct to protect her...even from himself. What if they made love and something happened to him? What if he left her carrying his child? He didn't worry that she'd abandon it as Blanche had Enid. But he could not bear the idea of Alys trying to carry on without him, alone and pregnant. Still, there were other ways....

"Stand still while I get these untangled." Gowain worked the laces free from collar to waist, exposing her thin chemise, but stopped Alys when she would have shrugged out of the wet robe. "Let me." The surroundings were less private, less comfortable, than he might have wished. He'd at least treat her with all the finesse he could muster. To that end, he tugged off her headdress and touched her braids. "I've dreamed of taking your hair down and spreading it over my pillow. That must wait for next time."

Alys shivered with delight as Gowain cupped her face and kissed her with devastating thoroughness. Dimly she was aware of his hands skimming over her shoulders, taking the robe with them. It settled into the water, a cloud of gray wool.

"What will you wear back?" he murmured against her mouth.

"The women hung the wash to dry in the back of the cave. I'll find something." She nipped at his lower lip, pleased by his low growl and the way his hands gripped her waist. She gasped when he lifted her out of the water and away from the sinking robe. The gasp became a soft moan as he slowly lowered her, letting her body slide down his till their eyes were level.

"Mmm." She looped her arms around his neck, glorying in the sensations. His muscles rippled, hard planes against the softness of her own body, with only the thin barrier of her chemise to keep skin from skin. "I want to feel you...all of you."

"It might be too much."

"I am fine," Alys said. Her blood ran like molten fire in her veins; her heart beat in double time against her ribs. The feelings were hers and his...tangled together. It didn't frighten her. It thrilled her. She tunneled her hands in his hair and kissed him with all the longing pent-up inside her.

Gowain responded to the frantic pressure of her mouth, the reins of his self-control fraying beneath her devastating combination of boldness and vulnerability. Untutored she might be, but her natural gift for giving, as well as taking, was more rousing than a courtesan's practiced wiles. He delighted in her soft gasp when his hand skimmed upward to cup one breast. "Perfect," he whispered, gently kneading the full, high mound. He longed to see as well as touch, but that would wait for next time when they'd hopefully have a bed and a locked door.

Alys cried out as his long, clever fingers plucked at the sensitive nipple. A sharp, desperate need throbbed through her, arrowing down to the secret recess of her body.

"You are so soft...so incredibly responsive." He waded

forward and set her on the sloping rock where she'd bathed on her solitary visits here.

Thinking he meant to end it, Alys clung to his neck. "Gowain, please don't leave me."

"I won't." He knelt beside her in the shallows, candle-light playing over the taut muscles in his neck and chest, his eyes nearly black with passion. "You make me so weak I can barely stand." He kissed her, cradling her head in one hand while the other roamed over her breasts, gently shaping and caressing them through the chemise till she thought she'd go mad with longing.

She shivered as his mouth left hers to stitch a line of stinging kisses down her neck. Before she could guess what he intended, his mouth closed over one aching peak. The heat, the sharp pleasure as he drew down on one throbbing nipple, made her arch upward. Hands tangling in his hair, she held him close. His name fell from her lips like a litany as sensation after sensation ripped through her. She could feel desire building, and nowhere did it throb more insistently than in the cleft at the juncture of her thighs.

She whimpered when he left her breast, sighed when his mouth moved on to pleasure the other aching peak. As his lips and tongue worked their magic on her, his hand slid over her hip and up under the hem of her chemise. His callused fingertips traced intricate patterns on her knee, her upper leg and, finally, the inner side of her thigh. Instinctively she opened for him, body tense, aching, waiting.

His first gentle touch, there where she wanted it most, made her gasp and shudder. Water lapped and eddied.

"Alys? Sweetheart, did I hurt you?"

Alys moaned in faint denial, not wanting to lose her focus on whatever was about to happen.

"Open your eyes, love," he coaxed. "I want to see you."

Alys lifted her lids, Gowain's face filling her vision. His features were stark and finely drawn, pupils dilated, nostrils flared. He looked as primitive and driven as some ancient conqueror. But she saw past that, to the tenderness in his eyes. Trust bloomed. "Gowain." She twined her arms around his neck. "I want you so," she blurted out.

"I am glad, for I want you," he whispered a heartbeat before his mouth closed over hers with a gentleness, a delicacy, that was all the more devastating because she sensed the dark hunger raging through him. He was protecting her...from himself was her last coherent thought before his fingers found the tiny nub that was the focus of the passion he'd roused in her.

Alys arched helplessly beneath his touch, her hips rising and falling to the rhythm he set. She sank deeper into the storm of swirling emotions. Hers, his...she didn't know or care where one left off and the other began. It was too much. It was not nearly enough. The coil inside her tightened, then shattered. She cried out with the wonder of it as passion shuddered through her. The sound muffled by Gowain's drugging kisses.

When the tide finally receded and she could think again, Alys realized Gowain had gotten them out of the water. She sat on his lap, towels draped over them.

"Oh, Gowain." She burrowed into his embrace.

"Are you all right, love?"

Was that a careless endearment, or did he love her? Did she love him? Nay, it was too soon, the idea too overwhelming. She shied from it as she had his touch. "I am all right. And you?"

"Fine." His voice was gruff.

Beneath her bottom, she felt a ridge that could have been stone, but wasn't. Innocent she might be, but she had been raised around breeding stock and she knew right well that what they had just done had left him unsatisfied and her still a maid. "Why?"

Gowain looked down at her, his skin ruddy in the pale light. "I did not want to get you with child."

Because of what had happened with Enid. Alys wanted

to protest. The fears she'd felt shimmering in him killed that urge. "But could I not, er, ease you as you did me?"

He managed a rusty chuckle. "Nay. The joy I got from your pleasure was enough. For now."

Alys took heart. "Will you sleep with me tonight?"

"Nay." He kissed her. "We'd not sleep a wink, and we both need to be rested for the journey." His smile faded. "Alys, I think I should leave you with Farmer Donald. He'll see you to Newstead or back to your family, which-ever—"

She placed her fingers over his mouth to silence him. "Nay. I'll not be parted from you. Not now. Not ever."

"I cannot bear the thought of placing you in danger."

"I will be fine. We will be fine. You will prevail." And once they were safely inside Malpas, she'd find a way to get word to her father about Ranulf. Gareth Sommerville was not one to let such injustice continue. He'd not only see to it that Ranulf paid a heavy fine for his actions, he'd make certain that Malpas was safe from reprisals.

"Come, we'd best see if we can find some clothes and get you back to your room," Gowain said gently, reluctantly.

Alys nodded glumly, counting the days till they could be together in every sense of the word.

They walked together across the stone bridge, clad in wrinkled garments, Gowain and his blond slut. 'Twas obvious from their flushed faces and swollen lips what they'd been doing in the bubbling pools.

Jealousy bit deep. They were so wrapped up in each other they gave no thought to who might have been listening to their loveplay, or might be watching now. 'Twas tempting to rush out from hiding and give Alys a shove over the edge. Into nothingness.

But Gowain would protect his highborn lover. Nay, the time was not yet right.

Soon, though, soon the Lady Alys must be eliminated.

* * *

The trip through the forests to Malpas took three days. Still, it was not as arduous as Gowain had feared it might be. He'd divided his forces into small groups for the journey, each consisting of a wagon and a few outriders disguised as farmers. If Ranulf did have patrols in the area, they'd see nothing more sinister than a succession of peasant families on their way to market. He and his fighters traveled a parallel course inside the tree line, hidden from sight but within striking distance in case of trouble.

Each night they camped in the woods, eating the cold foods Percy had prepared, sleeping lightly, if at all. The trek was hardest on the children, for whom the novelty of riding in the wagons soon gave way to restlessness. Alys did her best to keep the group with which she rode—including Enid and Birdie—entertained with stories.

In fact, if not for Alys, things might not have gone as smoothly as they had. Though she claimed little training in domestic matters, 'twas to Alys that people looked when they needed guidance in setting up camp or deciding on who would do what. Much to Maye's annoyance. When they reached Malpas, Gowain would have to somehow ease the tension between his friend and his love.

Trouble-free though the journey had been, Gowain drew a sigh of relief when the black peaks that guarded Malpas came into view. They made camp that last night on a rocky plateau two miles from the mountain pass that lead to Malpas. Here he planned to leave the women, the children and the horses not needed in the next step of his plan. Tempers were short, the mood was subdued. No one slept much. Just after midnight, Gowain and his fighting men left for the keep.

It lacked three hours till dawn when Gowain halted his troop of men and wagons at the base of the road leading up to Malpas. A chill wind moaned through the rocky canyons, bringing with it a hint of snow. The sound was fitting, somehow, for this was a wild land, raw and untamed, the jagged peaks of the mountains pressing in on all sides to block out the rest of the world.

Ahead lay the only way through them, a narrow, twisting mountain pass abutted by sheer cliffs. Malpas, the conquering Normans had called it, for travelers were vulnerable to robbers and rock slides. The name had been given to the tower they built to guard the mouth of the pass.

Gowain tilted his head back and stared up at the keep. Huge and black against the roiling storm clouds, it crouched on the lip of the cliff. It was virtually unassailable, the only approach a steep, winding trail.

"Jesu, 'tis enough to give a man nightmares," Lang Gib remarked, drawing his cloak closer.

"Aye. Once we've taken her, there are none who will get us out again," Gowain said. Glancing over his shoulder, he ran a practiced eye over his band. Twenty hard-faced men, veterans of the campaigns in France, dressed in Ranulf's livery of green and gold, part of the stolen supplies. If some of the garments were ill-fitting, the guards at Malpas would not notice. Hired soldiers wore what they were given. The wagons and drivers were another matter and would bear the closest scrutiny.

Wheeling his horse, Gowain rode down the line for a final look. He nodded when he came abreast of the first wagon. Bertram handled the reins, his beefy body and plain face giving him the look of a farmer. Beneath his woolen cloak of de Crecy green, Gowain caught the gleam of mail and a long sword.

"Best keep that blade out of sight till you need it, Bertram. No carter would carry such a weapon."

Bertram nodded grimly and tucked the sword behind the seat.

Gowain continued on, testing the ropes that tied down the sacks of grain, prodding a keg or two with the tip of his sword. Satisfied, he rode back to the head of the column.

"Is all in order?" asked Lang Gib.

"Aye, no one would suspect we are anything but what we seem, the long-overdue relief supplies."

Gib's teeth flashed in the dark. "They say this time of night's when spirits prowl and men sleep deepest."

"Let's hope this lot is slow to gather their wits." Gowain raised a mailed fist and ordered the column forward. They climbed slowly up the cliff, riding at last under the shadow of the great keep, and stopping upon the narrow lip opposite the gate.

"Halt and state yer business," called a youthful voice. A single torch bobbed overhead in the topmost arrow slit of the gatehouse, glinting on a round helmet.

Good, he'd hoped the watch would be sparse. Gowain smiled grimly beneath his visor. "Is this Malpas Keep?"

"Aye. And who wants to know?"

"Sir Arthur of Hemp with the supply train," Gowain shouted.

"The hell ye say. We heard 'twas set upon by Black Gowain and his foul band."

"So it was, but our valiant lord recovered it and sent us hither to deliver it."

"Really?" The guard leaned out. "Damn, but the men'll be glad to see you."

"Lower the drawbridge and let us in, then."

"Can't...not without Captain Will Gulliver's orders."

"Fetch him, then, for I've no wish to spend the rest of the night out here freezing my arse off."

"He's given orders not to be wakened."

Damn. "It's been a long, thirsty ride to this misbegotten corner of the realm," Gowain growled. "If we have to wait on your captain, we'll broach a keg of ale and ease our parched throats."

The guard licked his lips. "Well..."

"What are you waiting for?" Gowain snarled and let go a string of curses that had the youth ducking back inside.

Long, anxious moments passed. Gowain pictured Darcy and the thirty men with him scaling the backside of the cliff. If they were detected before Gowain and his men were inside, they'd be slaughtered like sheep in a stock pen.

At last a wave of torches bobbed along the top of the gatehouse, and a furious red face glared down at them.

"Lift your helmet and let me see who it is demands entrance at this ungodly hour," the captain snarled. He didn't sound incompetent or dazed with sleep. Pity.

"You'll not know me." Gowain lifted his visor. "Lord Ranulf hired my men and me fresh off the boat from France."

"France, you say? Why?"

"He's finding it a bit hard to find men who will fight for him...given Black Gowain has killed so many."

The captain grunted and rubbed a hand over his dark chin. He wore a wrinkled tunic, and his hair whipped around in the bitter wind. "I'll let you in, but you'll be watched close till I've made certain all is in order." Over his shoulder, he bawled orders to let them in.

Scarcely had the wooden drawbridge thudded to earth before Gowain sent his men clattering over it. He remembered Malpas well, for his mother had loved the brooding hills, the simplicity of life here and had often brought him here with her. His mind shifted briefly from war. Was his mother here, roused from whatever chamber Ranulf kept her in?

God, he hoped she was alive and well.

They passed under the iron teeth of the portcullis, then veered right, up a narrow passageway overlooked by a walkway. Two men, arrows notched in their bowstrings, watched them till they rode through the second gate and into the inner ward.

His nerves brittle as glass, Gowain glanced around the bailey and counted a dozen soldiers. Some wore the wrinkled clothes they'd slept in, others struggled into mail shirts. All carried swords or had them close at hand. Pity. As he watched, things improved. A handful of men raced along the wall walk, coming from the back of the keep.

They gestured excitedly at the wagons lined up in the court-yard. With any luck, they had left posts at the back wall, clearing the way for Darcy's party.

"Well, let's see what you've brought." Captain Gulliver strode across the bailey, rubbing his hands together, either out of greed or to ward off the cold.

Gowain swung down, tugged off his helmet, but left on the chain-mail coif to cover his hair. Black hair was not that uncommon, but coupling it with the green eyes he could not hide might rouse the captain's suspicions. He looped Traveler's reins over the saddle's pommel, a signal to the war-trained horse not to stray, and joined the captain.

"Tally sticks," Will Gulliver barked, holding out a hand. His eyes glittered with unmistakable greed as they raked the mounds of supplies. He looked the sort to put his men on short rations, sell half their food and pocket the profit.

Gowain handed over the sticks, then leaned against one of the wagons, head down, as the captain evaluated them.

"Loosen the ropes," Gulliver said at length. "Let's see what His Lordship has sent."

Gowain untied the ropes that bound the grain sacks. The top ones were filled with flour, the rest would not bear careful scrutiny. "Will you count them now?"

"In the middle of the night with the snow beginning to fall?" The remark was natural, given the gooseflesh on the captain's fleshy neck and arms, but there was something in his expression that made Gowain smell a trap.

"Lord Ranulf led me to believe you were very careful about such things," Gowain said.

"Did he?" The captain smiled faintly.

Gowain decided to play a card of his own. "He also said I was to stand by while you made the count and report back to him any…discrepancy."

Gulliver flushed. "If there was anything missing from past shipments, 'twas the carters' fault."

"Mmm." More certain of his footing now, Gowain moved to undo the ropes on the second wagon. It was vitally important that the loads not be tied down. "This should only take a couple of hours, then we can both seek our beds."

"Hours?" the captain glared at the sky, which had begun to shower down bits of ice.

"Mmm." Gowain strode to the third cart, freed the ropes, then lifted a small keg from under the driver's seat. "I nearly forgot. Lord Ranulf sent along this keg of French wine for—"

"Hush!" The captain snatched the keg and looked around at his milling men. "No need to rouse the whole keep," he murmured to Gowain.

"Just so." Gowain nodded his head toward the lead wagon. "Shall we begin, then?"

Will Gulliver shifted the keg, then licked his lips. His beady little eyes narrowed. "You must be weary after your long journey. This tally could wait till you've rested."

Gowain grinned. Thank you, Alys, for thinking of the wine. "A bit of sleep would sharpen my eyes and wits, I suppose."

"Just so," the captain said heartily.

"John, step lively now and show Sir Arthur and his men where they may sleep for what remains of the night."

Gowain cleared his throat. "I appreciate your hospitality, Captain, but I fear my men must remain here."

"Here? Where?"

"With the wagons, of course." Gowain lowered his voice. "The carters look a shifty lot. Wouldn't do for them to make off with some of my lord's goods and get us both in trouble."

Gulliver's smile dimmed. "As you say." He turned away, keg tucked under his arm. "You lot, back to your posts!" he shouted at the men on the walkways.

Gowain's spirits plunged. Then he caught sight of a familiar figure slipping between the keep and the barracks building. Darcy was inside, and the alarm had not been raised.

"Will you take a cup of wine with me before you seek your pallet?" the captain asked Gowain.

Will Gulliver did not seem the sort to share his prize. Did he think to sweeten his take by eliminating him, Gowain wondered? "I will be in as soon as I've settled my men."

"They look right able to tuck themselves in, but suit yourself." The captain and his torchbearer left the courtyard.

"That went smooth as silk," Lang Gib muttered.

"We've not won yet." Still, Gowain felt a bit easier as he went to set in motion the next part of his plan. Like mummers in some courtly play, he and his men put on an elaborate show of bedding down for the night.

They pulled the wagons alongside the stables, where the overhang from the slate roof cast deep shadows. Six of the men stuck torches into the rocky soil in a ring around the wagons, then stood at attention beside them. The flickering light illuminated the guards, but made it even harder to see what was going on in the wagons behind them.

There, an ancient drama was being reenacted. In the same manner as the Trojans had once climbed from the belly of their gift horse, Gowain's men slit their way out of the grain sacks at the bottom of the pile and climbed down from the wagons.

"Damn, I thought I'd suffocate before we got here," Ralph grumbled, arching his back as he slipped from the wagon. "Did you have to stand there jawing with—?"

"Shut up." Gowain pulled him to the ground and held him there as one of Malpas's own guards walked past. The soldiers were more curious than suspicious; still, all it would take was one glimpse of something odd and they'd sound the alarm.

Ralph wrenched his arm free and rubbed it. "You've no call to haul me about like that."

"Then stay down and keep quiet." Gowain stood. "Everything seems in order, Gib. Will you take the first watch?''

"Aye." Lang Gib climbed up onto the seat of the lead wagon and stretched his long legs out in front of him.

"Halt, who goes there?" called the guard who had just walked past them. He stood by the end wagon, his sword out and leveled at Tom the Reeve's flour-covered middle.

Gowain caught his breath. Across the way, he saw Will Gulliver pause, then turn, the keg still in his arms.

No help for it. The time for secrecy was past.

A cry echoed down the mountains to the cluster of rocks where the women waited.

It had begun.

Alys closed her eyes on a brief prayer and heard it murmured by a dozen waiting comrades. "God keep them safe."

There was nothing to do then but huddle together, listening in mute horror and frustration to the muted clash of steel, the distant shrieks and cries.

Alys shuddered, arms wrapped about her trembling body. She wasn't afraid for herself. Gowain had left them with horses, supplies and Farmer Donald to guide them to Newstead should the attack fail. She was terrified something would happen to Gowain.

What a time to realize you loved someone, Alys thought, when he was far away, his life in peril. Or mayhap that was why the blinders had dropped from her eyes, because there was every chance she'd never see Gowain again.

"Angel!" Enid scrambled through the rocks and flung herself into Alys's arms.

For an instant, Alys was engulfed by the child's fear. She fought it with more ease this time. "You are supposed to be sleeping, sweetheart."

"Bad men are coming. Hear them?"

"They cannot hurt us. Your papa is punishing them."

"He is?" Enid settled back, her head resting on Alys's shoulder. "Story, p'ease." she demanded.

Alys sighed, in no mood to make up tales. "I'll sing you a song instead." She began to hum a simple hymn of faith and hope. By the time she reached the chorus, Bette and Bab had softly picked up the tune. When she finished, not only had Enid fallen asleep, but Alys felt, oddly, more at peace.

Her tranquillity was shattered moments later by a shout from Maye, who had insisted on standing watch on the rocks above them.

"Riders coming hard," she called in a hoarse whisper.

"Is it Gowain?" Alys asked.

"Nay."

Alys shivered. Had Gowain failed? Was this the garrison come to get them? "Can you make out who it is?"

"Nay. They carry no torches." She leapt down from the rocks. "Get to the horses, we'll make a run for it."

True, the horses had been left saddled in case they were needed, but Alys looked around at the stricken faces of the old men and helpless women, many with sleeping babes in their arms. "We'd not make a mile."

"We have to try," Maye snapped. "If Gowain has been captured, it's our duty to remain free and rescue him."

Alys debated for a moment, then shook her head. "Gowain must have sent whoever comes, else they'd not know where to find us."

"What say you?" Maye cried, turning to the others. "Will you come away with me, or stay to be captured?"

Bette looked around at the frightened faces, then stepped forward, Birdie clinging to her skirts, thumb in her mouth again. "We could not get away in time," she said gently.

"Hello the camp," called a male voice. Jean rode out of the night, his smile nearly blinding. "We've won."

"Is Gowain all right?" Alys asked quickly.

"Aye, that he is."

Maye pushed past Alys. "Then why did Gowain not come for me as he promised he would?"

Jean shifted uncomfortably and looked at Alys. "He is rounding up the last of the garrison soldiers. He bade me come fetch you...and the others," he added, glancing at Maye.

Maye stiffened. She glared at Alys, then turned on her heel. "Come, everyone. Gowain wants us at the keep."

Alys stood back and let Maye organize the march. Though one battle had been won, she sensed another brewing. She must prevent it from tainting Gowain's victory. Even if it meant swallowing her own pride.

Chapter Fifteen

The bailey was filled with smoke and the stench of blood, but the clash of steel and the screams of the dying had been replaced by the moans of the wounded. A few rebels numbered among them, but the garrison had borne the brunt of the injuries, largely due to the element of surprise.

Gowain walked slowly among them, his bloodied sword lowered but ready should someone spring up to attack. "Is this everyone?" he asked.

"Aye. Lang Gib's dealing with the ones who were holed up in the barracks." Darcy nodded toward the charred ruin of that building's west wall. Gowain had ordered it fired to force the soldiers into the open and hasten the end of the battle.

Gowain expelled sharply, his breath frosting in the cold air. "The keep?"

"The door's still shut. No one's been in or out since the fighting started. Do you think there's more of them inside?"

Gowain tallied the dead, and added to it the captured. "Likely. The supplies we brought would see twice this many men through the winter. Gulliver might be greedy enough to ask for that much, but Ranulf would know how many needed to be fed."

"Well, then. I suppose we'd best be at it." Darcy lowered his visor and hefted his sword. "Though if they're so chickenhearted as to stay within, they may not put up much fight."

Gowain nearly wished they would. The battle for Malpas had lasted less than half an hour, but he'd fought so fiercely, so desperately, that the battle lust still fired his blood. Nay, it was Ranulf he wanted to fight, he realized. But his conscience would not let him. The frustration seethed inside him like boiling water trapped in a covered kettle, coupled with the fear for his mother. "Let us go up, then, single file and slowly. If there's a trap set inside, we'll not rush in to spring it."

Darcy clapped a hand on his shoulders, eyes eloquent in the sockets of his helmet. "We will find your lady mother within."

"I pray so. If she's been harmed..." He turned to look at Will Gulliver, who was bloodied and battered, but still defiant. The captain had denied any knowledge of Lady Elen's whereabouts.

"Come. Let us get this over with. Jean will return soon with the women and children."

Gathering ten men behind them, Gowain and Darcy crossed to the covered wooden steps that led up to the entryway. He was still vaguely surprised that whoever was inside hadn't poured grease on the stairs and set them afire, effectively preventing the attackers from getting in. Surprised but grateful.

They crept up the stairs, as soundlessly as possible, peering out from behind their shields, swords ready. At the top, Gowain counted three and threw his shoulder against the door. It flew open. Momentum propelled him into the dark room.

"Wait, goddammit!" Darcy cried, hard on his heels.

Gowain launched himself to the right. Back against the wall, sword extended, he searched the dim room. The place stank worse than a castle garderobe at the end of winter, but he could see little save a few dark shapes that might be tables and benches. A single torch burned near the doorway that led to the upper floor, draping shadows into corners that might hold an enemy. The fire in the hearth on the opposite wall sputtered fitfully. Nothing moved in the gloom, but he sensed someone was there.

"Show yourself," Gowain demanded. "Lay down your arms and come forward, or we'll drag you from hiding and—"

He broke off as an old crone rose from behind a stack of trestles and hobbled toward him. "Mercy, sir," she whimpered.

Jesu, Mary and Joseph, don't let this be my mother, he prayed. It wasn't. Though nearly gray, the woman's long, frazzled braid had once been red, not black. The eyes she raised to him were a muddy brown, blank with fear.

Gowain lowered his sword. "Easy, we mean no harm."

"Damn, have your wits gone begging?" Darcy exclaimed. He put himself between Gowain and the woman, angrily motioning the rest of the men into the room. "Light brands and search the place. Go in pairs. Sing out loud and plain at the first sign of trouble."

"Sorry." Gowain exhaled, raised his visor and pinched the bridge of his nose. "I—"

"God have mercy!" The old crone crossed herself and backed away. "It's...it's Lord Gowain, risen from the dead."

Gowain managed a grim smile. "I'm not dead yet, old mother. Who are you?"

"Ciel."

The name meant nothing to him. "Did you know my mother, Lady Elen? Is she above stairs somewhere?"

"Gone," Ciel mumbled. "All gone away."

"Gone where? Did Ranulf send her somewhere?"

"Ranulf, here?" Ciel ducked her head and shivered, looking about like a rabbit caught in a trap.

"Nay. He's not here. You're safe enough. Do you know where Lady Elen went?" Gowain blinked against the sudden flare as his men thrust torches into the coals and ignited them.

The light dispersed the shadows, and showed no soldiers lurking there to ambush them. But the sight that met his eyes was not reassuring. Smoke blackened walls that had once gleamed with whitewash. The tables where he had his family had eaten many a meal were scarred and crusted with food. The rushes underfoot had been reduced to slime, and if he wasn't mistaken, something moved in it. Something he didn't want to examine too closely.

"It looks as though someone used the hall to keep pigs," Darcy muttered. "And it smells worse."

"Aye." Gowain turned back to Ciel. "About my mother." A chill ran down his spine when he scrutinized her unfocused eyes and filthy clothes. She looked mad, daft.

"Away. All gone away." Ciel turned and limped over to a pallet in the corner where she'd apparently been sleeping. She curled up on it and closed her eyes.

"You'll not get any sense from that one." Darcy said.

Gowain scrubbed a hand over his own eyes. The ache behind them was growing worse. "I'm going upstairs to look around."

"Wait till we're sure the place is safe."

"Do you think me too feeble to protect myself?"

"Nay, just preoccupied." Darcy grabbed a flickering torch from one of the wall rings. "Let's see what's what."

· They met Ralph Denys on the second-floor landing. "There's naught up here but four sleeping chambers, all empty. The captain was using the largest one by the looks. Didn't have much worth taking, though."

Gowain noted the bulge under Ralph's tunic and held out his hand. "Share and share alike."

"I told you there weren't nothing to take."

"Hand it over."

"So you can take the lion's share?"

"So Darcy can give it to Bertram to be recorded along with the rest of the spoils."

"I don't trust Darcy, neither."

"See here, you little worm." Darcy pushed past Gowain and grabbed Ralph by the tunic front. "I've put up with your bad temper because that's the way Gowain wants it, but I'll not have my own character vilified by the likes of you."

"Wait." Ralph's throat worked convulsively.

"Bertram is down in the bailey," Gowain said. "Take Ralph down to him, Darcy. See whatever he's got hidden is properly recorded on the tally sticks."

Darcy glared at Ralph, then at Gowain. "What'll you be doing while I'm about that?"

"Seeing what's left of my home." Gowain smiled grimly. "Ralph says the rooms are empty, so I should be safe enough."

"He might have been mistaken," Darcy grumbled, but he hauled the protesting Ralph away.

He might have been mistaken. Gowain clung to that faint hope as he pushed open the door to the master suite. "Mother?" he called softly.

No one answered, of course. And if Elen had been here, all traces of her gentle presence had been obliterated by the filth in which Will Gulliver had obviously preferred to live. From the gray, stained linen on the lumpy bed to the dirty clothes and filth accumulated in the corners, the room was a shambles.

Gowain strode to the window, trying to ignore the crunching of nameless items under his boot heels. He threw open the shutters and let in the cold air, but the stink of sour ale, unwashed clothes and despair still filled his nostrils.

She wasn't here.

Though he'd spoken little of it, he'd been certain his mother would be here. Why else would Ranulf be so determined to shut off Malpas and keep him from gaining the fortress? Spite? Aye, his half brother was capable of that, but 'twas unlike Ranulf to exert himself so forcibly for simple malice.

So why had he done it?

Sighing, Gowain tugged off his gauntlets and helmet, then dragged a hand through his wet hair. He was bone-weary, but the sun was only just breaking over the distant peaks, and he had a full day's work to do ere he rested. Still, he took a moment to stare out over the walls at the lands he'd dreamed about while in prison. They were wild, raw and inhospitable, yet the vastness, the dynamic power of rock soaring into sky, drew him. Nor was the estate as barren as it appeared.

In spring, there were fish to be had from the icy mountain rivers that wandered along the base of the cliffs. Summer coaxed grass from the high plateaus where the villages took their flocks of sheep and goats to graze. He remembered his mother tending herbs and vegetables in the gardens be-hind the keep. If they could last till the good weather came, there was a chance they could feed themselves. Till then, it would be a struggle.

But work and struggle he would. For this was his home. His land. He'd always been more at ease here at Malpas than at the larger, more luxurious Eastham. Memories of happier times filled him. He could remember sneaking into his parents' room when he was small and frightened of night things. They'd cuddle him between them and whisper soothing words. Their love for him, for each other, had been evident in everything they did. The pain of wondering if that love had been a lie throbbed like a fresh wound each time he thought of Ranulf's accusations.

Gowain pounded his fist on the stone sill. Nay. He could not, would not, believe it. Nor would he rest till he'd learned where his mother was. She must be alive, he thought, temper calming. Close as they'd been, he would know if she had died.

As soon as the keep was secured, he'd round up the servants and the men-at-arms and question each one. Start-

ing with that greedy pig Will Gulliver. Much as he detested
torture, he'd not shy away from using even that to get the
information he sought.

Gowain straightened as the wagons bearing the women
rumbled into the bailey. Forgetting all else, he immediately
looked for Alys. How he'd hated being separated from her
for even these few hours. His heart rolled over in his chest
when he spotted her, sitting in the rear of the lead wagon,
Enid on her lap. Joy filled him as he watched Alys lean
close to say something that made his wee Enid smile.

Dear God, how precious they both were. His dark
thoughts vanished. With Alys beside him, there was nothing he could not accomplish. Suddenly he ached with the
need to be with her, to welcome her to her home...their
home...to share his victory and his concern for his mother.
To kiss her and hold her.

Gowain grabbed up his helmet and raced for the stairs.

The first thing Alys noticed was the stench. It was
stronger even than the smell of smoke, bringing tears to
her eyes.

"Stinks," Enid said, nose wrinkling.

"That it does, love." Alys looked around the crowded
bailey. Gowain's men milled about, faces streaked with
soot, some sporting bloody rents in their makeshift armor.
Of Gowain, there was no sign. That worried her more than
any bad smells.

"Mayhap they had just cleaned out the jakes," Bette
said, holding the sleeve of her gown to her nose.

"That is usually done in spring," Alys said absently. She
had little training in domestic activities, but she was ob-
servant and knew the rituals of castle life. "Do you see
Gowain?"

"Nay, but there is my Bertram over by the wagons."
Bette gasped softly. "Is that blood on his tunic? He promised he'd not be in the fighting." She scrambled from the
wagon.

Alys stood and raked the bailey from keep to stables to the charred wall of what she supposed was the barracks. Splotches of blood spattered the hard-packed earth, mute proof that the victory had not come without price. A shiver slid down her spine. Pray God Gowain was uninjured. As she looked back at the three-story stone keep, he emerged from the covered stairwell. He was alive. Her heart cramped, then expanded on a joyous beat as she watched him stride through the chaos toward her.

He moved with a lithe, catlike grace that bespoke power and strength. His head was bare, black hair shiny as a raven's wing in the morning light. Against his tanned face, his eyes glittered like polished emeralds. They were full on her, alight with pride and something even more moving. Love.

The smoke and noise and stink seemed to fade away to nothing. Held in thrall by emotions too wonderful for words, Alys waited for him to reach her. When he did, when he stopped beside the wagon and caught hold of her waist, she sobbed his name and all but tumbled into his arms.

"Alys," he whispered, swinging her around in a circle as though she weighed nothing. "Alys, I was worried about you."

"Me." She choked back another sob. "I was safe in the hills. You were the one fighting.... Oh!" she exclaimed, catching sight of the blood on his left side. "You are hurt."

He blinked in surprise, set her on her feet and looked down at his gore-spattered mail. "Most of it is someone else's."

"Most?" Alys ran her gloved hands over his shoulders and down his chest. "Where are you cut?"

"Nowhere." He flexed his left arm and winced. "Just bruised, I think. Though a few of these devils put up quite a fight."

"Come inside," Alys ordered. "Take off your things and let me see for myself."

He grinned. "I'll gladly undress for you, sweet, but later. First I must see the prisoners are secure, set our own guards to patrol the walls, find wood to replace the barracks wall and question Gulliver again about my mother's whereabouts."

"Your mother? Is she not here?"

"Nay." The light in his eyes was snuffed out. "There is no sign of her above stairs, and the only servant I've yet seen is not sound of mind, I fear. All Ciel would say is that Mama has gone away. Damn. Where? Where can Ranulf have sent her?" His hands tightened on Alys's shoulders; his pain and fury buffeted her.

Alys wanted to cry out and twist away. But that would not help Gowain. Shivering, she bolstered her own defenses and blocked out the storm of his emotions. "Let me help" was her first thought. "I will question this Ciel myself. Mayhap she was frightened of so large and angry a warrior as you."

"That may be." His hold on her gentled, and she breathed a sigh of relief. "Damn," he whispered. "I forgot."

"I am fine," Alys said at once. Though how much longer her shield would have withstood his fury, she didn't know. "I am getting quite good at this." She smiled and stood on tiptoe to gently kiss his taut mouth. It softened instantly for her, all traces of his earlier trauma gone.

"Ah, Alys," he murmured when she let him up for air. "What would I do without you?"

"I am hoping you never want to find out," she teased.

"Nay, I am not such a fool as to give up the best thing that has ever happened to me." He sighed and looked around. "I fear the keep will want tidying."

"I will see to it," Alys said with a great deal more confidence than she felt. "What of the wounded?"

"There are some on both sides. A few of Ranulf's men are dead, but none of ours, I think. There has not been time for me to take a count." He looked over to the wagons, where Bertram stood with his arm around Bette. "Bertie may know."

Alys nodded. "Go about your business, and I will see to the wounded and the keep." What doubts she had about her abilities with the latter, she kept to herself. Gowain had enough to worry about without taking on her shortcomings as a chatelaine. Besides, if she was going to be his wife, she'd have to learn. Strangely, the idea was not as unpalatable as it had once been.

"My thanks, Alys. There is much to do and not much time before the foul weather is upon us." He kissed her lightly on the brow and strode away.

Alys turned back to the wagon, where Enid watched her with fear-filled eyes. "Come, sweetheart, let us go inside where it is warmer." She lifted the child down from the wagon, then turned to find Maye watching her narrowly.

"So, now you will be lady of the manor," Maye said flatly.

"Unless I am much mistaken about conditions inside, I will be lady of the wash buckets," Alys replied. She scanned the circle of anxious women and clinging children. "We've a bit of work ahead, but if we pull together, we can do it."

"Can't be worse than the caves were," Dame Dotty said.

"Let us hope not." Alys led the way across the bailey, with Bradley next—carrying both Enid and Birdie. The other women followed, likewise holding the smaller children above the mud and gore of the battle.

Braced though she was to expect the worst, when she stepped inside the hall, Alys gagged and halted in the doorway. The vast, cavernous room gaped back at her, stinking like a black maw full of rotted teeth. Behind her, the other women cried out in horror.

"Did they use this for a stable?" Bette exclaimed.

Maye added, "I've never seen, or smelled, the like."

"Nor I," Alys said weakly. But she'd been taught to face a challenge head-on. Swallowing hard, she ventured inside, her eyes wide with disbelief at the filth revealed by the harsh circles of torchlight. Heaven only knew what worse horrors were hidden in the shadows beyond. "Poor Gowain. How awful to find his home in such dreadful shape." Her resolve to improve things sharpened. "Well," she said, whirling back to face her likewise-outraged friends. "First let us find a relatively clean place for the children to stay and the wounded to be tended."

"I doubt such a thing exists," Maye grumbled. "But I will look about." She and two others went upstairs while Dame Dotty and Velma cleared off a table on which the children could sit.

Alys took one of the torches and ventured into the pantry that adjoined the hall, startling a family of rats who were dining on the scraps from some former meal. Her scream scattered the rats and brought in Bradley and Dickie of Newton. The boys accompanied her on a search of the rooms beyond, an empty storeroom and another chamber where the cook must have slept. Both were cleaner than the hall.

"We'll put the wounded in the storeroom, the children in the cook's bedchamber," Alys decided. She set Bradley and Dickie to sweeping them out and went back to the hall. As she stepped gingerly over the threshold, trying to ignore the squish and crunch underfoot, a wraith flew out of a darkened corner.

"Lady Elen?" A wrinkled face peered up at her, framed by a tangle of graying red hair.

"Nay," Alys said cautiously. "Are you Ciel?"

The woman blinked, then nodded. "Once I was."

Oh, dear, now she saw what Gowain had meant about the woman's feeble mind. "Do you serve here?"

"Once I did. Too old now. Even worms such as these don't want me about."

"Are there other servants here?"

"They weren't so lucky. No indeed."

"Did they die?"

"Gone. All gone away." Ciel looked around. "'Cept Malkin."

"Where is he?"

"Hiding." She rolled her eyes toward the timbered ceiling two stories above, showing enough of the whites to make Alys shiver. "Always hides when there's trouble. You best hide, too, else they'll take you away."

"Who? Who might take me away? And where?"

Ciel grinned, showing naked pink gums. "The devil. He's a pretty one, is Satan. Fair of hair, handsome as sin." She cackled and wandered off to crouch on a pallet by the fire.

Alys started to follow, but Maye and her party clattered down the stairs just then, bringing the news that the chambers in the upper two stories were near as filthy as the hall.

"What are your orders, my lady?" Maye asked.

Alys grinned ruefully and shook her head. "'Tis true I grew up in a fine home, but my family allowed me to pursue my healing arts instead of learning a chatelaine's duties. I know some of what should be done, but not the best way of doing it. Could you not take charge?" she asked Maye.

Maye's shoulders straightened. "Aye, I'd be pleased to."

"Fine. I'll see to the wounded, then come help you. I fear I'll not be good at much, but I do have some experience with a gardening rake and hoe."

Maye looked down at the slop on the floors and grimaced. "I think such skills will come in handy mucking out this place, but I'd not set you to something so beneath you."

"I fear we will all do things we'd just as soon not before Malpas is fit to inhabit. Still, 'tis in a good cause. Better a few days of hard work than a few minutes living in such filth."

"Amen to that," chorused the other women.

The sentiment set the tone of cooperation for what was surely the longest day of Alys's life.

* * *

The highborn bitch was important to Gowain.

More important, even, than this keep and his vow to make a home for the rebels.

That had been plain in the way he'd gazed into her eyes as he gently lifted her from the cart. Jesu, but he'd kissed her in front of the whole company.

'Twas sickening.

'Twas not to be borne.

Soon. Soon they had to pay.

Chapter Sixteen

It was nearly dark by the time Darcy herded Gowain up the stairs to the keep.

"I can eat while I work on the barracks wall," Gowain grumbled.

"Damn, we're both so tired we can scarcely put one foot in front of the other."

"There's still much that needs doing ere I can rest."

"Alys said she needed to see you."

"Oh. Why did you not say so in the first place?" Gowain quickened his pace. "Did she say what was wrong?"

"She did not."

Imagining all sorts of new catastrophes to add to the ones he'd already solved today, Gowain hurried through the dark, narrow entryway. At the door to the hall, he stopped and nearly turned back, certain he'd somehow wandered into the wrong place.

"Damn me," Darcy muttered. "'Tis a miracle."

That it was. Gowain rubbed his eyes and looked again at the bare, clean floor and the neat rows of cloth-covered tables. The walls were still soot-blackened, but a cheery fire leapt in the hearth. Cautiously he sniffed the air. It smelled of yeasty bread and roasted meat. "What happened?"

The door at the far end of the room opened, and a stream

of women filed in, led by Bette. Each bore a basket or platter and a weary smile. When Bette caught sight of Gowain, her smile widened. Over her shoulder, she called, "Alys, he's here."

His love bustled in, spied him and danced across the room. She wore a clean robe and a dazzling smile.

"What kept you?" she scolded, though her eyes were warm.

"I was busy...as you've obviously been."

"That we have. Come." She grabbed hold of his hand and led him to the table nearest the fire. "I hope this is all right," she whispered. "I did not think you'd want to set yourself above the others with a high table on a dais."

"Nay." Still dazed, he sat where she bade him and looked around. "I cannot believe this is the same hall I entered only a few hours ago. How was this miracle accomplished?"

"With a lot of sweat and hard work."

"Thank you." Gowain tugged her down beside him on the bench and kissed her.

Alys beamed at him. "I cannot take credit. 'Twas Maye who organized the work parties...and did the hardest tasks herself. Ah, here she is now."

Gowain stood as Maye walked up. Darcy held her hand in the crook of his arm, but her eyes were all for Gowain.

He sighed inwardly. If only he could make her understand that he was not for her. "Maye. Alys tells me I've you to thank for the transformation of Malpas's hall."

"Everyone helped. Even Alys," she added grudgingly.

"I did very little," Alys replied. "Wait till you see the wonders Maye's army wrought in the master chamber."

"I'm looking forward to it." Gowain waggled his brows at Alys, charmed by her blush. Beneath the table, he squeezed her hand. It squeezed back. The gesture of support, as natural as though they'd been together for years, moved him deeply.

He loved her, Gowain thought, as he'd never loved before. Aye, this was what love was about. 'Twas not only a few moments of sweet, hot passion, it was the caring. The sure knowledge that there was one person in the world who would understand it all, your pride, your hopes, your dreams and your fears. One person who would shoulder the burden with you.

For him, that was Alys. And thank God he'd found her. And he intended to keep her. Always.

"I had not dreamed the hall would be ready to host a victory celebration this eve," Gowain said, raising his voice so that all could hear. "But 'tis fitting, for we've achieved much today."

A cheer swept through the hall.

As he waited for the noise to die down, Gowain gazed out over the sea of smiling faces, people who'd become dear to him in the months they fought together. "Ranulf's soldiers are under guard in the storage building." The keep had no dungeon below it, for the original builders had not cared to dig through stone to hollow one out. "Repairs continue to make the barracks and stables fit for our use. There will be more days of hard work before we're done, but Malpas is ours."

Another cheer went up.

Gowain grinned. "There is something else I ask you to celebrate with me tonight." He gently raised Alys to her feet beside him. "Alys and I plan to wed."

The crowd in the hall went wild. Women laughed and clapped their hands. Men whistled and stomped their feet.

Maye made a choked sound and swayed.

Darcy caught her to him. "You have our best wishes," he said at once.

"Gowain?" Alys tugged on his hand.

He looked down at her, wounded by the panic he saw in her face. "You do not wish it?"

"You might have asked me first."

"I—I thought 'twas understood. I'd never have touched you if I didn't mean to wed you."

"But we didn't... That is, you didn't..." Her cheeks reddened.

Gowain chuckled, thinking how pretty she looked, all flushed and flustered. "Nor will I till we're wed. But I've not much patience when it comes to getting something I want." He bent to whisper in her ear, "And I want you very, very much."

"I want you, too." The spurt of temper fled her eyes, leaving them hazy with desires he shared.

"Good, we are agreed." He looked up and caught the sheen of Maye's tears, and his pleasure dimmed. "Maye, you have been my friend longer than anyone. I hope you wish me well."

She nodded, battling tears with pride. It showed in the way she straightened her spine and met his gaze. "I do. Now, if you'll excuse me, I'd best see where my Johnny is." She broke away from Darcy's grasp and fled.

Darcy started after her, but Alys called him back.

"There are some things a person does best alone. Give her a bit of time to grieve."

"If you think so," he said doubtfully.

Gowain once again turned his attention to the rest of his people. "As I said, we would like to wed, but 'tis likely to be some time before a priest can be coaxed into this remote corner. In times gone by, folk used to wed with a kiss and a promise to be true. We would like to follow that ancient custom, if you will bear witness for us."

The answer was an "Aye!" that made the rafters shake.

Alys stared thoughtfully at their joined hands, wishing she was as happy as his people seemed to be.

"Alys?" Gowain gazed at her, one brow quirked up.

"It does not seem...proper."

"To a great lord or lady, nay, but the common folk quite often wed in this way. Better that than to pay the legerwite fine for coupling without benefit of marriage."

She sighed and gave voice to her vague disquiet. If there could not be honesty between them, they'd be miserable.

"I do want you for a husband, only…only I wish my family was here."

"So do I," he said solemnly.

How thoughtless of her. Here she was whining because her beloved family was not here, while he had no idea if his mother was even alive. "There was no word where your mother might be?"

Gowain shook his head. "Gulliver says he does not know where she is, but I think he's lying and will question him later."

"I am sorry." She paused, considering what Ciel had said. "Malkin may know something. Did you find a man by that name?"

"A soldier?"

"A servant, I think. Ciel spoke of him."

Gowain rolled his eyes. "A figment of her addled mind."

"I think not. But as she also seems to have disappeared, I cannot pursue the matter."

"Tomorrow I mean to find out what Gulliver knows. I'll also take a troop down to the village on the bluffs. But tonight—" he grinned, and his gaze darkened "—tonight I mean to sleep in my own bed with my wife beside me. If you'll have me."

"I will," Alys said, loud and clear.

Gowain glanced up at the waiting crowd. "You heard her. By her own words, she seals her fate." He lifted her off her feet and kissed her hungrily, with the lusty roars of the crowd beating against his ears.

"You'd best let the lass up for air, or she'll fall in a swoon," Darcy commented.

Gowain wrenched his mouth away from the heaven of hers, having nearly forgotten they had an audience.

Everyone roared with laughter, which set the tone for the balance of the evening. They dined on bread and a savory stew of salted beef, washed down with Ranulf's ale.

When the bowls were wiped clean and the ale pitchers

emptied, Gowain stood and called silence. "I thank you all for your hard work and for your loyal support. I'll have need of both in the coming days if we are to prosper here. And I do mean for all of us to prosper." Unsheathing his sword, he raised it hilt first above his head, so the torchlight played on the gold cross formed by haft and blade. "I swear to you, by all that I hold most dear, that I will defend and protect you with the last breath of life in my body."

"Gowain! Gowain!" the people chanted.

"For Malpas and Lord Gowain!" someone shouted, and the rest took up the cry till it shook the old stone tower.

Tears burned in Gowain's eyes. It was the first time these people—this rebel horde he'd fashioned into a fighting force—had referred to him by his title. Though he'd never have asked it of them, it gladdened him to hear they considered him their lord. The feel of Alys's arm sliding around his waist completed the feeling of satisfaction. Clasping her close against his side, he whispered, "What say we take our leave?"

"Just like that? What of the bedding ceremony?" she asked, nibbling on her lower lip. "Will they not expect to come up and see me stripped of my clothes to prove I am without flaws?"

"Nay, they will just have to take my word on it." So, that was what had the little minx so nervous she twitched. Had they been wed as befitted his station, she doubtless would have been displayed for all to gawk at. Still grinning, he hustled his prize out of the hall and up the stairs.

Alys didn't relax even when they were inside the master chamber with the door barred behind them. The room was smaller than her own at Ransford, dominated by a four-posted bed, devoid of hangings till more could be made to replace the tatters that had hung there. The bed had looked large when she'd made it up earlier with fresh linens. Now it looked...intimidating.

Spinning away from it, she retreated to the far window and peered out through the cracks in the shutters. There was nothing to see, of course, except the wind-whipped torches set at intervals along the wall walk.

"What is it, sweetheart?" Gowain's voice came from close behind her. Too close.

She jumped when his hands landed on her shoulders.

"Never say you're afraid of me?" His emotions were so carefully controlled she could not sense his mood, though she strained to read it.

Honesty still seemed the wisest course. Especially since the secrets she kept from him weighed heavily on her conscience. "I am nervous, is all. It all happened so...so quickly."

"You regret agreeing to wed?" Now he was hurt.

That she couldn't bear. Turning, she rested her hands on his shoulders and looked up into his startlingly beautiful eyes. "I love you, Gowain. And I want to be with you."

"But?" he teased.

She didn't smile. "I hated seeing Maye hurt."

"As did I, but 'tis better she know how things stand. Besides, she has Darcy."

"Mmm," Alys said doubtfully.

"Trust me, love, this will work out best for all of us."

"I hope so." Because her head was spinning with fears and hopes, with excitement and trepidation, she laid it on his chest. The steady beat of his heart calmed her. The gentle stroking of his hands on her back soothed her.

"Better?" he asked after a long silence.

"Aye." She looked up, startled by his compassion. "You always seem to know what I need."

"That is part of love," he said simply.

She nodded, conscious of the change in his breathing, the subtle narrowing of his eyes. Something else flickered there, something hot and elemental. Like spark to kindling, it ignited an answering fire in her blood. Her body tingled with anticipation. She was suddenly, vividly, aware of the heavy silence in the room, broken only by the rasp of their breathing and the hiss of the fire in the hearth.

Outside, the wind moaned around the tower, rattling the shutters on their hinges. So, too, was her own life about to be shaken from its safe moorings.

"If you are afraid, Alys, if you have doubts…"

She had doubts aplenty, mostly about what would happen when their lovemaking took the next logical step. A physical joining. Would she be able to do it, or would her gift ruin everything?

"It does not have to be tonight," Gowain said gently. "We could wait." His big body trembled, and she knew how much the offer cost him. He'd do it for her, though; he'd deny the needs blazing in his eyes to make things easier for her.

"My nerves have made me foolish." She ducked her head. "You have seen me with little on and touched me, yet I wonder…"

"Your fears are not foolish to me." He took her chin and lifted it so that their eyes met again. "I do not claim to know what will happen when we…when I…" A flush ruddied his tanned skin. "When we become one. If you have even a moment of doubt or discomfort, you have only to say so, and I will stop."

She knew he would do it, no matter the cost to himself. Quickly stripping off her gloves, she let them fall to the floor, and with them went much of her self-doubt. They could do this…together. She framed his face, glorying in the heat that radiated from him. The heat and the love. "Let us to bed, then, husband." The word tasted sweet on her lips, as sweet as the kiss that followed her declaration.

His mouth moved hungrily on hers, while his hands tugged off her headdress and demolished the braids she'd spent half an hour fashioning before dinner. A feeling of elation filled her as her hair was set free. Her body seemed to swell with it. The heavy robe, the cloth barrier behind which she'd hidden for years, now seemed prickly and confining. Soon, he'd free her of that, too.

"I've dreamed of this," he murmured. His fingers tunneled into her hair, lightly abrading her scalp.

Alys shivered delicately as the tingling spread from the top of her head clear down to her toes. His mouth claimed hers again, hotter, hungrier than before. With a moan that was part surrender, part triumph, she opened for him, drawing an answering moan from him as her tongue dueled boldly with his. Aye, this was what she'd wanted, yearned for, yet scarcely believed she'd find. By the time he raised his head, she was clinging to him, senses dazed by the passion he'd roused in her.

"Oh, my love," he whispered, eyes so dark they were nearly black. "You fray my control with a few kisses."

My love, he'd called her. Could he break free of past betrayals and love her? She wanted that so much. "I'm not afraid." She touched his face, felt the rasp of his whiskers, the echoes of his love. Beneath the tenderness he showed her, a raw, primitive hunger prowled. Like some great beast, it strained to break free of his control. The faint tremors of his violent need, stirred something inside her. "Show me...teach me."

He kissed the center of her palm. "Remember, if you want me to stop, you have only to ask."

"I don't want you to stop. I want you to take off my gown."

"Alys!"

"Am I too bold?"

"Nay, but what if—?"

"I trust you," she said simply. "Please. I need you to touch me...the way you did at the pool."

His hands shook so badly she didn't think he'd ever get her laces undone. Oddly, his show of nerves settled her own qualms. By the time he'd unbuckled her wide leather belt, her pulse raced with pure excitement.

Murmuring her name, he slid his hands inside the open neckline, then over her shoulders and down her arms. The gown fell with a soft whisper to pool at her feet, leaving her standing there in a thigh-length chemise. She had only a moment to regret that she'd left behind in the caves the beautiful silk chemises her mother's maid had packed for the trip to Newstead.

"You are even more beautiful than my memories." His hands skimmed up her ribs to cup her breasts, stroking them through the thin wool. He absorbed her moan in a devastating kiss that turned her knees to water.

Helplessly she linked her arms around his neck and gave herself up to wave after wave of the most incredible feelings. His and hers mingled together. She became a creature of sensation, shivering deliciously as his long, clever fingers teased her sensitive nipples. Her blood shimmered and heated as the storm built inside her. Inside him. She recognized the unfocused yearnings as her own; the relentless fierceness as his. It should have frightened her; instead, it fed her hunger, fueled it as dry wood does a firestorm. Restless, she tried to wriggle closer to the storm's center. "I need you," she whispered.

"And I you, sweetheart." Gowain swept her into his arms, crossed to the bed in two strides and tumbled with her onto the rough blanket. "But we have all night," he murmured, dying for her, yet determined to go slowly, to savor their first time.

"I can't wait that long," said his imperious love.

Gowain chuckled, the humor easing his rampant need. For a long moment, he gazed down at her, struck by her beauty. The pale perfection of her delicate features, the banner of bright gold hair spilling across the coarse gray linen. The high, full breasts straining to be free of confinement, the slender legs he longed to have wrapped around his hips.

Mine, he thought. My love, my wife. His breathing quickened; his groin tightened in anticipation. Slowly, he reminded himself. Slowly, gently, and above all cautiously. He'd always tried to be a considerate lover, bringing his partner pleasure before seeking his own. But loving Alys would test his control as never before. "Would you like wine?" he asked, his mouth suddenly dry.

"I'd rather have you." She reached for him, and his good intentions were burned to a cinder by her kisses.

Groaning, Gowain surrendered to the fire. His hands raced over her, molding and caressing her warm, pliant body. Delicate muscles quivered and flexed beneath satiny skin. Soft moans of pleasure filled his senses, drove him higher. They rolled together across the wide bed, limbs tangling, hands tearing impatiently at her chemise, his tunic and hose.

When skin met bare skin, she jolted.

Gowain stilled, breath ragged, heart racing. It took only an instant for his mind to clear. Alys's gift. "Alys?"

Her face was level with his, flushed with arousal; her eyes were smoky with it, rounded with wonder. "Gowain. You are so beautiful." She stroked the black hair that swirled over his chest, fingers probing the thick ridge of muscles beneath. "So hard and strong."

"But can you not feel how much I want you?" he asked, his voice harsh with the arousal he could barely control.

She nodded, meeting his gaze evenly. "'Tis a powerful thing, like a hungry beast or a savage storm. It does not frighten." She wriggled closer, her peaked nipples stabbing his chest, grazing him with fire. They both moaned. "It makes me want you as much."

"Alys." Gowain slid his hands down her back and cupped her bottom, molding her against him. Hard to soft.

"Oh!" Alys shivered with delight as the fullness of his arousal met the empty cradle between her hips. Instinctively she rocked into it, dragging a hoarse groan from Gowain.

"Not yet, sweetheart." He stitched a line of stinging kisses down her neck and across her collarbone to the swell of her breast. "There's more...so much more I'd show you." His tongue laved one nipple, and then his mouth closed over it, drawing down with devastating thoroughness.

Alys cried his name, clutching his head as he feasted on her. She cried out again, this time in dismay when he lifted his mouth away, but it was only long enough to transfer his affections to the other aching peak. Molten heat washed through her as he suckled, raced down to coil in the juncture of her thighs. He knew it, too, for his fingers traced intricate patterns on her sensitized skin, coming closer and closer to where she wanted them most. She shifted her legs, silently urging him on.

Gowain shuddered, struggling to maintain some control over his rampaging desire. The feel of Alys coming apart in his arms nearly broke him. He wanted to part those slender legs and bury himself in her welcoming heat. But he held back, wanting her pleasure more than he did his own. His reward was her throaty groan as his fingers slipped by the silky hair of her mound to the treasure buried beneath. Deftly he touched the secret heart of her, smiling as candlelight played over her shocked expression. The surprise gave way to wonder and finally ecstasy as he led her over that first sensual peak.

Alys arched against his hand, moaning as release shuddered through her. It was even better than the time by the pool, but it still wasn't enough. She knew what she wanted, what she needed. Gowain. Opening her eyes, she saw him poised above her. His face was stark, nearly violent, the corded muscles of his neck and chest testimony to the effort he made to hold back. For her. The ache inside her intensified. "Gowain," she whispered, arms raised in mute plea. "I need you to fill the emptiness."

With a grown that was part aggression, part surrender, he parted her thighs and gave her what she wanted.

Alys cried out as pain lanced through her. Pleasure vanished, and there was only the rawness, the feeling of being stretched, violated. "Please," she whimpered.

"Oh, my love. I'm so sorry." He held himself perfectly still, muscles quivering with the effort to hold back.

She felt all that and more. She felt his love. Around her. Inside her. It was…magical.

"I'll stop."

"Wait." Her body clenched instinctively to keep him. He gasped, and a new feeling intruded. A storm of them. Passion and pleasure. Needs too long denied. A primitive urge to mate. His needs. And hers. Experimentally she moved her hips again. They both gasped this time, and the feelings strengthened. She wanted this. Wanted it so much. "Love me, Gowain," she murmured, twining her arms around his neck.

"I do…but…"

"No buts. Make me well and truly yours."

"You are," he said softly, and set about proving it. He kissed her brows, her nose, the sensitive hollow behind her ear. He whispered words of love and passion as he moved gently into her, the rhythm slow and easy, coaxing and seducing.

Alys sighed and clung to him. The sense of being invaded vanished on a wave of pure bliss. "This is like a dream come true," she murmured.

"Aye, it is," Gowain said. He'd traveled through hell to find a woman to whom he belonged as thoroughly as he did Alys. She was his soul mate, his other half. Feeling the first tiny flutters begin deep inside her, he lifted her hips and plunged faster, carrying them higher and higher. "I love you, Alys. Though I never thought to say the words, I do love you."

"And I, you." Alys cried his name as her body convulsed, waves of rapture shivering through her. Groaning, Gowain tightened his grip on her and rode out the storm. When it broke, he poured himself into her, heart and soul.

This time it was right and perfect. That was Gowain's last coherent thought before he drifted into oblivion.

Chapter Seventeen

"Time to get up," Gowain murmured into the tangle of blond hair on his shoulder. Judging by the angle of the sun against the shutters, it was already midmorning.

"Humph," it replied.

"I had no idea I'd wed such a grump." Grinning, he danced his fingers across her ribs.

"Stop that." She wriggled and batted at his hand. "How did you know I was ticklish?"

"Last night I learned all your secrets."

She turned her head, blowing a lock of hair from a most serious face. "Gowain, there is something—"

"No frowns in our marriage bed." He feared there'd be challenges and bad times aplenty to face before winter was over. Let them have this one happy day, at least. He kissed her, then, with all the tenderness inside him, glorying when she responded as eagerly as she had last night. "We should get up."

"Some of us already are," she teased, her silky thigh rubbing against the heavy length of his arousal.

His body jerked as though brushed with fire. His mind, however, still struggled. "You are new to this, Alys, and I'd not want to hurt you. 'Twas selfish of me to take you thrice last—"

"If I recall correctly, 'twas I who awakened you at dawn and forced myself upon you."

"Forced?" Gowain choked on a spurt of laughter.

"You should do that more often," she said softly.

"Be forced into carnal acts by a lovely woman?"

"Only if the woman is me, but I meant laugh."

His smile became a scowl. "I had little to laugh at till you came into my life. And thank God you did," he added as he drew her into his embrace.

"Amen to that." She snuggled against him, mind racing. Was it too soon to ask to send a note to her parents? Last night his mention of secrets had jolted her, made her realize that she'd withheld things from him that should be made known. But he was so prickly on the subject of noblemen. Mayhap she'd feed the truth to him a bit at a time, as if it were bitter medicine.

"Did you say Bertram had brought my pack in here?"

"Last night, while we supped. Over there." He angled his chin toward where two chests sat side by side.

"What is this?" Wrapping the sheet about her, she hopped out of bed and threw open the lid of one chest. It held her reference books, the other one her clothes and the velvet bag with her herbal journals. She turned and found Gowain propped up on one elbow, watching her. "You weren't supposed to bring all this."

"Those things are important to you."

His consideration made her feel even worse. Slipping the top journal out of the bag, she returned to the bed and handed it to him. "I wanted to show you my book."

"Very costly, this." He traced the gilt lettering with one finger. "Alys Sommerville is your full name, then." At her nod, he opened the book. "Who did the drawings of the plants?"

"I did. My mother is a goldsmith, and I inherited her talent for sketching, if not for working with metal."

"'Twas from her family, also, that you got your gift."

"Aye. Before she died, my great-aunt Cici tried to help me control it, but nothing worked till you helped me."

"You deserve the credit. I didn't think it would work."

She drank in his ruggedly handsome features and lean body, yet it was the intelligence in his eyes that drew her most of all. "You first gave me the idea to try it, and 'tis you I think about...focus my thoughts on...when I must touch another."

"I am glad you did, else this might not be possible." His kiss was slow, leisurely and thorough. "What do you feel?" he asked moments later. "Do you sense my thoughts?"

"Nay. But I do feel your passion. It feeds mine till sometimes I think I'll go mad if I don't have you at once."

He grinned. "How convenient. That's exactly how I feel."

"I know." Alys walked her fingers down his chest. They dipped into his navel and made him suck in the protest he'd been about to utter. "It gives me much joy."

He shuddered and his eyes shut, but he didn't attempt to stop her marauding fingers from reaching their objective. When they did, he groaned and bucked beneath her touch.

Alys smiled. He'd taught her that, the power of giving, as well as taking. Aye, he was a generous man, kind and patient. She relished being able to do for him as he had for her. Last night his hands had brought her to completion more times than she could count. Today, she would return the favor.

"Enough." Gowain flipped her onto her back, body caged on the mattress by his superior weight. His black hair flowing wild around his face and shoulders, eyes glittering with a dangerous light, he looked every inch the rebel leader. "So, the pupil thinks to best the teacher."

Desire twisted sharp and low in her belly. She wanted surrender...his. Then she realized that what she felt was him wanting her to bow. Never. She smiled up at him and took up the cudgel. "My study of healing has taught me that one can never know everything there is to know. I assume 'tis the same with this.'' She lightly grazed his ribs and flanks with her nails, then sank them delicately into his firm rump.

Gowain groaned and went taut as a bow, his eyes squeezed shut, his hands fisted in the pillow. When he opened his eyes, they were luminous with desire, edged with determination. ''Ah, I see the lady likes to make up her own rules. That is fine, for this is a game we will both win...eventually.'' Shifting slightly, he parted her smooth legs with his rougher ones and attacked where she was completely defenseless.

Alys cried out softly, arching off the bed as he filled her, slowly, inexorably. Her breath caught on a low sob, and was absorbed into his mouth as he kissed her. His tongue thrust against hers in lush counterpoint to the cadence of his hips. Needs shimmered and shifted. Now it was she who clutched, hands clenched in his hair as he moved down to feast on her breasts. He sucked greedily, the contractions echoed deep inside her, where the familiar heated coil grew unbearably tighter.

She reached out and felt the pressure build in him, too, swelling, aching, till it seemed he'd burst. Yet he waited, held back, plunging into her with measured strokes, each one carrying them higher, making them burn. She knew then why he waited, what he sought.

''Now!'' she cried, surrendering to the storm. It broke around her, in her. And, finally, in him. She felt it all happen, every wild, glorious bit of it. Shock drove her eyes open. All she saw was him, watching her, eyes filled with the same dazed wonder she was experiencing. ''Now we are one,'' she whispered as she tumbled down from the heights, held safe and secure in his arms.

''I love you, Alys,'' he murmured.

She tried to answer, but sleep claimed her.

When Alys woke next, she was alone in the big bed, huddled under a tangle of sheets and blankets. Without

Gowain's heat, the room was nearly freezing. At home, the servants came in early to rebuild the fire.

Nay, this was home, now, and if the fire needed tending, she'd do it herself.

Alys leapt out of bed and added a few sticks to the fire before breaking the ice on the bowl of water and washing her face. The rest would have to wait till the room was warmer, she thought as she struggled into her robe.

Likely Gowain thought he'd done her a favor by letting her sleep in, but there was much that wanted doing. Anxious as she was to embark on her first day as his wife, precious minutes were lost combing the tangles from her hair and fashioning a braid. As she stepped out into the corridor, a furtive movement at the other end caught her eye. The hall was gloomy, but she saw a figure slip into the room where what coin they had was stored.

Gowain had the only key. But this person was too short to be he. She decided to investigate. Through the partially open door, she heard rustling sounds. As she pushed the door open...

A bony hand grabbed her wrist and yanked her inside. Before she could scream, the other hand clamped over her mouth.

"Gotcha. I've been watching ye, waiting for a chance to repay Gowain," Ralph said silkily. His breath stank of onions and sour ale; his eyes gleamed maliciously. They were nothing to the sick, twisted triumph that emanated from him. "Know what happens to people that cross me?" He didn't have to tell her, she felt his rage, his grim determination to hurt her.

"Let me go," Alys mumbled into his grubby palm.

"Not just yet." Banding her close with one arm and keeping her mouth covered, he dragged her to the door. A quick peek outside, and he grinned. "No one about." He shouldered the door open and hauled her into the corridor, making, not for the stairs that went down to the great hall, but the ones that went up to the tower walkway.

What did he mean to do? Something bad, that much she knew. He hated her, wanted her dead; she read that, too. Panicked now, Alys fought back, ramming an elbow into his ribs, lashing out with both feet so that he was forced to take her whole weight.

He grunted in pain and staggered momentarily, then rallied. "Stop that." He kicked her back, numbing her left leg. "Try it again, and I'll bash you senseless against a wall."

He'd do it.

Alys slumped in his grip, dazed as much by the suddenness of the attack as by his vicious feelings. His mind was a vast cesspool of dark, evil thoughts. They swirled through her, trying to suck her down. As he half carried, half dragged, her up the stairs, she concentrated on closing herself off from him. It was hard. So much harder than anything else she'd done.

Her mind turned to Gowain. She concentrated on her memories of their night together. She thought about how good, kind and decent he was. She remembered his tenderness, and with her thoughts, built herself a barricade against Ralph's malevolence.

They reached the tower door. "Scream, and it'll be the last sound you make." Ralph transferred his bruising grip to her throat, opened the door and hauled her onto the walkway.

Cold air struck her, stealing her breath. The wind whistled around the crenellated tower, driving bits of snow. They stung like bee stings. "Why?" she gasped past the pressure of his hand.

"To make him pay," Ralph growled. "He took what was mine. I'm taking what's his. All of it. Much as I can get." He looked over the edge, grunted and herded her along till he found a spot that suited him.

"Do you intend to ransom me?" She was shaking so badly she could hardly form the words. Keep him talking, was her only thought. Surely someone would come looking for her.

"Don't be daft. He's not got the coin. Revenge, that's all I want." Ralph spat, the glob of spittle turning to ice as it sailed over the wall and into the nothingness beyond.

Alys had the sick feeling she'd soon be following it.

"Enough talk. Can't stand here all day. Got things to do before I leave." With no more warning than that, Ralph grabbed hold of her arms, lifted her to the top of the wall and shoved her over.

Alys screamed again and again as she slid down the slick slate roof. But no sound came out. Whoosh, and she was over the edge, falling into nothingness.

Her bottom struck the sill of the window just below. She gasped and slid off. Desperate, she grabbed for it, and her fingers caught and held. The action nearly pulled her arm from its socket. Pain lanced. She clenched her teeth, twisted and grabbed hold with her other hand, too.

Swallowing hard, she looked down…down…down. She was on the back of the keep, the part of the building that stuck out over the ravine. There'd be no rescue from below. And likely none from above. Her fingers slipped a bit.

"I tell you, I do not know where Lady Elen is," Gulliver insisted. His faced was battered and bloodied. A result of the battle, not any "persuasion" Gowain had applied—yet.

"Was she here?" Gowain fingered a wickedly sharp knife, letting the torchlight play over the blade.

Gulliver swallowed. Sweat beaded on his forehead, despite the chill of the darkened storage building. He and his men were tied hand and foot to the hut's support pillars. "Aye. So I'm told. Soon after Lord Warren died. I was not castellan here, though. By the time I came, the lady was gone."

"Did Ranulf take her someplace else?"

"I do not know." His sharp, crafty gaze challenged Gowain.

Temper snapping, Gowain turned the blade with lightning quickness and pressed it against the captain's throat. "I want to know what Ranulf has done with her."

"If you kill me, I can tell you nothing."

"Ah, but during my two years in de Grise's dungeons, I learned there were ways to prolong the dying, to make a man beg for death. Shall I show you?"

Gulliver made an inarticulate sound, afraid even to swallow for fear of nicking himself.

"Gowain?" Darcy laid a hand on his shoulder. "Chaffin has just ridden in with news."

"Chaffin, here?" The news must be dire indeed to bring him so far from Eastham. Gowain stood and glared at Gulliver.

"Shall I take over here?" Darcy asked, smiling grimly.

Gowain shook his head. "Let him stew awhile."

Rob Chaffin was waiting for Gowain in the yard outside the stables, and the news he brought was indeed bad.

"The Earl of Winchester has outlawed you."

"Who is he to do that? Of what am I accused?"

"Gareth Sommerville is the king's high justice."

"Sommerville?" Gowain's gut clenched. He knew that name. Had seen it this morn on Alys's journal.

"Aye. There's more. The crime of which you stand accused is murder. You did kill, in cold blood, according to the writ, one Lady Alys Sommerville. The earl's daughter."

"She's an earl's daughter," Gowain repeated, appalled.

"Not only that, she was, is, Ranulf's betrothed."

Gowain gasped and sank onto the stone mounting block. He looked around blindly at the keep where last night they'd wed themselves before witnesses. Was this the reason Alys had been less than enthusiastic about the impromptu ceremony? Because she already had a husband? "She is his bride?"

"His intended bride," Rob Chaffin amended.

"Don't split hairs with me." A betrothal was as binding as a wedding, the couple joined in all but body. He had the fleeting thought that he'd bedded her first, his brother's wife. It was no balm to his injured pride, his dashed dreams.

"Where is Ranulf now?" Gowain asked in a dead voice.

"He comes, with an army augmented by the earl's forces. 'Tis said Lord Gareth himself rides with them, despite a barely healed broken leg."

"Does he know we've taken Malpas?"

"I do not think so."

Gowain nodded. If Blanche's betrayal had broken his heart, Alys's had torn it from his chest. Beaten and bloodied inside, he wanted to run away, to hide and grieve in private for this terrible loss. But he could not. Ranulf would soon learn where he was and try to pry them from Malpas. There was much to be done.

Gowain forced himself to stand. Carefully controlling every muscle and nerve, he clapped Rob Chaffin on the shoulder. "My thanks for your timely warning."

Chaffin nodded grimly. "I'd like to stay and fight with you." When Gowain protested, he added, "I do not think there is more information I can glean from Eastham. The stand will be made here, and you'll need every man."

Gowain couldn't dispute that. "All right, I—"

A scream rang out, stilling the activity in the bailey. It came again, long and high. A woman's scream. Alys?

Gowain was up before the sound faded. "Where did that come from?" he asked Bertram, who was tallying supplies.

"Round the back, I think."

They raced around the side of the keep to the gardens that had once been his mother's pride, overgrown now with a sea of dry brown weeds.

"I do not see—" Gowain began.

"Look! Up there!"

A woman dangled from the upper story, clinging to a ledge by her hands. Gowain instantly recognized the wheaten braids and the full robe billowing in the icy wind.

Alys!

All thought of what he'd just learned vanished on a wave of fear so strong it choked him.

"Dear God! How did she get there?" Bertram cried.

"How can we get her down? Jean, Lang Gib, get some blankets, anything to break her fall. Whose window is that?"

"M-Maye's, I think."

Gowain paled. Had Maye pushed Alys out the window?

The shutters above Alys opened, and Maye looked out. Despite the distance, he could read her shock. Immediately she leaned out and reached for Alys.

"What's she doing?" Bertram said. "She can't hope to pull Alys up from there."

"Nay, but she can hold her till I get there." Or Gowain prayed she could. Prayed as never before, racing across the bailey and up three flights of stairs. He arrived breathless, sweating, and scared to death.

"Help," Maye called weakly as he dashed into her room. She leaned half out the window, feet hooked around a heavy trunk.

Gowain leaned out beside her, slid his hands down her arms and grasped Alys's wrists. How slender they felt, how small and cold.

She looked up at him, eyes huge in her white face. Her lips were bloody where she'd bitten them.

"It's all right, love," he immediately said, his tone soothing. "I'll get you up." He locked his fingers around her fragile bones. "Ease off, now, Maye. I've got her." He waited only till Maye had moved out of the way, then slowly pulled Alys up, over the sill and into his arms.

"Oh, Gowain." She clung to him, trembling and sobbing.

He held her tight, shivering himself. It was a close thing. If Maye hadn't bought him time... "What happened?" he asked Maye.

"I don't know. I was just coming up from the hall, heard her scream and ran in." Her eyes were eloquent.

"Thank you," Gowain said simply.

"It was Ralph." Alys lifted her head from the security of his chest. "Ralph threw me off the roof."

"What?" Gowain exclaimed. "Why?"

The heat of his rage drove the cold from her body, made her speech steadier. "Revenge."

"He wanted to hurt me through you?" His anger turned darker.

"It is not your fault," she said gently.

"I should have protected you."

"We had no idea. He took me prisoner so easily because I never suspected he felt this way."

But he had. "I knew he hated me. Just not how much."

"You must not blame yourself."

"What kind of man am I if I cannot protect my wife?"

His tone set her teeth on edge. She tried to read him, but his mood was closed to her. "What is it, Gowain?"

He shook his head. "I think you should lie down. Come, I'll take you to our room." Temper simmered beneath the surface of his calm, solicitous manner. What had overset him?

"I've not thanked Maye." Alys turned to the woman who had been adversary and was now rescuer. "Thank you, Maye. I would surely have died if you hadn't come."

Maye smiled. "I'm just glad I was near enough to help."

"So am I." Things were still tense between them, but mayhap they'd ease in time. Alys forced a smile for the curious crowded in the doorway. Bette, Velma, and Ruby, cuddling a wide-eyed Enid.

"Angel." The little girl held out her arms.

"Alys is tired and has to rest," Gowain said. "Go with Ruby, and I'll come see you in a minute." He ruffled his daughter's inky curls, then herded Alys down the hall. His arm was around her shoulders, but his manner was distant and cold.

Or maybe it was just her. Her ears buzzed, and she

couldn't seem to stop shivering, even when Gowain gently tucked her into bed with the covers up about her chin.

She huddled there, watching him move about the room, wishing she knew what to say to break the terrible tension. The fire crackled, licking at the new wood he'd added. Liquid sizzled, and the smell of mulled wine filled the room.

"Drink this." He helped her sit, held the cup while she sipped the hot spiced wine. It paved a warm path to her belly, but didn't melt the block of ice in her chest.

"What has happened?" she asked at last.

He rose and paced to the hearth. "It will keep till you've rested and recovered from your ordeal." His fist slammed into the stone lintel above the fireplace. "Damn, I should have done something about Ralph weeks ago. The men are searching for him. He won't get away."

"You couldn't have known," Alys said, but she sensed that his anger was only partly directed at Ralph. "Please tell me what else troubles you. Is it Ranulf? Is he com—"

"Was that the plan?" he snapped, whirling on her.

"P-plan?"

He cursed violently, then began to pace like a caged beast. "What I do not understand is why you waited till I'd taken Malpas. It would have been simpler to ambush us on the road."

Alys sat up. "What are you talking about?"

"Your plans…yours and Ranulf's." The fury in his face was nothing to the pain burning in his eyes.

"I do not understand. I've made no plans with Ranulf."

The lips that had kissed her so sweetly hours ago curled with contempt. "Do you deny you are betrothed to him?"

"What? You cannot be serious." She saw he was. Desperate, Alys crawled out of bed and crossed to him, stripping off her gloves as she went. "I am not, nor have I ever been, betrothed to Ranulf." The hem of her robe brushed the toes of his boots, yet the gulf between them seemed miles wide. She touched his closed fist, wishing he had her gift for reading others. She touched him and felt nothing. Nothing at all.

Gowain glared at her hand, then slid his free. "Nay, well a warrant has been swore out, branding me an outlaw for having killed one Alys Sommerville, Ranulf's betrothed."

"Well, it is a lie. I am very much alive and have never been betrothed to—"

"A lie, you say. The warrant was issued by Gareth Sommerville, Earl of Winchester. Is he your father?"

Oh. Alys swallowed. "Aye, he is. I should have told you. I started to a dozen times, but..." She sighed. "At first, I feared you'd try to ransom me." The ache in her chest was so huge she could hardly go on. "Or even kill me if you knew I was one of the nobles you detested so thoroughly."

"So, it was all a sham to protect yourself?"

"Nay." She couldn't stop herself from reaching for him again. His hands were cold, so cold. "I love you, Gowain. That is as real as...as the night we spent—"

"Bed sport. Is that what you wanted?" he sneered. "A little slap and tickle with your outlaw lover before you settled down to marriage with my titled brother?"

"How can you jump to such a conclusion on such flimsy..."

"That was what Blanche wanted of me, too," he said, ignoring her question. "Bah, you highborn women are alike."

"I am not like her." Alys's temper stirred. "And I resent your implication that I am a loose woman."

His gaze gentled for just a moment. "Nay, I know you are not that." The furious mask slipped back into place. "When you wed my brother, do not tell him how you came to lose your maidenhead. He may not like knowing he was not the first."

"The matter will not come up," Alys said through clenched teeth. "Because I am not wedding Ranulf."

"Suit yourself." He spun and headed for the door.

"Where are you going?"

"To prepare for a siege. As I said, your father has declared me an outlaw. He and your betrothed are coming to try and take my castle. They'll find I keep what is mine."

"Wh-what of me?"

"If I thought you wouldn't betray our defenses, I'd let you go." His lip curled again. "As it is, you stay till this is settled. Who knows, mayhap I can ransom you back to them in exchange for Malpas."

As the door slammed behind him, Alys sank into the chair. Her throat ached with tears she was too heartsick to shed. How could things have gone so terribly awry?

Because Blanche's perfidy had poisoned Gowain's ability to trust. If he'd been thinking clearly, he'd have realized that since she wasn't dead, Ranulf must had duped her father into issuing that warrant. And he'd have believed her when she said she was not Ranulf's betrothed.

But Gowain was too hurt to think clearly.

I keep what is mine, Gowain had said.

Well, so did she. 'Twas said the Sommervilles loved only once, and that for life. She'd found her true love, and she was not giving him up. Somehow, she'd find a way to make him see the truth. She'd teach him to trust her.

Chapter Eighteen

Gowain stormed out of the keep, his mind in turmoil, his heart a dead weight in his chest.

Ranulf's wife. Not his.

The words played over and over in his head.

She'd lied to him, betrayed him.

God! He wanted to lash out at something. He wanted to kick and scream and rant till the fury boiling in him was spent.

"Gowain!" Darcy charged up. "I just heard what happened to Alys. Is she all right?"

"Aye. Women are like cats...they always land on their feet."

Darcy frowned. "What is it?"

Gowain dragged a hand through his hair. "Damn, I must be cursed where women are concerned." Slowly at first, the words like acid on his tongue, he gave Darcy the bad news.

"Ranulf's betrothed." Darcy pursed his lips. "That would explain why she was riding with him, I suppose, but I cannot imagine a kind, compassionate woman like Alys with such as him."

Gowain snorted. "Noble marriages are made for land and titles. Both of which Ranulf has."

"Mayhap she was forced to agree," Darcy said, brightening.

"Then why not tell me so? I would have understood. Hell, I would have supported her. Instead, she lies about why she was with Ranulf, then denies they are betrothed." His eyes narrowed. "The writ against me clearly states I'm charged with murdering Alys Sommerville, Ranulf's betrothed." Gowain dragged in a breath of cold air and exhaled. It didn't ease the pressure in his chest. Months it had taken him to get over Blanche's perfidy. But he hadn't really loved her. He hadn't known what love was till he met Alys. Alys. Even thinking her name brought a wave of pain.

"Wait. Alys isn't really dead," Darcy said. "All we need do when Lord Gareth's army comes is send his daughter out to him."

"What if this business with Alys is just an excuse to eliminate me? If we send her out, they may attack anyway. Especially when my dear half brother learns I've bedded his intended bride."

"Mmm. I had not thought about that. Still, I think you are being hasty in assuming she was part of Ranulf's—"

"I'd speak of it no more. We've a war to wage." Gowain studied the battlements, calculating how many men it would take to hold them if the attackers brought in siege engines.

"I had no luck with Gulliver. The man's tight-lipped as a clam. I'll wager he's hiding something, but whether 'tis your mother's whereabouts or not, I do not know."

"We'll have to try harsher measures, then. Just now, I'm more interested in finding Ralph Denys."

"Does Henry know where he is?"

"He was in the kitchen carrying in supplies for Percy. I'd swear he had nothing to do with Ralph's plans."

"Henry would have blurted it out if he did—"

The guard at the gate cried a warning. Both men swung about in time to see the man tumble from the walkway. In quick succession, the drawbridge crashed to earth, and a troop of horses charged out of the stables.

Will Gulliver rode the lead animal, Stork held before him like a shield.

"Stork!" Gowain cried, starting forward.

"Stay back, all of you," Gulliver warned. He held a knife to the boy's throat and spurred for the gate. Behind him scrambled ten of the soldiers Gowain's men had captured.

The last man in the tail grinned at Gowain as he sped by. 'Twas Ralph Denys. Clutched tight in his arms was a child.

"It's Maye's Johnny!" Darcy cried. He broke into a run. Too late to keep the man from leaving.

"To horse!" Gowain shouted when the last of the soldiers had thundered over the drawbridge.

Darcy grabbed hold of his arm. "They'll kill Stork and Johnny if we follow him."

Gowain was afraid they'd do it in any case. "We'll stay well back. They may leave them on the trail for us to pick up."

"Aye." Darcy's eyes reflected Gowain's fears. "I'll find Maye and tell her, but we'd best keep this from Velma."

Gowain quickly chose twenty men to accompany him, then went inside to arm for the mission. He heard the crying before he entered the hall, found Maye in Darcy's arms, sobbing uncontrollably. "Maye?" He touched her heaving shoulder and got no response. "We'll find him."

She lifted her head, her swollen eyes grim with hatred. "What kind of monster takes a child?"

A desperate one. "They have no reason to harm Johnny once he's gotten clean away. He'll set him down first chance he gets."

"He...he's always sneaking out to feed the horses," she said, fresh tears welling.

Gowain judged she was on the brink of shattering, and he had never felt more useless in his life. Maye had helped him countless times. Now she needed help, and he could think of nothing to offer save vague promises.

"Maye." Alys's gentle voice intruded. She slipped past Gowain and knelt beside the stricken woman. "I've brought you some hot wine. Drink it down." She held the cup and bullied Maye into finishing every drop.

Maye's lids were already drooping by the time Alys stood.

"What did you give her?" Gowain demanded.

Alys paled, then flushed. "It was not poison."

Gowain felt his own cheeks heat. "I didn't say it was."

"A sleeping draft." She looked down at the woman drowsing in Darcy's arms. "I pray that by the time she wakes, you'll have found her Johnny and Velma's brother."

"As do I," Gowain said awkwardly.

"Is there no hope?" she asked, and he guessed she didn't only mean for the young boys.

"You lied to me," Gowain snapped.

"Everything I told you was the truth."

"You said your father was a horse trainer."

"He is. Papa and Uncle Ruarke raise warhorses. He's also a member of the king's council and—"

"The court of chancery. In which capacity he has judged me guilty, set a price upon my head and ordered me killed by whosoever finds me first," Gowain said, voice curiously flat. Where before he'd worked at controlling his emotions, now he found he had none. He cared for nothing beyond finding Johnny and keeping his people safe from the hangman.

"Oh, you are being so thickheaded. Do you not see? 'Tis because he thinks you killed me," Alys said again. "When he learns I am alive, Papa will recant the writ and—"

"You are the one who is blind. This is all the justification Ranulf needs to gather an army and wipe us out. We'll be dead before 'tis learned you are alive. Excuses may be offered, but no one will care that a band of rebels were mistakenly killed.''

"We are ready to ride," Lang Gib called from the doorway.

"Let me grab my mail, and I will join you in the courtyard." Gowain murmured a few words to Darcy, but said nothing more to Alys before quitting the hall.

Darcy heaved a sigh, then stood with the sleeping Maye in his arms. "I'll take her to her room."

"I will be up directly to sit with her," Alys said bleakly. She waited, however, till Gowain had clattered down the stairs in full mail and gone out, shouting for his horse. The hall was oddly quiet, except for the speculative murmurs of those who'd witnessed the scene between Gowain and herself. If she looked up, she'd doubtless see the same contempt that had marred her early days with the rebel band.

Drained by the fight with Ralph and the arguments with Gowain, she sat staring morosely into the empty wine cup. She was nearly tempted to take a sleeping draft herself. Mayhap she'd wake up and find this had all been a horrible nightmare.

Nay, avoidance profited nothing. Besides, she had to help Maye. Duty prodded Alys to her feet. A hard chip plunked into the cup. She stared at the pebble. Were the rebels going to stone her here? Would it be crockery and rotted vegetables next?

A bit of bark fell straight down to land on the table beside her hand.

Reflexively Alys looked up. Just in time to see a blur of white vanish behind a crossbeam. A bird? A cat? She stared at the spot, stared so hard her eyes ached. There it was again. A face. Not one of the children, surely.

"I see you up there," she called softly. "Come down before you're hurt."

Nothing moved.

She called a little louder this time and caught movement farther along the beam. "Bradley, is that you?"

"Is what me?" the boy demanded from beside her.

Alys jumped. "Oh, you startled me. Look up there. Tell me if you see something."

Bradley walked across the room, looking up, scowling. "You there!" he shouted. "Assassin in the beams. I've got a crossbow, and if you don't show yourself at once, I'll use it."

His pronouncement caused a flurry of activity on the ground. Women grabbed their children and hustled them away. Two old men left off whittling wooden spoons and joined Bradley, knives extended as they scanned the overhead structure.

"I—I don't mean no harm," came a timorous voice.

Alys looked straight up into the frightened face of a wizened old man stretched out on the crosspiece above her. At least she thought it was a man. "Who are you?"

"M-Malkin of Malpas."

"Ah, Malkin. I've been wanting to meet you."

It took time to convince Bradley to bring a ladder, even longer to convince Malkin to descend it. Though he was frail and bent with age, his eyes were bird-bright in his wrinkled face.

"Ciel said you'd gone away," Alys remarked as she plied the man with food and drink.

"Her mind's gone," he said around a mouth of stew.

That was certainly true. The old woman was even now asleep before the hearth, curled up on the bare floor like a cat.

"Why did you hide?"

"So they wouldn't take me away. Not that an old husk like me'd do them much good, but they're getting desperate. Winter coming." He swallowed ale in noisy gulps.

"Who is they?"

"Bellamy's men. He's the mine reeve."

"What mine?"

"Up in the hills." Malkin stuffed his mouth full of bread, then chewed with it open.

Alys tried not to appear disgusted. "Whose mine is it?"

"Malpas's." Small bits of soggy bread flew about.

Alys ducked back and kept digging for information. "So this Bellamy has a mine, and he wants you to work for him."

"Don't know that he does."

"But you just said he did," Alys grumbled.

"Nay, I said he might want me, if'n he was desperate enough, or if'n someone died. Folk don't last long at the digging, you know. 'Specially the children."

"He has children working in his mine?"

"They're the best for it." Malkin picked at what teeth he had with a grimy finger. "Small, ye know, able to scoot into tiny holes and do the digging. And you don't have to worry much about them stealing, 'cause—"

"Stop." Alys rose and planted her hands on the table, carefully clear of Malkin's leavings. "This Bellamy steals children and forces them to dig...to dig what? What does he get from this mine of his?"

"Blue John."

"Blue... Oh, it's a purplish stone, isn't it?" Her mother had fashioned two goblets of the precious mineral as a gift when her oldest brother, Richard, wed his Mairi.

"They call it Blue John. Fetches a goodly sum in London, I've heard tell." He reached for another hunk of bread. "Oh, and the mine ain't Bellamy's mine. 'Tis Lord Ranulf's."

Ranulf's. The last piece of the puzzle fit horribly into place. No wonder Ranulf had cut Malpas off from the outside world. "What of Lady Elen? Do you know where she is?"

"Up to the mine, same as all the rest."

"His own stepmother?"

Malkin snorted. "She's able-bodied, and she caused a load of trouble here after Lord Warren died...trying to escape and riling the servants. Last time Lord Ranulf came, he took her off to the mines. Said he'd put all that fire to work for him instead of against him. I'd be there, too, 'cepting I'm too weak to do more than empty old Gulliver's slops and fetch his ale.''

Alys sat down and buried her face in her hands, but she could not shut out the picture of Lady Elen and the children laboring in Ranulf's deep, dark mine.

"Alys?'' Bab touched her shoulder, shocking her with a wave of concern. "What? What is it?''

"It's Velma. Her time's come. My mama says 'twas likely the shock when she heard Stork had been taken.''

Alys nodded and rose. 'Twas said babes picked the worst of times to come. God grant her the skill to help Velma through this. And then to win Gowain back.

It was dark and snowing heavily by the time the search party rode through Malpas's gates.

Bone-weary, Gowain dismounted and handed Traveler's reins to the stable boy. Eight hours in the saddle without seeing anything but a few faint tracks in the snow.

Darcy groaned and arched his back. "I say it could have been a false trail. There's no reason for Gulliver to head north into the hills, when Eastham and reinforcements lay to the south.''

"It makes as little sense as any of the rest of this,'' Gowain grumbled as they trooped up the stairs to the keep. They'd headed for the village first thing, thinking Gulliver might have hidden there. The place had been deserted. Nor did it appear the villagers had packed up and headed for a better place.

It looked as though they'd dropped everything and run. Gowain and his men had found clothes soaking in tubs, kettles of pottage cooked down to nothing on fires long since gone out. They might have been overrun by some enemy, for there was evidence of dried blood in one hut. There was no sign of looting, however. Whatever it was had happened months ago. Nor was this the only strange thing. They'd come across two farms and an isolated cottage, all likewise deserted. At one farm, a cow had died in its stall...of starvation.

Gowain crossed the entryway and peered into the hall. Two torches yet burned, one at each end of the room. They cast long shadows over the rows of sleeping bodies wrapped up in blankets.

"Guess I'll go up and see how Maye fares," Darcy whispered.

Gowain nodded glumly. "Tell her we will be back out looking at first light." Feet dragging, he sought his chamber. He half expected Alys to be waiting, wasn't certain whether he was relieved or disappointed to find she wasn't there.

Henry Denys was. He turned from emptying a steaming bucket into the tub set before a crackling fire.

"What are you doing here?" Gowain asked uneasily.

"Alys said I should keep the water hot and bring it up straight away when you rode in." His eyes clouded. "Do you know where Ralphie is? He wasn't at supper."

Gowain sighed and eased his hand away from his sword hilt. "I haven't seen him."

"Oh." Henry picked up the pair of wooden buckets. "Alys said he'd gone on patrol, and I shouldn't worry."

"Alys—" His throat tightened. "Alys is probably right."

"She left a pot of soup just off the fire, and there's bread and ale set there on the trunk. I was to tell you that, too."

"Thank you, Henry. I appreciate it."

Henry's simple face was all smiles. "Alys said you would." Buckets flapping against his sides, he lumbered out of the room.

Gowain closed the door and leaned back against it. The fire, the food, the hot bath. The signs of home he'd longed for all his life. The only thing missing was the woman.

Nay, he'd not weaken.

Straightening, he picked up the tray, set it within reach of the tub and began stripping off his sweaty clothes. Naked, he slipped into the water. The heat prickled into his frosted hands and toes. He sighed and settled his head against the rim, letting the hot water leach the aches from his weary body.

The creak of rusty hinges warned that his privacy was about to be disturbed. Darcy, no doubt—no one else would dare intrude without knocking. Lazily he lifted one eye. Both of them flew open as Alys bustled into the room.

She wore a bedrobe of some fluid blue fabric, and her hair flowed down her back like a golden waterfall. "Good eve, my lord. I trust the hot bath feels good," she said, as casually as though they'd been wed for years and no argument lay between them. Crossing to the bed, she bent to turn down the covers.

"What the hell are you doing in here?"

She glanced back over her shoulder, the pose as provocative as the light in her eyes. "I belong here. I'm your wife."

"You are Ranulf's betrothed."

She straightened, which was worse, for now he saw that the robe she wore clung sleekly to her body, emphasizing her narrow waist, her gently flared hips and the breasts whose taste he remembered all too well. "Nay. I am not. I am your wife."

"But the writ your father signed said—"

"We pledged ourselves to each other before witnesses. Do you not recall?"

"Of course I do, but I did not know you were already prom—"

"I was never betrothed to Ranulf." Hands on hips, she stalked to the side of the tub. The damn robe parted with every step, giving him a tantalizing glimpse of slim legs. Slim, bare legs. Was she bare all over? "Why do you refuse to believe me?"

Gowain gritted his teeth and tried to ignore the familiar changes taking place in his body just below the waterline. "You lied to me."

"Aye." Militant stance vanishing, she sighed. "That was a mistake on my part. At first, I kept silent out of fear, then…" She toyed with the ends of her belt. "Everything happened so quickly. One moment we were adversaries, the next, lovers." A becoming flush pinked her cheeks. "There never seemed to be a good time to say, 'Oh, by the way, my father is an earl.' Especially given your hostility toward noblemen. I thought…I thought to introduce the subject slowly."

Gowain wanted desperately to believe her, to believe in her. But old fears died hard. "If there was no betrothal, why would this honest father of yours claim there was?"

"I've given that much consideration, and I believe he must have been duped by Ranulf. 'Twould not be too difficult, I'm sorry to say, to find a priest who would draw up false papers."

"I suppose," Gowain muttered, unwilling to admit that he, too, had spent considerable time thinking about all this while searching for the boys.

"I swear it is true." Alys knelt beside the tub and placed a hand on his chest, right over his heart. Beneath her palm, she felt his slick muscles knot. A shiver coursed through his body and into hers. Passion chased the doubts from his eyes, turned them a smoky green. He no longer trusted her, but he still desired her. It was less than she wanted, for lust alone could not hold a complex man such as Gowain, but it was a start. "As true as the love I bear for you." She lowered her lips to his and waited, flesh barely brushing flesh, for him to accept what she offered.

"Alys." Gowain felt her bare hand on his chest and knew she was likely reading his every emotion, the love and desire that warred with caution and logic. He looked into her eyes, so close he could see the pupils dilate as passion flared, and saw no shadow of deceit or malice. Only love.

Her lips parted. "I am your wife, only yours."

"Only mine." Gowain tunneled his hands into her hair

and brought her mouth to his. Warm, soft and incredibly stirring, her lips moved in concert with his. Gently at first, then avidly, as needs built and surged.

Alys was barely aware of Gowain standing and carrying her to the bed. She gasped as he opened her robe and molded their bodies together. "You're wet and cold."

"Warm me, then," he whispered hoarsely. "Heal me."

Alys wrapped her arms around him, opening herself, body and soul. "Ah..." she sighed when he filled the emptiness inside her with the aching length of him. They moved together, tumbling across the sheets, limbs tangled, mouths met and held.

"I need you," he murmured, and showed her how much, setting a pace that made her whimper in delight. Her pleasure became his as she convulsed around him, drawing him with her into the fire.

Drained, sated, Gowain managed to roll onto his side, but kept her with him, their bodies still joined in the sweet aftermath. Never had he thought to find such oneness with any woman, he thought, senses filled with the scent of rosemary and Alys. His arm tightened possessively around her. "All right?"

"Mmm." Alys stirred, brushing the hair from her face. Her cheeks were flushed and sweat-dampened, her eyes hazy.

"I fear I was not as careful with you as I should have been. 'Tis easier by far to control my anger at others than to conceal my, er, baser needs from you. Did my lust frighten you?"

"Nay, 'tis quite stimulating." Alys stretched lazily, loving the slide of her smooth legs against his rougher ones, the press of his hard muscles against her soft breasts. She could feel his concern, too, and his love. "Our feelings must run in the same vein when we make love. Your desire feeds mine, till I'm wound tight as a spring. But frightened, never."

"I'm glad." He stroked her back, and sensed him drifting away into sleep he badly needed. But there were things she had to tell him before the morrow.

"You did not get any dinner," Alys said.

"I'll get something when my strength returns...next year."

Alys giggled, then propped her chin on his chest, her expression sober. "Much happened while you were out. I'm anxious to tell you everything, but Mama said you should never give a man news on an empty stomach."

"Bad news sits better on an empty stomach."

"Oh, this isn't bad. Velma had her babe tonight."

"And?"

She grinned. "It's a girl. Named Alys. The delivery went surprisingly well, considering. I used an herb I've been trying—" she broke off. "Well, that part likely won't interest you as much as the discussion I had with Malkin."

"Who is that?"

"Ciel's brother, as it turns out."

Gowain's raised brow said it all.

"Nay, his wits are not addled. He's old and a bit lame, which didn't stop him from climbing into the rafters to hide when you took the keep."

"What?"

Alys decided mayhap her mother had been right about the food. "Just a moment." Clothed in nothing but her hair, she trotted across the room and fetched the tray with Gowain's supper. The look in his eyes as she walked back to him made her blood heat again. "Do you think of that all the time?"

"Whenever I see you walking around nude," he replied. "Or any other way, come to think of it." He waggled his brows.

Alys chuckled. How good it was to see him at ease again. This morn, she'd thought their love doomed. With that disaster still fresh in her mind, 'twould be pleasant to explore the passion, the love, they roused so easily in each other. But this was no time for selfishness. She broke off a bit of bread and stuffed it into his mouth. "About Malkin. He says there are terrible things going on hereabouts."

"More of Ciel's disappearing people?"

"In a way." Alys took a sip of his ale, then launched into the story Malkin had told her.

"Ranulf!" Gowain snarled through his teeth when she was done. "'Tis a sin to wish my brother dead, but he must be stopped."

Chapter Nineteen

"Oh, my. It's absolutely beautiful." Alys turned in a slow circle, looking up at the domed ceiling of the cave, some five or six stories above them. Veins of sparkling minerals in a dozen jewel-like tones adorned the walls like paintings done by some giant artist.

"I do not know why I brought you," Gowain grumbled.

"In case there were wounded." Alys sobered. "Is the mine entrance much further along?"

"Just over the next ridge, if memory serves." On the ride here, Gowain had explained that the mine had been worked for centuries, as far back as the Roman occupation. His father had done little with the mines, because he could not bear to send people below the surface to grub like animals. "We'll leave the horses here and proceed on foot," he told the men who'd come with them. Thirty veterans of the French campaigns.

Single file, with Gowain in the lead, they crept up the narrow mountain trail. The wind had died down, but the pale afternoon sun held little warmth. Shivering, Alys drew the hood of her cloak close about her face and trudged on behind her husband. They'd mended the quarrel, but he now held himself a bit aloof from her. That was what he did with other people. She didn't like that at all. If only there was some way to prove she had not been betrothed to Ranulf.

"Down," Gowain whispered.

They'd reached the summit, where the trail broadened into a flat plateau. As one, the column went into a crouch and scuttled across the rocky tabletop like so many giant crabs.

"There it is," Gowain murmured.

The bottom dropped from Alys's stomach as she peered over the edge. It was a long, long way down. They were directly opposite the maw of a giant cavern. Four men in mail and helmets patrolled before the entrance. Another half dozen crouched around a small campfire, hands extended to warm them.

"Where are the children?" Alys asked.

"Likely inside working."

"How will you get past the guards to save them?" Alys asked.

"We'll come back at night. See those huts?"

She nodded. Just back under the roof of the cave sat a row of makeshift wooden hovels. Windowless, with blankets instead of doors, they leaned against each other for support, so feeble a light wind would knock them down.

"Likely that's where the mine workers sleep. The larger one on this end is probably for the soldiers who are not on duty. If we come late at night when the guards are drowsing at their posts, we can surround them."

"Oh, Gowain, look!" She clutched at his sleeve, pointing to the three men who'd walked out of the mines.

Will Gulliver, Ralph and a huge, bearded man who swaggered along like a bear looking for a fight.

"That must be Bellamy, the mine bailiff," Gowain said.

Alys shuddered. "He looks the sort to force children to work in that dreadful, airless pit."

Indeed, he had a barrel chest, thick arms and shoulders so bulky it seemed he had no neck. To emphasize the point, he was arguing with Gulliver, waving his burly arms and roaring curses. Ralph stepped forward, obviously in defense of his new cohort. Bellamy backhanded him into the cave wall. Ralph hit, crumpled and slid down to lie in a boneless heap.

Alys gasped. "Sweet Mary. Is he…dead?"

From the odd angle of his head, Gowain guessed his neck had been broken. "Ralph deserved well what he got."

"Idiot!" Bellamy shouted. "You should have gone for Ranulf!"

Gulliver said something, in protest or defense, and received a cuff that set him on his backside.

"Roberts!" Bellamy bawled. "Get ready to take a message to my lord at Eastham."

Gowain grinned. "One less man to face when we come back."

"Are you not worried Ranulf will bring reinforcements before you can return?"

"Ranulf is not at Eastham. He's out looking for me. By the time he gets word, I'll have his hostages safely at Malpas."

"And not a moment too soon. If this Bellamy is so violent toward Ralph and Gulliver, only think how he must have treated the poor people who work the mines."

Like his mother. His gut clenched. "We mustn't dwell on it, love. We'll soon have them out."

"When will we do it?"

"We won't." Gowain crawled back from the edge. "I will. You are going to stay at Malpas."

"But what if there are injured people?"

"We'll bring them to you. I brought you along this time on the off chance that this place was so isolated Ranulf would not mount a heavy guard." Gowain took her arm and led her down the trail toward their horses.

She sensed his preoccupation with the detail of the operation and held her tongue till they were mounted and on their way back to Malpas. "How soon will you make the attempt?"

"Tomorrow." He raised his visor and scowled at her. "And I want your promise you will not attempt to follow." It had been her threat to do just that that caused him to bring her along in the first place. That and the vain hope that they might find the children lightly guarded and rescue them today.

"I promise," Alys said. "But..."

Gowain quirked one brow. "Why do I think I am not going to like what comes next?"

Alys smiled, happy he was teasing her again. "Well, I was going to suggest we send a message to my father—"

"Nay."

"You've not even heard what I wanted to say."

"You want me to ask for his help."

Aye, partly. "I wanted to tell my parents that I am alive and well and wedded to you."

Gowain frowned.

"Imagine how grief-stricken they must be, thinking me dead."

"Aye."

"Had I known sooner, I'd have insisted on it." She beseeched him with her eyes. "Think how you'd feel if Enid was lost."

Gowain knew when he was beaten. "Very well, but—"

"Why do I think I am not going to like this?" she teased.

He didn't smile. "I do not want you to tell them where you are. Not till we have Malpas provisioned to withstand a siege."

"You think my father would attack us?"

"I think he would tell Ranulf, who would attack. Do not forget, I've been declared an outlaw, and could be killed on sight. No questions asked."

"Very well," Alys said. One step at a time.

"Gowain is at Malpas!" Ranulf roared. He looked at what was left of Farmer Donald and realized he'd get no more answers. But the last bit of knowledge he'd wrung from the man was enough.

Gowain had taken Malpas.

Ranulf spun on his heel and stalked to his horse. "Mount up. We return to camp." As the warhorse's mighty hooves ate up the muddy miles, his nerves settled.

Gowain had Malpas, but that did not mean he knew about the mine. He'd be too busy laying in supplies and preparing for a counterattack to care what was going on just beyond the next mountain. If Ranulf moved quickly, he could bring out as much ore as had been gathered and reinforce the mine's garrison.

By the time he cantered into camp, he had nearly recovered from the nasty shock. Just in time to receive another one.

A tent had been pitched in the center of his camp. A tent so grand and luxurious it made his new campaign tent look like a gypsy's castoff. No need to ask to whom the tent belonged. The red-and-black pennant flying from its peak told the tale.

Gareth Sommerville was here.

Ranulf ground his teeth together, dismounted and walked to the tent's entrance. The liveried soldiers at attention there bade him wait a moment, then lifted the flap and announced that Lord Ranulf craved an audience.

As though Sommerville were the bloody king.

"He bids you come in," the soldier said.

Ranulf shouldered his way through the billowing silk to find the earl seated in a chair, his mending leg elevated on a stool. He'd been reading, of all things.

"How goes the search for...for Alys's murderer?" he asked. Tears sprang to his eyes at the mention of his daughter's name.

"Not well," Ranulf grumbled. How was he going to get rid of the pesky earl while he went to the mines? Inspiration struck in that very instant. "I have had word Gowain has taken Malpas."

"I thought it was unassailable."

"To assault, not to treachery." He repeated Farmer Donald's tale of how it was done. "I suppose we will not get him out of there till his supplies are exhausted. And God knows it will be hard work maintaining a siege there in winter."

Gareth's midnight-brown eyes narrowed. "Do not worry. We'll soon rout the viper from his nest. We've come prepared for almost anything. This tent, and nearly all else I've brought with me, belongs to my brother, Ruarke. He's somewhere about, posting his men. He has with him the parts and pieces for a ram, catapult and siege towers."

"Excellent." Ranulf smiled for the first time in several long, hard days. "I shall leave the frontal assault to you and your brother, then, while I, er, scout around the back of the keep to make certain no one slips out that way."

"How long should it take them to go and come back again?" Alys asked for the hundredth time that day. She paced before the fire in the great hall, too restless even to work on her journal.

Malkin shrugged, plucked another wood curl off the horse he was whittling and tossed it into the fire. "Depends."

Alys looked at Bette, who was busily cutting down one of Alys's robes to make gowns for Birdie and Enid. The two women rolled their eyes. Malkin might be the only man who knew the land hereabouts, but it was harder than pulling teeth to get a straight answer from him.

"They left this morn," he went on. "Get there about now. Fight at dawn tomorrow. Gather the weans. Travel back. Depends on how quick they come, with the children and all."

Not before the day after tomorrow, then. Alys sighed and resumed her pacing. "I should have gone with them. No telling what condition those poor people will be in."

"Sad," Ciel said. "Sad shape." She sat at the table

watching Bette and occasionally offering a suggestion. Some were remarkably lucid.

Young Bradley burst into the hall. "There's a large troop moving up the valley toward the keep."

"Ranulf!" Alys gasped. What should they do? Gowain had taken most of the men with him, leaving Lang Gib and a small garrison to man the walls and maintain the watch.

"Lang Gib says we're to sit tight till Gowain comes back," Bradley added.

What else could they do? Still, Alys could not sit idly inside. She donned her cloak and went up to the wall walk.

"They're just coming abreast of us now," Lang Gib said.

Malpas Keep sat at the narrow end of a steep-sided gorge. Rather like the cork in a flask. If they had been so inclined, and had the archers, Gowain's men could have rained death and destruction down on the army passing beneath their noses. As it was, the defenders could do little but watch and wait to see what would happen.

"How will Gowain get back inside with them camped all around us?" Alys asked anxiously.

"Gowain's got near a hundred men with him. He could fight his way through their lines."

Alys thought about the men, women and children from the mine and shuddered. What would happen to them? What if Gowain could not protect them and fight Ranulf, too?"

"Bloody hell," Lang Gib snarled.

"What?" Alys looked down to see the army pass right by the base of the keep and continue up the gorge. "Do you think they are going to the mine?"

"Aye." Lang Gib swore again, his angular face twisting with frustrated rage. "I've got to get a message through to Gowain."

Alys spent a long, sleepless night in the big bed she'd shared with Gowain, wondering if Gib had found him.

True, Gowain had his best men with him, but he also had an unknown number of helpless people to protect, as well.

If anything should happen to him, she didn't think she'd want to go on. How odd that Gowain had become so vital to her in such a short time. Nay, it wasn't odd at all. He was the one person with whom she could truly bond, because, outward appearances to the contrary, he was honest, honorable and pure of heart. The only man who could stand the test of her gift.

Alys rose at dawn, hollow-eyed and frightened. Unable to stand the confinement of the hall and the sympathetic glances of those breaking their fast, she fled to the battlements. The stinging wind dried her tears, the sight of a lone hawk wheeling overhead steadied her. Gowain would prevail.

As she turned to go inside, a flash of light on steel caught her eye. And another. She raced back to the wall and spotted another army entering the gorge.

"Damn," exclaimed Bertram, who was taking his turn at guard duty. "Is that more of Ranulf's men?"

Alys strained to see. As they drew closer, she could plainly make out the pennant they flew.

"'Tis Papa! My papa's come!"

Alys ran down the stairs to the gatehouse. "Raise the drawbridge!" she cried.

Tom the Reeve glared at her. "Gowain told me that if Ranulf or his allies came, I was to keep the gates shut tight."

"But...but my father has come."

"Is he not the one who declared Gowain an outlaw?"

"Aye, but—"

Tom sniffed and went back to devouring his bread and ale.

Alys looked at the heavy winch that operated the drawbridge mechanism and knew she'd never be able to work it. Undaunted, she raced across the bailey and into the keep. She found Bertram at the table with Bette, Bab and Percy.

She quickly told them about her family, and especially her father. "He alone can help Gowain."

Bertram looked doubtful. "He declared Gowain an outlaw."

"And put a price on his head," Bette added.

"But—"

Maye wandered in just then. She looked so lost and wounded that Alys immediately went to her.

"Come join us," Alys said softly.

Maye nodded numbly and allowed herself to be led to the table. She took a sip of the ale Alys pressed on her, but barely touched the bread. "How soon will they be back?"

"Well..." Bertram shifted uneasily.

"What is it?" Maye asked. "What is wrong now?"

"Ranulf and his men marched by the keep this morn," Alys said gently. "They may be going to the mine."

"Oh, my God." Maye gripped the edge of the table. "We have to warn Gowain."

"Lang Gib left to do just that," Alys said.

"What if he isn't in time? What if Ranulf catches him?"

"What we need," Alys said, "is reinforcements."

"We'd best hope they are short of supplies," growled Ruarke Sommerville, hero of many an English battle against the French. "For there's no other way we'll pry them out of that keep."

"What of the ram and catapult?" Gareth asked.

Ruarke glanced up the sheer rock face to the stone tower crowning it like a fist shoved skyward. "Too far and wrong angle for the catapult. The stones would crash back on us." He studied the narrow, winding trail up the cliff. "There's no way we could provide protection for a ram."

"Are you saying Alys's murderer will go free?"

"Nay. We will find a way." Ruarke scowled at the keep, then studied the roadway again. He glanced sidelong at his older brother and grinned. "Mayhap we'll try intimidation first." Over his shoulder, he called, "Philippe, rig a flag of truce, ride up and tell the commander of yon keep that he has one hour to surrender before we send our battering ram to pound down their gate and our sappers to tunnel under their walls.''

Bertram and Tom Reeve, the senior members of Malpas's tiny garrison, went white when the Sommerville knight hailed the castle and called out His Lordship's terms.

''My lord offers full pardons and a promise that all who lay down their arms may leave with their weapons and valuables. All excepting Gowain FitzWarren.''

''This is ridiculous,'' Alys told the two men. ''You heard Sir Philippe. My father is only interested in Gowain...or at least he thinks he is. If you are afraid to open the gates and let them in, let me go out and speak with my father.''

''It can do no harm,'' Tom said hastily.

Bertram frowned. ''When he learns Gowain is not here, will your father pursue him to the mines?''

Alys certainly hoped so. ''When my father hears what Ranulf has done, he will pursue him, not Gowain or any of you.''

''Noblemen stick together,'' Tom muttered.

''I say we give Alys a chance,'' Maye said. ''If her father is as kind and compassionate as she is, we have naught to fear. Only look how much she has done for all of us.''

''Amen to that,'' Bette added. ''Would Velma be upstairs now nursing her wee daughter if not for Alys?''

''I suppose we have no choice,'' Tom grumbled.

''You will not regret it.'' Alys hugged them all, even sullen Tom, who really was as cross as he seemed. Then she grabbed a cloak and hurried down to the horse Bradley had saddled for her. Out the gate she raced and down the steep trail, her heart singing with joy.

She spotted her father at once, astride one of his gray warhorses, left leg sticking out at an odd angle. Poor Papa, how it must be paining him. She should have thought to have water heated for him.

"Halt!" cried the first of her father's soldiers. "State your name and purpose!"

Alys laughed and threw back the cowl of her cloak. "'Tis I, Lady Alys, seeking an audience with my father."

The poor lad's eyes bugged out. "You...you are dead."

"Obviously not." Alys cantered by him, making straight for her father and uncle. She marked the moment when they realized who she was. Shock. Disbelief. Then joy chased across very similar ruggedly handsome faces.

"Alys!" her father screamed. He kneed his horse forward to meet hers. They stopped side by side. He reached out and swept her into his arms, nearly toppling them both to the ground. That he didn't was a tribute to his strength and his horse's training.

Laughing and crying, Alys wrapped her arms around her father's neck and clung.

"Alys. Alys. I can scarcely believe it."

Alys leaned back and grinned. "I am alive and well, Papa. I fear Ranulf did deceive you...on several counts."

Tears streamed down the lines of her father's weathered face. "What happened? How come you to be here with this rebel, Gowain FitzWarren?" He glared up at the keep. "Does he think to escape punishment for his crimes by freeing you now? Or did you escape from that—"

"Hush, Papa. Gowain is more victim than anyone. Come up to the keep, and I will tell you all that has happened, but we cannot tarry long. Gowain has gone to the mines to save the people Ranulf has enslaved, but Ranulf passed by not long ago, and I am afraid he—"

"Slowly, Alys, you are losing me already."

"It is very simple, Papa. Ranulf has been exploiting his people. Gowain tried to stop him. He would have, too, only Gowain is too honorable to kill his brother, so Ranulf escaped. Then—"

"Alys." Her uncle Ruarke's deep voice intruded. "Start at the beginning. How did you come to be reported dead?

Whose body was in the casket Ranulf brought for us to bury?''

"God alone knows," Alys whispered. "As to how I came to be here, 'tis because I stopped to help a wounded boy, who mistook me for a nun. Which was fine, because—"

Uncle Ruarke laughed. "Whatever adventures you've had have not dampened your spirits, I see."

"Nay," her father said slowly. He looked at her with dawning wonder. "Alys. I am holding you in my arms."

"Aye, Papa. 'Tis another of the miracles that have befallen me, but there is no time to speak of it now. We must see if we can find the mines and save Gowain."

"Why would I want to save the man who kidnapped you?"

"Because he is my husband."

"Husband?" Her father gaped. "You wed a rebel? A murderer?"

"I wed a decent and honorable man. And I will save him, with or without your help."

Chapter Twenty

They slipped down from the hills in the dark hours just before dawn, their mail covered by wool tunics, their faces blackened with mud.

As Gowain had hoped, the guards on the outer perimeter were dozing at their posts and fell without a whimper. Signaling Jean to take the right side of the cavern, Gowain led his party in from the left. A pair of torches burned at either side of the wide entrance. By that faint light, he made out a score of men drowsing around a dying campfire. If his band could reach the soldiers before the alarm was sounded, this might yet be a bloodless victory for the rebels.

A few feet from their objective, a boot heel skittered on loose stones.

One of the soldiers roused. "Who goes there?" he called. The words ended in a soft gurgle as Art Jenkins's knife found its mark. But the damage was done. Another soldier gained his feet, drew his weapon. And another.

Gowain's sword hissed from its scabbard. He threw back his head and roared the ancient battle cry of the de Crecys. "For right and justice! To me! To me!"

The night erupted in sound and chaos as his men poured out of the darkness. Screaming wildly and brandishing their weapons they attacked the disconcerted soldiers like a band of berserkers. The soldiers fell back, some shouting for re-inforcements, others trying feebly to defend themselves.

"Quarter to all who yield!" Gowain shouted above the din.

"I'll kill the man who quits!" bellowed another. Bellamy charged into the fray, clad only in leather breeks but armed with a sword he knew how to wield. He felled one man and was beating back another before Gowain could finish his opponent and charge in to engage him.

Bellamy's first blow struck Gowain's blade and rever-berated up his arm, numbing it. Bloody hell. Teeth clenched, Gowain redoubled his efforts. His next flurry of thrusts forced Bellamy back, but the man regrouped and went on the attack, fury in his eyes, curses falling fast as his blade. Calling on years of experience, Gowain feinted and parried, looking for a fatal flaw in Bellamy's technique. Every man had one. Gowain had survived thus far by find-ing his opponent's and capitalizing on it.

There. Bellamy overcommitted when he thrust, leaving his left side unprotected.

Gowain retreated a step, waited for Bellamy to thrust, and drove in for the kill.

The mine reeve's eyes rounded with shock as Gowain's sword struck home. His mouth opened, but the only sound that came out was a hoarse groan. He collapsed in a heap at Gowain's feet.

Breathing hard, Gowain wheeled to assess the rest of the battle, just in time to see Darcy dispatch Gulliver. The sur-viving guards had surrendered, and now huddled together under the furious gaze of Jean and Robert Lakely.

"Damn," Gowain exclaimed. "That was close."

"Aye. They fought well." Darcy cleaned his blade on Gulliver's tunic and crossed to Gowain. "What next?"

"The huts." Gowain looked to the forlorn buildings. Not a peep had been heard from them during the brief, frantic fight.

Gowain crept up on the nearest one, with Darcy and six

others behind him. Standing to the side in case there were more soldiers inside, Gowain lifted the blanket-door.

A shovel handle jabbed out at him.

Swearing, Gowain grabbed it and pulled.

"Bloody hell!" exclaimed a youthful voice. Young Stork tumbled out, still grappling for the weapon.

"Hold, Stork!"

"Gowain!" The boy let go of the shovel and threw himself into Gowain's arms. Sobs racked his thin body. "I knew you'd come for us. I knew you'd not let us stay here."

"Easy, lad." Gowain held him and said to Darcy, "See who else is within."

Darcy nodded, his eyes misty, and disappeared inside the hut. Moments later, he emerged, carrying a crying Johnny, with six other children clinging to his massive legs.

All of Gowain's men had tears in their eyes by the time they'd finished liberating the people held hostage to work in Ranulf's mines. Most were strapping boys and young men, but a few of their fathers had been pressed into service, as well. The stories they told of beatings and deprivation, of long hours in the mines and cruel conditions, made Gowain wish he could kill Bellamy all over again.

Nay, 'twas Ranulf who was to blame. Ranulf who should pay. But Gowain knew there was little chance of that. Many in the land held that a lord could compel his people to work where he willed it. Some might decry Ranulf's harsh mea--sures, but the law, such as it was, would do little to stop him.

Gowain's victory was tainted by one thing. His mother had not been among the captives. One man, a shepherd from near Malpas, recalled she'd been at the keep when he was captured and impressed into digging for the Blue John.

"She were a prisoner there, my lord," the man mumbled. "Brought to the keep a few months after Lord Warren died, and kept under guard. I heard tell she tried more than once to escape."

That sounded like his mother, Gowain thought, heartsick and desperate to know what had become of her. It seemed that somewhere between the keep and the mine she had disappeared. Was Ranulf so depraved he'd actually murder his stepmother?

"We're ready to ride," Darcy said.

Gowain shoved aside his concern to deal with their present danger. When he had this lot safely back at Malpas, he'd decide how best to proceed. They had stripped Ranulf's men of their weapons, which would be useful in the defense of Malpas, but there was no time to bury them. Each of Gowain's men would ride double to carry the mine workers back to the keep.

Gowain had just swung into the saddle, with Stork riding pillion behind, when Lang Gib galloped up.

"Thank God, I didn't think I'd find this place again," Gib exclaimed. "Ranulf's troops came up the valley this afternoon. They bypassed Malpas. We feared they were on their way here."

"Damn." Gowain looked around, at the frightened victims of Ranulf's greed, at his men, who had already fought one battle tonight. The sun had risen over the rim of the plateau, casting pale winter light over the aftermath of last night's battle. Their best chance for survival lay in flight. "We'll go back up the trail to the caves where we waited before the attack. If Ranulf comes, we'll at least have high ground in our favor."

"Gowain, riders coming fast!" Jean shouted.

"Dismount!" Gowain cried, knowing it was futile to make a run uphill with the tired, overburdened horses. "We'll make our stand in the mine cavern."

They were in position, the horses and noncombatants well back in the cave, by the time they heard the troop approach.

Ranulf galloped into the clearing at the head of his men, took one look at the carnage and swore. As he drew rein, his mount danced, fighting the bit. "Gowain!" he roared. "Come out of there! Surrender at once!"

Gowain's heart sank when he saw how many men streamed in behind his half brother. A hundred, at least. They filled the level ground between the rocky outcropping and the cave's entrance. A hundred to thirty. They did not stand a chance. Oh, they could hold off a few sorties, kill a few of Ranulf's men. But they could never fight their way clear.

"Do you think there is a back way out of here?" Darcy asked.

"Not that I remember. 'Twould take too long to find, in any case." Gowain looked his friend in the eye. "What say you, shall we surrender and hope we can bargain for leniency for the children, or hold out as long as we can?"

"Normally, I'd fight to the last man." Darcy looked toward the back of the caves, where the others waited. Men and boys who had already been through so much. "But if there is any way we could return Maye's Johnny to her..."

Gowain nodded. "What terms do you offer?" he called.

"Terms?" Ranulf's laughter was harsh and sharp, ringing off the rocks. He lifted his visor and glared across the clearing at Gowain. "Why should I offer you anything?"

Gowain thought it over for a moment. Much as Ranulf wanted him dead, he also wanted his mine. The mine was vulnerable in one small way, he remembered from his youth. "If you do not, I'll fire the support timbers and collapse the mine shafts." Such a thing had happened once by accident.

Ranulf's face turned red as fire. A stream of hot oaths spewed from his lips.

Darcy grinned. "Can we do it?"

"Aye, if we use the huts for firewood, we can."

"What terms do you seek?" Ranulf snarled after a moment.

"Let us go free."

Ranulf laughed again, the sound ugly. "Not when I have

you right where I want you, Gowain FitzWarren.'' He paused for a heartbeat, then snapped, "They go, you stay."

"Nay," Darcy said hoarsely.

Gowain met his friend's outraged gaze as levelly as he could. "'Tis the only way. Ranulf knows he cannot let me go."

"Then we all stay."

"Nay. 'Tis foolish to die for just one man."

"We'll fire the mines," Darcy said mutinously.

"And die in the smoke?" Gowain shook his head. "I'd have done it...as a last act of desperation...but it would be suicide, and we both know it. This way, all of you will survive."

"I cannot let you make that sacrifice."

Gowain smiled. "The choice is not yours." He clapped Darcy on the shoulder. "I am counting on you to get everyone back to Malpas. Ranulf will doubtless be busy here for a day or so, setting things to right and collecting his gemstones. That should give you time to get away...back to the caves."

Darcy groaned. "I cannot go on without you."

"You must." Gowain's fingers dug into Darcy's flesh. "Think of Maye and Johnny and Alys." He shuddered inwardly, realizing he'd never see her again. Never hold her. The anguish was so great it nearly choked him. "I know she will look out for Enid, but if they should need anything..."

"I will make certain they want for nothing."

"Her family..." Gowain's throat closed, but it must be said. "She may want to return to her family."

"I will see she has an escort."

They both knew times would be difficult. The rebels would take what supplies they could with them, but food would be scarce. And likely once Ranulf had eliminated Gowain, he'd hunt down the rest of the band and kill them, too.

"What is your decision?" Ranulf shouted.

Gowain dropped his hand from Darcy and turned to face his brother across the sunlit clearing. The bright sky mocked his dark and desperate mood. "I will stay."

"Good." There was a wealth of malice in that word.

"But if you move in to take me before my people have gotten well away, I will fire the mine."

Ranulf sneered, "How little you trust me."

"How well I know you," Gowain countered. He looked back to his men and began giving the orders to march. They were as reluctant to leave him as Darcy was.

"Let me stay with you," Jean pleaded. "I could hide in the rocks and fight—"

"Darcy will need you to help get everyone back to the caves," Gowain said gently.

The children were frightened and confused, especially the ones who'd been longest at the mines. Young Stork helped bolster their nerve, telling them of the delights that awaited them at Malpas. Listening to the boy, Gowain felt a sense of failure. He'd rescued these people, only to have them join his band of hunted rebels. What would happen to them? Was Darcy leader enough to hold them together?

And what of Alys? Would she be all right without him? He knew how lost he'd be if the situation was reversed and something happened to her. Oh, my love. How short was our time together. If only I might hold you one more time.

Tears stinging his eyes, Gowain stood in the entrance to the caves and watched Darcy and the others mount up. Dread lay like a block of ice in his chest; his mouth was dry as dust. Would Ranulf really let them go? Or would he break his word? Gowain had started a large fire in the back of the first cavern, to serve as a warning to Ranulf. Yet he was acutely aware it might not be enough to stay his brother's hand.

Sure enough, just as Darcy gave the word to march, Ranulf ordered his men forward.

"Nay!" Gowain screamed. He started out of the cave.

Ranulf grinned and drew his sword. "See, he breaks his oath. He's trying to escape."

"I do not!" Gowain shouted.

"Seize him. Seize them all!" Ranulf cried.

"Hold, what passes here?" another voice roared out.

Gowain looked up as a column of men in red-and-black livery rode into the clearing behind Ranulf's. They were led by a knight in silver armor, astride a magnificent gray warhorse.

Ranulf wheeled his mount. "My lord, what do you here?"

"I've come to see what you are doing," replied the knight as he stopped in front of Ranulf.

"You are just in time to witness the capture of your daughter's murderer, Gowain FitzWarren."

Gowain blinked. So, this was Lord Gareth, the man who'd had him declared an outlaw. The man Alys said was good and fair. The small spurt of hope kindled by the troop's arrival died. It seemed she was wrong. The earl was firmly allied with Ranulf.

"Indeed." Gareth tugged off his helmet and handed it back to one of his squires. Resting his forearms on the saddle's pommel, he studied Gowain. 'Twas not hard to see where Alys had gotten her aristocratic features and fair coloring, for the earl was yet a handsome man. His eyes, dark as peat, stared so intently that Gowain felt he was being picked apart.

"So," the earl said at length. "This is the man you say murdered my Alys."

"Aye." Ranulf's chest puffed out. "I managed to trap him and his whole band here."

"Mmm. I thought they had taken Malpas Keep. What manner of place is this, and why are they here?"

"Wh-what? Oh, 'tis…'tis the caves where they made their headquarters," Ranulf stammered.

The earl snorted. "It seems a remote area from which to launch their predatory raids."

"Ah...the better to avoid capture."

"Mmm. And those children, are they outlaws, too?"

"I, er, believe they are." Ranulf glared at the boys who cowered in the arms of Gowain's men, as though daring them to speak up and dispute his statement.

Despite the dire circumstances, Gowain nearly laughed. His brother was making an obvious effort to impress the earl. Far from seeming impressed, the earl acted rather like a cat playing with a mouse. Against his will, Gowain found himself intrigued by Alys's father. He wondered how he'd come to be here, but decided against disrupting the delicate balance of things by asking.

"You saw Gowain kill my Alys?" Gareth asked suddenly.

"Aye." Ranulf shuddered. "'Twas terrible to see my beloved Alys raped to death before my very eyes."

Gowain jerked. "I did no such thing. I never—"

"I saw you!" Ranulf snarled. His fists curled into talons.

"Curious thing, that," the earl remarked. "For my daughter tells quite a different tale."

"What?" Ranulf exclaimed.

"Alys," called Lord Gareth. "We are in need of a witness to corroborate Ranulf's tale."

Alys rode out from behind the rocks, wearing a warm woolen cloak and a triumphant expression. Immediately her eyes sought and locked with Gowain's. So soft and full of love.

He smiled faintly, grateful at least to have seen her one last time.

"Jesu," Ranulf breathed. "'Tis a miracle."

"Indeed," the earl said. "But not of the sort you expect. Lord Ranulf, I charge you with murder, rape, kidnapping—"

"The hell you say." Ranulf spat. "Who accuses me?"

"The list is long...Percy Baker and Bertram the bailiff, who claim they were dispossessed, beaten and robbed by your order. Velma of Eastham, who claims you raped her. Dame Dotty of—''

"I am their lord. They are mine to do with as I want."

Lord Gareth shook his head. "Torture, murder and kidnapping are not part of your prerogative. But we will return to London and try your case there."

Ranulf's face drained of color. "You cannot be serious."

"I assure you, I am." Gareth's jaw tightened. "Your crimes are so appalling I am tempted to hang you here and now, but I am sworn to uphold the law, and would see you have a chance to defend yourself against these charges."

"Seize him! Take the earl!" Ranulf screamed.

"Ruarke?" Gareth inquired, without looking around.

"Have no fear, brother," replied a large knight who greatly resembled Lord Gareth. "His men are in no position to help, even if they'd wanted to." Indeed, an efficient band of men-at-arms were stripping Ranulf's men of their weapons under the watchful eye of this Lord Ruarke.

Gowain could scarcely believe his eyes. It was over? It was really over, and they had won?

From across the clearing, Alys watched Gowain's wariness give way to disbelief and finally wonder. Relief bubbled through her. It was going to be all right. They'd arrived in time, and her papa was setting things to right.

"I will not be tried like some petty thief," Ranulf exclaimed. "Gowain is the rebel, the outlaw. None of this would have happened if he hadn't come back." Before anyone could stop him, Ranulf slid from his horse and charged at Gowain, his sword flashing up in the sunlight.

"Papa, stop him. Gowain won't fight his brother." She urged her horse forward. Her father caught the bridle.

"Nay, Alys, you'll be hurt," Gareth said. "And look, Gowain has drawn his sword."

Indeed, Gowain had brought his blade up to counter Ranulf's furious blows. The clash of steel on steel reverberated off the mountains as the two men circled, Ranulf lunging wildly, Gowain parrying his vicious thrusts.

"Alys is right," Ruarke Sommerville said after a moment. "Gowain is defending himself, nothing more. Ranulf will soon figure this out and move in for the kill."

"We must stop them." Alys slid from the saddle, driven forward by the instinct to protect her love.

"Nay." With surprising agility, her father dismounted and blocked her path. "Stay here. Ruarke, make certain she does." Thrusting her into her uncle's arms, he limped toward the battling men, stopping a few feet away. "Lord Gowain. There is no shame in protecting yourself."

Dimly Gowain heard someone call his name, but he didn't look up, for all his energy was focused on staying one beat ahead of Ranulf's flashing blade. If he could just disarm him. But desperation increased Ranulf's strength a hundredfold. He fought with the fury and savagery of a wounded beast.

"Save yourself," the gruff voice demanded. "Think of Alys and your daughter."

"He won't kill me." Ranulf's voice was a rasp. "He won't." His eyes fastened on Gowain's, blazing with hatred.

Mad, Gowain thought. He is mad.

"But I will kill him, if it's the last thing I do." Ranulf sent his blade sliding down the length of Gowain's with stunning force, driving him back a step.

Gowain tripped on a rock and faltered. He felt his guard drop even as he struggled to regain his footing. This was it. Ranulf's blade flashed in the light, arching down in a deadly arch toward Gowain's neck. Gowain tensed, waited for the end.

Someone screamed.

It must have been him. Gowain waited for the pain.

It never came. Instead, Ranulf slowly collapsed in a heap at Gowain's feet.

Gowain swayed, staring at the sword that protruded from Ranulf's chest. A strong hand gripped his arm to steady him. Dazed, he looked up into the sympathetic face of the earl.

"I could not let him kill you," Gareth said softly. "Nor have his death on your conscience. Let me be both judge and executioner, for it would have ended no other way. Whether he died now, at the point of my sword, or two weeks hence in London on the gallows, he got what he deserved. Is that not justice?"

"Aye." Gowain dragged in a ragged breath. "Thank you, my lord earl. I did not expect…"

Alys rushed up, wrapped her arms around him and hugged him tight. "Oh, Gowain. I was so frightened."

"As was I." He looked over her head at her father's kind, compassionate face. "My thanks, sir." He swallowed and glanced at Ranulf's still face. "Still, I wish he had lived to tell me for certain what became of my mother."

"Your mother," Ranulf muttered, voice low and choked. "Al-always she came first. Even with my…my father." His eyes opened, but already they were glazing over.

Gowain crouched down, with one arm around Alys. "What did you do to my mother?"

"Nothing." Laughter wheezed in Ranulf's lungs. "She escaped…going…going to the mine. Never got there. Pity… I'd hoped Bellamy could…" He coughed and shuddered.

"She escaped," Gowain said in dazed disbelief.

"Hope she died…in W-Wales." The breath hissed from between his lips as he breathed his last.

Alys turned her face into Gowain's shoulder. "Oh, Gowain. I am sorry."

He stood slowly and looked around at those he had saved, Ranulf's victims. "At least Mama was not one of them. She was hardy and determined. I think she reached Wales. When I can, I'll try to find her people." But it would not be anytime soon.

The earl cleared his throat. "Let us get these children back to the keep, Lord Gowain, for it is starting to snow."

"Lord Gowain? It is long since anyone has called me that."

Gareth smiled. "You are now lord of Eastham and Malpas. A baron worthy of the title 'nobleman,' unless I miss my guess."

"That he is, Papa," Alys said. "He is the most honorable man I know, this rebel knight of mine."

Epilogue

Spring. The time of hope and renewal.

Sighing, Gowain drank deep of the air, warm and damp with the promise of rain. The winter had been long and cold, but sheltered inside Eastham's great stone walls, with the work of rebuilding the estate to occupy him, he had found the days passed swiftly. And the nights…

Gowain grinned in anticipation. They'd been gone for a week, taking building supplies to Darcy, who was castellan at Malpas. These six nights without Alys beside him had seemed long indeed. Not only was he anxious to see her, to hold her again, but he had news of Darcy and Maye he knew she'd relish.

"Almost home now," Jean remarked, cantering beside him on the winding road through the valley.

"Aye." Gowain looked ahead. The last rays of the setting sun bathed Eastham Castle in red-gold light, making the ancient towers glow as though touched by magic. In a way, he supposed, they were. The magic of Alys's love. How it had transformed his life in a few short months, awakening his soul the way the gentle spring rains did the seeds set deep in the soil.

"Do we go through the village or around, my lord?" inquired Dickie of Newton, squire-in-training.

"Through the village, Stor—er, Dickie, I've a mind to

see if they finished the new wall while we were gone,'' Gowain replied.

The wall of fieldstone and mortar was fine indeed, worthy of the buildings it encircled. A sense of pride filled Gowain as they trotted down the main street, past Bertram and Bette's new cottage with its fenced garden and thatch roof. Next to it stood Percy's bakeshop, sporting a new door and fresh whitewash.

"Looks far different than it did the first time we rode through here, does it not?" asked Jean.

"Aye." The whole village had been refurbished, the repairs paid for by the sale of the Blue John stones. All the families that had suffered under Ranulf's tyranny had been compensated in some way, and then Gowain had boarded up the mine.

"Me, I think the greatest difference is in the people. See how they bustle about their tasks with a quick step and a ready smile. Not that they can forget the pain and suffering inflicted on them by that fiend Ranulf, but with time it has faded."

"'Tis true, thank God." Enid's nightmares had faded, too. She still insisted on a night candle in her room, but her dreams these days were of puppies and sweet cakes, not bad men. They might never know what had been done to frighten Enid so, but Alys said it was enough that she'd put the past behind her, as had so many at Eastham. Gowain agreed with Alys, but still wished he'd punished Blanche's husband. When he thought of that bearded weasel claiming he had no idea where Enid was, when his own squire had visited the hut the night before...

"Welcome home, my lord!" Art Jenkins shouted down from the top of the wall as the drawbridge thudded to earth.

Gowain shook off his dark thoughts. "'Tis good to be home." Home. He savored the warm glow in his belly, the quickening of his heart as he looked up at the three square towers that made up Eastham. He had never dreamed the castle would one day be his, had balked at the idea when

Gareth proclaimed him lord of Eastham. After all, there was no proof of his legitimacy, but his father-by-marriage was even more stubborn than Alys when it came to seeing justice prevail.

"I have no doubt that Ranulf destroyed your parents' marriage lines," Gareth had grumbled. He'd not only insisted Eastham was Gowain's, he'd gotten King Richard to verify Gowain's right to the lands and titles, in writing.

Truly, Gareth Sommerville was a cut above most noblemen, a mark against which Gowain had taken to measuring his own performance as a lord. During the winter, messages had flowed back and forth between Eastham and Ransford. There were loving letters between daughter and parents, but more often, Gowain asked questions and guidance of the man he'd come to respect and admire.

"It seems you have guests," Jean remarked as they clattered into the bailey.

Gowain grunted, disappointed to see the stable thronged with strange horses. Guests meant it would be late in the evening before he had Alys all to himself. "Who would come visiting with the weather yet so unstable and the roads clogged with mud?" he muttered, stomping up the covered stairs to the entryway.

A wooden screen blocked the great hall, cutting down on drafts. From beyond it came the din of a great many people laughing and talking at once.

His pique vanished when he rounded the screen and spied his father-by-marriage with one arm around his lovely wife. He should have guessed it was Sommervilles, Gowain thought, no one else could make so much joyful noise. "Gareth! Arianna!" he cried, striding forward to welcome them.

Instantly he was engulfed in a wave of boisterous Sommervilles. He was hugged by Gareth and Alys's two brothers, Richard and William, and kissed by Lady Arianna.

"Our wives wanted to come, too," Richard explained when the noise died down. "But both are expecting again."

"My congratulations." His smile wavered a bit. Would that he and Alys could say the same. The fact that she had not yet quickened with child was the one blot on their otherwise happy lives. "What is the occasion?" he asked.

Gareth suddenly found the bottom of his cup interesting. The two boys scuffed their toes in the fresh rushes.

"Gowain," Arianna said, a trifle too brightly, "you look cold and tired. Come sit by the fire."

Oh. "What has Alys done?" he asked warily.

"Naught," all four said quickly.

"My, you've done wonders with this place since last I saw it," Gareth observed. "The new windows are splendid indeed, and the wall around the village looks most stout. The farmers we passed on the road were sleek as well-fed cats and full of smiles."

"Where is Alys?"

"She'll be down directly," said his mother-by-marriage. "She, ah, went up to fetch Enid."

"Is Enid sick?"

"Nay. Nay, she is fine." Arianna bit her lip.

Gowain frowned and started for the stairs. "I will just go up and make certain...."

Alys emerged from the stairwell, stopped dead in her tracks and said, "Oh, you are back."

So much for his warm welcome. "Is there some problem?"

"Nay." She bit her lip. "'Tis just that I wanted to have you all cleaned up first."

"For what? Am I to be the victim of another experiment?" They'd converted the old solar into a workroom, where two sisters brought in from Newstead copied over her precious herbal while Alys explored new remedies. He grinned at her family. "The tea she brewed for my cough turned my tongue blue."

Gareth chuckled. "She once tried on us a wrinkle cream that caused the skin to blister and peel. We all looked as though we'd been out in the sun too long."

"Knowledge does not come without a price," Alys murmured.

"What have you been up to?" Gowain asked.

Alys sighed. "There's no hope for it, I guess." She stepped onto the main floor and turned. "Mind your step, my lady."

An older woman stepped into the hall, Enid held in her arms. They had identical green eyes and soft smiles.

"Mama?" Gowain croaked. "Oh, God. Mama."

"Aye." Her smile turned misty. "Gowain, my love." She opened her other arm and enfolded him.

Tears streaming down his cheeks, Gowain hugged them both, his mother and his daughter. Both once lost to him and now returned. "Where have you been?" he asked when he'd mastered his voice. "How did you get here?"

"'Twas Lord Gareth's doing." Elen wiped her eyes on the sleeves of her gown, then dabbed at her son's cheeks.

Gareth materialized at Gowain's side, his face wet with happy tears. "My cousin's captain is Welsh. He sent word throughout the land that we were looking for your mother."

"Why did you not tell me she'd been found?"

"I didn't know," Gareth exclaimed defensively.

Elen laid a hand on Gowain's arm. "I was so overjoyed to hear you were alive and here in England, that instead of sending a message, I came back with the man. He had to stop at Ransford, so..." She shrugged. "The Sommervilles accompanied me here."

Gowain laughed and hugged her again. "Jesu, Mama, words cannot express my joy." His grin widened as Alys slipped her arm around his other side. "Surrounded by my three favorite women...and my beloved second family," he added, his gaze skimming over the sea of jubilant Sommervilles. "What more could a man wish for?"

Alys jerked, and he felt her slim body tremble against him, could have bitten his tongue. *Don't blame yourself, love,* he thought. But he knew she did. Damn, they must talk this out before the lack of a child caused a rift in their marriage. "I love you," he whispered in her ear, the words the only balm he could offer for her unspoken anguish.

"And I you," Alys whispered back. *I'm so sorry I've failed you,* she thought. What if she was never able to give him a son to carry on the proud heritage he'd fought so hard to reclaim?

"Dinner is ready, my lady," announced Velma, exuding a new confidence in her post as housekeeper.

Alys's spirits buoyed. Velma had survived a far worse fate than the lack of a child. She must stop feeling sorry for herself. "Come, let us eat," Alys said, smiling up at Gowain. She had found her one true love. 'Twas selfish to wish for more.

The meal was a fabulous success, despite the fact that Gowain had no time to change into the fine new tunic she'd laid out for him. Roasted fresh baby lamb and new peas bathed in butter were sweet indeed to palates dulled by a winter of salted meat and fish. Conversation flowed as freely as the fine Bordeaux wine her parents had brought with them.

"How did you manage to escape from Ranulf?" Gowain asked as soon as Richard, who was acting as Elen's dining companion, had offered a second toast to her safe return.

Elen laughed gaily. "'Twas the oldest trick in the world. We were traveling from Malpas to the mines, where Ranulf intended to incarcerate me. Because I'd made such a pest of myself by staging three escape attempts, the last of which nearly succeeded. You'd think they'd watch me carefully, but Ranulf thought me cowed by his tales of Bellamy's cruelty. Instead, they made me more desperate. I begged to get down and relieve myself. The moment his back was turned, I ran. Or so he thought." She giggled, eyes dancing. "Actually, I climbed a large oak and hid in the branches. 'Twas all I could do to keep from laughing as I watched them chase through the woods like a pack of addled hounds."

Alys shivered, thinking of her own abortive escape attempt. "Weren't you frightened in the woods alone? How did you find your way to Wales?"

"We Welsh grow up in the forests. And, too, I knew the lay of the land thereabouts, for I'd spent much time at Malpas. The farmers didn't like Ranulf at all. They gave me shelter, food for the journey, and even a guide to see me as far as the Welsh borders, where my uncle holds sway. Once into Wales, I merely waited to be found by my uncle's people. They gladly took me in. My only sorrow was in believing Gowain was dead."

"To Lady Elen," someone called out. Cups were raised and more good red wine was drunk down.

"Your father would be very proud of you," Lady Elen said when the cheering died away.

Alys's eyes misted again as she watched Gowain and his mother exchange loving glances. He needed a son.

She said as much to him hours later, when they were at last alone in their big chamber.

"'Tis as well we were wed in an unusual manner, for likely the church does not recognize our marriage, and you should have no trouble obtaining an…an annulment," Alys said shakily.

Gowain dropped the log he'd been about to add to the fire. Crouching before the hearth, he looked up at her with wounded eyes. "You desire to end our marriage?"

"It…it might be best." She turned away and moved to the window, her eyes so filled with tears the torches on the wall walk below blurred. How was she going to give him up?

"I am not giving you up!" Hard hands grasped her shoulders. Anger and pain burned through his control and hers.

Scorched, Alys cried out.

"Oh, love. I'm sorry," Gowain exclaimed, but he didn't let her go. He folded his arms around her and drew her into his embrace, emotions gentling to a wash of remorse. "I did not mean to hurt you, but you…you hurt me immeasurably. Say you did not mean what you said.''

"I…I do not want to go, but it might be best if you found a wife who could give you sons.''

"Ha! So that's what this is about.'' Gowain turned her to face him, tenderly lifting her chin so that he could settle a kiss on her trembling mouth. "Even if you and I never have children, I'll not let you go,'' he said slowly, as though speaking to an idiot.

"But—''

"No buts…not about this.'' Knowing action would suit his purpose better than words, Gowain swept her into his arms and carried her to the bed. She bounced once on the soft mattress before he tugged the formfitting surcoat off over her head.

"Gowain, I do not think this will solve anything.''

"This will solve everything.'' He tackled the laces that drew her undertunic close around her body. Desperation lent speed to fingers well familiar with getting his wife out of her clothes in short order. When he had her down to bare skin, he straightened to admire God's handiwork. "You are so beautiful it fair takes my breath away every time I look at you,'' he murmured.

Her lower lip trembled, and her coral-tipped breasts rose and fell with her ragged breathing. "What does it matter, if the vase is empty?'' she asked in an anguished whisper.

Gowain growled an oath, stripped off his own clothes and bundled them both under the covers. "Alys, you must stop this nonsense. You are not empty. You are full of goodness and kind—''

"But not full of life.''

Gowain sighed in exasperation. "I understand your pain, but six months of childlessness does not mean we'll never have any babes.'' He pulled her stiff body up against his, warming her chill flesh with his own. His hands moved up and down her spine, kneading, soothing, seducing. Still, he didn't relax when she molded her body to his with a sigh.

"It will be all right, sweetheart. We will stay here, in this bed till you quicken with my child."

"Surely you jest."

"Nay. I was never more serious in all my life." He stroked up to her breasts, teasing the nipples, making her gasp and twist slowly against him.

"What of food?"

"Velma will bring us our meals in bed. But for the moment, this little berry will satisfy me right well."

"Oh!" she cried as he began to devour her nipples. Matching contractions swept low in her belly, giving way to the familiar syrupy heat. "Oh, Gowain." Alys abandoned herself to the sensations he roused with his clever hands and mouth. He explored her everywhere, driving her up the first peak, and then the next, so that one release slammed into the next. Her eyes flew open in stunned surprise just as he levered himself up and slipped into her.

Hot as fire, sweet as the promise of forever, he loved her from the inside out. The pace he set was edged with desperation. She caught the fever, moved with it, taking him deeper, deeper, sipping at the frantic gasps that poured from his mouth into hers. "I love you. I love you," she chanted. He replied.

Each stroke tightened the spiral of needs tearing through her till she was well and truly lost. She could feel it welling, swelling, flowing between them so there was no telling where her pleasure ended and his began. 'Twas their gift to each other. Clinging to him, she gave herself over to the burning ecstasy, sucked up into a storm of pure bliss.

She cried out, heard his answering shout as he followed her over the edge. The light and the darkness swallowed them.

Numb, Alys thought, when she could think at all. She was numb and boneless, crushed beneath the massive weight of her husband and loving every minute of it, every inch of skin pressed tightly against skin.

"I should move," he mumbled.

"Nay, stay a moment. Let me savor the feel of... Oh."

"What is it?" When she didn't answer, he lifted his head from her shoulder. Concerned green eyes probed hers. "What?"

"I'm...I'm not certain. There is the strangest fluttering in my stomach."

"Mayhap it's me," he teased, but he rolled onto his side, gently withdrawing but keeping his arms around her. "Better?"

Alys shook her head, struggling to identify the vague sensation in her lower belly. "It feels as thought I've eaten butterflies for dinner."

"Bad lamb?" He came up on one elbow, frowning now. "Are you going to be ill? Do you want the chamber pot?"

"Nay, 'tis not like that. It's the strangest thing. I've never experienced it before, and yet it seems familiar somehow."

"Mayhap a patient had this sickness and you recall the feel of it because you touched them."

"Maybe." Alys frowned, thinking back. "It...it's like..." Her eyes rounded, and a tingle of hope raced down her spine. "It reminds me of the way Velma's tummy felt before Alys was born."

He stared at her smooth belly and the slender hand splayed protectively over it. "You mean we made a babe...just now?"

"I...I think so." Tears filled her eyes—happy tears, this time, not the countless private ones she'd shed each month when she knew she wasn't pregnant. "Isn't it wonderful?"

"Aye." Gowain put his hand over hers. "Wonderful." He kissed her with all the tenderness welling up inside him. "Do not get your hopes too high in case you are mistaken."

"I'm not. I can feel something going on." She frowned again. "Oh, dear, I guess I'll need to control this, or I'll have a very uneasy nine months."

"You can do it," Gowain said absently.

"What is it? Are you not pleased about the babe?"

"Aye, just a little disappointed. I'd rather looked forward to keeping you locked in here, naked and willing."

Alys grinned, put her arms around his neck and snuggled closer. "I'm naked and willing for you...always."

"Always. Aye, I like the sound of that." He kissed her, his mouth going from slow and tender to hot and drugging in an instant.

* * * * *

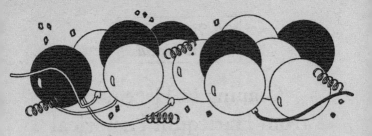

Ring in the New Year with

New Year's Resolution:
FAMILY

**This heartwarming collection of three
contemporary stories rings in the
New Year with babies, families and
the best of holiday romance.**

Add a dash of romance to your holiday celebrations
with this exciting new collection, featuring bestselling
authors **Barbara Bretton, Anne McAllister** and
Leandra Logan.

Available in December,
wherever Harlequin books are sold.

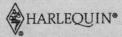

PHNY332

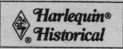

Harlequin® Historical

Coming in December
from Harlequin Historical

A Warrior's Bride

Award-winning author Margaret Moore
creates another exciting story
set in medieval times!

A WARRIOR'S BRIDE (ISBN 28995-2)
available wherever Harlequin Historicals are sold.

If you would like to order your copies of the books in the author's latest series, Most
Unsuitable…, *The Wastrel* (ISBN 28944-8), *The Dark Duke* (ISBN 28964-2) and *The
Rogue's Return* (ISBN 28976-6), please send your name, address, zip or postal code
along with a check or money order (please do not send cash) for $4.99 for each book
ordered ($5.99 in Canada), plus 75¢ postage and handling ($1.00 in Canada), payable
to Harlequin Books, to:

In the U.S.

3010 Walden Avenue
P.O. Box 1369
Buffalo, NY 14269-1369

In Canada

P.O. Box 609
Fort Erie, Ontario
L2A 5X3

Please specify book title(s) with your order.
Canadian residents add applicable federal and provincial taxes.

Look us up on-line at: http://www.romance.net

MM198

Christmastime...

When rediscovering
lost loves brings a
special comfort, and helping
to deliver a precious bundle
is a remarkable joy.

Comfort and Joy

brings you gifts
of love and romance
from four talented
Harlequin authors.

A brand-new Christmas collection,
available at your favorite retail store
in November 1997.

HARLEQUIN®

HPCJ266